WINDS OF EDEN

Following heavy casualties, General Townshend withdraws his exhausted troops to the town of Kut Al Amara, Iraq. His orders – to engage as many Turkish troops as possible in a siege situation. A relief force is hastily assembled, among them Charles Reid, Tom Mason and Michael Downe, for each of whom the advance is personal. Charles returns to the country where he lost the love of his life. Tom's brother John, an army surgeon, awaits execution. Michael's brother Harry, an army intelligence officer, is missing having never returned from his last mission. All three men wonder if they will ever see home and their wives again.

WINDS OF EDEN

WINDS OF EDEN

by

Catrin Collier

Magna Large Print Books
Long Preston, North Yorkshire,
BD23 4ND, England.

British Library Cataloguing in Publication Data.

A catalogue record of this book is
available from the British Library

ISBN   978-0-7505-4105-3

First published in Great Britain in 2014 by Accent Press Ltd.

Copyright © Catrin Collier 2014

Cover illustration © Accent Press

The moral right of the author has been asserted

Published in Large Print 2015 by arrangement with
Accent Press

Magna Large Print is an imprint of Library Magna Books Ltd.

Printed and bound in Great Britain by
T.J. (International) Ltd., Cornwall, PL28 8RW

"Heroes who shed their blood and lost their lives! You are now lying in the soil of a friendly country. Therefore rest in peace. There is no difference between the Johnnies and Mehmets to us where they lie side by side here in this country of ours. You, the mothers, who sent their sons from faraway countries, wipe away your tears; your sons are now lying in our bosom and are in peace. After having lost their lives on this land they have become our sons as well."

Mustafa Kemal Atatürk

**For my grandson
Alec John Nicholas Anderson
May he live in a peaceful world**

Chapter One

'Congratulations, Mr Downe.' The emissary from the War Office who'd introduced himself as 'Mr Smith' shook Michael's hand. 'Your editor, Mr Kenealy, assures me that, young as you are, he could find no better or more experienced man than you to be the *Mirror*'s war correspondent on the Mesopotamian Front. No doubt you'll see Mr Edmund Candler there. You could learn a great deal from him. He's not only the *Times* correspondent for the Expeditionary Force, but also the British Government's Official Eye-witness in Mesopotamia.'

'Thank you, sir. I'll look out for Mr Candler and do my utmost to deserve the trust Mr Kenealy and the *Mirror* have placed in me.'

'Make your dispatches accurate, as detailed as space allows no matter how unpalatable the truth, and you won't go wrong.'

'Something else to remember, Downe,' Mr Kenealy added, 'is that your dispatches will be heavily edited by the censor before they appear in the *Mirror*.'

'I've worked on the Western Front for the last year, sir,' Michael reminded him.

'Of course, you have. My apologies.'

'So, you know all about security, censorship,

and keeping up the troops' morale, Downe.' Mr Smith turned away from Michael and shook Mr Kenealy's hand. 'Lunch soon – but not today. I have to return to the office. A deluge of communiqués arrived this morning.'

'Is there any fresh news from Mesopotamia, sir?' Michael ventured.

'The Battle of Ctesiphon resulted in a stalemate.'

'I read that when it came in on tape from Reuter's two days ago, sir.'

'General Townshend and General Nureddin have retreated from the battlefield.'

'Both sides have given ground?' Michael was surprised.

'General Townshend had no choice. His supply lines were stretched too far. An army can't fight without food, water, and ammunition. The terrain's impossible. Either desert flat as a subaltern's wallet that affords no cover, or swamp and marsh that affords too much, flooded year round by water deep enough to drown a tired man. The country, coupled with the extremes of temperatures, makes soldiering in Mesopotamia hell. Townshend is aiming for a point on the Tigris where he can be supplied from Basra by river. Possibly, though it's by no means certain yet, at Kut-al-Amara.'

Encouraged by 'Mr Smith's' frank reply, Michael asked, 'Are all the casualty lists in from Ctesiphon, sir?'

'More were coming in this morning when I left the office. You have someone there?'

'My brother, sir.'

14

'An officer?'

'Lieutenant Colonel Henry Downe, sir.'

'The political officer?'

'Yes, sir.'

Mr Smith gave a rare smile. 'We are acquainted with Harry Downe and his exploits in the War Office. Sir Percy Cox, the Chief Political Officer with the Indian Expeditionary Force, speaks highly of him. So, you're off to join your hero brother. I envy you, boy. General Townshend is a fine man, a fine leader. A few months from now I dare say you'll be marching alongside him and your brother into Baghdad. What a headline that will make for you to write for the readers of the *Daily Mirror* to read over their breakfasts.'

'Yes, sir. Thank you, sir.' Michael knew he was being over-effusive but after hearing Harry praised, he couldn't help himself.

'No need to see me out, Kenealy. I know the way.' Mr Smith opened the office door. The noise of the newsroom blasted in, a cacophony of almost battlefield proportions. Typewriter keys being hit and hit hard interspersed with the slam of carriage returns. The whirr of tape machines mixed with the staccato of hobnailed boots skidding over the wooden floor, as errand boys charged from one end of the hall to the other. Reporters were shouting, checking facts, and announcing updates above the squeak of the tea trolley's wheels as it rolled from desk to desk.

'By the way, Downe,' Mr Smith raised his voice so he could be heard. 'How old did you say you were?'

'I didn't, sir.'

'He's twenty-three,' Mr Kenealy revealed.

'This is a young man's war. Bad news for us veterans who've been put out to grass, Kenealy. Good luck, Downe.'

'Thank you, sir.' Michael watched the civil servant raise his hat in salute as he sailed past the journalists hammering out copy.

'Good chap Mr ... Smith.' Mr Kenealy closed the door and the noise subsided. 'Passes on a lot of useful leads.' He went to his desk, opened a drawer, and removed a wallet-sized folder. He handed it to Michael. 'Travel warrants. You're leaving for France tonight on the midnight boat train from St Pancras, sailing out of Marseilles next Sunday, which should give you a couple of days' respite to enjoy the French fleshpots. This,' he handed him a stiff-backed card, 'identifies the bearer as a journalist of the *Daily Mirror*. These,' he passed over a brown envelope bearing an official government stamp, 'are your War Office papers designating you war correspondent posted to the Indian Expeditionary Force, Mesopotamia. Just as the Western Front, you have carte blanche to join any company you see fit, and go wherever the action and your instincts take you, provided you...'

'Don't get in the way of, compromise, or hinder military operations, sir.'

'I keep forgetting you know more about active service than me. To my shame, every time I look at you I see a schoolboy not a veteran, Downe. Forgive me. Age has never given way to youth graciously, preferring to see the young as immature and inexperienced. You've probably seen

16

more action in the last six months than I did as a correspondent during the entire second Boer War. Do you have everything you need in the way of tropical kit?'

'Thanks to my *Mirror* expense account, the Army and Navy Stores, and Gamages, sir.'

'Stout trunk?'

'The one you recommended, sir. The War Office steel cabin trunk, guaranteed airtight and insect-proof.'

'Whether it will stand up to Mesopotamian flies is another matter. I've heard they're cunning little blighters. Mosquito nets with wooden frame including a fine mesh net for sand flies?'

'Yes, sir.'

'Canvas bath? Field washstand?'

'Plus a twenty-pound tent for my bearer when I get one. Forty-pound for me, folding table and chairs – in short the entire kit prescribed by HQ Simla for officers of the Indian Army, as I'm going to be with them, if not one of them.'

Alexander Kenealy nodded approval. 'Not sure if you have one of these, but I thought it might prove useful.' He handed Michael a writing attaché case. 'It has a safety ink bottle, something every war correspondent should own.'

Michael was touched by his editor's generosity. Turned down by the army as unfit due to a childhood leg injury he'd applied for a position as a reporter. The transition from a desk in his father's bank to war correspondent hadn't been smooth. Any idea he'd had that journalism would be an easy option was shattered the first time Kenealy had bawled him out for submitting

17

verbose, over-emotional dispatches from France.

'I don't know what to say, sir.' Michael ran his hands over the leather grained case.

'As you'll be the one doing the work on the ground, least we can do is give you the tools for the job. I put a couple of boxes of horseshoe nibs in there. The ink reservoir on them is useful although I wouldn't go as far as to endorse the manufacturer's claim it's sufficient to write a whole letter.' He hesitated. 'Downe, I know your brother's in Mesopotamia, but are you absolutely certain this is the assignment for you? I've heard the Indian Office has made a complete cock-up there, especially with supply lines. The men are short of kit, food, ammunition, and other essentials they need to drive out Johnny Turk. The weather's foul, either unbearably hot or cold, and in the rainy season the whole country floods and turns to mud. You could stay on the Western Front.'

'No. Thank you, sir, but no.' Michael was resolute.

'Not sure I understand. You're not long married. Mrs Downe is too pretty a girl to be left alone in London for months on end. If you return to France you can always nip over the channel during the quiet times to deliver your dispatches and see her.'

'She's busy with war work, sir. My parents' and parents-in-law's estates have lost so many workers to the army she spends most of her time in the country, dividing her time between Clyneswood and Stouthall. In fact she's there now.'

'Surely not working in the fields?'

18

'She helps with book-keeping and oversees the fulfilment of requisitions of agricultural produce for the War Office.'

'King and Empire are demanding a great deal of your generation, Downe, women as well as men. I'm proud of you. All of you, for stepping up to the call. I won't keep you. I don't doubt you have plans for your last day in Blighty.'

'I'm meeting my sister for lunch and we're dining with our cousin. He received his orders yesterday.'

'For France?'

'Marseilles, sir. I'm not the only one in the family with a brother in Mesopotamia.'

'I hope you find your brother and cousin well in the East, Downe. Good luck, goodbye, and safe return.'

'Thank you for your help and advice, sir. I would never have made war correspondent without the training you gave me.'

'All I did was knock raw material into the shape the *Mirror* demands. I won't burden you with cautions, Downe. After the Western Front you know what you'll be up against. I do however have one piece of advice. A war correspondent's brief is to accurately record within censorship guidelines, and that's all. Don't take unnecessary risks. No heroics. I want to see you back here, sound in wind and limb the moment the peace treaties are signed.'

'I'll be back, sir.' Michael opened the attaché case and stowed his identity papers and travel documents inside. He shook his editor's hand and left.

Alexander watched Michael make his way through the newsroom. Downe was popular in a quiet, self-effacing way. Everyone wanted to wish him well and shake his hand. Given what he'd heard about the failings of the India Office and rampant disease in the Mesopotamian Expeditionary Force he only hoped he hadn't sent the boy to his death.

Ritz Hotel, London, Tuesday 30th November 1915

Tom Mason took the key from the bellboy and handed him sixpence.

'Thank you, sir. If you and your wife need theatre tickets...'

'We won't be needing any, thank you.' Tom hung the '*Do not disturb*' outside the door, closed it in the boy's face and locked it. 'Well, Mrs Captain Dr William Scott, alone at last.' He raised his eyebrows.

Clarissa Amey dropped her handbag and coat on the nearest chair. 'Just who is Captain Dr William Scott?'

'A boring physician I've thankfully left behind on the Western Front. What do you think of the room?'

'Luxurious and extravagant. We could have gone to the usual place, Tom.'

'Bayswater's too drab to say goodbye. Besides, nothing's too good for my girl.' He wrapped his arms around her, pulled her close, and kissed her long and thoroughly.

Clarissa wanted to ask him if she *was* 'his girl'

when he allowed her to breathe again, but mindful of an article she'd read in *Woman's Weekly* about 'sending your loved one off with a smile' she refrained. How could she demand Tom give her any assurance about his feelings for her, or their future together, when he was going off to war?

Since she'd been promoted to ward sister, the reality of what the men who marched away were forced to face had become all too apparent. The strain of nursing the smashed and broken bodies of young men who would never be whole again, and listening to their screams as they relived the horrors of the battlefield in their nightmares, had been almost more than she could bear. Especially when she thought of Tom and her brother Stephen.

'You're pensive, sweetheart?'

'Sorry. Thinking about the list of sister's duties Matron gave me,' she lied.

'Don't, not until after midnight.' He gave her a winsome smile.

'Is that the time your boat train leaves?'

'From St Pancras. Here, I bought you something to remember me by.' He took a jeweller's box from his greatcoat and handed it to her before hanging his coat in the wardrobe.

Her heart pounded when she saw the small blue leather box. She hadn't dared voice her hope, but she'd dreamed of an engagement ring, or at the very least a locket with a photograph she could wear close to her heart. Something she could show her family and friends with a casual – 'My boy at the front gave me this when he said goodbye.'

21

She opened the box. A pair of beautiful sapphire earrings twinkled up at her, reflecting the light from the electric lamps.

Tom read the expression on her face. 'If you don't like them the jeweller said he'd exchange them.'

'They're beautiful, Tom. It's just that...'

'What?'

How could she even begin to tell him she would have preferred something less expensive, more personal? 'They're lovely, Tom.' She closed the box, 'But they remind me you'll soon be gone.'

'Not for,' he looked at his wristwatch, 'almost twelve hours.'

A knock at the door disturbed them.

'Our champagne and caviar. Get undressed, darling, so we can start making memories.'

She bathed her eyes in the bathroom while he dealt with the waiter.

Kettner's Restaurant, Soho, London, Tuesday 30th November 1915

'So, you did it. You managed to get yourself posted to Mesopotamia.' Dr Georgiana Downe eyed her brother Michael across their table.

'You look as though you don't know whether to kiss or thump me.'

'Definitely thump you. As a war correspondent, you're in an even better position than me to know what Mesopotamia's like. I don't doubt you've read the dispatches as well as Harry's letters.'

'As much as the correspondents and Harry are

allowed to put in them,' Michael picked up the wine list.

'There was a huge battle there a couple of days ago with heavy casualties. Our forces...'

Michael looked over his shoulder before lowering his voice. 'Have tactically withdrawn.'

'In God's name...'

'Now you're blaspheming.'

'Since when have you turned into St Michael?'

'War correspondents are not saints.'

'Only a saint would volunteer for a hell-hole. Isn't it enough that I have one brother there? Do you have to emulate every stupid thing Harry does? You could have stayed in the bank.'

'With Britain at war?'

'I accept you want to do your bit. But a war correspondent? With a badly broken leg which never healed properly that prevents you from running. What do you do when the shells start falling?'

'Duck. If they're close, there's no point in running. If they're not, chances are you'll end up in their path.'

Exasperated, Georgiana reached for her cigarettes. 'Like Harry you have an answer for everything.'

'I don't, but I do know we're both worried sick about him. I need to be with him, Georgie, so I can see how he's bearing up.'

'Mesopotamia's vast. What are the odds of you being sent anywhere near Harry?'

'That's the beauty of being a war correspondent. I won't be "sent" anywhere. I can go where I like, even into the thick of the action.'

'Great, knowing Harry, that's exactly where he'll be. It will be comforting to know you were killed together.'

'Neither of us will be killed, Georgie. Once I'm there, I'll check his whereabouts with HQ and travel to wherever he's stationed. I'll write to you as soon as I see him. Then you can stop worrying.'

'You know what Harry and I are like. I'm not just his sister. I'm his twin. Whatever affects him affects me. I know he's unhappy, desperately so, but I don't think it's the war. It could be something to do with his wife. He didn't mention Furja in his last few letters.'

Michael smiled. 'Only Harry could marry a Bedouin. He sounded so happy when he first wrote to us about her, but if he's been on active service he might not have seen her for a while.'

'It's possible, I suppose.'

'I've often wondered if Harry married his Arab and you married Gwilym just to annoy our parents.'

Georgiana rarely mentioned her brief marriage to a Welsh coalminer. A pacifist, he'd volunteered for Red Cross duties in France. His death within a week of arrival at the Western Front was still raw.

'When I fell in love with Gwilym, I thought only of myself – and Gwilym. Children should live their lives the way they want without paying heed to their parents, especially when the said parents are antiquated remnants of another age.'

'Don't let Father catch you saying that.'

'He's so hidebound he's positively Neanderthal. He'd keep me at the back of the cave cooking, cleaning, and skinning his kills if he could.'

Michael laughed at Georgiana's depiction of their immaculately turned-out, meticulous, and correct army officer father as a primitive hunter. 'Let's forget the parents and Harry for now. Enjoy a damned good lunch – on me – and spend the afternoon doing whatever you want before we have to change to dine with Tom, Clarissa and Helen.'

'What time's your train out?'

'Midnight. Until then I forbid you to think further than five minutes ahead.' He read the menu and summoned the waitress. 'I'll order for both of us. How does stuffed herring rolls, followed by roast sirloin, Yorkshire pudding, roast potatoes, and Brussels sprouts, finished off with blackberry and apple pie with cream sound?'

'Leaden.' She turned to the waitress, 'I'll have the herring rolls to start, the cold beef, pickles and tomato salad...'

'You must have blackberry and apple pie and cream,' Michael broke in. 'I don't want to be the only stuffed piggy.'

'And the pie,' Georgiana capitulated.

Michael summoned the wine waiter. He ordered vintage claret to go with the food and cherry brandy to be served with Viennese coffees after dessert.

'You and your sweet tooth,' Georgiana teased. 'I remember the cook's screams whenever she caught you and Harry in the pantry, spoons in hands dipping into her pots of preserves. It's a wonder any survived for the breakfast table.'

'It was always Harry's idea, but then most of

25

the fun things we did were. Where do you want to go after lunch?'

'As it will be your last afternoon in London for a while, it's your choice.'

'National Portrait Gallery,' he said decisively.

'You're only saying that because it's one of my favourite places.'

'Is it so awful of a man to want to please his big sister?'

'I've tickets for the Adelphi for a matinee of *Hi Jinks*.'

'Fat lot of good they are on a Tuesday when matinée days are Wednesdays and Saturdays.'

'Except when management's laid on a special performance for wounded and convalescent soldiers.' She pulled the tickets from her pocket.

'I couldn't take a serviceman's seat.'

'You wouldn't. So few soldiers are fit enough to leave the hospitals we were given double the number of tickets we could use. I telephoned the theatre. They were so delighted at the prospect of having a war correspondent witness their generosity they offered us a box. Unless of course you're too embarrassed to be seen with your big sister.'

'I'd be honoured to accompany you, Dr Downe.' He leaned back as the waitress set their stuffed herring rolls on the table.

'You sound exactly like Harry. Deferential to the point of sarcasm.' She fell serious. 'Michael, tell me to shut up if you like, but you and Lucy...'

'Shut up.'

'Is your marriage beyond salvaging?'

'Yes.'

'You rushed into it.'

'I did. I regret it. If you want to say "I told you so..."'

'I don't. Can I help?'

'Not unless you can magic Lucy off the planet. No, that's unfair. I don't wish her dead or ill, only a million miles away from me. Permanently.'

'Have you seen her?'

'Not since my last leave five months ago.'

'You haven't been to Clyneswood?'

'Not since I returned from France the day before yesterday, and, before you ask, we haven't corresponded for five months.'

'Have you told our parents?'

'They'd have to be blind not to notice we can't stand one another.'

'Do you intend to divorce her?'

'When I'm back in this country for longer than a week I'll talk to a solicitor. But that's the problem, isn't it, Georgie? While King and Country need us body and soul we can't make plans to do anything personal, and won't be in a position to until "after the war".'

Chapter Two

The Ritz, London, early evening, Tuesday 30th November 1915

Damp from his bath, Tom padded naked into the bedroom. He looked at Clarissa lying in bed, and without warning yanked the covers from her.

Naked and irritated, she shouted, 'Tom!' before grabbing the sheet and tugging it to her chin.

'That's like sealing the cake tin after the cake's been eaten.'

'Now I'm a cake?'

'A luscious strawberry and cream sponge.' He peeled back the sheet, nuzzled her bare back, and slipped his hand between her thighs. 'Why so coy? Especially after what we've been doing for the past six hours?'

'I'm cold,' she lied. His attitude to nudity was casual, hers wasn't, and she knew he thought her prudish.

'I could give you a hot bath.'

'I'm not a child.'

'As I discovered earlier.' He lifted the sheet and slapped her buttocks lightly. 'Time to rise and make yourself beautiful, Mrs Scott. I've booked a table for seven thirty.'

'Our last dinner.'

'Please, don't get maudlin. I hope you have a dress that will complement those earrings.'

'As it happens, I do.' Furious with herself for allowing the façade of happy, compliant girl-friend to drop, she pulled the sheet from the bed, wrapped it around herself and went to her week-end bag. She unbuckled the clasp and pulled out a midnight blue lace evening gown.

'Scratchy lace.'

'Uncrushable lace.'

'Bath, woman. I need a drink before Mike, Georgie, and Helen get here and there's no champagne left.'

'Ten minutes.'

'Make it five.' He caught the end of the sheet and pulled it from her grasp.

'Tom...'

'Can't blame a man for wanting to admire the view.'

Swallowing her irritation she drew closer to him. He pushed her away. 'I'm clean and about to get dressed. Get a move on.'

It took all her powers of forbearance to remember she'd promised herself to do whatever it took to send him off with a smile on his face.

Dining Room, the Ritz, London, evening, Tuesday 30th November 1915

Tom rose from his chair, kissed Georgiana and shook Michael's hand when they joined him, Clarissa, and Helen Stroud at their table. 'Did you get the posting you wanted, Michael?' Mindful of the 'careless talk' directives, he didn't mention the destination.

29

'He did,' Georgiana confirmed.

'Well done you.' Dr Helen Stroud, who was Georgiana's closest friend and knew Michael well, rose from the table and kissed Michael's cheek. 'Every time I see you I think you look more like Harry's twin than Georgie.' She indicated the empty chair next to hers.

Michael took it. 'I keep forgetting you knew Harry?'

'All the female medical students exiled to the Royal Free Hospital lest they contaminate male students with their girl bacteria knew Harry. He made quite an impact on the medical parts of the city the year he pretended to study medicine.'

'My brother John had a stock of Harry stories about that year,' Tom signalled to the wine waiter.

'If they were scurrilous they were probably true,' Helen qualified.

'Dressing corpses and wheeling them into lectures, hiding body parts in professors' studies, painting spots on himself when he wanted to get out of doing anything he didn't want to...'

'Which was often,' Helen interrupted. 'Considering they were cousins you couldn't meet two more different men than John and Harry. I felt sorry for John having to share rooms with Harry. John was so serious and dedicated. When he finished training everyone agreed he was a brilliant doctor.'

'Whereas Harry is still making an impact. From what I heard today, this time it's for the right reasons. He's been mentioned in dispatches.'

'Perhaps he's found his niche in war and mayhem,' Helen observed.

'More like they're allowing him to run wild with the natives.' Tom glanced down the wine list. 'Champagne all round to drink with the meal and moonlight fizz cocktails to put us in the mood for the evening?'

'Sounds good,' Georgiana agreed.

Michael took the menu the waitress handed him. 'Palestine soup and roast goose, please.' He looked enquiringly at the others.

'We've all ordered,' Tom informed him.

'In that case please double the order,' Georgiana said to the waitress.

'No dessert?' Tom raised his eyebrows.

'After what Michael and I ate for lunch, we won't have room.'

'Lunch was hours ago. I'll have the chestnut cream and cheese fingers, please.' Michael returned the menu to the waitress.

'Lunch might have been hours ago but we've done nothing since except sit in a theatre box.'

'What did you see, Georgie?' Clarissa asked.

'*Hi Jinks.*'

'I'm green with envy. Do tell what it was like?' Clarissa begged.

'Brilliant!' Michael couldn't say more because he'd spent the whole show thinking about what lay ahead in Mesopotamia.

'Was it really brilliant?' Clarissa pressed.

'So...' Helen turned to Michael, while Georgiana was talking theatre to the others. 'Have you heard from Harry lately?'

'Not for over two months, but, given the news this week, that's hardly surprising. Although I

31

was told today it's not a defeat, it's a...'

'Strategic withdrawal,' Tom finished for him. 'As you well know, we've had a lot of those of the Western Front.'

'I've been trying to explain to Clarissa how busy the men are and how often the mail goes astray.' Georgiana kicked Tom under the table.

'You'd think men would have nothing to do when they spend all day sitting in a trench waiting to be shelled but the brass never let up. It's spit and polish day and night.' Tom knew he'd failed to sound convincing when he caught Georgiana's eye.

Clarissa sipped her cocktail. 'My brother used to write home every week when he was posted to Basra before the war. Sometimes his letters took six months or more to arrive but at least we received them. Then he was always complaining how bored he was. When war broke out and his unit was absorbed by Indian Expeditionary Force D he stopped complaining, but we haven't had a single letter from him now, for over four months. My mother and I have pored over the casualty lists until we see double. Stephen isn't on any of them, thank God, but I wish the *Times* would use larger font.'

'If they did, they'd have to make the newspaper as thick as Kelly's directory,' Helen observed, 'and that would be unpatriotic. A waste of valuable paper.'

'You mentioned a withdrawal, Michael. That has to be good, doesn't it? It's not like a defeat,' Clarissa pleaded. 'It's so the troops can regroup and attack again.'

'Of course they can.' Georgiana was finding it increasingly difficult to be patient with Clarissa given her own mounting concerns about Harry, John and Charles.

'Has anyone heard from John, I think he'd be a better bet than Harry to keep in touch with home?' Helen made an effort to sound casual. She'd been close to John Mason during his student days, just how close, neither she nor John had revealed to anyone before he'd left to take a post in the Indian Army Medical Service. Seeing his younger brother Tom had rekindled memories. Tom was as tall, well-built and handsome, but, unlike John, she'd noticed Tom was aware of his good looks.

'Like Clarissa with her brother, we haven't heard from John in months,' Tom revealed.

'I told you it was the mail, Clarissa.' Georgiana finished her cocktail. The wine waiter removed her glass.

'Do you have a relative in Mesopotamia, Helen?' Tom asked.

'I don't know anyone there except John, Harry, and Charles Reid.'

'You've met Charles too?' Michael asked.

'John and I had dinner with him and Harry the night before the three of them sailed to take their commissions in the Indian Army. John wrote to me a few times from India but his letters were always slow in travelling. I received a Christmas card from him in August 1913 that had been sent in November 1912.'

'My mother commented that John's last few letters seemed strange but that wasn't surprising.

He was marching across country when he wrote them and there was a high incidence of disease and heat stroke among the troops. In medical terms that means no rest for doctors. He probably left personal things like writing home until bedtime when he was sleeping on his feet and hardly knew what he was doing.'

Georgiana didn't disagree with Tom, although she couldn't imagine careful, methodical John leaving anything as important as a letter home until he was too tired to think. Especially knowing his mother would read every word at least ten times over.

'I heard John married?' Helen ventured.

'Maud Perry, a colonel's daughter at the beginning of the war. He met her in India.' Tom confirmed.

'No one in the family knows a thing about her,' Georgiana said, 'other than to use Charles's words, "she's pretty".'

'She's with him?' Helen continued to fish.

'Not in the front line, but living in a mission in Basra.'

'As it's a Presbyterian mission, we hope she's not overly religious.' Tom patted his pockets.

'Looking for your travel warrant?' Michael asked.

'Checking I have my wallet, I did say tonight was on me.'

'We can all afford to chip in,' Georgiana said.

'As I'm sailing to the back end of beyond for months, if not years, I'll soon have nothing to spend my money on, so I may as well splash out now.'

'I had dinner with Uncle Reid last night at his club. He told me exactly where your "back end of beyond is".' Georgiana glared at Michael. 'You knew?'

'I knew,' he admitted.

'You're both leaving from St Pancras tonight?'

'Midnight train,' Michael confirmed.

'It will be good to have a bridge partner who knows how I play,' Tom declared.

Georgiana stopped listening. She'd heard the bravado too often to believe it.

'Anywhere has to be better than France.' 'It'll be a picnic in the desert.' 'We'll be home in good time for next Christmas.' 'The Turks haven't a clue how to fight.' 'One of our troops is worth a dozen Axis soldiers.'

She was tired of the platitudes. Tired, of doctoring and operating on smashed young bodies, but most of all she was tired of war and patriotic forced gaiety.

St Pancras station, 11.50 p.m., Tuesday 30th November 1915

Georgiana hugged Michael, holding him close so he couldn't see her face – or her tears.

'Write as often as you can. If you're lucky enough to find Harry, give him my special love and tell him to hurry home because I can't bear the thought of him in danger or having to live any longer without seeing him.'

Michael suppressed a tide of emotion. 'I will.'

'Don't forget to give Harry, John and Charles

35

the Fortnum and Mason hampers I bought this afternoon. They should have been delivered to the train by now...'

'I'm sure they're on board with the rest of my luggage, Georgie. I'll hand them out if they survive the crossing although I wish you'd settled on smaller boxes. Any thoughts I had on not needing a bearer disappeared the moment I saw how much you were intent on dumping on me.'

'If the food's at risk of spoiling...'

'I'll feed it to my travelling companions.' He gripped her shoulders and pushed her at arms' length so he could look her in the eye. 'Stop worrying, Georgie. We'll all be back in one piece as soon as we've licked the opposition.'

'Take care of yourself, little brother.'

'If you agree to do the same, big sister.'

The stationmaster blew the first whistle. Helen had stood tactfully back to allow Georgiana and Michael to say their goodbyes in privacy. She joined them when the porters started closing the carriage doors.

'Don't worry about Georgie, Michael. We'll both be too busy to get up to any mischief, but not too busy to read your columns in the *Mirror*.'

'Greater love hath no friend than they forsake the *Times* for the *Mirror* for a journalist's sake.'

'I won't forsake the *Times*, just read both papers. Take care of this,' she handed him an envelope. 'Give it to John if you see him.'

'I will, Helen.' He pocketed the letter, stepped on to the train, gave Georgiana's hand one last squeeze, released, it and disappeared inside. He pushed down the window of the carriage and shouted down to where Tom was locked in Clarissa's arms.

'Do I have to go to war on my own?'

Tom wiped the tears from Clarissa's eyes with the thumbs of his leather-gloved hands. 'Take care, Clary.'

'You'll write?'

'I'll write, but don't sit in waiting for letters. Go out and have as fine a time as wartime London will allow.' He left her, jumped on board and walked to the carriage where Michael was hanging out of the window.

The final whistle blew. The train steamed and began to move slowly out of the station. Georgiana stood and waved until she could no longer see Michael's hand waving back. When the last puff of smoke dissipated, Helen linked her arms into Georgiana's and Clarissa's.

'I have a bottle of brandy in my rooms and I'm not on duty until the night shift tomorrow. Anyone care for a nightcap or two or three or four?'

'Me please,' Georgiana accepted gratefully.

'Me too,' Clarissa added.

'While we drink, we'll talk about hats, the latest skirt lengths, shoes, and *Hi Jinks* because you saw it today, Georgie. When we tire of that we'll discuss what we'll wear and who we'll dance with at the hospital Christmas balls. The one topic we will not think about or discuss under pain of severe forfeit is the war. Understood!'

'It would be lovely if we could forget it for a few hours,' Clarissa agreed.

They walked out of the station into a group of

eager, excited recruits fresh from training, embarking for France. Georgiana didn't have to look far to see the long line of ambulances. She knew from the times she'd attended the medical convoys, the maimed and wounded were always unloaded at the back of the railway stations. Out of sight of 'new blood' lest it 'rattle' them before they reached the front.

Despite Helen's exhortation that they wouldn't think about the war, she couldn't help recalling the pages of close-printed casualty lists she'd seen in the *Times* that morning.

First List – Second List – Officers – Ranks – 'The Killed' 'The Died of Wounds' 'The Missing' 'The Dangerously Wounded' 'Wounded-Shock-Shell' 'Wounded-Concussion-Shell' 'Wounded and Missing' – she felt the last category must be torture for relatives and friends as there was no indication who was wounded and who was missing in the closely printed lists of names that followed.

'Taken prisoner' 'Wounded' 'Accidentally Killed' – that meant the family received less compensation than if their loved one had been killed in battle – 'Died of Wounds' ... British, Canadian, Australian, Newfoundland Contingent, New Zealand, South African, and whenever she reached the end of the names and thought there couldn't possibly be any more, the evening paper was delivered to the doctors' rest room with a new and even longer tally.

She glanced back at the volunteers crowding through the station doors and wondered how many of the impossibly young, fresh-faced boys were destined to be wrapped in army blankets and lowered into pits dug in French soil before New Year's Eve ushered in 1916.

Chapter Three

Marseille, Sunday 5th December 1915

'The *Royal George,* Sahib Downe. Sami and I have placed your and Sahib Mason's luggage marked "Wanted on Voyage" in your cabin. The rest we personally stowed all safe in the hold.' Adjabi pointed to a transport vessel moored alongside a ship filled with Gurkhas.

'Thank you, Adjabi.' Michael and Tom had acquired bearers within twenty-four hours of reporting to the duty officer at Marseilles. Heavy casualties among Indian Army officers in France had cast many bearers adrift. Reliant on their "officer" for wages, they needed to be placed to draw army rations and uniform. Anxious to avoid a second winter in France, Adjabi and Sami had left the front and made their way south as soon as they heard transports were heading east out of the port. Aware that 'Eastward Bound' could mean anywhere in East Africa, Egypt, Salonika, Gallipoli, or India, they hoped for warmth, if not home.

Michael had a feeling both Indians would be disappointed when they found themselves in Mesopotamia.

'Do you know where we're heading?' An officer

of the Black Watch greeted Tom when he set foot on the deck.

'East?' Tom answered.

'Even I know that much.' The lieutenant turned away in disgust.

'There's a whole bundle of different regimental uniforms for a single transport,' Michael observed. 'Isn't that the 61st Howitzer Battery?'

'It is,' Tom agreed. 'The Indian troops seem to be in high spirits.'

'Their Izzat is high. Welcome aboard.' The man extended his hand. 'Captain Boris Bell, 6th Indian Cavalry.'

'Captain Tom Mason, British Field Ambulance Medical Corps.' Tom shook Boris's hand.

'Michael Downe, war correspondent.'

'War correspondent to where?' Captain Bell enquired artfully.

'East,' Michael hedged.

Boris laughed. 'You've been trained well, but once word gets out we've a war correspondent on board who knows where we're bound, you'll be mobbed.'

'Not until we're at sea and then it won't matter.'

'If you'll excuse us, we're off to hide in our cabin until we cast off.' Tom touched his cap to Bell and followed Sami to the inside decks.

After a route march down endless metal-walled corridors the bearer proudly opened a door. 'I trust the sahibs will be comfortable in here.'

Michael inspected the cramped quarters which were a quarter of the size of the preserves pantry in Clyneswood. A double bunk filled half the space, a drop-down table hung from wall to bunk

40

beneath the porthole. Beneath it, their bearers had stowed their kit bags, Tom's regulation sword and helmet case and his medical bag.

Michael asked, 'What's Izzat, Adjabi?'

'Dignity and honour, Sahib.'

'The India troops have dignity and honour?' Tom checked.

'They are pleased to be leaving the cold of a French winter to go east, sahib. East will be warmer than this. It will also be nearer home, and the fighting will be better.'

'How can fighting be better?' Tom was bemused.

'In France, the sahibs who fight underground are killed in holes like my Captain Bennett was. I've heard the sahibs who fight in the air or on the water are also killed. In the east I've been told that war is carried on according to the old methods, on the ground like civilised soldiers. That has to be much better.'

'I hope you're right, Adjabi, although I've yet to see any evidence of civilised behaviour in war.' Michael dropped his attaché case on the bottom bunk.

'The Indian troops say we should reach Basra within the month, do you think they're right, Sahib?'

'Who told them we're going to Basra?' Tom demanded.

'That is what they say, Sahib. That General Townshend has got himself and his troops into a pickle and a jam because he ran out of supplies and we are going there to take him and his men what they need. But first we have to fight and

41

overcome the Turks who have built a circle around them.'

Michael laughed.

'Even before the war, John wrote from India that the bearers always knew more about what was going on than the officers.' Hemmed in by their bearers and Michael, Tom climbed on the top bunk and stretched out.

'Would the sahibs like tea?' Sami flattened himself against the wall when Adjabi opened the inward-facing door.

'Please, Sami,' Tom answered, 'and any biscuits or cake on offer.'

'Adjabi and I will forage, Sahibs.' The bearers left.

Tom's disembodied voice floated down to Michael. 'Do you think we should tip off intelligence? Tell them to give up paying spies in favour of planting an agent among the bearers. That way we'll know everything that's about to happen before it does.'

'I was thinking of moving down to the Indian deck so I could get the news before I write my copy.'

'An excellent idea. I might actually have enough room to breathe if you do.'

'Considering I'm half your size, you've no cause for complaint.'

'I can't help my size and I'm not complaining about you but the accommodation.' Tom stretched down his hand and offered Michael a pack of Golden Dawn and a box of Lucifers. 'Smoke?'

'Thanks.' Michael took one and handed the pack and matches back up. 'You think a tent's going to be roomier than this?'

'At least we won't have to share.'

Michael remembered Harry's description of camping in the desert. How the only saving grace in blistering heat, freezing cold, and relentless rain was the companionship of his fellows. He wondered how long it would be before he and Tom felt the same way.

Kut al Amara, Thursday 9th December 1915

Major Warren Crabbe approached the northeastern bank of the Tigris shortly after dawn. The last of the Punjabis were gingerly withdrawing from the dug-outs that had guarded an exposed – as it had turned out dangerously exposed – makeshift boat bridge. One of the first things the engineers had done after the Expeditionary Force had occupied Kut was cobble together the bridge from battered danack rafts lashed together with forty-foot beams and liberal lengths of Major Sandes the chief engineer's first-class manila rope.

Crabbe found Sandes standing at a safe distance from the bridge monitoring the Punjabis' retreat. He joined him, and together they watched the column's painfully slow progress from the floating planking on to a sandbank that had been pounded into quicksand.

'My men worked all night in freezing water to secure that last twenty-yard stretch of bridge for the retreat and it's still not stable,' Sandes complained.

Crabbe decided there was no way he could

deliver the message he carried tactfully, so he plunged in. 'General Townshend has received orders from General Nixon in Basra HQ.'

'And?' Sandes, whose men had worked tirelessly to improve the defences and sanitation in Kut since the Force had retreated to the town, sensed bad news.

'General Nixon and HQ believe that Indian Expeditionary Force D...'

'Namely us.'

'Would do more good digging in and engaging the Turks in a siege situation, than retreating downstream. They've issued finite orders for us to do so, on the premise that we'd tie up more of the Turks' troops and resources if we remain exactly where we are.'

'So we're not following the cavalry, camelry, and tanks and are being abandoned here to rot?' Sandes winced when a young Punjabi took a bullet in his back from a sniper and fell into the river. He was hauled out quickly but not before one of his rescuers was also hit.

'Rotting implies inaction. We're here to take Turkish bullets and brave Turkish artillery shells and bombs.' Crabbe ducked instinctively as a sniper shot whistled from what until a few minutes ago had been the Punjabi-manned defensive lines. 'I've also been instructed to order you to dismantle that magnificent boat bridge before it's commandeered by the enemy and used by them to access our defences.'

'Has Command any idea of the work I and my men put into building that bridge?'

'The precise orders the staff told me to convey

are, "Major Sandes is to demolish the bridge the moment the last of the Punjabis are safe behind our lines lest the enemy utilise the structure."'

'I'd like to see the red collars destroy their work willingly. Oh dear, I forgot,' Sandes said caustically, 'the staff don't do anything as demeaning as work.'

'I have another order for you.'

'Yes?' Major Sandes eyed Crabbe warily.

'General Townshend would like you to build a pontoon bridge a mile downstream connecting the fort to the right-hand bank of the river.'

'This boat bridge is built. It's as serviceable a bridge as he's likely to get given the materials I have to work with.'

'The orders are "It's to be constructed a mile downstream".'

'Why?'

Crabbe offered Sandes his pack of cigarettes. 'You have your choice of two rumours.'

'The first?'

'In the case of an overwhelming attack by superior Turkish forces, General Townshend can retire our force to the right bank and from there we can make our way downstream and on to Ali Gharbi.'

'In direct contradiction of Nixon's orders for us to keep Johnny Turk tied up here. I discount that rumour.' Sandes produced a box of Lucifers and lit their cigarettes. 'What's the other?'

'General Townshend's intention is to use the bridge as a thoroughfare to either bank so our force can engage the enemy on either side of the river.'

45

'As that rumour suggests imminent battle, I don't like it. The staff do realise I'll need infantry cover for my men while they dismantle this bridge and construct another?'

'I asked. The request was refused.'

'They want me and my men to play sitting duck targets for Turkish snipers?'

'Brass has taken the line that the men are exhausted and need to rest. Orders have come down that the only duties to be carried out are the bare, necessary minimum to secure the town.'

'What about my exhausted men?' Sandes raged.

'It's common knowledge engineers don't require rest, sleep, or food, but if you promise to keep quiet about it, I'll find you some Dorsets who aren't afraid of shooting Turks.'

'"Keep quiet" – "Off the record" – that's all I'm hearing. Do the brass ever move outside of their improvised HQ and temporary messes to take a look at the hole we've dug ourselves into?'

'Not that I've seen.'

'Why did I join the Engineers? Why didn't I demand a cushy berth with the red tab collar brigade?'

'Because you're not the shirking sort? I'll round up volunteers to cover your men.' Crabbe tossed his cigarette to the ground and headed for the forward trench the Dorsets were digging.

'Crabbe?'

'Yes?'

'Thank you.'

Georgiana charged into the foyer of the nurses' home. Breathlessly she gasped, 'Is Clarissa Amey still here?'

The porter left his desk and opened the inner door that led to the rooms. 'Sister Amey went upstairs to pack half an hour ago, Dr Downe. We were all very sorry...'

Georgiana didn't wait for him to finish his sentence. She ran through the door and up two flights of stairs. Panting, she knocked on Clarissa's door. When there was no reply she tried the handle.

Clarissa was sitting on her bed. An open tapestry weekend bag was beside her, a jumble of clothes on her lap. White-faced, dry-eyed, she was staring into space.

Georgiana shrugged off her wet coat and gloves and tossed them to the floor. She kneeled and grasped Clarissa's hands. 'I'm so sorry, Clary. What can I do?'

Clarissa's eyes were wide, burning with unshed tears. 'I have to go home.' She spoke slowly, mechanically.

'I'll help you pack and go with you.'

'You're on duty.'

'I've organised cover. I don't have to return to the hospital until midday tomorrow. I came as soon as I heard you'd had a personal telephone call on the ward.'

Everyone knew the only calls Matron allowed the switchboard to put through to working staff were ones that conveyed news of family bereavement.

'My father said Stephen was killed in the battle of Ctesiphon on the 22nd November. That's over two weeks ago. For seventeen days I've been complaining Stephen hasn't written and all that time he was dead and couldn't ... couldn't...'

Realising Clarissa was in shock Georgiana took her coat from the back of the door and wrapped it around her.

'I'll help you pack. Then we'll get a cab to the station.'

'You'll come with me.' Clarissa gripped Georgiana's hand.

'Of course.'

'You have to help me.'

'Any way I can, Clary.'

'My father said I have to come home.'

'That's understandable. Your parents will want to arrange a memorial service for Stephen.'

'You don't understand, Georgie. My father says my mother's had a nervous collapse and as Penny's married and Stephen's gone, I have to be the one to stay at home and look after her. He insists my duty as a daughter takes precedence over my career.'

Kut al Amara, Friday 10th December 1915

'Almost done, sir.' Lieutenant Davies saluted Major Sandes and Crabbe as they approached the river. 'Men are tightening the lashings on the pontoons now.'

'Planks look uneven.' Sandes squinted sideways.

'Captain Harris's men are seeing to that, sir.'

'It's as fine a pontoon bridge as I've ever seen, Major Sandes,' Crabbe complimented.

'Breakfast for the workers, gentlemen?' Captain Peter Smythe strolled down the riverbank with a basket of rolls. Behind him, his bearer carried a tray of tin mugs and two jugs of steaming coffee.

'You Dorsets know how to live.' Sandes helped himself to a roll.

'Where did you get this?' Crabbe asked.

'Norfolks' mess. I told their cook that their officers had been out all night helping Major Sandes.'

'They haven't been near here.'

'I know that and you know that. The Norfolks' cooks didn't.'

'I like your style, Smythe.' Sandes stared as a wave of Turkish infantry headed by an officer brandishing his sword rushed the far side of his bridge.

'Bollocks!' Crabbe yelled to one of the Dorset privates, 'Evans, get to HQ. Tell them we're under attack.'

'Sergeant Lane,' Peter shouted in the direction of the fort. 'Troops out of the front trench. Now!'

'To the fray, gentlemen.' Sandes unbuckled his pistol.

'The only way to stop them is to demolish the bridge, sir.' Lieutenant Matthews picked up a fifty-pound gun cotton charge.

'Not at this end. It'll be an invitation to use the remains on the far bank as a bridging point.'

'Then we'll have to blow it up on the opposite bank.' Peter took a second gun cotton charge from a private.

'It would be suicide to go over there,' Sandes warned.

'Want to try your luck?' Peter grinned at Matthews. The two of them jumped into a boat.

'Idiots!' Crabbe shouted after them. He pulled Sandes into a sandbagged dugout.

Peter and Mathews reached the centre of the river to be met by a barrage of Turkish gunfire.

Major-General Mellis charged up harrying a contingent of reinforcements. 'Covering fire! Pin Johnny Turk down! Into the forward trenches!' he ordered, before joining Crabbe and Sandes in the dugout. He indicated the mass of Turkish snipers on the opposite bank. 'We'll have to wait until nightfall to destroy your bridge Sandes. Crabbe, organise volunteers from the sappers, miners and Gurkhas and find two officers to go over to the opposite bank with them tonight.'

'The officers will be easy, sir.' Crabbe looked to where Peter and Matthews were lying low in their boat, scanning the bridge with binoculars.

Kut al Amara, nightfall, Friday 10th December 1915

Peter watched the sun turn from gold to red as it sank slowly to the horizon. He was mentally and physically drained. The Turkish snipers hadn't let up since their main force had abandoned their failed attack on the bridge early that morning. As a result, over two hundred British troops had been stretchered into the town. The fortunate to the makeshift improvised hospitals set up by the medics, the less fortunate to the mortuaries.

50

When the Turks had attacked he'd been prepared to fight a battalion single-handed without covering fire, but interminably long hours spent lying in the bottom of the boat before he and Matthews had managed to paddle back to the home bank, had sapped his enthusiasm and energy.

Crabbe slithered down the bank on elbows and knees to where Peter and Lieutenants Mathews and Sweet were waiting. 'Ready?' he whispered.

Peter nodded. He and the two lieutenants waded into the river alongside the poised and waiting Gurkhas. Before they could push out the first boat, the Turkish fusillade started up again. Bullets hailed into the water around them.

Within seconds covering fire from the 2nd and 7th Gurkhas whistled over their heads.

'Mellis's men,' Mathews breathed.

Peter dropped the gun cotton charges into a boat and pushed it towards the centre of the river. Clinging to the stern, he and his two fellow officers headed for the opposite bank. Behind them two boats steered by volunteers from the ranks floated in their wake.

'We've sent those men on a suicide mission,' Sandes declared when Crabbe crawled back into the dugout.

'Smythe's come through worse.'

'Didn't it occur to the bloody brass when they ordered me to build that pontoon bridge that the Turks would see it as an invitation to visit?'

'Possibly they thought you needed something to occupy yourself and your men.'

'I know just how I'd like to occupy myself.'

51

'Engineering officers are not permitted to blow up HQ.'

'More's the pity.'

They stood side by side, peering over the sand-bags. Tense minutes ticked past as they strained their eyes monitoring the shadowy figures of the small party pushing boats packed with explosive to the opposite bank.

'Suicide!' Sandes reiterated as a bullet hit a Gurkha. The man fell back into the river. His body was carried downstream.

A voice resounded behind them. 'If they'll succeed there'll be a medal in it for the officer in charge.'

Crabbe turned. Colonel George Perry had entered the dugout.

Crabbe couldn't resist answering. 'Medals lose their gloss when they're pinned on a corpse, Colonel Perry.'

Perry snorted and moved on. The first explosion rent the air.

'They did it!' Sandes grabbed Crabbe's shoulder as his bridge was thrown high and splintered in the air. 'They bloody well did it!'

'They're back, sir. Look.' A private pointed to Peter who was dragging the wounded Gurkha out of the water. Close behind him were the sodden figures of Lieutenants Alec Matthews and Roy Sweet.

Chapter Four

Lansing Memorial Mission, Basra, Saturday 25th December 1915

'All day people have been asking me. "How can we celebrate Christmas with so many men dead?"' The Reverend Butler looked down the table to where his wife, Dr Theo Wallace, Theo's sister Angela Smythe, and Dr Picard were sitting. 'I can only repeat to you what I said to them. It's cold comfort after the news that was brought to our door yesterday, but God's mercy knows no bounds. Unfortunately neither does man's in-humanity to man. We have, all of us, been placed here, in this town, this country, at this time, by God. It is His will that we offer comfort and assistance to our fellow man to the best of our abilities. As for what has happened. It cannot be changed. All we can do is remember the souls of Lieutenant Colonel Harry Downe and Captain John Mason along with those of every other brave man who has fallen, in our private prayers, and pray that God extends his mercy to the cour-ageous men who are besieged at Kut al Amara, including Angela's beloved husband, Peter. So,' he solemnly filled their glasses from the wine decanter, 'please, join me in a toast to Lieutenant Colonel Harry Downe, Captain John Mason and all absent friends.'

Blinded by tears, Angela rose to her feet and raised her glass along with the others.

'Two more toasts, ladies and gentlemen before we drain our glasses. To the new life that joined us yesterday by God's will. A posthumous son for Captain Mason, and our guest Mrs Maud Mason. And to peace. May it grace the world in 1916.'

As Angela echoed the toast of 'Peace' she recalled the troops she'd seen disembarking at the town's wharves. Sepoys and sappers from India and the Western Front, senior officers in splendid dress uniforms and behind them crates of guns, ammunition and stores destined to feed the war effort.

She couldn't help wondering if peace would return to Mesopotamia – or anywhere in the world. Or if she'd ever see Peter in this life again.

Kut al Amara, Saturday 25th December 1915

Warren Crabbe and Peter Smythe left the improvised mess of the Dorsets after the last post-Christmas dinner toasts had been drunk and all the bottles the steward had permitted to be opened for the occasion, emptied.

'Leg still bothering you?' Crabbe asked when he noticed Peter limp out of what had been a carpet shop before their regiment had evicted the merchant and taken over the building.

'When it hits the cold,' Peter admitted.

'That will teach you to blow up a bridge when you're under it.'

'You would have found a better way?'

They heard General Charles Townshend's baritone accompanied by his inevitable banjo-playing echoing from the sheikh's house he'd requisitioned. The general exhibited a taste for all things French, and officers who'd been invited into his private quarters swore the mud walls of the room he entertained in were festooned with risqué pictures cut from *La Vie Parisienne*.

'Alphonse is on good form tonight,' Peter commented.

Crabbe stopped walking and listened. 'The Black Cat, or as the general with his penchant for all things French would say, *Le Chat Noir.*'

'Your accent is improving.'

'Thanks to the French I hear in the mess every time Townshend's name is mentioned. Why do officers refer to him as "Alphonse" when the men call him "Charlie"?'

'Possibly because Charlie is more British and French isn't taught in council schools,' Peter suggested.

'My Glasgow slum school didn't even teach English.'

'I've noticed,' Peter joked.

'I'll talk to you when you've mastered the tongue of Robbie Burns, my boy.'

'Frankly, given the noises you Scots produce I'd rather not try.'

They headed north-east through the rod-straight avenues Sandes and his engineers had hacked through the higgledy-piggledy, cheek-by-jowl housing in Kut. Walls had been torn down and the holes covered by matting, their owners' protests silenced by liberal donations of silver rupees from General Townshend's war chest. The result was a prospective battlefield within the town where communications could be carried by runners from one battalion to another and troops swiftly deployed to any area under attack if – or what was more likely – when the Turks broke through the outer defences.

Their boots scuffed the unmade roads as they avoided stinking pools of stagnant effluents. They passed mud-brick houses and clumps of palm. On their right, at the eastern edge of town, the ink-black outline of the town's gibbet stood high above the riverbank, reminding Peter of a woodcut illustration he'd seen in a book of medieval torture.

By tacit agreement they shouldered their kitbags and quickened their steps.

'It's cold enough to addle a man's brains and frost his eyes.' Peter pulled his muffler higher over his face.

'Not to mention shrivel his balls. There I go, showing my gutter origins again.' Crabbe was a phenomenon rare in the British Army until the onset of war had decimated the ranks of officers. He was a 'ranker', a private who'd risen beyond sergeant to second lieutenant and on to major by dint of brilliant soldiering.

'I've been meaning to ask. Do you ever regret leaving the ranks?' Peter side-stepped to avoid a mound of slimy, foul-smelling, mouldering vegetable waste.

'I did until peacetime soldiering became wartime soldiering. It's easier for an officer to accept a ranker when he sees one ducking the same bullets. What hurt the most was the reaction of the non-commissioned officers. I felt orphaned when they told me I was no longer welcome in the sergeants' mess.'

'As an officer they never allowed me in, but judging by the noise emanating from their quarters on celebration nights, the non-coms know how to enjoy themselves.'

'That they do,' Crabbe agreed.

'Talking of the mess, why did I agree to leave a nice warm room to accompany you on this mission of mercy?'

'Because you're kind.'

'More like the mess was so warm I'd forgotten how cold it is out here. It only seems like yesterday we were complaining it was hot enough to fry eggs in the sun, not to mention our boots and brains. Now it's too damned cold for penguins.'

'How many of those have you seen lately?' Crabbe asked.

'Don't be pedantic. Why the hell do we have to fight in this cursed land of extremes?'

'Because king and country put us here.' Crabbe, the elder by more than twenty years, answered philosophically.

'They should have put us somewhere else.'

'Like the Western Front?'

'At least we'd be within kicking distance of Piccadilly. I've forgotten what London looks like.'

'You'd only see it if you were given Blighty leave.'

'Leave – what's that?' Peter feigned innocence.

'It's described in your officer's handbook.'

'Johnny Leigh collected all the ones he could

57

find in our billet last night to feed the stove.'

'Did they keep you warm?' Crabbe enquired.

'Not for long.'

They continued past the ordnance and a row of private houses that had been knocked into a single building by the engineers and transformed into a general hospital by the Medical Service. The entire street had been commandeered. The bank and exchange was now a dressing station for the sepoys and the largest private house requisitioned and converted into an officers' hospital.

Mules, awaiting transfer to the cooks, brayed in the makeshift slaughter house as they skirted the Indian and Gurkha billets.

'I could get used to this quiet,' Crabbe commented.

'Quiet! Can't you hear the screams of the Turkish wounded in no-man's-land?' Peter winced when an agonising, earsplitting cry rent the air.

'Turkish bastards, leaving their own out there to die,' Crabbe cursed. 'Damn them to hell for starting a show on Christmas morning and firing on us when we attempted to retrieve their wounded.'

'I was on duty in the observation post at the fort.' Peter referred to the defences built by the army's civilian contractors, Lynch Brothers, in November. Adjacent to the front-line defences, the Dorsets used it to house their ammunition and field hospital.

'I heard it was hell there.'

'It wasn't pleasant,' Peter replied. 'Shortly after dawn broke I watched a Turkish officer crawl inch by inch from our lines to theirs. It took the poor beggar over two hours. When he reached the parapet of the Turkish front line, they left him hanging. All it would have taken was a tug from a friendly hand to pull him in.'

'Johnny Turk is thick-skinned, thick-headed and heartless when it comes to the plight of their wounded. Let's hope their attitude doesn't extend to our injured. God alone knows how many of ours fell into their hands after Ctesiphon.'

Peter recalled the hospital barges that had been cut loose from the burning gun boats blown up by Turkish artillery. He'd seen them drift towards the Turkish lines and feared for the fate of their human cargo, even before he'd seen the callous casual brutality the Turks meted out to their own injured.

Crabbe walked past the brick kilns into the second lines. The Anglican priest, Reverend Harald Spooner, was holding an impromptu service in a dugout. His altar was a dried milk box, a tin plate did duty as paten for the cream cracker host, and a brandy flask the cup, a score of officers and men crowded around him as he led them in a rendition of *Hark the Herald Angels Sing*. Further down the line they heard voices raised in a discordant version of *Silent Night*.

'Bizarre to be singing about heavenly peace when the entire world is at war. Especially when we're losing the best of our officers and men to the daily Turkish fusillade. There's no letup for the burial parties. The damned brass...'

'Steady, Smythe. Ranks' ears.' Crabbe whispered. 'We're all upset and capable of unravelling, but don't let anyone in command hear you talk like that. Think of the men. In a siege situation, morale is everything. You brought the cigarettes as well as the bottles?'

'Now you ask me?'

'Now I thought of it. After weeks of tight rations that whisky's gone straight to my head.'

'One tot?' Smythe was incredulous.

'That's all it took. Even that liberal helping of festive Donkey à la lamb didn't help.'

'We'll be relieved before we have to eat the horses, won't we?'

'You worried about Harry's Dorset and Somerset?'

'Bizarre, isn't it,' Smythe agreed. 'After what's happened to Harry, all I can think of is saving his horses.'

'Possibly because it's the only thing we can do for him now. Middle line ahead,' Crabbe warned. 'Remember, morale first, second, third, and last. No defeatist talk.'

They stopped at a gun emplacement manned by the Dorsets. The sappers had hung a reed curtain in front of the trench opening, carpeted it with a cheap rug from the bazaar and embellished the walls with palm leaves and crayoned illustrated texts.

GOD BLESS OUR MUD HOME,

MERRY CHRISTMAS AND PLENTY OF TURKS,

and below the decorated papers,

EXCURSIONS TO KUT AL AMARA ON CHRISTMAS DAY AND BOXING DAY BY ARRANGEMENT.

'I would knock, but you can't on reeds. Officers

begging admittance.' Crabbe pushed aside the curtain.

A sergeant, corporal, and half a dozen privates snapped to attention.

Crabbe lifted his kit bag from his shoulders and set it on the mat. 'At ease.'

'Welcome, Major Crabbe, Captain Smythe, sirs, and a Merry Christmas,' the sergeant offered them a tin plate that held half a dozen crackers.

'We would pour you a drink, sirs, but all we have is chlorinated Tigris water with a dash of lime. You're welcome to try it.' Private Evans picked up his flask and tin mug in readiness.

'We're here to offer you Christmas cheer, not the other way round.' Crabbe eyed a line of socks pinned to the side of the trench with tent pegs. One had no foot and a wag, he suspected Private Evans, had placed a bucket beneath it with another crayoned sign,

THANK YOU SANTA. OVERFLOW TO FALL BELOW.

Peter crouched down, opened his kit bag and fumbled through the contents with his mittened hands. He pulled out five packs of cigarettes, a couple of bars of chocolate and a bottle of Turkish brandy and placed them in the pail.

'Thank you, sirs. That's jolly nice of you,' Sergeant Lane picked up the brandy.

'Never thought I'd see Santa wearing an officer's uniform, Major Crabbe, Captain Smythe.'

'He comes in all guises, Private Evans. These are from the late Lieutenant Colonel Downe's personal private store, and they're to be shared between two dozen.'

'We'll drink a toast to him, sirs. May he find a good stock of brandy as well as peace in heaven.' Private Evans took the cigarettes from the pail and handed them out.

'Amen to that,' Crabbe voice wavered with suppressed emotion.

Peter averted his eyes. 'We have more Dorset dugouts to visit, so if you'll excuse us.'

'Yes, sirs. Thank you, sirs, and Merry Christmas.'

Peter and Crabbe continued walking to the outer defences to a tuneless '*For they are jolly good-fellas...*'

When they reached the front line they distributed the store of cigarettes, whisky, brandy and chocolate they'd taken from Harry's private supply and supplemented with donations they'd begged from fellow officers.

They passed sappers trying to divest themselves of dirt accumulated during a day spent digging, deepening, and widening the trenches that had become 'home'. Men with torn and bloodied hands and faces who'd returned from laying swathes of barbed wire in no-man's-land, waiting their turn for a bucket of cold water and sliver of soap. They stepped over corporals and privates curled in blankets who were trying to sleep on the damp, frozen ground.

Peter tripped as they left the forward line to enter the fort to be greeted by, 'I'm not a bloody football.'

He crouched down, slid back the shutter that concealed the flame of his oil lamp, and saw a hump of soldier swathed in full uniform, blankets, muffler, mittens, balaclava, and boots stretched on the ground.

'And we're not bloody privates, private!' Crabbe snarled.

'Sorry, sirs.' The man recognised Crabbe's voice and jumped up. 'I wasn't expecting anyone to come along here.'

'Not on picket duty, are you, corporal?' Crabbe questioned.

Sleeping on duty was a capital offence, punishment to be carried out immediately.

'No, sir. Just finished duty in a forward redoubt, sir. It's taking in water so I thought I'd find somewhere drier to kip.'

Crabbe gave the man a pack of cigarettes and a bar of chocolate. 'There's brandy up the line. Glad to see you kept your boots on.'

To the medics' annoyance a command had been passed down on Christmas Eve ordering the ranks to keep their boots on day and night, and not to remove them under any circumstances and penalty of court martial. The doctors had warned that adherence could lead to crippling infections, but the staff had ignored the advice.

Peter glanced over his shoulder at the corporal as the man rolled himself, chocolate, and cigarettes back into the blanket and returned to his spot in the leeward side of the trench.

'That order about keeping our boots on?'

'You on the doctors' side?' Crabbe asked.

'Not on anyone's side, just wondering if it was it passed down because HQ is expecting Johnny Turk to attack any minute and don't want us to lose any time dressing before fighting them off. Or do they want us to keep them on so we can run away the instant we hear them coming.'

'With the Turks in front of a loop of the Tigris that covers our back and both flanks where the hell do you think we can we run to except the guns in Johnny Turk's front line?' Crabbe demanded.

'To join the fishes.'

'I don't think the brass has mass suicide in mind for Force D.'

'Too quick and painless? And before you take me to task again about morale that was a joke.' Peter took the last of the cigarettes from his kitbag. 'After giving this lot away we'd better be relieved soon. If we're not, the price of these is going to rocket sky high. Always supposing we have any left at all.'

'I was in the wireless room this morning. Relief Force is assembling at Ali Gharbi. That's only 56 miles away. The weather is fine...'

'And cold.'

'Thank you for that. I would never have guessed. According to HQ Basra there's absolutely no reason why the Relief Force shouldn't arrive here early in January.'

'You believe that?' Peter sought reassurance.

'I do, and if you don't want to drive yourself mad, you should too,' Crabbe advised.

Chapter Five

Furja's house, Basra, morning, Thursday 30th December 1915

Hasan Mahmoud was lying on a divan, his pain evident in the creases of what could be seen of his face below the bandages that covered his right eye.

'You feel like company?' Mitkhal whispered from the doorway, reluctant to disturb his friend if he was close to sleep.

'If it's yours.'

Mitkhal sank down on the cushions opposite the divan. He unscrewed the top of a metal flask and passed it over. Hasan took it from him with his left hand. The stump – all that remained of his right – was swathed in linen.

'Furja said you slept most of yesterday afternoon and evening.'

'I did.' Hasan took a draught of brandy and handed the flask back to Mitkhal. 'Which is probably why I didn't sleep last night.'

'Drink enough of this, and you'll sleep tonight.' Mitkhal returned the flask.

'When I sleep I dream...'

'Of what?' Mitkhal was cautious. He'd discussed Hasan's dreams with Furja. She was adamant. Other than the life he'd lived with her, their children and Mitkhal, her husband's past was best left forgotten. He'd agreed, but he'd also voiced reservations, doubting that it was possible for a man to truly forget the major part of his life.

'The desert. Always the desert,' Hasan murmured through cracked lips. 'I feel at home there.'

'Not surprising, given the number of times we've ridden across it.' Mitkhal reached for his tobacco pouch.

'Where were we going?'

'Travelling out of and into Ibn Shalan's camp. Looking for hostile Bakhtairi Khans and Bani Lam who wished the tribe ill. Watching soldiers...'

'Turkish or British?'

'As you've discovered, both enjoy torturing Arabs and Bedawi in particular.'

'I was riding a horse in my dream. A magnificent grey. It had a strange name – Dorset.' Hasan's remaining eye shone, light grey, probing into Mitkhal's.

'That was your mount's name.'

'What does it mean?'

Mitkhal shrugged. 'Who knows, you acquired the name along with the mare. You won it gambling with British officers.'

'I remember another, almost as good called Somerset. Do I still own them?'

'You left them up river before the Turks took you.'

'I remember being captured. I was riding a camel.'

'A poor beast that is all the poorer now for being in the care of the Turkish bastards,' Mitkhal finished rolling the cigarette, and handed it to Hasan.

'My horses? Are they with the Turk or the British?'

'Who knows?'

'I dreamed of a house, upriver where the land is fertile. It was surrounded by grazing, lush enough for horses. I was breeding greys, beautiful animals that my children – and yours – could ride...'

'That really is a dream, Hasan. Perhaps a dream of the future, but still a dream,' Mitkhal interrupted. 'This is the only house you live in, and it's your wife's.'

'We have no other?'

'You had a black tent in Shalan's camp in the desert until Shalan forced you to divorce Furja so she could marry Ali Mansur.'

'Why did Shalan make me divorce Furja?'

'Desert politics. Ali Mansur had more guns than you and Shalan wanted to marry Ali Mansur's sister.' Lying came easily to Mitkhal. He'd done it all his life. But his heart always quickened when Hasan was the recipient of his fabrications.

'Shalan would kill us if we tried to return to his camp?' Hasan asked.

'Without a doubt. Me for helping Furja leave his camp and her husband Ali Mansur, you for disobeying his orders not to attempt to see her.'

'And the children and Furja and Gutne?'

'Would be sent out into the desert without food and water to die. We cannot return to Shalan's camp, Hasan. Or allow anyone to know other than a few trusted friends like Zabba that Furja bought this house for us to hide in. There is no foretelling what Shalan would do if he discovers us in Basra.'

Hasan finished his cigarette and stubbed it on a

clay tile. 'The Turks asked me questions about the British defences in Kut. Did I leave my horses in the town?'

'I was here with Furja and Gutne when you rode out of Kut on your camel so I don't know for certain, but if I had to guess, I'd say you left your horses in the town.'

'If they are half as magnificent as they appear in my dreams I need to go up river and find them.'

'The Turks are fighting the British upriver.'

'All the more reason to find my horses before they are shot or injured in the shelling.'

'In all probability they are already dead, my husband.' Furja entered the room.

Hasan lifted his head to look at her. 'I have to be sure.'

'You are not going anywhere until you are well again.'

'I will go.' Mitkhal rose to his feet.

Furja laid a hand on Mitkhal's arm. 'No one is leaving this house. It is too dangerous. Between the war, the Turks, the British and my father...'

Mitkhal interrupted. 'Your father won't be looking for me on the river, Furja.'

'My father will be looking for you, me and Hasan everywhere, Mitkhal. He knows it was you who helped me flee Ali Mansur. I will not allow you to leave Gutne, your son and the safety of this house to search for horses that are most likely stolen or dead.'

'Furja is right.' Hasan moved restlessly on the divan. 'Horses like the ones in my dreams will be stolen and long gone.'

Gutne joined them, 'The doctor is here, Hasan.'

'Good, he can give you a draught that will enable to sleep through the night and then perhaps you will stop turning day into night and night into day, my husband.' Furja rearranged the cushions Mitkhal had sat on.

Mitkhal followed Gutne out of the door.

'You're not really thinking of going upriver to look for Hasan's horses, are you?' Gutne asked as soon as they were out of earshot.

'I was made to roam the open desert not sit behind the walls of a town.'

'We're safe here,' she reminded.

'We're imprisoned. I can't bear to sit back doing nothing except watch Hasan suffer. He's getting no better and he knows it. If only I'd managed to get him out of that Turkish camp sooner...'

'You did well to get him out at all.'

'I rescued a shell, not a man.'

'Mitkhal...'

He ignored her and walked into the courtyard. Gutne stayed on the terrace and watched him sit on one of the benches. He pulled the flask from his robes and drank. She heard the doctor talking to Furja in the room behind her.

The doctor left, and a few moments later Furja joined her.

'Hasan has a fever.'

'He will fight it as he has fought everything else,' Gutne assured her.

'And if he recovers? We can't keep our men locked up forever, Gutne.' There was resignation as well as sadness in Furja's voice.

'Aren't you afraid that if Hasan leaves, he'll

remember he was a British officer?'

'Terrified,' Furja conceded. 'But I have him for now, and for a while longer. The doctor has forbidden him to exert himself until all signs of fever have abated and he is completely well. That won't be for months.'

'Pity the doctor cannot forbid Mitkhal to leave.'

'I'll remind Mitkhal of his duty to you and his son, Gutne.' Furja moved to the door.

'Save your breath, Furja,' Gutne advised. 'You'd have more success caging a lion.'

The Basra Club, Thursday 30th December 1915

Charles Reid waved to Angela Smythe when he saw her walk through the door into the club. He didn't rise to meet her. Despite the best efforts of the medics in Basra's military hospital, his leg wound hadn't healed. Crippling pains shot from his ankle to his thigh every time he tried to stand, which was why he'd been rolled into the club in a wheelchair, and given strict instructions not to leave it.

'You look very elegant,' he complimented her, when Angela joined him at the prime table he'd commandeered next to the stove.

'As elegant as a Basra Jewish tailor's idea of Paris fashion allows. Sorry I'm late. I returned to the mission to disinfect myself and change after my stint in the Lansing so I'd be safe to touch.' She kissed his cheek.

Basra's military medical resources had been overwhelmed by the tide of British casualties that

70

had flooded downstream after the Battle of Ctesiphon, so the Turkish POW and native wounded had been diverted to the Lansing Memorial Hospital, a charitable institution financed and run by an American Baptist mission. Angela's brother, Dr Theodore Wallace, worked there under the direction of Dr Picard. As inundated as the British Military facilities, every available pair of hands in the mission had been roped in to help at the Lansing. Even Angela's, although she usually taught in the mission school.

'Disinfect – fever's broken out?' Charles signalled to the waiter.

'No, thank heaven. Since the cold weather began we haven't had a single fever case that wasn't rooted in wound infection. But a Turkish POW has developed gas gangrene.'

'Poor man, and poor you having to quarantine him and scrub out the ward.'

'When I left, Sister Margaret was barking orders louder than any sergeant major and Theo and Dr Picard were cowering at their desks in their office. Neither is brave enough to stand up to her.' She frowned. 'I was amazed when I received your invitation.'

'Colonel Allan prescribed the outing. He thought it would "cheer me up".'

'Doesn't he realise that everyone who knew Harry and John Mason has been devastated by their deaths?'

'Yes, but sending me here will brighten the atmosphere in the ward for the other patients.'

'Are you sure you should be walking about?'

71

She was concerned by the pain lines etched deep around Charles's eyes and the way his hand shook when he offered her a cigarette.

'I'm not walking, I'm wheeling. A man can't lie in bed for ever. Colonel Allan gave me a three-hour pass as a test as well as a treat. If I – or rather my leg – behaves he intends to discharge me at the beginning of next week.'

'To convalesce in India?'

He shook his head. 'My wound isn't severe enough to warrant a spell of leave.'

'Rubbish! You sure you're not playing truant?'

'Absolutely. Ask Colonel Allan if you don't believe me.'

'I will the next time I see him,' she asserted. 'You're obviously sick. I bet he only let you come here as an experiment because he needs your bed for an officer who's freezing in one of the ancillary tents outside the hospital. If you don't survive he gets your bed, if you do, he still gets the bed early next week. You're a kill or cure venture.'

'I love the way you Americans murder the English language. I am no longer "sick" as you so quaintly put it. If I'm discharged next week, I won't even be a convalescent but officially fit for duty.'

'That I don't believe.'

'Provided they let me keep this chair, I'm quite capable of sitting behind a desk and pushing papers from one side to another. It might not be interesting or even constructive, but it's all the brass has been doing in Basra HQ since Ctesiphon.'

'Have you found somewhere to stay if you're

discharged from the hospital?'

'Major Chalmers offered me a room in his bungalow.' The waiter appeared. 'Whisky, sherry, brandy, gin?' Charles asked her.

'A gin and tonic would be lovely, thank you. It's been a long foul day.'

'A double gin and tonic for the lady and I'll have another brandy and soda please on my account.'

The waiter went to the bar.

'Two brandy and sodas after your last bout of fever?' Angela admonished him.

'Three brandies, to be mathematically exact. They brought me here early.'

'You're yellow.'

'When Harry saw me before Ctesiphon he said if it was spring he could lose me in the daffodil meadow in Clyneswood.'

'That sounds so like Harry.' She smiled at a memory she didn't voice. 'Clyneswood – is that the house where Harry grew up?'

'It's beautiful.' Charles's eyes misted. 'As is John's family home, Stouthall. Harry's family home is Tudor. It dates back to the Elizabethan age. John's is newer, only two hundred years old. I envied both of them their family history and their lives occupying the same rooms their ancestors had done for centuries.'

'Every family has a history.'

'My father's, his father's, and so on back to caveman days is army camps and soldiering. My father bought a house close to Clyneswood when he retired from the Indian army. It's nice enough from the outside. Inside it's military quarters.

There's nothing there that couldn't have come out of a kitbag apart from the furniture and that's good-quality, dull, and unimaginative. Replicas of the pieces in every officers' mess in the Empire. But enough of me, John, and Harry. You look exhausted,' Charles moved so the waiter could set down their drinks. 'I know Sister Margaret's a slave driver and your brother and Dr Picard exacting, but surely you can stop working in the hospital now? All the Turkish casualties who are still breathing are down from Ctesiphon and there won't be any more fighting until we go upstream to relieve Kut. Your pupils must be missing you.'

'Not in the Christmas and New Year holidays, they're not. But Theo did say at the end of my shift that I can return to teaching when the spring term starts next week.'

Charles held his finger to his lips.

A middle-aged major wearing the insignia of the 6th Poona Division was booming loud enough to be heard above an artillery barrage. 'I don't know why we put up with civilians in this club. Treating the place as if it's their own...'

'You brave enough to tell him this is a civilian club whose members graciously allow officers to use the facilities?'

'Not me. Like Theo and Dr Picard, I'm a coward.' She reached for her gin and tonic. 'There are a lot of officers here fresh off the boat. Would I be right in assuming the push upstream to relieve Kut is imminent?'

Charles lowered his voice. 'I've heard we won't be going up to get Peter and the others out until we have sufficient manpower and arms to do the

74

job properly.'

'Too late for Harry and Captain Mason.'

Charles gripped his glass so tightly she thought it would shatter.

'I'm sorry. I won't mention their names again.'

'That would be worse. As though we were trying to deny they'd lived.' Charles swallowed his brandy and immediately felt light-headed. Given his weakened state he realised if he didn't slow up he'd soon be too drunk to stand. He wondered if that's what Colonel Allan had had in mind when he'd insisted on the wheelchair. 'I received a letter this morning from one of Harry's friends, Major Warren Crabbe. This was enclosed for you.' He handed her a postcard. On one side was a sketch of a soldier lolling beneath a palm tree, glass in one hand, slice of cake in the other. Whoever had drawn the sketch, she knew it wasn't Peter. His artistic skills only extended as far as matchstick men. On the back, next to her name and address, Peter had scrawled,

Christmas Greetings from Kut. Am well and missing you, all my love as ever, Peter.

Angela stared at the postcard. It had been in Peter's hands only a few days ago. He'd written he loved her – she wished she could turn the clock back and accompany it on a return journey through the besieging lines of Turkish troops. Watch Peter write it, hug him. Tell him no matter what, they would survive the war somehow and build a good life together...

'Do you know Major Warren Crabbe?' Charles's voice intruded on her thoughts.

'I've met him. Like Peter and Harry he was

75

stationed here before the war.' She didn't look up from the postcard but ran her fingers over the surface. She knew she was being ridiculous but she couldn't help feeling that in touching it, she was in some way reaching her husband.

'The lieutenant who brought the letter to the hospital said Crabbe entrusted it to one of the ghulams who've been smuggling communications out of Kut. I dread to think how much he had to pay the man to carry it.'

'Did Major Crabbe say anything about the conditions in Kut?' Angela asked.

'Not really,' Charles fudged. 'He wanted me to know that although Harry's posted "missing" there's no hope he's alive. Before the Turkish blockade was raised, Townshend sent the tanks and the cavalry south under the command of Lieutenant Colonel Leachman. Harry went out shortly afterwards. He was in native robes and accompanied by two Arab ghulams. Our sentries heard snipers in the Turk forward posts. One of the ghulams returned with Harry's bloodied robes. He told Crabbe Harry had been killed by the first volley.'

'So there's absolutely no chance that Harry survived and was taken prisoner?'

'None, I'm afraid,' Charles confirmed. 'Crabbe asked me to write to Harry's family because he didn't want them to cling to false hope.'

'Did he mention Captain Mason?' Angela asked.

'No.'

'Don't you think that's odd?'

'The letter took some time to get to me. It was dated the second week of December. John died

76

of fever. It's possible he hadn't even been taken ill when Crabbe wrote.'

'In which case you think Captain Mason would have written to you about Harry, not Major Crabbe.'

'John wouldn't have had time to breathe. No doctor would, once the wounded reached the aid stations inside Kut.'

She stared into her glass. 'I can't believe I'll never see Harry or Captain Mason again.'

Charles downed his brandy in silence.

'Reverend Butler asked me to enquire if you'd like him to organise a memorial service for Harry. He had so many friends in the town.'

Charles smiled at the thought of the gamblers and whores in Abdul's piling into the austere confines of the mission chapel. 'Most of Harry's friends are too scurrilous for the Reverend and Mrs Butler to want in their chapel.'

'Reverend Butler is broad-minded.'

'Broad-minded enough to allow Mohammedans, Jews, Bedouin, and ladies of the night into his pews?'

'Perhaps not,' Angela allowed. 'But that was Harry. He made friends with everyone he met. Have you heard anything from his wife or his bearer, Mitkhal? The handsome Arab who looks like a bandit?'

'I haven't heard from him. You know about Harry's wife?' Charles was surprised.

'I know he married a Bedouin.'

'He told you?'

'Maud did. She said she and John honeymooned in Harry's father-in-law's house, here in

Basra before the war. If you know where she is, Charles, I'd like to call on her.'

'I've never met her but the fact that Harry kept her separate from the rest of the people in his life suggests he knows we wouldn't have mixed.'

'Maud said she was a sheikh's daughter and her father made Harry promise he'd never ask her to live among Europeans. Harry had no choice but to keep her away from us.'

'But not John and Maud, at least not after Maud's mother's death.' Charles had always sensed that Harry and John had not been entirely truthful about the death of Emily Perry.

Emily had died the night she, Maud, he, and John had arrived in Basra from India. They'd shared a wonderful and memorable summer. Emily and Maud had been sent to visit friends there by Maud's father, in the hope that Maud would find a suitable officer husband. John had fallen in love with Maud the first time he'd caught sight of her. He'd shocked John by falling in love with Maud's mother, Emily.

His love had been reciprocated but Emily had insisted on keeping their affair secret and returning to her husband in Basra. Having no choice but to comply with Emily's wishes, he'd left Basra for England the morning before John's wedding

When he'd heard that Emily had died from a scorpion bite shortly after his departure, he'd been suspicious. Especially when he'd discovered Emily's body had been found outside Harry's bungalow barely an hour after he'd left it.

Angela disturbed his train of thought. 'Personally I can't understand this segregation between races. We're born equal...'

'According to the American Declaration of Independence,' Charles broke in, 'but the truth is some races don't want to mix. There's more animosity between the Hindus, Muslims, and Sikhs than between Indian and Anglo-Saxon.' He felt uncomfortable even as he said it. His life had been saved after Ctesiphon by his Indian bearer. A bearer he'd since discovered was his half-brother.

'An excuse Anglo-Saxons use to safeguard their superiority complex.'

'Is that a repetition of American philosophy or do you really believe what you just said?'

'I most definitely believe it,' Angela insisted.

'Are you saying that Americans don't believe they outshine every other nationality?'

'How can we, when you British constantly remind us that your education, history, and sense of fair play are vastly superior?'

'Touché.' He touched his glass to hers. 'Remind me to continue this discussion when my head isn't quite so fuzzy from brandy and painkillers.'

'If you should see Harry's bearer, will you ask him to call on me at the mission please, Charles?'

'If you want me to.'

'Do you think he knows Harry's dead?'

'Given how close they were, he either knows or was killed alongside him.' Needing to change the subject from Harry and John, he asked, 'Has Maud settled on a name for her baby?'

'She was undecided when I left this morning.'

'She's not going to name him after John?'

'Not when the whole of Basra knows the baby isn't John's child.'

'Has the father appeared?'

'Not that I've seen.' Maud had confided to Angela that her baby was the result of rape. Theo confirmed that Maud had reported a rape to an Indian Army doctor, but Angela didn't feel she should pass on the information, even to Charles. It was Maud's secret, not hers to tell. 'Will you dine at the mission tonight? Reverend and Mrs Butler would love to see you.'

'Thank you for the invitation but I invited Chalmers to dine with me here in return for offering to put me up. And here he is.'

'Mrs Smythe, Reid. Good evening.' Richard Chalmers joined them.

Angela finished her drink. 'If you'll excuse me, I must go. Given Mrs Butler's cook's temper, I dare not be late for dinner.'

'I'll escort you,' Charles offered.

'In your wheelchair?'

'Tough luck, Charles. That prerogative falls to me.' Richard Chalmers offered Angela his arm.

'Thank you, Major Chalmers, but my brother said he'd pick me up here at six and it's five past now. Thank you for the lovely drink, Charles.' Angela kissed his cheek. 'Take care and visit us soon. You too, Major Chalmers. The Butlers would love to meet you.'

'Reid gets a kiss and I don't,' Chalmers joked.

'A small one, all I can spare from Peter's ration.' She brushed her lips across Major Chalmers's cheek and almost ran from the room.

Her marriage to Peter had been far from idyllic,

but close proximity to any man in uniform who exuded authority and the unique British officer's scent of starch, leather oil, tooth powder, and shaving soap kindled memories, and the realisation just how much she missed Peter's presence in her life.

Chapter Six

Lansing Memorial Mission, Basra, late evening Thursday 30th December 1915

Angela knocked on the door of Maud's bedroom, opening it at Maud's 'Come'.

Maud was sitting in a chair, reading. The native nursemaid she'd employed to look after her child was feeding her six-day-old son from a glass baby's bottle.

Maud set her book aside. 'Did you see Charles?' The last person Maud wanted to hear about was Charles Reid, but as Angela had told her she was meeting him in the Basra Club, she didn't want to risk exciting Angela's suspicions that something was amiss between her and John's childhood friend.

'Yes.'

'How is he?'

'In a wheelchair, but well in himself considering what he's been through. He asked after you and the baby.'

'Really?' Maud was surprised.

81

'He asked if you'd named him.'

'I have.' Maud glanced at the baby. His eyes had grown heavy and his body was relaxed. He lolled away from the bottle, his mouth still full of milk.

'Would you like me to wind him and get him down so the nurse can wash the bottle?' Angela offered.

'If you like.'

Angela spoke to the nursemaid in Arabic. The woman handed the baby over and left the room.

'I thought I'd call him Robin after my mother's father. I never knew him. He died when Mother was twelve, but she spoke fondly of him.'

'Robin John?' Angela suggested.

'Just Robin. As John and I didn't live together for over a year before he was born I'm reverting to my maiden name. He'll be Robin Perry so the Masons won't have further cause to be angry with me.'

'Have they written to you?'

'Not since I received official notification of John's death. There hasn't been time for mail from England to reach here. John's parents and his sister wrote regularly after our marriage. It was hard to read the letters they sent after John was posted to the front. They assumed I was a perfect wife and John was a fortunate man. I've finally found the courage to tell them the truth.' She pointed to three envelopes on her travelling desk. 'The third letter is for John's brother. I don't have his address but I've written to him care of his parents.'

'You can't tell them the baby isn't John's,'

Angela protested. 'There's no point now John's dead.'

'There's every point, Angela. I can't allow them to believe that my baby is their grandchild and nephew.'

Angela set the baby down in the crib and tucked the shawl around him. 'Most women would.'

'Not women people talk about. British military society is merciless towards those who've broken their rules. I'm not sure how long I can stay here when it's obvious the baby can't possibly be John's. There's gossip about me. Gossip that will, if it hasn't already, affect the reputation of the mission.'

'No one in the mission takes any notice of gossip, Maud.'

'You can't ignore the fact that Harriet agreed to look after me before the baby was born, only to change her mind after he arrived.' Maud had been hurt by Harriet's change of heart. Harriet had been her mother's maid in England, accompanied her to India after her marriage, and accepted the post of ladies' maid to her after her mother's death.

'Harriet's pregnant,' Angela reminded her.

'One or two months,' Maud dismissed the comment. 'Nothing that would have prevented her from helping me.'

Harriet had married Sergeant Greening shortly after Charles had dragged Maud and Harriet to Basra from India in the hope of silencing rumours in the Indian army about Maud's adulterous exploits. Harriet hadn't remained with Maud long after their arrival, and Maud had wondered if Harriet's sudden marriage had more to do with distancing herself from her mistress's tainted reputation than love for Sergeant Greening.

'I've heard Harriet is suffering badly from morning sickness.' Angela said in the maid's defence.

'Face it, Angela, the only military wife to pay a call on me since Robin's birth is Colonel Allan's, and she felt duty bound as her husband had delivered him.'

'The others are probably observing etiquette. Isn't it usual to wait ten days before visiting a new mother?'

'They won't come,' Maud declared. 'Reverend and Mrs Butler have been very kind but I can't continue to impose on their hospitality.'

'Do you want to go back to England?'

'"Go back"? I've never set foot in the country and don't know a soul there.'

'India?'

'The gossip is bad here; it would be unbearable there. I'd be totally ostracised. Here at least I have you and the Butlers.'

'You should talk to Reverend and Mrs Butler,' Angela advised. 'They found your services in running the mission invaluable before the baby was born, so please don't make any decisions without consulting them.'

'After all they've done for me and the baby, it would ill-mannered not to. Has Charles heard anything from Kut?'

Maud's father, Colonel George Perry, was with the beleaguered force and Angela assumed Maud was hoping for news of him. 'Charles received a letter from Major Crabbe that was smuggled out, but the major only mentioned Harry. He wrote that a ghulam witnessed Harry's death and there was no hope.'

'Poor Harry. I can't bear to think how many more will pay the ultimate price.'

'Neither can I.' Angela shivered at the thought of Peter marooned in Kut. 'Can I get you anything?'

'No, thank you, Angela.' Maud left the chair and hugged her. 'You've been very kind.'

Angela opened the door and hesitated. 'Promise me you won't take any notice of the gossips, Maud?'

'I can't promise that, Angela. I wouldn't mind if their poison was only directed at me, but their vicious tongues are hurting the Butlers, the mission, you, Theo, and Dr Picard, and that's hard to take.'

Angela had never been a good liar and she'd run out of comforting things to say. 'See you in the morning, Maud. Sleep well.'

'You too, Angela, and thank you.'

'For what?'

'Being a friend when I desperately need one.'

Basra, early morning, Friday 31st December 1915

The ranking Transport Officer, Major Perkins, faced Tom square on, blocking his exit from the gangplank. 'I don't care how many brothers you have stationed with the Indian Expeditionary Force, Captain Mason. You have twelve hours. If

85

you are on this wharf any later than six o'clock this evening you will be declared AWOL. Do I make myself clear?'

'Perfectly, sir.' Tom paused just long enough after the 'perfectly' and before the 'sir' to let the officer know what he thought of him.

'Do we know our destination, sir?' Michael enquired from behind Tom.

Major Perkins eyed Michael's civilian clothes. 'And you are?'

'War correspondent, sir.'

'Which paper?'

'*Daily Mirror*, sir.

'Never read it. On a need-to-know basis, your destination is "upstream".'

'Thank you, sir.' Michael didn't pause between his words but he knew, from Harry's tutoring, the exact inflection to transform 'sir' into an insult.

Distracted by a sepoy who'd unloaded officers' kits on to a cart destined for other use, Major Perkins left them.

'Ten guineas says he was a civil servant in peacetime.' Tom stepped down from the gang-plank of the shallow-draught vessel that had brought them up from the Shatt-al-Arab, where they'd had to leave the deep draught *Royal George*.

'You'll get no takers.' A slim one-armed man joined them on the quayside. Tom and Michael had enjoyed the company of Edmund Candler, the official eye-witness and *Times* and *Manchester Guardian* correspondent on the voyage.

'Do you think Major Perkins knows our destination any more than we do?' Tom enquired.

'Upstream,' Candler repeated with a smile.

Michael looked along the wharf. A few clumps of palm broke the line of unprepossessing, low-built, mud brick buildings.

'Dear God, Harry called Basra the Piccadilly of Mesopotamia. What the hell have we let ourselves in for?' He swatted ineffectually at a swarm of flies.

'You know Harry's sense of humour.' Tom removed his topee and waved it in front of his face.

'See you later, gentlemen.' Edmund Candler headed away from the wharf.

'Upstream,' Tom shouted after him.

'You have orders, sirs?' Adjabi and Sami appeared from the second gangplank where the bearers and sepoys were disembarking.

'Our kit secure?' Tom checked.

'All locked, sirs, in the secure hold,' Sami confirmed.

'Then you can take the day off to look around Basra,' Tom said.

'You too, Adjabi, but be back here at five thirty,' Michael warned.

The bearers bowed and ran off in the direction of the rooftops behind the quayside palms and buildings.

'It's cooler than I expected,' Michael observed.

'That's because it's winter. If you've any sense you'll get yourself posted out of Mesopotamia before summer.' Richard Chalmers climbed out of a carriage and introduced himself. 'Welcome to Mesopotamia, even if you are a civilian,' he noted Michael's suit.'

'Thank you.' Michael shook his hand.

'I'm here to meet my cousin Boris Bell. You

probably came in on the same boat. Do you know him?'

'Of course they do.' Boris joined them 'You look ten years older than when I last saw you a year ago, Richard.'

'Nothing like a compliment from a cousin. You all bound for Ali Gharbi tonight?'

'All we've been told is upstream,' Tom replied.

'Good men. Someone's got to get Townshend out of Kut.'

'Out of – he's trapped?' Michael asked.

'Where've you been, man?'

'On board a ship getting here for the last month,' Tom explained.

'You weren't in radio contact?'

'The captain was. He didn't believe in sharing information.' Michael dropped his attaché case. 'When we left London, Townshend had just fallen back from Ctesiphon.'

'He retired to Kut al Amara. The Turkish forces now under the command of a German, Baron von der Goltz, have him pinned down in the town.'

'Any news on casualties?' Tom asked. 'We both have brothers with Townshend.'

'Officers?' Chalmers took a packet of Camel cigarettes from his pocket and offered them to Tom and Michael.

'My brother, John Mason, is a major in the Medical Corps.'

'My brother is a political officer, Lieutenant Colonel Harry Downe.'

Richard Chalmers was adept at concealing his emotions. 'I'm bunking with a friend of theirs, or I will be when he's discharged from hospital:

Major Charles Reid.'

'Charles is here, not with Townshend?' Tom's spirits rose. His brother was so close to Charles and Harry he had sudden hopes of finding all three in Basra.

'Charles was wounded at Ctesiphon. He's in hospital but on the mend.'

'Where's the hospital?' Michael picked up his attaché case.

'It's on the way to my quarters where I've had my bearer prepare a feast for Boris, not that he deserves it.'

'After what I've been forced to eat to survive on voyage I deserve every ounce of sustenance you've scavenged. Hope there's a decent vintage to wash it down.'

'You can hope.' Richard smiled at Boris's crest-fallen expression. 'Cousins!' he clapped his arm around Boris's shoulders. 'Appears this sideshow is something of a family occasion for all of us.'

Military Hospital, Basra, morning, Friday 31st December 1915

Michael and Tom heard Charles's shouts even before they entered the hospital. A young medic backed out of the ward as they approached.

He nodded to Richard, said 'I refused to discharge him,' and disappeared.

Richard strode into the ward. 'Smile, best manners called for, Charles, you have visitors.'

Charles looked up, saw Michael, and murmured, 'Harry.'

'Michael.' Michael held out his hand. 'It's good to see you, Charles.'

Charles struggled to regain his composure. 'It's good to see you, and Tom, too.' He turned to Tom. 'You resemble John but not enough to be mistaken for him, whereas Michael ... what the hell are you both doing here?'

'We got in half an hour ago,' Tom revealed, 'met Major Chalmers on the wharf and he kindly brought us here. Where are John and Harry? Are they in Basra too?'

Richard went to the door. 'I can't leave my cousin in the carriage when he only has a day here. I'll leave you to your reunion, Charles. See you later.'

Charles didn't blame Richard for retreating. If the situation had been reversed he'd have done the same thing. He waved a goodbye and turned to Michael. 'You're not in uniform?'

Michael pulled up a chair and lowered his voice so as not to disturb the other patients. 'The army rejected me because of my leg. I'm war correspondent for the *Mirror*. We only just heard about Kut being besieged.'

'When we left London they were calling it "General Townshend's strategic withdrawal". Are John and Harry with him?' Tom pulled up another chair.

'Are John and Harry in Kut?' Michael reiterated when Charles didn't answer.

Charles gripped his metal bed head until his knuckles turned white. 'They're dead.'

'Dead!' Michael began to shake. 'Both of them?'

'Both of them,' Charles confirmed.

90

'They can't be. Not Harry...'

Charles started talking. Once he began he couldn't stop. He knew exactly how Tom and Michael felt. He hadn't wanted to believe Harry and John were dead either. They'd been far more than friends. They'd been an integral part of him – his life – his childhood and the best part of him had died with them.

'Townshend arrived at Kut on December 3rd. On the 4th and 5th he sent his aeroplanes and all his river craft except the gunboats *Firefly* and *Sumana* downstream. On the 6th Leachman led out the cavalry and tanks. Most made it to Ali Gharbi. Townshend sent fourteen hundred Turkish prisoners here. He's been left with nine or ten thousand fighting men. With camp followers there are fifteen thousand on his ration muster but two thousand of those are sick. He faces a Turkish force, estimated by aeroplane reconnaissance, of twenty-five thousand infantry, cavalry, and camelry, thirty-one mobile guns, and seven heavy guns, plus thousands of Arabs. On the 9th Nureddin demanded Townshend surrender. Townshend refused. Since then the garrison's been under bombardment. Townshend asked permission to retreat, but General Nixon refused...'

'I don't want a bloody military report. I want to know what happened to Harry.' Michael was so pale Tom thought he was about to pass out.

'Harry left Kut a couple of hours after Leachman. He was in Arab robes, accompanied by Arab ghulams.'

'He was sent to spy on the Turks?' Michael guessed.

'That's what political officers do and Harry was damned good at it.'

'He always did like dressing up.' Tom regretted the fatuous remark as soon as he made it.

'After war broke out Harry alternated spying on the Turks and Arabs with fighting alongside us. According to Harry's friend Crabbe,' Charles rummaged in his locker, produced Crabbe's letter, and handed it to Michael, 'Harry was ambushed after he and his ghulams left our lines. One ghulam returned with Harry's bloodied robes. He told the CO that Harry and the second ghulam fell at the first volley and he'd seen their bodies. Crabbe had no doubt from the ghulam's account that Harry was dead.'

'If they were behind Turkish lines they could have been taken prisoner...'

'An eye-witness said Harry was dead, Michael.' Charles couldn't bring himself to utter any of the platitudes that littered last letters home. 'He died instantly.' 'He didn't suffer.' 'The end was swift and painless'.

He'd resorted to them himself when the deceased soldier's end had been anything but dignified, swift, or pain-free.

'John?' Tom demanded.

'Died of fever in Kut after Nureddin raised the siege. Crabbe knew Harry and John well. Harry was incredibly popular, as was John. I find it difficult to believe I'll never see them again. It must be much worse for you to arrive here to be told they're dead. I wrote to you, your parents, Georgie, and Lucy but you obviously left England before my letters arrived.'

Michael finished reading Crabbe's letter and handed it to Tom. 'There's no hope, no hope at all.' It wasn't a question.

Charles opened his locker again and brought out a metal flask. He filled the top with brandy, handed it to Michael, and gave Tom the flask. Tom refilled Michael's cup after he emptied it.

'How soon are we going in to relieve Kut?' Tom screwed the top back on the flask.

'I've heard that Townshend only has supplies for four more weeks of siege. Our forces are gathering at Ali Gharbi. From there the plan is to advance, relieve Kut, and move on to take Baghdad. I'm guessing the next show will be within the next week and somewhere between Ali Gharbi and Kut.'

'The Turks?' Michael asked.

'Dug in and well equipped. They haven't let up. They inflicted major assaults on Kut on the 24th and 25th. Two days ago the Turks requested an armistice to bury their dead. We sent up planes for reconnaissance. Estimates put their dead at over two thousand. Townshend wired Nixon that ours were four hundred including seventeen officers.

'I suppose we'll find out more when we go upstream.' Tom returned the flask to Charles.

'What time's your boat leaving?'

'Six.'

'As a war correspondent, I'm hoping to beg a ride,' Michael added.

'The brass will offer you anything you want, on condition you show them your dispatches before you send them,' Charles warned.

'What about John's wife?' Tom asked. 'Is she

still in Basra?'

Charles hesitated before answering, 'She is.'

'Don't tell me there's more bad news. Is she ill...'

'She had a baby on Christmas Eve.'

'My mother will be pleased. Did John know?'

'He knew she was pregnant. Maud was notified of his death before the birth. She's living in the Baptist mission attached to the Lansing Memorial Hospital if you want to see her.'

'I'd like to.'

'I'll go with you.'

'You're not fit enough.' Tom looked at Charles with a professional eye.

'They let me out in a wheelchair last night; they can do it again now. You should come with us, Michael. The people there knew Harry as well as John. They'd be pleased to see you but there's one thing you should both know before we leave. The baby is Maud's but it's not John's. Your sister-in-law is a whore, Tom.'

Chapter Seven

Kut al Amara, Friday 31st December 1915

'I joined the bloody army to fight. Not to burrow in bloody holes and live like a bloody rabbit. I dig in bloody dirt. I live in bloody dirt. I eat bloody dirt. I sleep on bloody dirt. I even feel like a bloody rabbit. Look at my strong back legs and big ears.'

94

Private Bert Evans helped carry Sergeant Lane inside the house that had been commandeered by Townshend's 6th Division as an aid station for the front lines.

'Just how many "bloodies" can you get in one sentence, Private Evans?' Major David Knight of the Indian Medical service held open the door of the room that did duty as dressing area.

'A lot more than I just said, sir,' Bert continued unabashed as he and his companion hauled Sergeant Lane inside and dumped him on a chair. 'The "bloodies" are for you, sir. Usually I'm less polite.'

'I don't doubt it.' David Knight examined the bullet wound in the sergeant's shoulder. Lead shot was embedded in his collarbone. Blood and bone splinters had sprayed over his tunic. 'Matthews?' David called for the orderly.

'Sir.' He appeared in the doorway.

'Clean this up, and warn the duty orderly I'll need the theatre in the non-coms and ranks hospital to operate.'

'Sir.' Matthews called to the duty orderly before picking up a bowl, a jug of boiled water, gauze pads, and scissors.

'Johnny Turk's starting the fusillade early today. He usually holds back until four o'clock,' Knight tipped water into a bowl, took a bar of carbolic soap and began scrubbing his hands.

'Judging by the bullets flying our way, the opposition's brought some keen snipers up the line, sir. The minute they see an officer's cap or stripes on a non-com's sleeve they let rip and unlike Petulant Fanny they usually hit their target.'

95

On the right bank of the Tigris the Turks had set up a trench mortar that fired noisy 15-inch bronze shells. All aimed at the same spot, slightly ahead of the British redoubts, but 'Petulant Fanny', as the troops had christened the mortar, had yet to hit rank, file, or a single military target.

John Mason's bearer Dira ran in, shouting, 'Officer coming, Sahib Knight. Badly wounded.'

Two stretcher-bearers from the 6th Poona Division burst in carrying Major Cleck-Heaton. Blood covered the right side of the major's face from a head wound that was still pumping.

'Couldn't have happened to a nicer officer,' Knight muttered.

'Sir?' Matthews was unsure he'd heard correctly.

'Bowl and swabs, Matthews, the shoulder wound will have to wait.'

'Bloody officers always get in first,' Bert swore.

'Another comment like that, Private Evans, will see you on a charge. Head wound takes precedence over shoulder wound, whether the head wound's a sepoy, private, or colonel,' David snapped. 'Set the major on that table.'

David soaked a pad of gauze in the bowl Matthews held for him and swabbed Cleck-Heaton's face. The bullet had entered just below his right eye socket. But Dira had failed to notice the bullet hole in the major's chest.

'Prepare the major for surgery, Matthews. Dira, tell the orderlies to get the theatre ready in the officers' hospital. Then fetch Sergeant Greening and his prisoner. There's only one doctor who'd dare operate on that chest wound.'

'He finished a fifteen-hour shift two hours ago, sir,' Matthews reminded him.

'I know but he's the only one with enough surgical experience to tackle this. Go, Dira. Tell him the patient's Cleck-Heaton, and I wouldn't blame him for refusing to come.'

Dira left the building. He kept his head low. Although the aid station and hospitals were well behind the lines, many areas of the town were within the sights of the Turkish forward posts across the river and within range of their snipers, if not their major guns. He passed a rickety, irregular row of squalid, crumbling mud brick houses. Women were squatting in front of them, gathered around mud ovens, cooking their thick pancake 'kababs'. Grubby children played in the dirt beside them. Half a dozen older girls were grinding corn in shallow stone bowls. As soon as they had enough to mix to a paste they carried it in their hands to the women nearest the stoves. Immersed in their task, the locals didn't even glance up at Dira as he ran to the end of the street.

The building HQ had requisitioned for use as a prison was mud brick. It appeared to be crumbling but there were sturdy iron bars at every window and the door was metal. Dira banged on it with his closed fist. It was opened by a sergeant from the Mahrattas. Dira stepped into the mud-walled and -floored room to be instantly over-whelmed by the stench of raw sewage. Four Indian sepoys were sitting around a table. A bunch of keys, a charcoal-fuelled burner with kettle, a tray of mugs, and a set of dice lay in front of them.

'Cha?' the sergeant offered Dira.

Dira kept his lips tightly closed and tried not to breathe too deeply. He shook his head. 'Thank you, but no. I'm in a hurry.'

Knowing what Dira wanted, the sergeant lit an oil lamp and handed it to him along with the keys.

Dira unlocked a metal door set in a side wall. It opened on a steep stone staircase that wound down to the cellar. As he began his descent the reek of damp and excrement intensified. The temperature plummeted to the freezing low that made sleep impossible at night. At the foot of the winding stair was a two-metre-square hallway. It held a chair, army cot, and low-burning oil lamp. Sergeant Greening of the 2nd Dorsets was stretched out on the cot, wrapped in his uniform, greatcoat, boots and two blankets.

Dira shook him.

The sergeant opened one eye and squinted. 'I'm dead.'

'You're talking.'

'I'm a talking corpse.'

'Major Knight sent for your prisoner. It's urgent. Major Cleck-Heaton has been badly wounded.'

'That's bloody marvellous, Dira. Do you mind if we celebrate later when I'm not tired.'

'Major Knight said you're to bring your prisoner at once.'

'That's bloody rich.'

'Sahib Knight says Major Cleck-Heaton's only hope is your prisoner.'

'If Cleck-Heaton had had his way the man who's been asked to save him would have been

98

shot by a firing squad, weeks ago. Let's pretend that's what happened. Inform Major Knight that Major Cleck-Heaton has no saviour to call on.'

'I've been given orders.'

Realising Dira was about to lose his temper, Sergeant Greening rose slowly from the cot so as not to topple it. 'Keep your hair on.' He filched the keys from his belt and unlocked the only door in the hall. He picked up the oil lamp and stepped into an ice-cold, windowless cell.

'Major Mason, sir, Major Knight has sent for you. Major Cleck-Heaton has been wounded. Major Knight says you're the only one who can save him.'

British Military Hospital, Basra, Friday 31st December 1915

After ten minutes of heated argument and intervention by a senior medical officer who'd known and respected John in India, Charles was given permission to visit the Lansing Memorial Mission with Tom and Michael. An orderly was sent to summon a carriage while Charles dressed. When Charles was ready, he refused to sit in a wheelchair. The Indian orderly who'd helped him don his uniform settled the discussion by simply lifting Charles into the chair and wheeling him to the door.

To Charles's annoyance the orderly also hoisted him into the carriage and pushed the chair in after him. Wracked by pain, exhausted by the effort it had taken to dress and reach the outside,

Charles sank back in the seat.

'Leg wound followed by fever?' Tom climbed in and sat on the bench seat opposite Charles.

'It appears that you, like your brother, never stop being a doctor,' Charles snapped.

'Am I right?'

'Not entirely. I had fever before I was wounded as well as after.'

'You're lucky to be in one piece, and you're not helping yourself by fighting medical advice. Model patients who follow their doctors' instructions recover more quickly,' Tom remonstrated.

'Model patients are sent to recuperate in India. I have friends in Kut with Townshend. Someone has to get them out.'

'Not a major who's unfit for duty,' Tom declared. 'Charles...'

Tired of banter, Charles ran his hand over the leather upholstery. 'This old landau looks like the one Harry won from a sheikh in a card game before the war.'

'Lieutenant Colonel Downe's carriage. Yes, sir. It belonged to Lieutenant Colonel Downe.' The driver nodded.

'He sold it to you?' Charles asked.

'Not sold, sir. I drive it for the owner,' the man replied.

'If you drive it for the owner Lieutenant Colonel Downe must have sold it,' Charles pressed him.

'Lieutenant Colonel Downe gave it to the new owner, sir.'

'That's Harry,' Michael joined them and closed the door. 'Easy come, easy go. He never set store by material things.'

'It's Abdul's carriage now?' Charles guessed.

'I drive it for the owner, sir,' the man repeated.

'You'll wait for us at the mission.'

'I will have to charge you for the time, sir.'

'No discount given to Lieutenant Colonel Downe's friends?'

'Sorry, sir. None, sir.' The driver turned his head and concentrated on the road ahead.

In an effort to distract Michael and Tom who were both still absorbing the tragic news, Charles pointed to a two-storey building set in a palm grove. 'That's the Lansing Memorial Hospital. The mission's just ahead.'

'Did Harry visit the mission often?' Michael sat forward to get a better view.

'Yes. One of Harry's close friends, Peter Smythe, a captain in the Dorsets who was stationed in Basra with him before the war, married an American who lives here, Angela Wallace, now Smythe. Her brother Theo works in the Lansing Hospital. If he's home you'll be able to talk tropical diseases with him, Tom.'

'John knew Angela and her brother as well as Harry?' Tom checked.

'He did,' Charles confirmed,

'Were they close?'

'Not that close, but only because John spent most of his time upstream and not in Basra.'

'Why is Maud living here and not in married quarters?' Tom questioned.

'She shared quarters with John's colonel's wife. When Colonel Hale died of fever, his widow returned to England and Angela invited Maud to move in here.'

'John was a major, didn't his rank warrant married quarters for his wife?'

'There was a shortage,' Charles hedged.

'None of the other wives wanted Maud living with them?'

Charles wondered how much he could tell Tom about the events of the past two years without breaking the confidences John and Harry had entrusted to him.

'Charles, we're going to be at the mission in a few minutes,' Tom remonstrated. 'If there's something you're holding back, now's the time to tell me because if this place is anything like the hotbed of gossip most military stations are, I'm going to find out, and frankly I'd rather hear whatever it is from you.'

Charles capitulated. 'John was on honeymoon in Basra when war broke out. He was recalled to India and took Maud with him. He left her in India when he was posted to the Expeditionary Force, a force Harry and the men stationed here were absorbed into. I was sent here from the Western Front last March. I travelled via India to get acclimatised. As soon as I walked off the boat I heard rumours about Maud.'

'You were told she had a lover?' Tom pressed.

'Several, I've no idea how much of what I heard was true, but one thing was certain, she'd scandalized Anglo-Indian Society.'

'Did you hear any names?'

'A few,' Charles acknowledged. 'One officer in particular who was killed in action here in Mesopotamia. There was also a Portuguese business-man...' Charles couldn't bring himself to mention the natives. 'Unfortunately I wasn't the only one who'd heard. John knew about the gossip before I arrived in April. Although he was eligible for leave he didn't apply. Instead he volunteered to march from Ahwaz to Amara over the desert in the full heat of summer. When he reached Shaiba he had a fever. Harry and Peter dragged him back here. They wouldn't have succeeded if John had been conscious. Harry told me that Maud visited John in the hospital to tell him she was pregnant. As they hadn't lived together since John left India in September 1914 he knew he couldn't be the father.'

'Were they ever happy?' Tom asked.

'Presumably, or John wouldn't have married her. They honeymooned in Harry's father-in-law's house here in Basra. From something Harry said I believe there was animosity between Maud and Harry's wife. I've heard Maud refer to her as "Harry's native concubine".'

'Have you met Harry's wife?' Michael looked up as they drew alongside the Mission House.

'No. Angela Smythe asked if I'd seen Harry's orderly, Mitkhal. He's Arab, huge, with the face of a brigand. He was totally devoted to Harry. She was hoping he could take her to Harry's wife.'

'Where would I find this Mitkhal?' Michael opened the carriage door and unrolled the steps.

'If Mitkhal's still alive, which I doubt, as I can't see him standing back and watching Harry take a bullet, Abdul might know. He runs a coffee house, brothel, and gambling house on the quay that caters for British officers as well as natives.'

'Is he the same Abdul who owns this carriage?'

'The same.' Charles glanced at the driver. He knew the man was listening to every word they were saying.

Michael lifted down the wheelchair.

'I'll be damned before I'll wheel myself into the mission in that contraption,' Charles snarled.

'Then be damned. Because you're in no condition to fight one of us, let alone two.' Tom stepped down and reached back inside the carriage to lift Charles out.

Lansing Memorial Mission, Basra, Friday 31st December 1915

'It's not Harry, Angela. It's his brother Michael.' Charles had reluctantly submitted to being pushed in the chair. 'He's in civvies because he's a war correspondent. Mrs Angela Smythe, meet Michael Downe, and Captain Tom Mason, a doctor like his brother John. Michael, Tom, this is your brothers' and my very good friend, Mrs Angela Smythe.'

'You're so like Harry.' Tears started in the corners of Angela's eyes. 'I can see your resemblance to your brother, Captain Mason, but it's not as startling as Mr Downe's to Harry. Please come in, we'll be having lunch shortly, you must join us.'

Chapter Eight

Train, London Paddington to the West Country, Friday 31st December 1915

Helen, Clarissa, and Georgiana found an empty first-class carriage out of London Paddington and spread their bags, coats and hats over the bench seats to discourage anyone else from entering. Georgiana sat next to the window. Not that there was much to see. The day was as grey and despondent as her mood. Rain was falling, not in a torrent, but in a steady icy drizzle that clouded the glass and misted the scenery.

Dressed in mourning, all three were shattered by grief. They were travelling to Clyneswood and the estate chapel where John and Harry's memorial service would be held that afternoon. The day before, they'd attended the memorial service for Clarissa's brother Stephen in Brighton. The emotional strain of coping with their grief as well as that of others, and the knowledge that they would never see their loved ones in life again, had taken its toll. Even the well-meaning 'last letters' from regimental officers had hurt more than helped.

Clarissa's eyes were red and there were dark circles beneath them in stark contrast to the pallor of her cheeks. Georgiana was as pale, her eyes as haunted, but there was a defiant tilt to her chin.

'Please, don't keep telling me to accept Harry's death, Helen, because I won't. I'm his twin. That's much more than a sister. Since nursery days I've always known whenever something good or bad is happening to Harry. Whether I'm with him or not, I've felt it here.' She laid her hand on her chest. 'So I'd know, absolutely know, if he was dead and he's not.'

'You told me you felt something was happening to Harry early in December,' Helen reminded her. 'You said you didn't sleep for nights...'

'I didn't,' Georgiana was fierce in her assertion. 'But whatever it was he survived.'

'What I can't stand is this absolute void – this nothingness,' Clarissa asserted. 'I have to look at a photograph of Stephen to remember what he was like, yet we grew up together. Spent every day together until we went to separate schools. As children, all he did was torment me. When we grew up he delighted in teasing me. Then he joined the army and went to India and Basra. He used to write regularly before the war. Once the fighting started, he stopped. Every time I saw my mother she complained she never heard from him ... and now ... now he's gone.'

Georgiana laid her hand over Clarissa's.

'Elizabeth Wells, the medium, visited me. She said she could contact Stephen...'

'Steer clear of Elizabeth Wells and her spiritualist groups, Clary,' Helen warned. 'She preys on the vulnerable and tells them what they want to hear. Not the truth.'

'But if she really can communicate with loved ones who've passed over to the other side...'

106

'Have you any idea what the "other side" is like?' Helen interrupted.

'No.'

'Neither have I. I'm not even sure it exists, but, if does,' Helen moved closer to Clarissa and wrapped her arm around her shoulders, 'and the dead are able to contact us, I believe they'd do it in more direct ways than knocking on tables in a roomful of strangers, or spelling out words with a moving glass.'

'You're always so down-to-earth, Helen.'

'Not always.' Helen thought of John. How she'd prayed that he'd send her a sign from beyond the grave that 'something' – some spirit – some essence – survived death. But there'd only been the cold realisation that death was a one-way door that opened on to bleak, blank eternity.

Clarissa started talking again. 'I sent for a form to join the Queen Alexandra Imperial Nursing Corps. I know they're looking for nurses to go to Mesopotamia because Fanny Gould told me they were when I bumped into her three weeks ago in a Lyons tea shop. She joined them when war broke out. She'd just finished a tour of duty on the Western Front and was waiting for new orders. She knew Stephen was in Mesopotamia and asked me what he thought of the place. She said she might be there soon because she and a few of the people she'd been working with had been issued with summer kit.'

'She's just as likely to be posted to Egypt, East Africa, or India,' Helen pointed out. 'Even if you did join the QAINC, Clary, and were by some miracle sent to Mesopotamia, what do you think you could do there?'

'Look for Stephen's grave. As the telegram said he died of wounds there must be one.'

'Given the number of casualties at the Battle of Ctesiphon, he was probably buried in a mass grave,' Helen warned.

'Even so, there'd have to be a marker,' Clarissa countered, refusing to think of the alternative. 'Anyway, it's all rather academic. My father absolutely refuses to allow me to carry on nursing. He insists I have to return home to run the house and care for Mother.'

'Your parents have a cook and a maid. I saw them.'

'And a housekeeper,' Clarissa added.

'Georgie told me that your father was pressurizing you to give up your career. It amazes me how parents can be so selfish as to deny their daughter her vocation, particularly when that daughter has worked so hard to achieve success. Doubly so in wartime with the shortage of labour and every hospital in the country stretched to the limit, because so many staff are in the services.'

'My mother's nerves have never been strong. With Stephen gone there's only me and my sister, Penny, and she can't help my parents because she's expecting her second baby in April.'

'She's the one you introduced us to at Stephen's memorial service, whose husband is a teacher?' Helen checked.

'Yes.'

'Do they live near your parents?'

'About a mile away.'

'Then my advice to you is: do what you want,

Clary, not what your father and mother demand. They have three servants, they don't need another. Join the QAINC. You're over twenty-one, you're a damned good nurse, and you could save a lot of lives wherever you're sent, be it Mesopotamia or elsewhere.'

'It's easy for you to say that, Helen,' Clarissa protested. 'You've no family...'

'Whatever gave you that idea?' Helen broke in.

'You never talk about them.'

'If I don't talk about them it's for a reason. My parents consider a female doctor in the family a disgrace. Fortunately my grandmother left me enough money to finance my training at the London School of Medicine for women.'

Clarissa was shocked. 'Don't you miss your family?'

'As much as they miss me,' Helen replied ambiguously. 'I keep in touch with one of my brothers. Although we're both doctors, he's the success story of the family. I'm the one they never speak of. You want to nurse in the army, Clarissa, do it.' Helen looked at Georgiana. 'You're remarkably quiet. No words of wisdom on following your calling?'

'Other than there comes a time in everyone's life when they have to do what they think best, irrespective of what others say, no. I admire you for wanting to go to Mesopotamia, Clarissa. I hope you find Stephen's grave.'

'Thank you.'

Helen studied Georgiana. 'You're trying to work out how you can travel to Mesopotamia to look for Harry, aren't you?'

'Yes.'

'Think, Georgie, how on earth are you going to get there? The military may accept nurses behind the lines, but they'll never accept a female doctor.'

'I'm not expecting them to.'

'You'll never get a berth on a boat.'

'Never is a word you taught me to ignore, Helen.' Georgiana looked out of the window at the sodden winter fields and dripping hedgerows. Clarissa wasn't the only one who knew the army was recruiting nurses for Mesopotamia. She'd applied to join the QAINC an hour after she received the telegram from her father to tell her Harry had been posted missing, presumed killed.

Her godfather, General Reid, would be at the memorial service. He'd been appointed to a senior position in War Office. She'd decided to ask him to pull strings to get her accepted by the corps and find her a berth on the first boat to Basra. She'd never canvassed him for anything before. Once he saw just how intent she was on going to Mesopotamia he could hardly refuse to help her find Harry.

Could he?

Lansing Memorial Mission, Basra, Friday 31st December 1915

'More cabinet pudding, Captain Mason? Mr Downe?' Mrs Butler attracted the attention of the maid who carried the dish to the opposite end of the table where Michael and Tom were sitting.

'No thank you, Mrs Butler, I couldn't eat another thing,' Michael refused. 'That was a marvellous meal. I can see why my brother and John visited every time they were in Basra. Wonderful company, good conversation, excellent food, splendid surroundings – it feels as though we've landed in an oasis of civilisation after our voyage. It must have seemed like heaven to them after soldiering in the desert.'

'You have the same pleasing manners as Harry, Mr Downe.'

'If you called my brother Harry, you must call me Michael.'

Tom shook his head as the maid proffered him the dish. 'I agree with Michael, Mrs Butler. After what we've been eating the last month, this meal is nectar. It was kind of you to invite us to lunch.'

'Not at all. As Major Reid knows, your brothers were good friends to us and the Mission. We knew Harry better than Major Mason only because he spent more time in Basra. He was generous with his contributions and supportive of our work.'

'Although there were times when my wife and I were afraid to ask quite where Harry found some of the things he donated to our cause,' Reverend Butler qualified.

'Harry knew some very odd people who could lay their hands on even odder things,' Charles added.

'One of the best gifts he brought us was twelve boxes of Kay's soap shortly after the Turks retreated from the town. At the time you couldn't buy soap at any price simply because it wasn't available.'

'The Turks took all the soap with them when

111

they left?' Michael was amused by the thought.

'As there was none to be found they must have. Angela,' Mrs Butler turned to her as she carried a tray into the room. 'Did Maud eat her lunch?'

'Most of it.' Angela had left the dining room after pudding had been served, to take Maud her dessert. 'I told Maud you'd like to see her, Captain Mason. She's free now. I can take you to her if you've finished your meal.'

'Thank you.' Tom crumpled his napkin and left it on his plate as he rose from the table.

'We have to hurry back to the hospital, Captain Mason. If we don't see you again before you leave Basra, good luck upstream,' Theo offered Tom his hand.

Tom shook it. 'It was good to meet you. Thank you for enlightening me about the tropical diseases I can expect to encounter.'

'This is a vicious country. After three years I'm still not sure what's worse, the pestilential heat of summer, the flies, the floods or the cold nights of winter.' Theo lowered his voice. 'Try not to tire Maud. She's had a difficult time adjusting to motherhood. It's not a week since the birth and she's not strong, physically or mentally.'

'I won't keep her long.' Tom turned to his host and Dr Picard. 'Thank you for the conversation and the insights into this country. I'm sure they'll be very useful.'

'Our pleasure.' The men left.

'I'll keep the coffee warm for your return, Captain Mason, unless you'd prefer to drink it with Mrs Mason,' Mrs Butler offered.

'I'd like to join you, Mrs Butler.'

Angela led Tom through the hall down a corridor and knocked on a door.

'Come in.'

The voice was feminine, soft, low, and educated. Tom tried not to like it. Angela opened the door and stepped back.

'You're not staying?' Tom was surprised.

'Maud said she'd prefer to see you alone but to observe propriety the nursemaid will remain in the room. She doesn't speak English.'

Tom hesitated but he couldn't think of anything else to call his brother's wife. 'If that's what Mrs Mason wants.' He stepped inside and glanced around. The room was small, simply furnished, how he'd imagined a nun's cell would look, although he'd never been in one.

A plain wooden bed faced out from the back wall. A washstand stood to the right, a bedside cabinet to the left. Next to the cabinet was a wardrobe. A travelling trunk had been pushed against the footboard of the bed. Two upright chairs were set either side of a desk in front of the window that also did duty as a table, judging by a jug of water and bowl of fruit. A cot and upholstered chair completed the furniture. The walls were white-washed brick, the floor plain wood.

A young woman in a drab grey wool dress and white apron was sitting in the upholstered chair. A middle-aged native woman attired in black, who Tom presumed was the nursemaid, was seated in an alcove that jutted into the garden. She was darning a pile of socks. The cot was next to her, not Maud. He glanced inside. All he could see was a small pink nose and above it a shock of the palest blonde hair.

'Please, sit down, Captain Mason.'

Tom picked up one of the upright chairs, swung it away from the desk and placed it at the furthest point in the room from Maud's chair that space permitted.

The breath caught in Maud's throat and tears started in her eyes. John had done the self-same thing the only time he'd visited her at the mission. It had been the last time she'd seen him before Colonel Allan had arrived to tell her that her husband had died in Kut.

Neither she nor Tom said anything for a few moments. All Tom had heard about Maud before Charles had broken the news of her infidelity was an off-hand comment Charles had made when he'd returned from India before leaving for the Western Front.

'John's wife is very pretty.'

Plainly dressed, her fair hair screwed into a knot at the nape of her neck, with a thin face and figure and pale blue eyes, Maud didn't strike him as pretty. Not when Tom compared her to Clarissa Amey's exotic dark-eyed beauty. In fact Maud looked so colourless and nondescript he wondered why his brother had been attracted to her.

She broke the silence. 'There are strong similarities between you and John, Captain Mason.'

'Height and build,' he acknowledged. 'We both followed our father in that respect but my hair is darker than John's and there's no trace of my mother's auburn in it.'

After what Charles had told him about Maud's

infidelity, he wanted to shout at her, be angry with her on John's behalf. His brother – the man he'd looked up to all his life – was rotting in his grave years before his time while his unfaithful wife was sitting calmly and quietly with her bastard, apparently unmoved by his death.

'I saw you arrive through the window. I thought Harry's brother was Harry.'

'They've always been alike.' Tom knew he was being terse but he couldn't stop himself.

'Captain Mason, I've no doubt you've heard that your brother and I were living apart before his death and I don't mean because of the war.'

'I know exactly what you mean.'

'John wrote to you?'

'He never mentioned anything personal after he left India. Not about his marriage or you. I assumed, wrongly, because you'd been separated by war.'

'I wrote to you but you wouldn't have had time to receive my letter before you left England.'

'I didn't.'

'You've heard that I was unfaithful to your brother?'

'Within an hour of landing in Basra.' Tom saw no point in mentioning Charles's name.

'You've also heard that my baby isn't John's?'

'Yes.'

'He isn't,' she confirmed. 'I have no excuse. I deeply regret my actions and I deeply regret hurting John.'

'Why were you unfaithful to my brother?' When she didn't reply he asked, 'Was John a bad husband?'

115

'On the contrary, he was an excellent husband. I have absolutely no excuse for my behaviour, other than one day he was there, the next he wasn't, and I was lonely.'

'He went to war, not a gentlemen-only picnic.' Tom was embarrassed to see the nursemaid look up when he raised his voice.

'I was weak. There were other men. I offer no explanation and expect no sympathy. All I can do is apologise to you for my behaviour, as I did to John.'

'When did you last see him?'

'Twenty-eighth of June this year. He called after he was discharged from hospital following a bout of fever. As soon as he found a doctor prepared to certify him fit for duty he volunteered to go upstream. He left Basra on the eighth of July but he didn't visit me again, nor did I expect him to.' She opened a drawer in the desk, removed an envelope and handed it to him. 'This is John's last letter to me. It was sent out of Kut as the Turks were raising the siege. I have no right to keep it. If you or anyone in your family would like it, please take it.'

Tom removed the single sheet of paper.

December 15th 1915

Dear Maud

I hope you get this. I haven't long to live. I trust you won't waste time grieving for me. I'm not in pain and as Charles and Harry have gone there doesn't seem a great deal left to live for. Write to my brother Tom care of my father. He has the authority to administer my estate and will arrange payment of the annuity I set up for you. If it will help, you may name the child after me. Thank you for the happy times. There were some, John Mason.

'John thought Charles was dead?'

'It was understandable if he knew Charles had been wounded. Charles arrived in Basra after a horrendous journey on a filthy ship with no food, water, sanitation, or medicines. Most of the men on that vessel died on route or shortly after arrival.'

'Did you write to my father?' Tom asked.

'Not about the annuity. After what I did, I don't deserve John's money or anything that was his. I won't be accepting the widow's pension from the army.'

'What will you live on?'

'Harry sold some jewellery for me.'

'Jewellery John gave you?'

'No. Jewellery another man gave me.' She stared at him through yet another silence. 'I don't expect you or anyone in John's family to accept me or keep me.'

'If you don't take the army's widow's pension or private annuity the money will be lost. No one else in the family can claim it so you may as well have it.' He left the chair and walked away from her to the window so he could look at the garden instead of her face. 'Will you name the child after John as he said you could?'

'No. I've reverted to my maiden name, Perry, and I've named my son after my grandfather. Robin, so he'll be known as Robin Perry.'

He held out the letter to her.

117

'If you don't want it you could send it to your mother.'

'She would appreciate it.' He was aware she'd picked up on his inference that she wouldn't. He folded the letter back into its envelope and pocketed it.

'You can't hate me any more than I hate myself, Captain Mason.'

'After I was told of the way you'd behaved towards my brother I thought of a great many things to say to you – now I'm actually with you, I can't even begin to convey my feelings. I'm not even sure what I want to say, other than I'll mourn John and Harry and miss them every day for the rest of my life.'

'You won't be the only one, Captain Mason. Although I didn't know John, or Harry, for as long as you did, I knew both of them, I like to think well. And I love...' she fought the catch in her throat, 'loved John.'

If she'd intended to invoke his pity by crying, her tears had the opposite effect.

'What about the father of your child? Will you marry him?'

'He's dead,' she lied.

'Will you continue to live here at the mission?'

'If you're wondering if I know I'm imposing on the Butlers' charity and goodwill as well as creating problems for them, I am. I'm also aware I'm the object of scandal and derision in British military society. No one has called on me except Colonel Allan's wife. My mother's maid, Harriet, who married a sergeant now in Kut, agreed to look after me and my baby before he was born.

She changed her mind after the birth. I presume because she couldn't withstand the social pressure.'

'You resent her for it?'

'If the situation had been reversed, I wouldn't have behaved differently. I'm as much a coward as the next woman.'

'So you'll return to England?'

'I've never lived there.'

'India then?'

'I have no plans, Captain Mason. I have sufficient money to live quietly for a while. I intend to try to find some way of supporting myself and my child, but I'm not sure where. As I've already said, if you want an assurance that I won't be asking you or your family for anything. You have it.'

'You're not wearing a wedding ring.'

'I gave it to Harry the last time I saw him and asked him to give it to John. Could you do me one favour please, Captain Mason.'

He waited.

'Would you please ask Major Reid if he'll see me? I won't detain him long.'

'I will ask – Mrs – Perry.'

'My deepest sympathies on the loss of your brother, and your close friend Harry, Captain Mason.'

'If my father hasn't already done so, I'll write to the family lawyer about the annuity. John arranged it after he asked you to marry him. It's considerable. A thousand a year if I remember correctly, but being John he made provision for a lump sum to be payable and a lesser annuity in case you wanted to buy a house. Take it and John's army pension. Better you use it to educate the child than allow the money to go to waste, which it will if you don't claim it.'

'I'll think about it, Captain Mason.'

Tom realised he couldn't say anything more to his brother's widow that would make her feel worse than she already did. He closed the door behind him.

Lansing Memorial Mission, Basra, Friday 31st December 1915

Michael pushed Charles to Maud's door a few minutes later and wheeled him in. Maud closed the door as soon as Charles was inside.

Charles was shocked. The last thing he'd expected to see was Maud in a drab gown with her hair dressed in a fashion befitting an elderly spinster. He carried many images of her. The beautiful golden-haired, innocent-eyed virgin who'd entranced John; the happy fiancée, glittering like an angel in a white beaded gown when she and her mother, Emily, had joined him and John at the captain's table on the voyage to Basra. And, finally, the crimson-gowned bejewelled siren, exuding more sex than a Rag full of whores who'd scandalised British military society with her blatant and indiscriminate affairs among officers, Portuguese, and – it was rumoured – natives.

'Why do you want to see me, Maud?' Charles demanded.

'I don't.' Her blue eyes gazed unashamedly into

his. 'Of choice I never want to see you again.'

'Then why ask Tom to bring me here?'

'I thought you might want to see your son.'

Chapter Nine

Kut al Amara, Friday 31st December 1915

Major Warren Crabbe had never been a patient man. He clutched a file as he paced the length of corridor that been designated 'waiting area' in HQ. Twenty-four steps east to west. Twenty-four steps west to east. At the western end of the corridor he heard the thud of crates being moved, the ring of metal on metal, the rip of ammunition boxes being torn open and sappers cursing.

Command had evacuated the native population from the entire street, and requisitioned every building. The one next door to HQ was being used as an ordnance depot by the Norfolks and Hampshires manning the second lines. The coarse gibes of the ranks mingled with the cries of street vendors in the market beside the mosque behind the building.

Crabbe had been waiting for an hour. He knew the brigadier would have seen him right away if he'd arrived early that morning, but he'd wanted to avoid Colonel Perry, who'd been designated chief supply officer and consequently been given a desk in HQ. The only way to ensure he wouldn't run into him was to wait until mid-afternoon.

Perry had established a routine the first week of the siege and stuck rigidly to it since. He put in an appearance in HQ sometime during the morning, lunched in the Dorsets' officers' mess, and left at precisely three o'clock for the Norfolks' mess, where he played bridge with his opposite numbers from the Norfolks, Hampshires, and Kents until five o'clock.

At four o'clock Crabbe heard the rattle of teacups behind one of the doors. A second lieutenant appeared and saluted. 'The brigadier will see you now, sir.'

Crabbe marched in and snapped to attention.

The brigadier set down his pen. 'Close the door behind you, Lieutenant Miles, and see that Major Crabbe and I aren't disturbed.'

'Sir.' The subaltern left.

'At ease, Crabbe, and take a seat. You here about Mason?'

'Yes, sir.' Crabbe sat in the visitor's chair.

'I hear he saved Cleck-Heaton's life this morning.'

'That might be a bit strong, sir. There's no doubt Major Cleck-Heaton would have been handed to a burial party if Major Mason hadn't operated, but it's by no means certain he'll survive.'

'That's why I insisted a side room be prepared on the second floor of the officers' hospital for Major Mason while he's acting senior surgeon. He needs to be within easy reach of his patients. It's ludicrous to keep an able-bodied member of the force imprisoned in a damp cellar while we're under siege. Doubly ludicrous when that officer is a medic.'

'I wondered who'd arranged the transfer of Major Mason's billet to the officers' hospital, sir. Thank you. I've seen the room. It's healthier than the cellar.'

'I've heard you're the master of the understatement, Crabbe. You represented Mason at his court martial?'

'Yes, sir.'

'I was busy organizing the defences at the time so I'm not fully conversant with the facts of the case. Update me, and tell me why you chose to represent a man accused of disobeying orders, and inciting mutiny and murder.'

Crabbe knew, as did everyone who was acquainted with Colonel Perry, that Perry was the instigator of the charges against John Mason. Cleck-Heaton had formally pressed the allegations and taken them to command, but he'd done so at Perry's behest. The relationship between Perry and Cleck-Heaton ran deeper than friendship. Cleck-Heaton's family had money. Perry's considerable influence in the India Office. Given Cleck-Heaton's shortcomings as an officer it had become obvious he'd owed his commission to something other than his intellect.

'We're not in a courtroom, Major Crabbe. You're not under oath and no one is making a record,' the brigadier prompted.

'Major Cleck-Heaton went to the Forward Aid Station during the battle of Ctesiphon when he heard that Major Mason was refusing to evacuate the wounded to Baghdad.'

'We never reached Baghdad.'

'Major Mason knew we hadn't progressed

beyond Ctesiphon, sir. That's why he refused to obey the order when it was passed down.'

'If he hadn't disobeyed it, the Turks would have picked off the wounded and their escorts. The death toll would have been worse than it was.'

'It would have, sir.'

'Continue.'

'I wasn't witness to the argument between Major Cleck-Heaton and Major Mason, sir. Major Cleck-Heaton testified that Major Mason lost his temper, and as a result released the pressure on a sub-lieutenant's severed artery. The officer died. Major Cleck-Heaton insisted the charge of murder of Sub-Lieutenant Stephen Amey be added to the charges of disobeying an order, and inciting mutiny.'

'I know from experience a severed artery is almost always fatal in battle conditions. Now I understand why you chose to defend Mason. Were you aware I'm acquainted with Major Mason?'

'No, sir.'

'He was senior medical officer on General Gorringe's hundred-mile march across the desert from Ahwaz to Amara at the height of the hot season. More than half the force went down with sun or heatstroke, the other half with dysentery. I don't think Mason slept day or night while the sick needed his attention.'

'I know him well, sir. He won't rest while a man needs care he can deliver.'

'He also displayed remarkable tact when General Gorringe treated the medics abominably, informing them he could do a better job of treating the sick and wounded with patent medicines.'

It was common knowledge that officers as well as men despised Gorringe for his arrogance, but Warren Crabbe had learned never to agree with a superior officer's criticism of another, no matter how well-founded. In his experience the most casual comment could be misinterpreted and twisted at a later date to suit a hidden agenda.

'I believe Major Mason to be innocent of all the charges levied against him, sir. I am here to formally request that the findings of the court-martial be set aside until such time as the court proceedings and sentence can be reviewed.'

'I take it you mean after the siege has been lifted, Crabbe?'

'Yes, sir. I believe only then can sufficient time and attention be given to determine the veracity or otherwise of the evidence against Major Mason.'

'As Mason's defending officer, you have the relevant papers?'

'Yes, sir.' Crabbe handed the brigadier the file he'd brought with him.

'I'll study your report and get back to you. Meanwhile, given the high incidence of sickness in the town, and the fact that Turkish snipers are hitting an average of one to two hundred unlucky souls a day, I'll lift all restrictions on Major Mason's movements except...' the brigadier paused, 'the armed escort. I won't get that past Colonel Perry until a formal review has been held. Sergeant Greening is still guarding Mason?'

'Yes, sir.'

'Mason tolerates Greening's presence?'

'Yes, sir.' Crabbe didn't elaborate although John and the sergeant had become firm friends, despite the situation and disparity in rank and class.

The brigadier reached for a notepad. He wrote three letters, stamped them with the date, his official stamp and signed them. He placed them in separate envelopes and handed two Crabbe. 'These state Major Mason has the freedom to go wherever he chooses in Kut or the forward defences provided he's accompanied by his guard. It also states Major Mason is no longer to be treated as a prisoner but as an officer and doctor of Indian Expeditionary Force D. His sentence to be reviewed after the relief of Kut. I will keep one copy and ask General Townshend to countersign it. Give one of those to Mason. Tell him to keep it on him at all times in case he is challenged by Colonel Perry – or any other officer. The third copy I suggest you file in a safe place where it's likely to survive bombardment or attack.'

'Thank you, sir.' Having achieved more than he'd hoped for Crabbe went to the door.

'Before you leave, Major Crabbe, and this is completely off the record. Just what the hell happened between Major Mason and Colonel Perry for Perry to want Mason shot?'

'You said this is confidential between the two of us, Brigadier?'

'You have my word.'

'Major Mason married Colonel Perry's daughter the evening of her mother's death. The colonel was drunk at his wife's funeral. Afterwards he locked himself in his quarters. Major Mason and Lieutenant Colonel Downe...'

The brigadier smiled. 'I miss that man. Every time Harry Downe's name came up, the brass seemed unsure whether to shoot or promote him.'

'Either way you couldn't help liking the man, sir.'

'We could do with him here. If he went out, just once, in his Arab skirts he'd find out exactly how many locals are in cahoots with the Turks.'

'We don't need Harry to tell us that, Brigadier. The entire native population of Kut are with the Ottoman Empire.'

'To return to the situation between Major Mason and Colonel Perry?' the brigadier prompted.

'Major Mason and Lieutenant Colonel Downe broke down the door of Colonel Perry's bungalow to fetch Miss Perry's – now Mrs Mason's – trunk so she could travel to India with Major Mason after their marriage. Rumour has it the speed of the marriage annoyed Colonel Perry but as the colonel was behaving erratically Major Mason felt he couldn't leave Miss Perry with him.'

'I heard some odd things about Mrs Perry's death.'

'It was a scorpion bite, sir. One of the small yellow ones. Major Mason said their bite was invariably fatal.'

'He attended Mrs Perry?'

'Yes, sir. Her body was found between the Perrys' bungalow and Lieutenant Colonel Downe's quarters. Major Mason was staying with Lieutenant Colonel Downe that night as his and Maud Perry's wedding was arranged for the following day.'

'Who found Mrs Perry?'

'Lieutenant Colonel Downe, sir. He was

returning from the dock after seeing a friend off on leave.'

The brigadier held up the envelope he'd kept. 'Thank you for enlightening me, Crabbe. I'll telegraph the information in this letter to General Nixon's office today and ensure everyone in command knows Mason's sentence has been postponed.'

'Thank you, sir.'

'Am I right in thinking that Colonel Perry has already transmitted news of Mason's death to his wife and family?'

'Yes, sir.'

'Ask Major Mason if he wants me to telegraph the news of his remarkable recovery.'

'I will, sir.'

'One last thing, Major Crabbe, and this is on the record. You can tell Major Mason from me, he is fortunate in his friends. You're not the only officer who's been in here demanding his reinstatement to rank and duties.'

Abdul's coffee shop, Basra, Friday 31st December 1915

The windows of the coffee shop were shrouded in cheap silk, the interior dark, fogged by tobacco and hashish smoke. Men in native robes sat, crowded around small tables, playing backgammon, eating dates, spitting out seeds, and drinking thick-grained Turkish coffee from miniature, doll-sized cups. The clink of backgammon tiles and hubbub of voices was deafening. The stench of male sweat intermingled with roasting coffee beans and burning incense was nauseating.

Abdul bowed before Charles, Tom, and Michael, but his gaze was fixed on Michael.

'My heart was desolate when I heard Lieutenant Colonel Downe had been killed. I have said many prayers for his soul.' Abdul ushered them out of the noisy public area into his office. Like Charles and Maud, he'd mistaken Michael for Harry and had been distraught when Charles had enlightened him.

The office was small, furnished Arabic-style with low divans and cushions covered with bright tapestries. The tables were raised barely four inches from the ground. A young man brought in a tray of coffee and pastries. When Charles saw Tom and Michael trying to curl their legs under themselves to sit on a divan he was glad of his wheelchair.

Abdul dismissed the servant, closed the door, and unlocked a chest in the corner of the room. He rummaged in its depths and extracted an envelope which he presented to Michael.

'Lieutenant Colonel Downe left this to be given to a friend in case he was killed.'

Michael turned it over. Written on the outside, in Harry's large-lettered scrawl, was *To be delivered to Major John Mason or Major Charles Reid or Captain Peter Smythe in the event of my death. Harry Downe.*

Below it were two lines of Arabic writing.

'What does this say?' Michael asked Abdul.

'Or to be given to my faithful friend Mitkhal.'

'Mitkhal was Harry's bearer,' Charles explained.

'Mitkhal was Lieutenant Colonel Downe's friend, Major Reid, not his servant,' Abdul corrected.

'Have you seen Mitkhal lately, Abdul?' Charles asked.

'I have not seen him since last June, Major Reid.'

'He wasn't here with Harry in November?'

'No, Major.'

'That's strange,' Charles murmured, 'they were practically inseparable.'

'You're not an officer like your brother, Mr Downe?' Abdul asked.

'No, a war correspondent. I write accounts of the battles for the English newspapers,' he added when he saw the confused expression on Abdul's face. He opened the letter and read the single page it contained. 'It's Harry's will. He left everything apart from a set of jewellery to his wife and daughters.'

'Harry has children!' Charles was shocked by the idea of his friend fathering mixed-race children.

'Twin girls.' Michael carried on reading. 'He has a strongbox in the bank.'

'Who did he leave the jewellery to?' Tom recalled Maud telling him Harry had sold a set of jewellery 'another man' had given her.

'Maud.'

'Why on earth would Harry leave Maud jewellery?' Charles spoke more sharply than he'd intended.

'Maud told me Harry had sold jewellery for her,' Tom revealed. 'If Maud had said to him, as she did to me, that she didn't want to touch any of John's money, it would be like Harry to pretend to sell her jewellery to give her enough to live on.'

'Abdul, have you any idea where Harry's wife is?' Michael asked.

'No, sir. I never met her.'

'But you know her name?'

'I know she is the daughter of Sheikh Ibn Shalan.'

'Ibn Shalan is?' Michael pressed.

'A powerful sheikh no man wants to annoy, sir.'

'Where does he live?'

'He has houses in Basra and in Baghdad, but like all Bedouin his true home is the desert. It was in the desert Hasan Mahmoud was born and it was where he made his home.'

Michael asked. 'Who is Hasan Mahmoud?'

'His English name is Harry Downe, sir, but his true name is Hasan Mahmoud.'

'Harry's Bedouin identity,' Charles explained.

Michael tried and failed to imagine his brother masquerading as an Arab. 'Could Harry really pass himself off as Bedouin?'

'My Arab customers who did not know him well never suspected he was British, Mr Downe,' Abdul replied.

'Once he put on his Arab robes you wouldn't give him a second glance,' Charles agreed. 'Every man in the Dorsets has a story about mistaking Harry for an Arab and either almost shooting him or seeing someone try. Did Harry leave anything with you except this letter, Abdul?'

'Not with me. There may be something in

131

Lieutenant Colonel Downe's room. It's how he left it. No one has been it apart from the women to clean it. If you want to look at it, you are welcome.'

'Thank you, I would.' Charles left his wheelchair at the foot of the inner staircase and, leaning heavily on the banister, followed Abdul up the stairs. Tom and Michael climbed up behind them.

Abdul produced a bunch of keys from his robe, inserted one in a lock, and opened a door. He removed the key he'd used from the ring and handed it to Michael. 'Don't forget to lock the room and return the key to me when you leave.'

'I won't.' Michael looked inside. 'You kept my brother's trunk?'

'Nothing has been taken from this room since Hasan left. He was a good friend to me. War is chaos. Some people are reported dead who still live. I cannot imagine Hasan dead. I intend to keep his room like this until the war ends. If he does not appear then...' Abdul left without finishing his sentence.

Michael entered the room. A divan draped in camel hair rugs was pushed into the corner closest to the stove. A military chest secured by a large iron padlock stood next to it. A second unlocked chest stood behind the door. A plain wooden table and two chairs completed the furnishings.

'By the look of this place, Harry lived simply.' Tom went to the window.

'I watched him prepare to ride out into the desert from Amara,' Charles said. 'He was in Arab robes, and carried a saddlebag that contained a handful of dates, a skin of water, a couple of gold sovereigns minted in 1872, his gun, sword, and knife. I took him to task for not wearing his identity discs, he said he was careful to have nothing on him that a native wouldn't carry. He not only lived with the Bedouin, he lived like them.'

Michael lifted the lid on the unlocked chest. He removed a set of Arab robes, headdress, sandals, soap, tooth powder, toothbrush, hairbrush, underclothes, and a bottle of brandy.

Tom pulled at the padlock on the military chest. 'Do you want me to ask Abdul if he has the key for this?'

'If Abdul had the key he would have given it to us.' Charles released his grip on the door and lowered himself on to one of the chairs.

Tom examined the padlock.

'I'll open it.' Michael thrust his hand into his pocket and brought out what looked like a pocket knife. He opened it up and extracted a slim blade.

'I didn't know you could pick locks as well as Harry.' Tom watched him set to work.

'It was Harry who taught me. I give him full marks. This is not an easy lock to pick.'

'Too complicated for you?'

'I didn't say that.'

Five minutes later Michael lifted the lid. He took out a medium-sized wooden box and handed it to Tom who opened it.

'There are a couple of hundred gold sovereigns in here.'

'Anything else?' Michael asked.

'Just the coins.'

Michael lifted out another, smaller square box that appeared to be a block of solid wood. He ran his fingers over the sides, testing the surface and pressing the corners. Moments later a tiny secret drawer slid open. Inside was a key. 'Looks like we found the key to the safety deposit box Harry mentioned in his will.' Michael slipped it into his wallet.

'Is there anything in there that might lead us to Harry's wife?' Tom asked.

'Nothing, just the two boxes.' Michael sat back on his heels. 'It's not much to show for a life.'

'No,' Charles murmured. 'Not much at all.'

Chapter Ten

Gray Mackenzie & Co, Basra, Friday 31st December 1915

'We only have an hour before Michael and I have to be at the wharf,' Tom warned Charles as they entered the bank.

'Wheel me to the office door and leave the talking to me.' Charles straightened his cap. His features hardened, and he was transformed from helpless invalid to authoritative officer. He rapped the glass inner door with his cane and motioned Michael to open it at the occupier's 'come'.

'Major.' The man behind the desk rose when the entered. 'Anthony Smith, how can I help you?'

'We're here to check Lieutenant Colonel Downe's safety deposit box.' Charles took the letter Crabbe had sent him from his pocket and handed it over. 'Notification of Lieutenant Colonel Downe's death from a fellow officer. His brother has his will. We have the key.'

Anthony read the papers. 'We were all upset to hear of Lieutenant Colonel Downe's death. He was a popular visitor here. My condolences, Mr Downe. The family resemblance is remarkable.'

'Thank you.' Michael reached for his wallet and extracted the key.

Mr Smith rang a bell and an elderly clerk appeared. 'Escort these gentlemen to the bank vault, Friedman. Give them Lieutenant Colonel Downe's safety deposit box, and any assistance they require.'

Less than five minutes after entering the building they were in the vault. Friedman showed them Harry's box but it took the combined strength of Tom and Michael to lift it on to the table. Friedman tactfully moved to a desk at the door, opened a ledger, and pretended to study it.

Michael produced the key and lifted the lid. He removed a black ledger and a leather jeweller's case to reveal a mass of sovereigns.

Tom whistled. 'Looks like Harry saved his pennies.'

Michael opened the ledger. 'According to an entry Harry made last November there were 6,000 but there's an entry below his I can't decipher. It looks like Arabic.'

Charles examined the jeweller's case. Set on indented beds of cream velvet were a ruby and diamond necklace, tiara, ring, earrings, and four bracelets, two large enough to be worn above the elbow, two smaller ones below. He'd seen the set before. Maud had been wearing them the evening he'd called on her in India and told her he was taking her to Basra – and John. He could even remember their conversation, the obdurate look on her face when she'd announced: *'I'm not going.'*

His voice, bitter angry resonated through his mind. *'You'll board that ship if I have to drag you up the gangplank by your hair. You said life is short. A tour of duty on the Western Front has shown me just how short – and painful. But some pain can be avoided. You're not going to hurt John any more than you already have. Whether he lives for another month or sixty years he's going to be as happy as a whore like you can make him.'*

He'd succeeded in dragging Maud to Basra but he hadn't succeeded in alleviating John's further pain. John had called on Maud only once in Basra. To inform her he was divorcing her.

Tom interrupted Charles's thoughts. 'These look as though they belong in an empress's collection.' He picked up one of the three-inch long earrings.

'Only if you're talking about a pagan empress,' Charles concurred. 'They're too ostentatious for any modern woman. If you trust them with me, Michael, I'll see Maud gets them.'

'Of course I trust you, but can we be sure this is the set Harry intended for Maud?' Michael was wary of giving Harry's possessions to anyone except his wife.

'I saw Maud wearing them in India. She admitted John hadn't given them to her.'

136

'My brother has better taste.' Tom replaced the earring in the box. 'I'm guessing instead of selling them, Harry gave her what he thought they were worth.'

Michael carried the ledger over to the clerk. 'Do you read Arabic, Mr Friedman?'

'Yes, sir.'

'Could you please tell me what this says?' He pointed to the last entry in the ledger.

'It appears to have been made by Lieutenant Colonel Downe's wife, sir.'

'She comes here?'

'She has done, sir.'

'To do what?'

'That I couldn't tell you, sir. Gray Mackenzie & Co prides itself on client confidentiality.'

'She accessed this box?' Michael pressed him.

'Yes, sir. She had a key and a signed letter of permission from Lieutenant Colonel Downe.'

'You have the letter?'

'A copy I made, sir.' Friedman handed it to Michael.

'Dated last November before the Battle of Ctesiphon.' Michael couldn't conceal his disappointment. A more recent date might have meant that Harry had by some miracle survived the Turkish ambush. 'Did she take out money?'

'According to this notation, yes, sir.'

'How much?'

'A thousand sovereigns.'

'What would that buy in Basra?' Michael asked.

'A great deal, sir.'

'A house?'

'A fine one, sir.'

'Do you have Mrs Downe's address?'

The man flicked through the ledger. 'No, sir. Only the time of her visit. Eight o'clock, Tuesday morning. 7th December. She was accompanied only by a woman. Veiled, of course. No man-servant, which was unusual. I remember thinking at the time he must have been upriver with the lieutenant colonel.'

'How long did she spend here?'

The clerk checked the ledger again. 'No more than ten minutes, sir.'

'Will you notify me if she comes again?'

'Aside from the fact that I've been ordered to give you every assistance, it would be my pleasure, sir. Will you be staying in Basra?'

Michael thought for a moment. 'Tom, would you mind going upstream alone? I'll stay on for a few days to talk to people in HQ and write a background piece on the campaign for the *Mirror*.'

'While you try to find Harry's wife and daughters?' Tom surmised.

'That too, if I'm lucky,' Michael returned the ledger to the box and locked it.

Kut Al Amara, Friday 31st December 1915

Major Warren Crabbe left HQ, turned down the lane that connected number 1 and number 1A alleyways and entered the Officers' Hospital. Two second lieutenants were in the room designated as an aid station. One was having a shoulder wound dressed by Matthews, the other bathing a graze left by a bullet that had nicked his earlobe.

138

He knew both men. When they'd arrived to join Force D six months before, he'd called them 'Eton Wet Bobs' the ultimate derogatory term applied by seasoned officers to the newly commissioned. After Ctesiphon, they'd lost their round-faced, wide-eyed innocent look. Now both had the lean, uncompromising appearance of battle-hardened men.

'Stop wearing your officers' caps and insignia within the sights of the Turkish snipers, or learn to duck,' Crabbe advised.

'If we'd ducked any lower we'd be under the worms,' one of them retorted.

'Best you know your place. Major Knight around?' Crabbe asked Matthews.

'In the main ward, sir.'

Crabbe walked across the corridor and opened the door. David Knight was sitting in the curtained alcove he grandly referred to as his 'office' although all it held was a travelling desk, a chair, and a shelf of forms and ledgers. Every one of the beds in the room was occupied. From what he could see of the occupants' faces, more by fever patients than the wounded.

'I swear you have a bloodhound's nose that enables you to sniff out a fresh brew of tea over a mile radius, Crabbe. I've just sent Dira to make a pot.'

'Where's John?'

'Checking Cleck-Heaton. We've left the bastard in a room next to the operating theatre in case John has to go back in. The shrapnel Cleck-Heaton took did serious damage to the blood vessels supplying his lungs.'

'Swine doesn't deserve medical care.' Crabbe handed Knight one of the envelopes the brigadier had given him.

'As a doctor I can't agree with you, as John's friend and fellow officer I do. What's this?'

'Read it and I'll put some brandy in our tea to celebrate.' Crabbe took a flask from his top pocket.

Dira brought a tray into the alcove.

'Can you bring a chair and an extra cup please, Dira, for Major Crabbe? And tell Major Mason tea's ready.'

'Yes, sir.

Knight read the letter. 'How the hell did you manage this, Crabbe?'

'By asking.'

'Come on, you must have traded something?'

'Like what? Everyone knows the brigadier is as straight as a ramrod.'

'I'm amazed.'

'What's amazing?' John joined them. Skeletally thin as a result of campaigning in the worst of the heat, overwork, and his brandy addiction, John was a shadow of the man Harry had introduced to Crabbe when he'd arrived in Basra to marry Maud in July 1914.

'See for yourself,' Crabbe handed him the letter.

John read it. 'So, I'm not likely to be shot at dawn any sunrise soon.'

'That has to be good, doesn't it?' Crabbe hadn't been looking for praise for his efforts on John's behalf, but he'd hoped for a more enthusiastic response.

'Yes, sorry, that was remiss of me. Thank you,

140

Crabbe. I know how hard you've worked for this. I'm grateful for everything you've done for me, and at no little risk to your own career.'

'Hardly. I reckon I've been promoted just about as high as a ranker can expect.'

'It's good news for you, John, the hospital, and me.' Knight took the flask from Crabbe and poured liberal helpings into all three teacups. 'This means that I, and the other medics, can get the occasional hour's sleep. If I was the emotional kind, Crabbe, I'd kiss you.'

'I'm glad you're not.' Crabbe handed John an envelope. 'The brigadier made three copies. He told me to make sure you carried one with you at all times in case a sycophant of Perry's or Cleck-Heaton's questions your right to roam. He's asking Townshend to countersign the copy he kept and is telegraphing the contents to Nixon in Basra. He ordered me to keep the third copy safe. The brigadier wants to know if you'd like a message sent out on the wireless to tell your family you're alive.'

'What did you say?'

'That it would be your decision.'

John thought of his parents, his brother Tom, and sister Lucy. He loved them dearly but he was closest to his mother and brother. Both would have been devastated by the news of his death but he knew them well enough to realise, given time, they'd follow his father's example and take the news of his demise in typical British fashion – stiff-upper-lipped and stoical. Not because it was expected of them but because it was the way they dealt with every misfortune life threw at them that they were powerless to alter. It would be cruel to give them hope when Kut could be overrun today – tomorrow – next week – and he could be killed or really die of fever. Or, if the brass took it into their heads to countermand the brigadier's lenience – shot. As for Maud, he didn't doubt she'd already ensnared another man to dance attendance on her. One who might even believe he was the father of her child.

'Given the number of casualties we've admitted between the ranks, non-coms, and officers' hospitals today, it might be as well if we keep the news of my miraculous recovery inside Kut. I'd hate to give my family hope only for them to receive a second telegram if I succumb.'

'Probably as well,' Crabbe agreed. 'I'm beginning to think it will come as a surprise to the brass and the outside world if any of us survive this rat trap.'

The quayside, Basra, Friday December 31st 1915

Tom held out his hand. Michael shook it.

'You'll take care of yourself?'

'For the few days it will take me to gather background information before following you upstream.' Michael looked over Tom's shoulder at the hillock Adjabi and Sami had built from his trunk, bags, and packages. 'Is that everything of mine, Adjabi?'

'Everything, Sahib,' Adjabi answered.

'You've left the Fortnum hampers for Captain Mason?'

'Apart from the one you left for Captain Reid, yes, sir.'

'You'll be seeing Sami again very shortly,' Michael said in amusement as Adjabi embraced Tom's bearer.

'Nothing is certain in this world, Sahib.'

'Sami, find me a comfortable berth on board and a chair with a view of the riverbank,' Tom ordered. He turned back to Michael. 'I don't like the thought of you living in that Arab brothel.'

'Coffee shop,' Michael corrected. 'It was good enough for Harry.'

'Harry had odd tastes that shouldn't be taken as a recommendation. If you asked Richard Chalmers I'm sure he'd find you a bed in military quarters.'

'Old war correspondent adage. The further from the brass you get, the more accurate the rumours.'

'Then beg a bed from the Butlers at the mission.'

'No fear, they'll have me singing hymns every night after supper. I'll be fine at Abdul's.'

'I'm not so sure.'

'Harry was.'

'Harry spoke Arabic and passed as a native.'

'I can learn Arabic.'

'In a few days?'

The boat engines coughed and wheezed before bursting into life, drowning out hope of further conversation.

Michael shook Tom's hand again. Sami appeared at the top of the gangplank. Tom left the quay and joined him. The plank was hauled on board. Michael turned his back on the troops lining the lower decks of the paddle steamer and walked over to Adjabi.

'You stay with the luggage, I'll find us rooms.' He crossed the quay and entered the coffee house.

Abdul's coffee shop, Basra, Friday 31st December 1915

'No, sir, you cannot have your brother's room.' Abdul was obdurate.

'You said Harry had paid you for the year.'

'To keep his room for him or his ghost. I have other very good rooms. A big one for you, a small one for your servant, sir. The very best rooms in my house.'

Michael hesitated.

'I will show them to you. Come. You will find nothing better in the whole of Basra. Not in military quarters or a private hotel. Come, sir.'

Michael followed Abdul up the stairs into a sparsely furnished room almost identical to the one Harry had occupied. Abdul opened a connecting door. 'This will be for your servant, sir.'

Michael looked into a cubicle that held a bed and travelling washstand.

'As you see, sir, two doors. One to the passage outside so your servant need not disturb you with his comings and goings, and one to your room for when you need him.'

'How much?'

'A sovereign a week for you, half a sovereign for your servant.'

Michael remained silent. It was a trick he'd learned from Harry.

'With the services of a girl thrown in.'

'I don't need a girl.'

'You will when you see the ones I have on offer.'

Michael resisted the temptation to argue.

'All the food you can eat.'

Michael said nothing.

'All the food your servant can eat.'

Michael returned Abdul's stare.

'I see you are as hard at bargaining as Hasan. One sovereign a week for both of you.'

Michael still didn't say anything.

'Two sovereigns for both of you for one month.'

Michael finally spoke. 'I'm unlikely to be here a month.'

'But you'll want me to keep your things for you when you go to fight the Turk?'

'You can put them in Harry's room.' Michael slipped his hand into his pocket. 'Half a sovereign for my servant and myself for one week. We'll talk again then, if I haven't left.'

'Where are you going, sir?' Abdul asked as Michael walked back towards the stairs.

'To fetch my bearer and my luggage.'

'I have people to do that, sir. Stay in your room, rest. I will have fresh fruit and warm water for washing sent up.'

Michael waited until Abdul left before going to the door. He looked down the passageway. Harry's room was at the opposite end of the corridor with the landing and stairs between them. He wondered if his rooms really were 'the very best' or simply the furthest from Harry's. If that were the case, why would Abdul want him as far away from them as possible?

Abdul went downstairs. He saw one of his barmen, Latif, leaving by a side door. He didn't need to ask where he was going. He knew. He beckoned to the doorman. 'Summon my carriage. The closed one. Now.'

Zabba's house, Basra, Friday 31st December 1915

Zabba didn't rise when a servant showed Abdul into her private sitting room, but she extended her hand. He kissed her fingers before sitting opposite her and taking the glass of tea her manservant handed him.

'Two visits in a month, Abdul. People will begin to talk about us,' Zabba joked. 'To what do I owe the pleasure of your company?'

'What else, other than business. I need a girl.'

'You have a coffee house full of them.'

'I need a clever one who can speak English. You train your girls not only to service the English but to talk to them.'

'They know how to entertain British officers,' she acknowledged.

'I need one now, right away.'

'Why the urgency.'

'Hasan's brother is in Basra.'

Zabba sat upright and leaned as far forward as far as her bulk would allow. 'A soldier?'

'No. A writer for newspapers. He will be going upstream soon.'

'Cox...'

146

'Knows he's here or he will shortly. He pays a man in my employ to give him news.'

'You allow that?'

'I take care Cox's spy only conveys what I want Cox to know.'

'Do you think Hasan's brother knows what the British intend for this country?'

'If he doesn't, he may soon. The way everyone who knew Hasan looks at him, he will be trusted by many, just as Hasan was trusted. Do you have a girl I can buy?'

'A girl you want to use as a spy?'

'Yes.'

'If she gives you information you will share it with me?'

'Yes.'

'You haven't forgotten how to lie, Abdul.'

'You know I keep my word, Zabba,' Abdul protested.

'You will keep your word, just as you will keep any useful information the girl gives you to yourself until it is so old it is worthless.'

'Zabba...'

Zabba waved him to silence. 'This brother of Hasan's, he is young?'

'He could be Hasan's twin.'

Zabba thought for a moment. 'I will not sell you a girl, Abdul but I will lend you one. You can pay her for her services, but she remains my property.'

'I would prefer to buy her.'

'Then go elsewhere. There are many girls for sale in Basra.'

'Not trained whores who can speak English.'

147

'My terms or none, Abdul.'

'Very well, I agree. She will remain yours but I will pay her for her services.'

Zabba turned to her manservant. 'Find Kalla and bring her to me.'

Chapter Eleven

Furja's house, Basra, Friday 31st December 1915

Mitkhal stood in the doorway of Hasan's bedroom and watched the doctor drip opium into his friend's mouth. Hasan's face was flushed with fever and pain as he tossed and turned on the divan. Occasionally he moaned or whimpered. The worst was when he screamed. Nothing intelligible, just sheer agonising cries of absolute terror. When that happened, Mitkhal knew Hasan was transported back to the tent where the Turks had tortured him.

'He will live through this, Mitkhal.' Furja materialised like a ghost at his elbow. 'I cannot believe Allah would allow you to bring him back to us only for us to lose him to death.'

'Dorset. Here! Dorset!'

The doctor looked up. 'Do you know what he's saying?'

'He's calling for his horse.' Mitkhal didn't explain to the doctor that Hasan's words had been clear – and in English.

Furja met Mitkhal's steady gaze. 'Hasan's

delirious. He doesn't know what he's saying.'

'Or what language he's speaking?' Mitkhal murmured too low for the doctor to hear. He stepped outside the room. 'I'll get his horses.'

'Mitkhal...'

'Forgive me, Furja, but I can't stay idle in this house and watch Hasan suffer. If he sees Dorset...'

'A horse won't heal him,' Furja remonstrated.

'Maybe not, but he's asking for the mare and the only thing I can do for him right now is find her.' Mitkhal left the room, went into his own quarters and picked up his empty saddlebags. He took them out into the courtyard and set them on a stone bench.

Gutne joined him and handed him a package wrapped in palm leaves. 'Bread flaps and dates.'

Unable to meet her look, which he knew would be full of reproach; he unbuckled one of the bags and tucked it inside. 'Thank you.'

Furja joined them 'Hasan's flask. I've filled it with Turkish brandy. Hasan says French is better...'

'But Bedawi should be grateful for what they're given. Thank you, Furja.' Mitkhal thrust it into a hidden pocket inside his abba before fastening his coat.

'Mitkhal, I wish you'd stay.'

'You know what Hasan thinks of those horses.'

'No horse is worth a man's life.' Furja sat on the bench.

'Harry...'

'Hasan,' Furja swiftly corrected Mitkhal. 'If he heard you...'

'I'm sorry, Furja, but he spoke English.'

'He was raving and we agreed we'd do everything we could to help him forget his previous life.'

'I'll try not to let it happen again.'

They started nervously at a knock on the iron-reinforced wooden door that separated Furja's house from Zabba's. It was the only door that connected to the outside world. The first thing Furja had done after moving in was hire a trustworthy builder Zabba had recommended to brick up all the other doors that connected with the street or Zabba's house, including the ones in the garden walls.

'Farik.' Mitkhal called to the gatekeeper who was in the kitchen.

He came and opened the small eye-level grille. 'Zabba.'

'Let her in, Farik,' Furja ordered.

Zabba waddled in slowly and embraced Furja and Gutne.

'Welcome, Zabba.' Furja indicated the sitting room that opened off the courtyard. 'Farik, bring refreshments and tell the doctor where I'll be if there's any change in Hasan's condition. Mitkhal, Gutne, please join us. Bantu can look after the children. They'll not wake for an hour yet.'

'Someone is going somewhere?' Zabba noticed the saddlebags as she passed the bench.

'I am.' Mitkhal went ahead and pulled out a comfortable chair for Zabba.

Zabba lowered herself into it. 'I know I usually visit first thing in the morning before my household is awake, Mitkhal, but there is no need to

150

look suspicious. I was careful leaving my quarters. No one will miss me or come looking for me. I usually sleep for an hour or two before the evening begins.'

'But something is wrong. You wouldn't have come here otherwise.'

'Not something bad, but something you should know. Hasan's brother is in Basra. According to Abdul the resemblance between them is remarkable.' She told them why Abdul had visited her and the little Abdul had gleaned about Michael Downe. 'He's looking for you, Furja, and you, Mitkhal. He's been asking everyone he meets if they know where you are.'

'Just as well Abdul doesn't know,' Furja said.

'Abdul wouldn't tell anyone, even if he did know,' Mitkhal countered.

'Not even if he was offered money?'

'Not even then, Furja.' Mitkhal turned to Zabba. 'How long is Michael Downe staying in Basra?'

'He intends to follow the soldiers upriver in the next few days. Everyone knows there's going to be a major battle there soon between the British and the Turks.' She remembered the saddlebags. 'You're going upriver too?'

'I'm going upstream, but not because of Michael Downe. This is the first I've heard of him. Hasan is concerned for his horses. I promised I would look for them.'

'If you travel you may be recognised. One of the British may see you, or one of Ibn Shalan's men, and that will be the end of you. If they torture you and you reveal the secret of this house, it will also be the end of the lives of everyone here.'

151

'I would never betray Furja, Gutne, or the children.'

'I know you wouldn't, Mitkhal, no matter what it cost you, because you are as stubborn as Hasan. But you'd still be risking your own life. It's not worth it, not for horses,' Furja insisted.

'Some things are worth taking a risk for, Furja.'

'If you won't be dissuaded, Mitkhal, my cousin has a boat. He's leaving Basra tomorrow. I could ask him to take you upriver with him.' Zabba accepted the tea Farik handed her.

'Your cousin who visits battlefields to pick up the weapons of the fallen so he can sell them to the sheikhs?' Mitkhal guessed.

'The same cousin.'

'He'll take me upriver without telling Shalan, or anyone else who asks, the identity of his passenger?'

'He will, because he knows better than to cross me. But that doesn't mean he'll take you without payment. He'll charge full rate.'

'For a passenger or a fugitive?' Mitkhal asked.

'He's my cousin.'

'Fugitive rate,' Mitkhal said wryly.

Zabba smiled and her chin wobbled. 'We poor people have to make a living.'

'You'll need money, Mitkhal,' Furja warned.

'What's in Abdul's will be enough.'

'Are you sure?'

'I'm sure.' He eyed Zabba. 'You said Abdul wanted a girl for Hasan's brother.'

'One who spoke English so she could spy on him. I gave him Kalla.'

'Gave him?' Mitkhal repeated.

152

'I explained she has regular customers and will have to return here one or two days a week to keep her appointments.'

'And when she does, she'll inform you of everything's she's learned about the British plans from Hasan's brother?' Fuija suggested.

'I doubt it will be much. From what the officers say after a few glasses of brandy, I don't think even British command knows their plans. Mitkhal, do you want to travel upriver with my cousin or not?'

'It will be quicker than by horse or camel, so yes, thank you. What time will he be leaving?'

'All I know is tomorrow. He's eating with me this evening. If you visit me at midnight you can make arrangements with him.'

'How far upriver will he be going?'

'As far as Kut al Amara.'

'Sailing on the Tigris?'

'He's not a fool, Mitkhal. He'll be travelling the back way through the canals and the Shatt-el-Hai. Less risk of being stopped and searched by the British military.'

It took Furja to say what they were all thinking. 'But more risk of being stopped by the Marsh Arabs, who'd slaughter a man for his abba, let alone a boat.'

Zabba rose from her chair. 'My cousin is used to dealing with Marsh Arabs. I guarantee you'll reach Kut in one piece, Mitkhal. However, travelling downriver with horses, especially if they're good ones, may be a little trickier.'

'It was good to have someone from home to talk to. We could have dinner in the Basra Club every night until you go upstream,' Charles suggested.

'Provided they allow you out of the hospital again.' Michael helped Charles from his chair into the landau.

'They will,' Charles muttered through gritted teeth.

Richard Chalmers folded the chair and placed it on the floor of the carriage. He held the door open. 'We'll drop you off at Abdul's on our way to the hospital, Michael.'

'No, thank you. I've seen enough of Basra to know it's out of your way. Besides, I'd like to get my bearings and explore the town by night. Am I right in thinking that, if I stay on this road, I'll reach the quay and Abdul's?'

'In about ten minutes, but don't deviate or wander up any alleys,' Charles warned. 'The natives are aware that British officers are armed, but there's a criminal element that might consider a European in civvies a soft target with a fat wallet.'

'My wallet is anything but,' Michael refuted.

'Only by your standards, not those of the natives,' Richard cautioned. 'We'd be happier if you'd let us give you a lift.'

'I'll be fine. I'll call in the hospital to see you tomorrow, Charles.' Michael shivered when icy air hit his lungs and he walked briskly in an effort to keep warm. The street was narrow, hemmed in by high mud brick walls pierced at intervals by close-fitting wooden doors. Lamps burned in niches set alongside them. Michael couldn't see keyholes and presumed the doors were bolted or barred on the inside and manned by a doorkeeper.

Rubbish was piled below the walls. It stank abominably and dark, foul liquid oozed from it, forming puddles he tried to avoid.

The road widened when it approached the river bank. The quay came into view and the high walls were supplanted by shop fronts on the landward side. Most were shuttered, but a stall selling dried dates and figs was open, lit by smoking oil lamps. The stallholder shouted and stepped out to greet him. Michael shook his head to indicate he didn't want to buy anything.

Undeterred the man ran towards him. Michael sidestepped, but the man caught him and began speaking at speed in Arabic. Michael extricated himself and backed towards Abdul's. Grinning, still talking, the man followed. When they were within earshot of the coffee shop the doorman called out to the stallholder. When Michael saw the man freeze and tears appear on his cheeks, he realised he'd been mistaken for his brother – yet again.

'You look so like Hasan you will have to get used to it, my friend.' Abdul, who'd watched the proceedings from the window, pulled a chair out from his table for Michael.

Michael sank down, loosened his muffler, removed his gloves, opened his overcoat and held his hands out to the stove to warm them.

Abdul clicked his fingers at a waiter. He brought over a bottle of brandy and two glasses. Abdul filled both and handed one to Michael.

'You've just begun to realise Hasan is dead.'

'How did you know?'

'I see the pain in your eyes, my friend. He was a brother to me too.' Abdul raised his glass. 'To Hasan.'

Michael emptied his glass. Abdul refilled it and his own.

'To Mesopotamia. May the country oust all the interlopers who wish to take it and make it their own.'

Michael hesitated but after a moment's reflection diplomatically joined in the toast. 'I thought Muslims didn't drink alcohol,' he commented when Abdul filled their glasses a third time.

'Some do, some don't. Some drink to honour their friends. Hasan was my true friend even if he was born a ferenghi.'

'Ferenghi?'

'Like Hasan when he first came here, you have much to learn about my country, our ways and our language. A ferenghi is a foreigner.'

Exhausted after a long day, devastated by Harry's death, overwhelmed by the unfamiliarity of his surroundings, Michael was tempted to go upstairs and pack his bags. Then he remembered his brief as war correspondent. If he felt like a fish out of water, what were the feelings of the men who'd been ordered into this theatre of war without any prior knowledge of the country or its inhabitants?

'You say you're here to write about the war for the newspapers, Mr Downe. So you won't be doing any fighting?'

'No,' Michael confirmed.

'Not at all?

'I'm here to watch, not fight. Please, tell me about my brother, did he stay here often?'

'He lived here whenever he was in Basra.'

'With his...' Michael recalled Abdul's vehement denial that Harry's bearer was his servant, '...friend.'

'Mitkhal lived here too.'

'You said Harry's father in law had a house in Basra. Do you know where?'

'No.' Abdul left the table.

'Someone must know...'

'It's not wise to ask questions about important people,' Abdul pushed the brandy bottle towards Michael's glass and went into his office. He closed the door behind him.

'To annoy Abdul is to flirt with danger, Mr Downe. He knows some very odd people.' Theo Wallace approached the table.

'I didn't set out to irritate him.'

'Like all Arabs, he frequently sees insult where none was intended. Mind if I join you?'

'I'd be glad of your company.'

Theo picked up the bottle of brandy and waylaid a waiter. 'Bring me a glass, please?'

'That's Abdul's brandy.'

'Don't worry, I'll put it on my expenses.'

The waiter returned with the glass and two plates of snacks.

'Sesame and date balls and fig halva soaked in honey. Thank you.' Theo pushed one of the plates towards Michael and filled his glass.

'No, thank you, I dined well in the Basra Club.'

'And you found your way to Abdul's after-

157

wards. I congratulate you, from one end of Basra's social spectrum to another on your first evening. What led you here?'

'My room. I've moved in.'

'You are aware it's a brothel?' Theo filled his glass and topped up Michael's.

'So everyone keeps saying but I've yet to see a girl.'

'Abdul keeps them at the back of the building, behind a well-guarded door on the second floor, lest anyone try sampling the goods without paying. He also owns a building behind this one as well, where the brandy is cheaper but coarser and the girls older and somewhat plain. It's popular with the ranks, but I don't recommend it.'

'You know a great deal about Abdul's business,' Michael commented.

'Professional interest. I check out his girls on a weekly basis. Medically, that is,' Theo explained. 'I recommend them. They're pliant, trained to satisfy, and if you've any doubts about disease there's a box of French letters in every room. Apparently courtesy of a suggestion your cousin John Mason made to Abdul.'

'John visited this place?'

'To check the girls. Before Ctesiphon the Indian Medical Service did the honours, but after Ctesiphon their medics were too busy so Abdul approached the Lansing.' He finished his brandy and winked at Michael. 'It has its perks, which I'm off to enjoy. I'm surprised to see you still in Basra?'

'I'm hoping to track down my sister-in-law, Harry's Arab wife. Don't suppose you have any idea where she is?'

'Unfortunately, no. I never met her. You've spoken to my sister about her?'

'Yes, she couldn't help me. But I only have a day or two to search for her before I head upstream.'

'To report on the top secret "show" everyone is talking about. Good luck, Michael, I hope to see you again before you leave. If you'd like a tour of the Lansing Memorial Hospital, please call in. I can give you a couple of paragraphs of copy designed to keep the donations flowing in.'

'I can't see the readers of the *Mirror* donating to a medical facility that treats the enemy.'

'We treat natives, too, Mr Downe, including women and children. They can be real pocket-book-openers.' Theo rose from his seat. 'Excuse me. I hate to keep ladies waiting.'

Michael finished his drink and left the table. Before he walked away the waiter cleared the bottle of brandy, plates of uneaten sweetmeats and glasses.

Lightheaded from the uneasy mixture of Abdul's brandy and the Chianti he'd drunk with his meal in the Basra Club, he went to his room. He knocked on the door of Adjabi's cupboard and opened it. His bearer was sound asleep on his divan. Closing the door he turned. He'd left the shutters open. Moonlight streamed in illuminating a figure in Arab robes sitting in the corner behind the door.

Michael's breath caught in his throat. 'Harry?' he whispered.

'No, Mr Downe.' The man rose and stretched out his hand. 'Sir Percival Cox, Secretary to the Government of India and Political Resident in

159

the Gulf. Until his death, Lieutenant Colonel Downe was under my direct command. I'd appreciate a word.'

Chapter Twelve

Kut al Amara, Friday 31st December 1915

'This is becoming a habit,' Peter Smythe complained as he, Crabbe, and Sub-Lieutenant Philip Marsh – who, unfortunately for him, had been posted to Nasiriyeh a day before the battle of Ctesiphon – stepped down into the front line trench where the Dorsets faced the Turks across the barbed-wire-strewn wasteland of no-man's-land.

'Someone has to keep up the men's morale, and as the brass are busy guarding their personal supplies of whisky, brandy, and cigars, it falls to us lowly officers.' Crabbe saluted a private on sentry duty.

'Password, sir.'

'Wellington,' Crabbe answered.

'Thank you, sir. Nice of you to call. Don't suppose you've any New Year's cheer tucked away in your pockets for us poor sappers?'

'Evans put you up to asking, Roberts?'

'He did, sir, but we're all hoping.'

'Hope away, Roberts. The only New Year cheer you'll get until we're relieved is a slice of mule with whatever you find growing around here as vegetable substitute.'

'That's not a cheery thought, sir.'

'This is not a cheery place,' Peter Smythe countered.

'Please, can one of you sirs tell us poor sappers why we're here?' Private Evans feigned subservience.

'The stock answer is serving king and country,' Crabbe answered.

'We know that, sir. What we can't fathom is why any king, let alone one as good and kind as ours, would want us here. From what I've seen this country's no good to man, beast, or anyone used to living in Buckingham Palace. It's certainly no good to anyone from Ynysybwl.'

'Ynys-a-where?' Peter had trouble repeating the name.

'Ynysybwl, sir. It's a nice little village outside Pontypridd in Wales. Not much there other than mountains, the pit where my father works, and a couple of shops. But it has a railway station for those who want to get away for a few hours and some nice pubs for them that wants to stay. It would be my pleasure to show you around when we get out of here. The barmaids...'

'That's enough, Evans. Officers don't want to hear about your village. Nice to see you up and about, Lieutenant Marsh, sir. I trust your wound has healed.' Sergeant Lane stepped out of a canvas roofed dugout and saluted the officers.

'It's better than yours by the size of that bandage on your shoulder, Sergeant Lane,' Philip answered.

'You sure you should be here and not in the

161

hospital, Sergeant Lane?' Crabbe questioned.

'Someone has to keep the boys on their toes, sir. Give them five minutes rest and they'll take five days if you let them.'

'As long as you're not watching them at the cost of your health, sergeant.' Peter pulled out a pack of Golden Dawn and offered them around before he and Lieutenant Marsh turned right towards the fort that marked the North East boundary of the Front.

Crabbe lit Sergeant Lane's cigarette. 'The men really all right?'

'They grumble as only sappers can, sir.'

'But?' Crabbe waited.

'It's none of my business, sir, but if I was an officer I'd take a look at the lines around Brigade HQ. There was a bit of a ruckus there half hour ago among the sepoys. I couldn't tell what they were shouting. Only that one or two sounded as though they needed to keep their hair on.'

'Thanks for the tip,' Crabbe called to Smythe and Marsh. 'We're making a detour.' They turned back and joined him.

'All quiet here, Major Crabbe, sir,' Lieutenant Ash reported as they entered one of the "linking" trenches between the first line and the second manned by the Kents and Hampshires.

'But not further on?' Crabbe suggested.

'Sepoys been a bit noisy around the Norfolks' HQ, sir.'

'Drew the short straw, Ash,' Philip Marsh crowed.

'It'll be your turn next week, Marsh,' Ash retorted. 'You can't play the wounded soldier

162

for ever.'

'I hope the Turks will be as sleepy on my duty as they are on yours.'

'Ssh.' Crabbe unbuckled his revolver holster and moved forward. Peter Smythe saw a shadow on the river bank. He rose above the parapet to take a better look. A shot rang out and he crumpled to the ground.

Lieutenant Ash shouted, 'Bastard's reloading.'

Philip Marsh unbuckled his revolver. He saw the silhouette of a sepoy, aimed and fired. The Indian screamed and dropped his weapon.

Crabbe crouched beside Peter. 'Where are you hit?'

'My arm. It's not serious.'

Crabbe shouted, 'Stretcher-bearer!'

A major from the Indian 103rd Infantry ran up to the sepoy, dragged him into the trench and threw him down alongside Crabbe.

The sepoy fell to his knees. 'I am Muslim, Sahib Major. Tell them I am Muslim,' he pleaded. 'Those are my brothers on the other side. I cannot kill my brothers. I want to join them...'

'You'll be doing that soon enough but not on any side on this earth, you bloody fool,' the major snapped. 'Beasely, Warrington?'

A sergeant and sub lieutenant appeared.

'Get this bastard to Brigade HQ and convene a court martial. Ash, Crabbe, Marsh, you're witnesses. How's that poor beggar?'

'In need of the hospital.' Crabbe put pressure on Peter's wound and helped him to his feet.

'What will happen to me, Sahib?' the sepoy begged.

'Wounding an officer while trying to desert? You'll be shot at sunrise,' the major declared. He shouted down the second line. 'Where's that bloody medic? Doesn't he realise it's an officer in need of assistance.'

Basra, Friday 31st December 1915

Michael shook Cox's hand before striking a Lucifer and lighting the oil lamp. The flame sent shadows dancing around the rooms, throwing Sir Percy Cox's face into dark, sardonic profile when he moved his chair away from the pool of light.

Cox lifted an attaché case from the floor and extracted a file.

'Is this about Harry, sir?' Michael ventured.

'It's about you, Mr Downe. I believe you could be useful to us.'

'The military, sir?'

'King and Empire, Downe.'

'When I volunteered for the army, sir, I was rejected.'

'On physical grounds. A leg injury incurred in childhood, when you fell from a tree in the middle of the night.'

Michael looked at him in surprise.

'Correct?'

'Yes, sir.'

You studied German and French at school, passed all your examinations with distinctions, unlike your brother Harry, and went on to read History at Cambridge. Education completed you accepted your father's invitation to join him at

164

Allan and Downe's Bank. Earlier this year you married your cousin, Lucinda Mason. A month after the outbreak of war you applied for a position as war correspondent to the *Daily Mirror*. Posted to France, you requested a transfer to the Mesopotamian Front. Your request was granted at the beginning of December.'

'You know a great deal about me, sir.'

'I know a great deal more than those basic facts, Mr Downe. You met a Mr Smith in your editor's offices the day you left England. He telegraphed me, alerted me to your talents, and suggested you might prove useful to the Political Department of the Indian Expeditionary Force.'

'As I've already pointed out, sir, I have no military experience.'

'Few political officers have...' Cox paused, and Michael sensed he was choosing his words carefully, 'what you would call a conventional military background, Mr Downe. In fact blind obedience is a disadvantage in the field of politics. Take your brother for example. His military career was hardly exemplary before he joined us. I've recruited archaeologists, journalists, engineers, and naval officers, among others, and the one characteristic they all had in common was the ability to think for themselves, especially when they were in a tight corner.'

'Harry was always at his most inventive when he was in trouble.' Michael smiled in spite of the emotionally crippling pain that struck whenever he thought of his brother.

'It was precisely that trait that made him a brilliant political officer. Every success the Indian

Expeditionary Force achieved until Ctesiphon owed something to his efforts. He averted several disasters and saved more lives than he was aware of.'

'Perhaps because he spoke fluent Arabic and could pass as a native.'

'That undoubtedly helped, but Arabic can be learned, Mr Downe. As for passing as a native,' the political officer indicated Michael's divan.

Michael hadn't noticed the robes laid on the camel-hair rug that covered it. He picked them up. 'These look like the ones in the chest in Harry's room.'

'I brought them in. Wearing those and the headdress you would be indistinguishable from your brother, Mr Downe. The resemblance will open doors closed to officers of His Majesty's Army, including myself. As for the Arabic, your brother became fluent in a matter of months. I could assign you a syce who has proved himself an excellent Arabic tutor.'

'I have a bearer.'

'When you go upstream you will need horses, and horses require a syce to care for them, Mr Downe.' Cox rose to his feet. 'You don't have to give me an answer now. Meet me in the Basra Club the day after tomorrow. One o'clock.'

'Would you expect me to give up my post as the *Mirror's* war correspondent?'

'No, Mr Downe. It affords excellent cover for any tasks we might assign you. We would of course pay you for your services, initially at a captain's pay rate.'

'I am more concerned about being able to fulfil

my duty to my country than remuneration and I'm still not sure what I can do to help you,' Michael demurred.

'Spoken like your brother, Mr Downe. You resemble him in more ways than appearance. As for fulfilling your duty, I wouldn't have invited you to join us if I wasn't certain that you will do just that. To your own detriment, if the situation calls for sacrifice.' He went to the door.

'My brother... Do you know where I can find his wife?' Michael asked.

'Unfortunately not, Mr Downe. She appears to have gone to ground.'

'In Basra?'

'Or the desert.'

'Major Reid mentioned Harry had an Arab friend.'

'He had several, Mr Downe.'

'He mentioned a name – Mitkhal.'

'They were close,' the political officer acknowledged.

'Do you know where he is?'

'Like Mrs Downe, he appears to have gone to ground.'

'He's alive?' Michael persisted.

'I've heard nothing to indicate that he's dead.'

'Could you get a message to him?'

'I can try.'

'Could you please tell him that Harry's brother is staying in Abdul's for the next day or two and he'd like to see him?'

'I make no promises, Mr Downe, but I'll try.' He shook Michael's hand, opened the door, and strode down the corridor to the head of the stairs. Michael followed him as far as the landing.

He turned his back on the stairs and looked down at the inner courtyard. It was enclosed on all four sides by the building. Several hooded oil lamps burned, illuminating carved stone and wooden benches set on marble tiles. Potted palms drooped; sad winter victims of the buffeting wind and rain. A brass-headed marble fountain was caked with rotting foliage, but it took little imagination to picture the garden in summer, cool and inviting in the shade of the high walls.

He looked up. There were no drapes at any of the windows that overlooked the inner yard. Theo Wallace was standing in front of bed in a room diagonally opposite. Two dark-haired women, both naked, were kneeling before him on the divan. The women were doing things he'd seen depicted in the pornographic postcards his fellow students had passed around his college. Things he'd never imagined any woman doing willingly to a man, yet both of Theo's 'ladies' were smiling as broadly as Theo who was obviously enjoying their ministrations.

'Mr Downe?'

Embarrassed at being caught playing the voyeur, Michael started. Abdul was behind him.

'I was seeing a visitor out...' Michael glanced at the empty staircase.

Abdul ignored his explanation. 'I've brought you a girl. If you don't find her pleasing I can show you a selection.'

'No, thank you,' Michael stammered. 'I don't need a girl.'

168

'If you'd prefer a boy...'

'No! Neither–' Michael could feel colour flooding into his cheeks.

Abdul barked an order. A girl moved out of the shadows.

'Take her or view some others, Mr Downe. You'd disrespect my hospitality if you refuse.'

Michael recalled Theo Wallace's warnings about annoying Abdul but he simply couldn't look the girl in the eye.

'I speak English, Mr Downe, and I would try to make you as happy as I did my captain before he was killed.'

Michael looked up from the bare henna-painted feet of the young girl. Dressed in a simple red robe, her most striking feature was her enormous brown eyes.

'Mr Downe?'

Michael nodded to Abdul and managed a murmured, 'Thank you.'

'You are Mr Downe's for as long as he stays here, Kalla.'

The girl replied in Arabic.

'Can I send a servant with anything else you require, Mr Downe? Food, drink?'

'No, thank you.' Michael opened the door of his room, the girl followed. She closed the door behind them and removed her robe.

'Kalla...' embarrassed by her nudity, Michael faltered.

'You don't find me pretty?'

'Very pretty.'

'You were watching Dr Theo and his girls. I could send for another girl...'

'No!'

'Then I will try to be enough for you, Mr Downe.'

Chapter Thirteen

London, Saturday 1st January 1916

Georgiana entered the exclusive, masculine confines of the gentlemen's club and picked her way around mounds of luggage to the desk. The vestibule, stairs, and main hall were crowded with men in military uniforms. The navy was rubbing shoulders with the cavalry, infantry and flying corps, and all appeared to be either coming or going through the double doors that led on to St James's Street. She pitied the sprinkling of sober-suited civil servants, who looked positively drab in comparison to the men in uniform.

'May I help you, ma'am?' The clerk, who'd acquired the manners of senior royalty during thirty years of service in the club, looked down his long nose as though he were vetting her for a position below stairs.

'Miss Downe for General Reid.' Georgiana had learned not to use the title of Dr in the environs of male conclaves. It led to mirth or raised eyebrows and she wasn't in the mood to combat either.

'Miss Downe, my apologies, I didn't recognise you.'

'Like everyone out there I'm pretending to be a fish.' Georgiana peeled off her rain-sodden hat and coat.

'Yes, madam.' He didn't evince the flicker of a smile. 'Bellboy, relieve Miss Downe of her outdoor garments.'

A uniformed boy left the head of the line assembled to the left of the desk, rushed forward, and took Georgiana' s umbrella, coat, and hat.

'We will acquaint General Reid of your presence, Miss Downe. Please take a seat in the ladies' waiting room. Boy.' The clerk summoned the second in line.

'I know the way, thank you.' Georgiana walked into the bland characterless room. It held a row of upright mahogany chairs and a low table, nothing else. No pictures adorned the walls, no magazines littered the table. There weren't even curtains at the windows.

The clerk moved in slow, unhurried motion as he wrote a note, folded it into an envelope, addressed it, and placed it on a silver tray before handing it to the boy. The boy walked away from the desk ringing a bell and calling,

'Message for General Reid. Message for General Reid'

The clerk walked to the door of the ladies waiting room, ignored Georgiana and closed it, softly but firmly. It opened a few minutes later and her godfather entered.

She left her seat. 'Uncle Reid, it's good of you to stand me lunch here.'

'Not at all, Georgie. Glad you could make it. We'll eat better in the club dining room than any restaurant in these days of food shortages and requisitions. The staff still have time to look after the older members, although the committee have taken on so many new members the club is more like the Tottenham Court Road these days than the oasis of calm and quiet it used to be before the war.'

'Like everywhere in London, it's full of people coming and going.' She took her godfather's arm. 'As for doubts about the quality of the food, mine were laid to rest when I saw men from the War Office Agricultural Department heading upstairs.'

'You recognised them?'

'They dined at Clyneswood the last time I was home.'

'Your father was probably softening them up in the hope of hanging on to enough breeding stock to replenish his barns and cowsheds.'

They walked up the stairs into the mahogany-panelled dining room. The head waiter glided across the polished floor to greet them.

'General Reid, always a pleasure. Ma'am, sir.' He pulled out a chair for Georgiana and when she was seated, unfolded the linen 'slipper' in front of her place setting and shook it over her lap.

'Would you like to order now, General?'

'I think so. What do you say, Georgie?'

'Fine.' All she wanted was the preliminaries to be over with so she could ask her godfather if he'd managed to get her a berth on a Mesopotamia-bound ship.

The waiter leaned conspiratorially towards the

General. 'May I suggest menu number one, General? The potato soup, halibut collards, roast goose, cranberry sauce, mashed potatoes, cauliflower, and for dessert honeycomb mould and devilled almonds.' He handed them leather-bound menu holders.

'You may, but I'll take roast potatoes instead of mashed and you know I can't stand cauliflower. Tastes like wallpaper paste.'

'I could substitute peas and carrots, sir.'

'Good man. Menu suit you, Georgie?'

'Yes, thank you, Uncle Reid.' She glanced around as she handed back the unopened folder.

The room was full of middle-aged and elderly men. A few were accompanied by women young enough to be their daughters, in some cases granddaughters. Georgiana had seen the sceptical look in the head waiter's eyes the first time she'd visited the club and the general had introduced her as his "goddaughter". It had taken a dinner with her father and Dr Mason for the waiter to realise that some club members did choose to eat at the club with family and friends.

The wine waiter appeared.

'I know you'll tell me it shouldn't be drunk with goose, but we'll have the 1909 claret and a bottle of the house champagne. Unless you have a preference, Georgie?'

Georgiana was growing increasingly impatient and wondered if she'd ever be left alone with her godfather.

'Fine,' she repeated.

'You'd think a young girl would be more enthusiastic about champagne, wouldn't you, Henry?'

173

'May I suggest aperitifs on the house, General?'

'Suggest away when it's on the house,' the General answered. 'Georgie?'

'Yes, please.' She didn't care whether she drank seawater or ate sawdust. All she wanted to know was whether or not her godfather had managed to get her into the Queen Alexander Imperial Nursing Corps.

The wine waiter clicked his fingers. A junior waiter appeared and filled their sherry glasses.

'Thank you,' Georgiana took her glass and touched it to the General's.

'What are we toasting?' he asked.

'My joining the QAINC.'

'I'll discuss that with you in a moment.'

Determined not to be deflected, she said, 'In that case we'll drink to a swift end to the war.'

'Won't be this year, I'm afraid.'

'Next.'

'Probably not even then.'

'Dear God, how many more young men have to be sacrificed?'

'If we can advance the line in France, break the siege of Kut; smash the Germans in East Africa...'

She interrupted. 'Did you get me a berth on the ship that's heading for...'

'Don't say it.'

She looked over her shoulder. 'You think there are spies in the club?'

He tapped his nose again with his forefinger. 'Can't be too careful.'

'Did you get me a berth?' she reiterated impatiently.

'I tried my best, Georgie. If you were a nurse I

174

could have swung it but you know what the military think of female doctors.'

'I'm better qualified and more use to the wounded than any nurse.'

'You don't have to convince me, Georgie, but I'm afraid this particular scheme of yours has hit barbed wire. There's absolutely no way I can get you to Mesopotamia. I talked it over with your father and your Uncle Mason.'

'They didn't need to know.'

'I couldn't keep your plans from your father. He and Dr Mason are my oldest and closest friends.'

'My plans are no concern of my father's.'

'They are when you enlist my help. Your father was furious that you'd even asked me to try to arrange your passage.'

'He would be.'

'Think of him and your mother, Georgie. They've lost Harry...'

'Harry's alive,' she contradicted vehemently.

'I was about to remind you that Michael's out there. They have no idea when, if ever, they'll see him again. If by some miracle you're right and Harry is alive, Michael and Tom will find him.'

'They'll be too busy writing reports and doctoring the sick to look.'

'Georgie, please, don't blame your parents and everyone who loves you for wanting to keep you in London. You're doing sterling work for the war effort, here, caring for the wounded.'

'Last week I was moved from surgery on to the women's medical ward in the London Royal Free Hospital. A fat lot of good I'm contributing to

175

the war effort there.'

'I thought you were a surgical registrar.'

'I was, until a male doctor invalided from the front took my job.'

'You can't think of him as taking your job, Georgie. Rather think that by working in the Royal Free Hospital you've freed a man for the front. That's what war is about. The men go off to fight. The women stay at home...'

'And worry themselves sick?'

'Bit unfair I know, while the men cover themselves in glory.'

'In this war more men are being covered in the mud and blood of the Western Front and the deserts of Mesopotamia and Gallipoli than glory,' she said bitterly.

He patted her hand. 'Doctoring men or women, you're doing vital work where you are, Georgie. My advice to you is, forget Mesopotamia. Concentrate on what you're doing here.'

Their soup arrived.

Her godfather looked across at her. 'I did try to get you into the nursing corps, Georgie.'

'I believe you.'

'You have to give up any idea you have of joining the QAINC.'

'Uncle Reid...'

'I asked, Georgie.'

'Did you really?' she challenged.

'I did.' The General set down his spoon. 'Everyone I spoke to was sympathetic.'

'But unhelpful?'

'Georgie, you have to understand women have no place in war. It can get brutal out there.

176

People die.'

'After a year spent in surgery there is nothing you can tell me about death that I don't already know.'

'There is a difference between someone dying peacefully in surgery and being blown apart on a battlefield.'

'Surgery – peaceful!'

'You know what I mean.'

'As a nurse I wouldn't even be allowed on a battlefield to get "blown apart". Hospitals are in safe areas behind the lines even in Mesopotamia...' Georgiana was interrupted mid-flow by a short, immaculately dressed man who stopped at their table to shake hands with General Reid. Turning from her godfather to her he closed his fingers over hers and bowed.

General Reid rose to his feet. 'Mr...'

'Smith.' The man supplied.

'Mr Smith and I work together at the War Office,' General Reid explained. 'May I present my goddaughter, Dr Georgiana Downe, Mr Smith.'

'A pleasure, Dr Downe. I didn't mean to encroach on your privacy, General.' Mr Smith looked around the crowded restaurant. 'So this is where you hide yourself at lunchtime? I can't say I blame you, the food here has a formidable reputation.'

'Please, Mr Smith, join us.' To Georgiana's annoyance, her godfather put an end to their argument by signalling to the waiter.

Another chair, place setting and menu were produced and in less than a minute, Mr Smith was sitting alongside Georgiana sipping sherry.

'It's a pleasure to meet you after hearing so much about you, Dr Downe.'

'My godfather told you I was a doctor?'

'He's very proud of you, Dr Downe.'

'Don't look so shocked, Georgie. I am proud of you and not above boasting about your accomplishments.' General Reid signalled to the waiter, who hurried to the table to remove his and Georgiana's soup bowls.

Mr Smith returned the menu to the waiter unopened. 'General Reid has a penchant for seeking out the best. Bring me a duplicate of his order.'

'Yes, sir.'

The junior wine waiter filled their wine and water glasses and left them.

'My goddaughter is disappointed that I can't call in enough favours to get her into the QAINC,' General Reid revealed.

Mr Smith shook out his napkin and tucked a corner into a napkin holder he clipped to his collar.

'Isn't nursing a backward step for a qualified doctor, Dr Downe? Bit like a general taking a subaltern's post.'

'Wouldn't the general take the post if it was the only way open to him to search for a member of his family declared missing in action?' Georgiana countered.

'General Reid told me that you're convinced your brother Lieutenant Colonel Downe is alive somewhere in Mesopotamia.'

'I am.'

'I can verify that your godfather has canvassed

178

everyone with influence in the Mesopotamian theatre on your brother's behalf, Dr Downe, unfortunately to no avail.'

'I failed to glean any more information than your father received, Georgie,' the general confirmed.

'I also verify that he spoke to the people in charge of the QAINC.' Mr Smith's soup arrived. He took a spoonful and blotted his upper lip with his napkin.

'And?' Georgiana prompted.

'They were horrified at the thought of a woman doctor, let alone one who wanted to masquerade as a nurse,' the General divulged. 'So please, Georgie, we'll have no more talk from you of berths on Mesopotamia-bound ships or the QAINC, if you please. Let's just enjoy this lunch.'

The Mission, Basra, Sunday 2nd January 1916

Charles chose to visit Maud on Sunday morning when he hoped the Reverend Butler and the entire mission household would be attending church services. But not all the mission staff were in the chapel. An Arab maid answered the door and showed him into Maud's room. He limped in awkwardly on crutches, his movements hampered by the attaché case he carried.

Maud was sitting in the same upholstered chair he'd seen her sitting in before. The nursemaid was still darning socks in the alcove, with the baby's cot next to her. Not Maud. He wondered if any of them had moved since the last time he was in the room.

Maud set her sewing aside when she saw him. 'Please, sit down, Charles, before you fall down.'

He accepted her offer of a chair and propped his crutches against the wall.

'I never expected to see you here again after the way you walked out last Friday.'

'I was in shock. Do you really expect me to believe I'm the father of your child?'

'You've had a memory lapse, Charles?'

'It was once...'

'Once is all it takes. Forgive me for being crude, but I assure you that you are the only man I fornicated with after I left India. There's been no one since. But I have no intention of arguing Robin's paternity with you. It's a matter of complete indifference to me whether you believe me or not.'

'Then why tell me I'm Robin's father, Maud?'

'I assumed – it appears wrongly – that you'd like to know you have a child.'

'Were you hoping I'd pay for his keep – and yours?'

'No. Absolutely not. The baby is mine and my responsibility. Emotionally and financially.'

'When it comes to emotions I hope you take more care of his than you did of John's. As for financially, this should help?' He took the jewellery case Tom and Michael had found in Harry's safety deposit box from his case and set it on the table.

She stared at it.

'It was yours?'

'It was,' she conceded. 'I didn't expect to see it again.'

'Or these?' he opened the case. 'I recognised them the moment I saw them.'

'You've seen them before?'

'You were wearing them when I called on you in India, the night before we sailed for here.'

'You mean, the night before you dragged me here.' The blood red rubies in their glittering gold and diamond settings caught the light and sparkled on the bed of oyster velvet. Maud flicked the lid closed. 'Harry sold them for me. He gave me the money.'

'If Harry had sold them I wouldn't have them,' Charles said.

'Where did you get them?'

'Harry's safety deposit box at Gray Mackenzie & Co.'

'Why would Harry have a safety deposit box?'

'To store his valuables while he was at the front. Michael's trying to find Harry's Arab wife. We went to Abdul's to ask if he knew where she was. He gave us a copy of Harry's will.'

'Harry gave his will to an Arab?' Maud was shocked.

'John and I were upstream with most of the force. There wouldn't have been many people around and Abdul, like Harry's wife, is Arab.'

'He could have left his will with Reverend Butler or Theo.'

'He left it with Abdul, Maud. He obviously trusted the man. Abdul showed us Harry's room. We found the key to the security box there. Under the terms of Harry's will,' he pointed to the jewellery, 'these are to be given to you.'

'Harry never sold them?'

'It looks that way.'

'But Harry gave me a great deal of money for them. I couldn't possibly keep the money and the jewels.'

'It's what Harry intended.'

'I doubt Harry intended to die,' Maud retorted.

'None of us intend to die, Maud, but every soldier has to be prepared to do just that. Take the jewels. Harry wouldn't have mentioned them in his will if he didn't want you to have them.'

'They're his. They should go with the rest of his estate.'

'The only other beneficiary Harry named is his wife and so far Michael's had no luck in tracking her down.'

'Where is Michael looking for her?'

'Here, in Basra. He didn't go up river with Tom. He's renting a room in Abdul's as Harry did. He's been interviewing people in HQ and writing articles on morale and our determination to re-lieve the Indian Expeditionary Force holed up in Kut.'

'How is the force hoping to accomplish that?'

'That's classified military information.'

'Angela is beside herself with concern over Peter.'

'We'll get him – and the others out.' Thinking of John and Harry and how any attempt to break the siege would come too late for them, he leaned forward and looked into the cot so she couldn't read the expression in his eyes. 'You're deter-mined to bring up this child alone?'

'If you want him, Charles, take him.'

'I'm hardly in a position to care for a baby.'

She indicated the woman sitting next to the cot. 'I've hired a nursemaid. I'll continue to pay her wages if you move her into a military bungalow.'

'Why would I move a child that's not related to me into military quarters?'

'The orphaned son of your best friend shouldn't raise too many eyebrows.'

'People note dates, Maud. Everyone knows the child isn't John's. I assume you have candidates for lover, husband, and fatherhood duties hovering around you. There wasn't a shortage in India.'

'There's no one.' She picked up the box from the table and handed it to him. 'Please take the jewels. I couldn't manage without the money Harry gave me. If I took them back I'd feel as though I'd accepted charity. Give them to Michael.'

'I doubt he'd find them useful upstream.'

'He could pass them on to Harry's sister.'

'I know Harry's sister. She wouldn't want or wear them.'

'Then tell Michael to sell them and give the money to Harry's wife when he finds her,' she suggested in exasperation.

'They're yours, Maud. You find someone to buy them.'

'I couldn't find anyone, which is why I gave them to Harry.'

'It appears Harry couldn't find anyone who wanted them either.' Charles opened the box again and looked at them. 'Tom said you told him you were living on the proceeds of a jewellery sale. You never did tell me who gave you these. Was it

D'Arbez?' He referred to the Portuguese plant-
ation owner and trader whose name he'd heard
linked with Maud's.'

'What if it was?'

'Payment for services rendered?' he taunted.

'Believe what you will.'

'Tainted ill-gotten gains, antique, and in their
way quite magnificent. They probably once belonged to an Empress or at the very least a
Maharani.' He snapped the box shut, returned it
to the table, and reached for his crutches. 'Keep
them. Wear them when you have a settled life
again, Maud. And you will. Scum always rises to
the top. They may attract a man looking for a
wife who doesn't know who or what you are.'

'And your son?'

'If I thought for one minute he was really mine,
I'd be concerned for his fate. As it is, I couldn't
give a damn. Find some other dupe, Maud. One
who's stupid enough to believe your lies.'

Chapter Fourteen

The Basra Club, Sunday 2nd January 1916

A steward waylaid Michael when he walked into
the Basra Club at twelve forty-five. He eyed his
civilian clothes with the disparaging expression
Michael had come to expect, not from the
military, but the civilians who served them.

'Are you a member of the Basra Club, sir?'

Michael wished he'd acquired Harry's aptitude for telling convincing lies. 'No.'

'I regret to say, sir, affiliated status of the Club has only been extended to officers serving in His Majesty's Forces.'

'I am here to meet an officer. Colonel...'

The steward interrupted him. 'I have a list of expected guests, sir. Your name?'

'Michael Downe.'

'If you'd care to follow me, sir.'

Michael glanced into the dining room and lounge as they passed the open doors but failed to spot the political officer's lean figure.

'This way, sir.' The steward prompted. He led Michael down a corridor, up a staircase and through a passageway into the back of the building. He opened a door.

Sir Percival Cox and two majors were standing in front of a desk blanketed with layers of maps.

Cox checked his pocket watch. 'Mr Downe, I wasn't expecting you for another ten minutes.'

'I could wait downstairs, sir.'

'Not necessary.' Cox addressed the officers. 'I believe we've finished here, gentlemen.'

'If you have no further orders for us, sir.'

'Not at present. Report to my office six hundred hours tomorrow.'

'Understood, sir.' One of the officers gathered the maps, and proceeded to roll them into a leather tube.

'Take a seat, Mr Downe.' Cox pointed to rattan chairs grouped around a cane table. After the officers left, he picked up two glasses and set them next to a samovar on the table.

'Have you made a decision, Mr Downe?'

'If you really believe I can be of service to you, and my country, I accept.'

'Good man.' The political officer filled the glasses with tea. He pushed one and a bowl of sugar cubes in front of Michael.

'Should I prove a disappointment...'

'If you're one-tenth of the man your brother was, Mr Downe, you won't. Given your cover as a journalist you'll be excused uniform, although as I've already said, you'll be commissioned and paid as a captain. You'll report to me directly.'

'Will my commission be generally known, sir?'

'No, and your fellow political officers will only be told on a need-to-know basis. Commissions in the Political service aren't like those in the army. They're more of a...' Cox chose his words with circumspection, 'an honorary title. Useful when you meet the occasional regimental blockhead who might be tempted to try to pull seniority on you. You're attached only to the Political Service and we work in the shadows, Mr Downe. The less the regular army knows about us the better. All our senior officers, myself included, are Lieutenant Colonels in name and pay grade. Ranking with the Political Service is very much dependent on the respect a man earns.' He changed the subject abruptly. 'You'll receive a visitor at Abdul's this afternoon. An Arab Syce, Daoud. He's made an appointment for you to visit a native horse trader at sixteen hundred hours.'

'You were certain I'd accept your offer?'

'You were turned down by the military yet you persisted until you discovered a way to serve. It was obvious you'd accept my proposal, Mr Downe. Daoud will help you select your horses. Most officers have at least four. The country upriver is hard on them, especially with the rainy season about to start. I can vouch for Daoud's honesty. He's been working for the Political Office for some time. When do you leave to join the forces upriver?'

'Tomorrow morning.'

'When you reach the camp and begin interviewing, pay particular attention to the Arab irregulars. Find out which tribe they're from. Daoud will interpret.'

'Wouldn't he be better off going in alone?'

'To talk to the Arab tribesmen, yes. But I'd like you to talk to their leaders.'

'They don't know me.'

'When they recognise your resemblance to your brother they'll want to sympathise with you on your loss.'

Michael was taken aback, 'You want me to use Harry's death as an introduction?'

'To influential sheikhs, yes, Mr Downe. We're at war. I'm prepared to use every weapon at my disposal to fight it, including the friendships forged by our fallen heroes. It's essential the Arabs your brother courted and won to our cause remain on our side.' Cox's eyes were grey, cold, the colour of tempered steel. 'As well as speaking to the natives, I'd appreciate you gauging the attitude of the Relief Force officers towards those in command.'

'Any names in particular you want me to look out for, sir?'

'Best you go upstream with no pre-conceived

ideas, Downe. Do you know any men stationed there?'

'My cousin Tom Mason is a captain seconded to the Indian Medical Service. We travelled here together. He went upriver on Friday evening.'

'No one else?'

'The officers on the transport that brought me here. There may be people I was in school or university with, but none I'm aware of.'

'Have arrangements been made for you to telegraph your reports to your editor?'

'I'll be allowed to use the wireless when it is not needed for military communications, sir.'

Cox smiled. 'Be prepared to telegraph in the early hours of the morning, Mr Downe.'

'It wouldn't be the first time, sir. I reported from...'

'The Western Front, I'm aware of your last posting, Mr Downe.'

'Do I send my reports to you by wireless, sir?'

'Good Lord, no! I have a network of couriers. Daoud knows them all. Should you be separated from Daoud for any reason you can send non-sensitive reports downstream in the mailbag for HQ. Anything sensitive you keep to yourself until you can be certain that it will reach me personally. All communiqués forwarded in the general mail must be marked "personal" to me with my name, rank, and number.'

'I'll be certain to do that, sir.'

'It's common knowledge that a show upstream is imminent. Townshend will be out of supplies by the end of the month. The sooner we extricate him and his command the sooner we can begin the campaign to take Baghdad. I hope to be in Ali Gharbi myself shortly. Should you have any queries before my arrival, ask Daoud. He's acquainted with the precious few natives on our side, also the untrustworthy open to bribery, and those who'd slit our throats given half a chance. Did your brother write to you?'

'Not often and rarely about military matters.'

'That's no reflection on you, or your relationship with him, Mr Downe. As your brother well knew, nothing contentious or military would get past the censor. The problem is, we're not only fighting the Turks who are desperately trying to cling on to their empire, but almost the entire population of this country. The Arabs are baying for independence.'

'Are they likely to get it, sir?'

The political officer's eyes narrowed. 'Not from the Turks.'

'Us?'

'It would be premature to discuss the future of Mesopotamia before we've driven out the Turk, Downe.'

'So we have no plans for the country?'

'You've accepted a position as a captain in the Political Office, Downe. Despite your cover as a journalist, this meeting and our conversation, like all our future conversations, are entirely off the record. So forget any thoughts you might have had about publishing any part of anything said by me.'

Michael resisted the temptation to argue that his position as a journalist was more than a cover. 'I understand, sir.'

'I trust you do, Downe, or our acquaintance will be a brief one.'

'It would help if I knew the Indian Office's long-term plans for Mesopotamia, sir,' Michael ventured.

'You've heard something?'

'Rumours, sir.'

'Elucidate?'

'A letter that was sent to an M.P.'

'It's well known that there are people, in the Indian Office, Westminster and the military, even in my own department, with plans for Mesopotamia.'

'I read Sir William Willcocks' argument for annexing the country for India, sir. He suggested irrigating the southern lower reaches of the desert around Amara and Basra with water from the Tigris and Euphrates until it rivals the north for fertility. He also suggested that this new agricultural land could be populated with surplus Indians from the Punjab who would, and I quote, "transform Lower Mesopotamia into one of the largest granaries of the world." Presumably with the aim of creating a new colony for India?'

'The Indian Office has made no secret of its expansionist plans,' Cox agreed.

'Are the Arabs aware of these plans, sir?' Michael asked.

'To be frank, Downe, it's not something I've discussed with them, or would wish to. I trust you're not thinking of bringing the matter up in conversation with any sheikhs you meet.'

'No, sir. But there was a paragraph in the proposition I found disturbing.'

'Which one?'

'It stated that the Arab population would gladly accept British rule through the Indian Office as they did at Basra before the war. Harry was here, and he never mentioned British rule of any part of the Ottoman Empire, or "glad acceptance by the natives".'

'You said he never wrote about the war.'

'This was before the war, sir. I'm just looking for confirmation that the Indian Office sees Mesopotamia as a future colony of our eastern empire.'

'I wouldn't go as far as to say that's how the Indian Office sees the future of this country, Downe. Like you, I've heard it argued that skilful irrigation could transform the arid nature of the lower reaches of the desert around Basra. My deputy even suggested we wouldn't even have to garrison the country as the land could be leased or gifted to native Indian Army veterans who'd form a territorial defensive militia should the Arabs prove difficult, which in my opinion they most definitely would if the Indian Office imported overlords. Mesopotamia is very different to India, as your brother well knew. The Bedouin may be nomadic, but they are neither disorganised nor weak. Two attributes I believe the Indian Office equate with their nomadic lifestyle.'

'So the political future of Mesopotamia has yet to be decided sir?' Michael tried not to sound disingenuous.

'As I've already said, first we have to drive out the Turks. There's no point in even discussing the matter until we've accomplished that much.' Cox refilled their tea glasses.

191

Michael sensed Cox wanted to end the interview but there was one subject he hadn't yet broached. 'Have you managed to locate my brother's bearer, sir?'

'I sent a message out on the native grapevine. Hopefully he will hear it.'

'If he should contact you, I'd be grateful if you'd let me know.'

'Of course.'

'Captain Reid informed me that my brother was shot by a Turkish sniper.'

'That's correct.'

'Does anyone know what happened to his body?'

'Other than his corpse fell into Turkish hands, no. There are many unmarked graves in the desert, Mr Downe. I usually say that is a situation that will be rectified at the end of the war, but not in your brother's case. He left Kut to spy on the Turks. He was dressed in native robes and carried nothing that could identify him as a British officer. Not even his identification tags. There's no way of distinguishing his body from any other, even if it should be found.'

'Thank you for your honesty, sir.' Michael left his chair. 'I have copy to deliver before I go upstream. Please excuse me.'

'You won't forget to meet Daoud in Abdul's.'

'At four o'clock. I won't forget, sir.'

Kut al Amara, Sunday 2nd January 1916

'You're picking up a fair collection of scars. Out to impress your lady with tall tales of hard fought battles, Smythe?' John Mason quipped as he passed him and Knight in the officers' aid station.

'If I ever see her again,' Peter moaned.

'No defeatist talk allowed.' John filled a bowl with water from a jug and proceeded to scrub his hands.

'Only officers to hear it.'

'Officers as depressed as the ranks, despite the dictates of the brass that it's our duty to bolster morale.' Knight was attempting to tweeze a bone fragment from Peter Smythe's shoulder that had proved stubborn when the wound had first been dressed. 'How's Cleck-Heaton?' he asked John.

'Sitting up. Uncommunicative.' John reached for a towel.

'Must be difficult to say "thank you for saving my life" to a man you wanted shot.' Peter winced when Knight dug too deeply.

'Sirs,' John's orderly Dira appeared at the door. 'Stretcher-bearers have brought in a sepoy with a head wound.'

'Take over here, John. I'll go to the Indian hospital.'

'Any reason, Knight?'

'You've only half an hour of your shift to go and I've just come on duty. Besides, this bone splinter is proving more elusive than the carp in my father's lake.' Knight handed John the tweezers and left the chair. 'Snipers busy, Dira?'

'No more than usual, Sahib sir, but from the casualty lists it seems they prefer to aim at the English and Indian officers, than at the ranks, sir.'

'Wipe that grin off your face, Dira, before the

brass suggest you change uniforms with us.'

Dira's smile broadened. 'Yes, sir, Sahib Knight.'

John sat on the stool Knight had vacated and dipped the tweezers into a cup of antiseptic. 'You need to keep this wound clean, Smythe. Get it dressed here night and morning.'

'It's infected?'

'It's looking messy.'

'That a technical term?'

John frowned as tried to get a grip on the sliver. 'Try to eat some of the weeds the cooks serve as vegetable substitute. It's anyone's guess what they are or what effect they're having on our digestive systems but malnutrition, scurvy, and the unsanitary conditions are playing havoc with recovery rates from wounds, so anything's worth a try.'

'I'll be fine.'

'I wish I had a guinea for every time I've heard that lately. Another injury like this and you'll be heading downstream to your lovely lady as soon as we're relieved.'

'I wish I could look forward to that reunion.'

'You're worried about what happened in Qurna last August?' John asked.

'You probably remember more of what happened than me.'

'You'd been in battle, you were shell-shocked. You lashed out in your sleep...'

'And damn near killed my wife. You saw what I did to her. You treated her after I beat her.'

'In your sleep,' John reiterated.

'There's no guarantee I won't do the same again.'

'You haven't attacked anyone other than a Turk

194

sleeping – or awake – since that night.'

'How can you be sure?' Peter demanded.

'Because I asked Crabbe to keep an eye on you and he would have told me if you had.'

'Even in my sleep I'm aware that Crabbe, and his Webley revolver are only a couple of feet from my head.'

'You could always ask Angela – Mrs Smythe – to lock you in a separate bedroom at night if you're worried about a recurrence when you see her again,' John finally managed to gain a purchase on the bone splinter.

'I am worried,' Peter admitted, 'and for that reason alone I'm dreading us being relieved.'

'Have you considered we might not be?'

Peter looked John in the eye. 'You think we'll be forced to surrender?'

'It's a possibility and forewarned is forearmed. The food's running out and the sepoys ... let's just say there's been an increase in the number coming into the aid stations with gunshot wounds.'

'Self-inflicted, feet and hands,' Peter guessed. 'Cowardly beggars! Are the rumours of Turkish reinforcements being brought in true?'

'You have more time than me to monitor the Turkish lines. Are they?'

'Every time I look out over no-man's-land, all I see are rows after rows of the bastards. We won't stand a chance if Constantinople send another brigade to join them.'

'Which is why I try to spend all my time in here. Success at last.' John dropped the bone splinter into a kidney dish. 'I'm the proverbial coward who's afraid to look.'

'That I don't believe. A lesser man would be a gibbering idiot after what you've been through since Nasiriyeh.'

'I doubt it,' John dismissed. 'The instinct for survival is inbuilt in us all.'

'Let's hope it's in Townshend, and if the worst does come to the worst, that he opts for surrender, not a futile last attack.' Peter felt in his pockets for his cigarettes. 'If he surrenders you do realise that will mean the end of the war for all of us?'

'And God knows how many years in a Turkish prison camp.' John deliberately moved the conversation away from their plight. 'Have you seen Harry's horses?'

'Oddly enough I mentioned them to Crabbe earlier. If you'll excuse me from duty I'll see if I can find them.'

John washed his hands again and reached for a notepad. 'The "excused duty" is easy. I'd be grateful if you would look for them. Harry adored his horses and I can't bear the thought of them ending up on a plate in the mess.'

'I know there's talk of eating mules but surely we won't have to eat the cavalry horses?' Peter questioned.

'That depends on how long we're dug in here and how long the animal feed holds out. Last I heard it's dangerously low and they're thinking of giving it to the Indian troops to supplement their rations because they're refusing to eat mule or horseflesh.'

'Silly beggars.'

'This is not for general consumption but the Indian Medical Service has advised General Townshend – not for the first time – to search the town and stockpile all foodstuffs found in the native warehouses and shops under military authority.'

'Rationing?'

'Full rations at the moment but if we're not relieved in a week or two it might have to be cut by a third,' John warned.

'I heard that the brigadier advised a search of the town for hidden stockpiles when we arrived. General Townshend refused on the grounds that the natives were restless enough and he was afraid a house to house search would push them over the edge. It would have been better if we'd sent them packing when we reached here. As it is we have to feed them as well as ourselves.'

'It was Cox who persuaded Townshend not to expel the native population in the middle of winter. It's the British way. We care for the underdog.' John handed Peter the note he'd scrawled.

'Word from HQ is the Relief Force is assembling at Ali Gharbi only 56 miles away. Given the Generals' penchant for delay I hope they make a move towards us before the rainy season.'

'Which will start any day now,' Crabbe walked in. 'And when it does, it will bring floods, in which case we'll all be floating out of our trenches downriver to Basra. Us, Turk, Arab...'

'Floating and fighting.' Peter fell serious. 'The sappers can't understand why we're in this Godforsaken place.'

'No one's given me a reason that makes sense.'

John dropped the tweezers back into the antiseptic.

'It doesn't pay to think deeply about anything in this man's army,' Crabbe studied Peter's wound. 'That looks distinctly off-colour.'

'John called it messy. You'll have me down as a case of gas gangrene next.'

'Not if I can help it.' John irrigated Peter's wound one final time before reaching for a square of gauze.

'Major Mason, they've just brought Captain Leigh in with a neck wound.'

'I'm there, Matthews. Send an orderly in to bandage Captain Smythe.' John went to the door. 'You won't forget to look for Harry's horses, Peter?'

'He won't need to, I've found them,' Crabbe announced.

'You could have told us.' John remonstrated.

'I came straight here after talking to the Norfolks' syce. They're in the Norfolks' stables.'

'Who put them there?' Peter demanded indignantly.

'Perry.'

'The thieving bastard!' Peter jumped out of the chair.

'Sit until the orderly's had a chance to put a bandage on that,' John ordered.

'Someone needs to have a word with Perry.'

'That's Colonel Perry to you, Captain Smythe. Unfortunately he outranks us all,' Crabbe reminded him.

'His rank doesn't give him the right to take Harry's horses,' Peter protested.

'Unfortunately Harry purloined Perry's polo ponies and used them to swim the river at Amara. He reminded the syce of the incident when the syce suggested that Dorset and Somerset should be taken to the Dorset's stables.'

'You going to try arguing with Perry?' John looked at Crabbe.

'I'm on my way to see him.'

'Give me a few minutes and I'll go with you,' Peter said.

'Any advice from you about Perry's soft spots would be welcome,' Crabbe said as John walked to the door.

'The only advice I can give you is that my father-in-law has no soft spots that I know of. Good luck to both of you. You'll need it.'

Chapter Fifteen

London, Sunday 2nd January 1916

'That was one interminable, boring sermon. After one hour, twenty-two minutes, and thirty seconds of Reverend Brooke's pontificating...'

'You timed it?' Clarissa asked Georgiana as they left the church after evensong.

'On the wristwatch Uncle Reid bought me as consolation prize for being rejected by the QAINC.' Georgiana pulled back her glove so Clarissa could admire it. 'I fail to understand what Jesus resisting temptation in the deserts of Israel has to do with the length of women's skirts. Does the Reverend believe men have so little self-control they can be driven wild by the sight of a woman's ankle and a glimpse of her calf?'

'Shh, not so loud!' Rain started spotting. Clarissa opened her umbrella.

Georgiana ignored an audible 'Blasphemy' and parried disapproving glares from a group of elderly women. She linked arms with Clarissa as they walked ahead. 'It's going to be horrid without you.'

'You'll have Helen. Both of you will be too busy to miss me.'

'Busy and envious. Truth be told, absolutely green.'

'I'm sorry your godfather couldn't organise you a berth or a posting to the QAINC, but I promise, Georgie, the moment I step on Mesopotamian soil I'll start asking about Harry.'

'Bless you.'

'You'll post these for me tomorrow?' Clarissa handed the umbrella to Georgiana, opened her bag, and pulled out two letters.

'One for your parents,' Georgiana guessed.

'The other for my sister. I hope they'll understand why I had leave.'

'We've been through that a hundred times, Clary. If they don't, it's their problem, not yours.' Georgiana took the letters and stowed them inside her handbag. 'You'll write?'

'As often as I can.'

'Don't put up with any nonsense from that cousin of mine when you catch up with him.'

'Nonsense?' Clarissa echoed.

'There'll be military chaplains even in Mesopotamia. Drag Tom to the altar. He's dilly-dallied
enough.'

'You want Tom to marry me in Mesopotamia in
the middle of a war even if it means I'll lose my
commission in the QAINC?'

'After the way he's treated you, yes.'

'Georgie, the last thing I need right now is
another lecture on how Tom takes me for
granted.'

'He does,' Georgiana declared.

'I know, but…'

'You love him so much you're happy to allow
him to use you as a doormat?'

'This war is awful for the men.'

'Some men, granted, but not quite so awful for
doctors. Aid stations and military hospitals aren't
frontline trenches, Clary, and you're forgetting
this war is just as foul for the women.'

'Things might have been different if Tom hadn't
put in for a transfer from France. Two leaves last
year wasn't much but now he's in Mesopotamia
it's hopeless.'

'You'll be there shortly.'

'That doesn't mean I'll see him. We were given
a lecture on what to expect when we reach there.
Basra has been secured by our troops. All the
fighting is expected to take place two hundred
miles or more upriver. We've been drafted in to
take the place of the medical staff in the military
facilities who are being sent to the front. Given
Tom's experience in France, he's bound to be
posted to a field hospital or aid station.'

Georgiana frowned. 'You have written to him to

201

tell him you'll soon be in Mesopotamia ... you haven't, have you?' she pressed when Clarissa didn't answer.

'Everything's so uncertain. We've been warned that if we're needed in Egypt or Africa we could be diverted. And, we have to go to India en route. Something about thinning our blood in readiness for the heat. Even if I'd written to tell Tom I was on my way, I wouldn't have been able to give him any idea what month, let alone week, I can expect to land.'

'I'd give a year's pay to see Tom's face when you finally catch up with him.'

'You think he'll be pleased to see me?'

'Of course.'

Clarissa picked up on a momentary hesitation. 'You're not sure?'

'He'll be shocked, but when he's had time to recover, he'll be delighted.' Georgiana gave her a hug. 'You've finished your packing?'

'The one small case I'm allowed to take beside the kit I've been issued.'

'I'm going to miss you, Clary. The late-night suppers, after afternoon shifts. The teas before the night shifts. The outings on our days off, but most of all having you to confide in and listen to my moans.' They reached the steps that led up to the nurses' hostel. Georgiana stopped and embraced her.

Clarissa shook her head when Georgiana tried to hand over the umbrella. 'Keep it. If you don't, I'll only have to leave it behind in the hostel.'

'Harry wrote that it doesn't rain cats and dogs in Mesopotamia but camels and elephants.'

'In which case this poor thing would break under the strain.'

Georgiana took it. 'Thank you. I'll think of you whenever I use it, which given this weather will be pretty much every day. We'll have a huge celebration when you get back. You, me, Helen, Tom, Mike – and,' she hesitated before determinedly adding, 'Harry. Tea in Claridges followed by dinner in Kettner's, and from there dancing until dawn wherever's open.'

'I doubt we'll all be together until after the war is over.'

'Precisely, then we can start living again, and making plans for a future without interference from the War Office or anyone else.'

Clarissa almost said 'if we survive' but kept the thought to herself. She crossed her fingers superstitiously. 'Do you want me to give Tom your love?'

'Only a reminder to look after you. But you can give Michael and...' It was Georgiana's turn to cross her fingers. '...Harry my love. What time are you leaving?'

'Six o'clock boat train from Victoria tomorrow morning.'

'Something for you to read on the way.' Georgiana took a pocketbook from her bag. 'A collection of Saki's short stories. They never fail to make me smile.'

'Georgie...'

'Nothing more to be said, Clary. I hate goodbyes.' Georgiana walked away quickly.

When she reached her front door she saw a man standing on the step, holding an umbrella so low it obscured his face. He turned when she approached, lifted his umbrella and raised his hat.

'Good evening, Dr Downe.'

She recognised him as the man who'd joined her and her godfather for lunch in the club. 'Good evening, Mr Smith. Are you visiting someone in this building?'

'You, if you'll allow me to, Dr Downe.'

Georgiana unlocked the door. 'My rooms are on the third floor, Mr Smith. Apologies for the climb.'

'It will be worth it if you can offer me tea. Earl Grey would be very acceptable.'

'You sound just like my godfather. Do they teach the direct approach in the War Office?'

'Encourage, not teach, Dr Downe. Polite niceties consume valuable time.'

Georgiana led the way up the stairs to her rooms and unlocked the door. 'My sitting room.' She showed him into a small room, furnished with a sofa, two upright chairs, and table. After lighting an electric standard lamp, she pulled aside a curtain to reveal a sink, cupboard, and shelf that held an electric chafing dish and hotplate.

'I have Earl Grey tea, but no milk. I do however have a lemon.'

'I prefer my tea black with lemon and no sugar, thank you.'

She filled the kettle and placed it on the hotplate. 'Please sit down.'

He sat on one of the upright chairs. She knelt in the hearth, struck a match, and held it to her temperamental gas fire. It blew out almost instantly and she had to strike another four before she succeeded in lighting it.

'A wet Sunday evening is an odd time to visit someone you've met only once, in the hope of receiving a cup of Earl Grey, Mr Smith?' She left the hearth, washed her hands, set out a tray with cutlery and crockery and sliced the lemon.

'I see it's not just the staff of the War Office who can be accused of the direct approach, Dr Downe.'

'As you said, it saves time. Something I've discovered for myself, especially when a patient haemorrhages during surgery.'

'Very well, let's cut to the chase, as they say in hunting circles. Would you be interested in a surgical post in a charitable institution?'

'Thank you for bringing the post to my attention, Mr Smith, but I am anxious to contribute more, not less to the war effort. I doubt any charitable institution, admirable as it might be, would further that aim.'

'The charitable institution is in Basra.'

Georgiana stared at the kettle. It was beginning to steam. She tried to think beyond the mention of Basra. 'The military would never allow a female doctor into any hospital that treats army personnel, even a charitable one.'

'They wouldn't,' he agreed. 'At least not British military personnel, but there are other facilities in need of physicians. Have you heard of the Lansing Memorial Hospital?'

'Harry mentioned the Lansing Memorial in one of his letters. Isn't it a charity operated by Americans?'

'It is. They run a school, a Baptist church and

have set up various committees in Basra with the aim of alleviating distress among the poorest inhabitants of the town. They also fund a hospital the Indian Medical Service has found invaluable. The Lansing Memorial not only caters for locals but also cares for wounded Turkish prisoners of war that we haven't the staff or resources to treat. Two doctors work there, one American, one French, and four trained nurses. They also welcome the services of volunteers.'

'You think they'd employ me as a doctor? I have independent means so they wouldn't have to pay my passage or my salary...'

'Should you accept the post, your passage and salary would be paid, Dr Downe, but not by American Baptists,' he interrupted. 'As I said, the Indian Medical Service has reason to be grateful to the Lansing Memorial. Your salary would be paid by the War Office in reparation for the Lansing Memorial's services in caring for our Turkish POWs and aiding our war effort.'

'So I would be employed by the War Office?'

'Not directly.' He didn't elucidate. 'After meeting you in the club, I took the liberty of telegraphing Lieutenant Colonel Cox, the Chief Political Officer with the Indian Expeditionary Force.'

'He was my brother Harry's immediate superior.'

'So I understand. I informed him of your determination to travel to Mesopotamia to look for your brother. It was Lieutenant Colonel Cox who suggested we offer your services to the Lansing. We are indebted to them, not only because in caring for the enemy wounded they free our

resources but because their doctors work in close collaboration with the Indian Medical Service and supply drugs and medical supplies when our facilities run short.'

The kettle began to whistle but Georgiana made no move towards it. 'You're certain the Lansing Memorial would employ a female doctor?'

'They would welcome you, Dr Downe. They rely on donations, therefore the gift of a doctor, female or male, salary-free would be considered a bonus. Lieutenant Colonel Cox spoke to Dr Picard, who runs the hospital, personally. The Reverend and Mrs Butler who oversee the mission have offered you food and accommodation should you decide to take the post.' The whistle escalated to screaming pitch.

Georgiana walked over to the hotplate, filled the teapot, and carried it to the table.

'You did want to go to Mesopotamia, Dr Downe?' Mr Smith checked.

'More than anything.'

'I'm offering you an opportunity to do so.'

'I accept, Mr Smith.'

'If you need time to discuss the matter with your parents or your godfather...'

'I don't, Mr Smith, because I know what their reaction will be.'

'They would attempt to dissuade you?'

'When it come to my father that's an understatement.' She poured the tea and offered him the saucer of lemon slices. He took one and dropped it into his cup.

'Transport to Mesopotamia has been arranged for you with a convoy of nurses. The train leaves

Victoria at six o'clock tomorrow morning. I regret you won't have much time to prepare for the journey.'

Mesopotamia! She was really going to Mesopotamia – and Harry! 'I need to write letters, to my parents, godfather, and the hospital board, and to pack.' She looked around. 'I'll have to vacate these rooms but I have a friend who will store my things and settle up with the landlord. I'll telephone her now.'

'You don't have to contact her or the board. I will make all the necessary arrangements with the hospital and your landlord.'

'Thank you, but in case you need assistance, I'll give you the address of my friend, Dr Helen Stroud. She has a spare room and will take my books, reading lamp, and personal items.'

'Your tropical kit will be on board the train.'

'The correct size?'

'The size of your hospital garments. You can take only one small case with personal items. I will be here tomorrow morning at five o'clock with a cab to convey you to the station.'

'Thank you.' She picked up her teacup.

'There is something that you could do for your country, while you're in Basra, Dr Downe.'

All Georgiana could think about was Harry. She didn't have to rely on Clarissa to look for her brother. If Harry was alive and still in Mesopotamia she'd find him... 'What's that, Mr Smith?'

'We'd like you to keep a log of visitors to the mission.'

'You want me to spy on my hosts?'

'Spy is a strong word, Dr Downe. We're at war.

As your brother well knew and understood. The British Empire has ... how can I put this ... certain interests in Mesopotamia.'

'Like the Anglo-Persian Oil Company?'

'That is certainly one of them, but there are others that are exciting interest not only among our enemies but our allies. We're not alone in the area. There are French emissaries, Americans, Dutch...'

'You would like me to report on any visitors to the mission from those countries.'

'We would like you to report every visitor, Dr Downe.' He sensed her reluctance. 'It would not be onerous. Basra is a small town. You will meet many of our military officers socially, including Lieutenant Colonel Cox. All that would be required of you is a little conversation.'

'Nothing written?'

'Nothing so formal, Dr Downe.' He finished his tea, and rose to his feet. 'I knew the Empire could reply on you. Until tomorrow morning, Dr Downe.'

Chapter Sixteen

Basra, early morning, Monday 3rd January 1916

Michael woke with a start. Disorientated, uncertain of his surroundings, he sat up and looked around. He'd left a small oil lamp burning in a niche beside the door. Its glow cast his shadow large, looming like a theatrical ghost on the lime-washed wall.

His luggage was piled high in the corner, reminding him that in a few hours he'd be travelling upstream. He heard someone breathing beside him, and looked down on Kalla.

Even asleep she was beautiful. Her long black eyelashes grazed her sleep-flushed cheeks. Her mouth, wide-lipped, sensuous, appeared to be smiling. If she was dreaming, it was a happy one.

She'd taught him more about the pleasures of the body in a few days than he would have believed possible. She'd also brought the comforting realisation that the failure of his marriage wasn't entirely down to him and his 'unreasonable demands', as Lucy would have had him believe. In fact his 'unreasonable demands' had been accepted gratefully and graciously without shame or false modesty by Kalla who had no compunction about requesting more of the same.

He was tempted to rouse her but he heard the sound that had woken him again. Footsteps padding lightly along the wooden floor of the landing.

He reached for his pocket watch and opened it. Three a.m. He crept from the bed, pulled on his trousers, and opened the door to Adjabi's cubicle.

His bearer was stretched out on his divan under a pile of camel-hair blankets. Michael whispered his name. When Adjabi didn't stir, he went to the door that opened into the corridor, muffling the latch with his fingers, he opened it a crack and peered out.

The door to Harry's room was open. A figure emerged swathed in a black cloak and headdress. Whoever it was paused to lock the door with a key and turned. Michael stepped back smartly lest he be seen.

He returned to his own room, picked up his multi-purpose 'tool' from the table where he'd left it, and lifted the lamp from the niche. He heard footsteps again. This time heading down the stairs.

He opened his door gingerly. The landing was deserted. Shading the lamp's flame with his hand he crept to the top of the stairs in time to see the cloaked figure acknowledge Abdul who was sitting at his customary table with a waiter, the inevitable backgammon board between them. The front door opened and closed. The only sounds that broke the silence were the bubble of the hookah and the backgammon tiles clicking on the board.

Careful to continue shading the lamp, Michael stole along the corridor to the door of Harry's room. It was locked but the lock was simpler than the one on his brother's trunk. He picked it in a few seconds, slipped inside the room, set the lamp on the floor and closed the door. The room appeared to be unchanged from his last visit.

He opened the trunk that had contained Harry's clothes. It was as he'd expected after Cox had taken the native dress to his room, empty. He set about picking the lock on the second chest. It didn't take him as long as it had the first time. When he'd done, he opened the lid and removed the two boxes. The one that had held two hundred sovereigns by Tom's estimate was empty. Not a single coin remained.

He examined the second box that had held the key to the safety deposit box. The key was buttoned into his wallet but he checked to see if the box held any other secrets. After ten minutes of poking and pressing he decided if it did, he couldn't find them.

He replaced everything as he'd found it. Sat for a moment and imagined his brother in the room. Harry had a wife that, everyone agreed, never visited him here. Was this simply an 'office'? A place Harry conducted 'business' away from the home he shared with his wife and children.

What kind of business did political officers undertake that required clandestine meetings? Was the mysterious figure he'd seen Harry's wife or his elusive friend Mitkhal? The disappearance of the sovereigns suggested one or the other needed money. Money he could give them if he knew where they were.

Then he remembered the five thousand sovereigns that remained in the safety deposit box. They didn't need his money when they had Harry's to draw on. He was too tired to think straight. He glanced around the room to make sure he hadn't disturbed anything, checked the corridor to make sure it was empty and spent a moment locking the door before returning to his own room.

Kalla was sitting up in bed. 'I missed you. Where have you been?'

'I thought I heard a noise.'

'Many people live in this house. They all make noises.'

'As I've discovered.' He stripped off his trousers and climbed back into bed. She moved close to him, her skin cool as silk against his. He wrapped his arm around her shoulders and pulled her close until her breasts nestled against his chest.

'Do you have to go up the river today?' she whispered.

'I'm a war correspondent. My editor will be wondering whether I'm ever going to get to the front.'

'Take me with you?' she pleaded.

'To the front?'

'Yes, to the front.'

'I can't. No women are allowed at the front.'

'Other officers take their mistresses with them. They call them cooks and maids.'

'Believe me, there will be no women where I'm going.'

'Please, Michael,' she wheedled. 'It's been good for me to have a kind man like you to look after me.' She slipped her hand between his thighs.

He was tired, he needed sleep, but he was enjoying her caresses too much to stop her.

'You've been good to me too, Kalla, but I can't take you with me.' He kissed the top of her head. 'Will you be here when I get back?'

'That is up to my mistress.'

'Your mistress? I thought you worked for Abdul.'

'She loaned me to Abdul because I speak English.'

'Loaned you ... this mistress owns you?'

'Yes.'

'You are a slave?'

'Of course.'

He was shocked but the more he thought about it the more it he realised how naïve he'd been. Kalla was obviously practised in the arts of sex, but he doubted many women would willingly opt for the life of a whore if they had a comfortable alternative.

'Why did your mistress loan you to Abdul?'

'Because he wanted a girl who could speak English.'

'Why?'

She made no attempt to answer him.'

'Tell me?'

'I've already said too much.'

'You are here to spy on me?' Given the brief he'd received from Cox he could see irony in the situation.

'All Arabs, including Abdul and my mistress, want to know what the British intend to do with Mesopotamia if you should win the war.'

'They think I know the secrets of government!' he laughed.

'You are a writer, for the newspapers, they think you know everything.'

'I wish I did. Believe me, Kalla, I know no more than you.'

'Please,' she begged, 'take me with you. I will do anything you ask, cook, clean, fetch, carry...'

'I have a syce and a bearer.'

'I don't want to return to my mistress. She will sell me to other men, and it will be hard to love them after you.'

'I'm sorry, Kalla. If I could take you with me, I would. But it's impossible.' He thought for a moment. 'How much would it take to buy your freedom?'

'More than I will ever earn.'

'I will talk to Abdul tomorrow. Ask him if you can stay here, in this room, while I'm upstream.'

'You would ask Abdul that for me?'

'I'll pay the rent in advance and give you some English sovereigns in case you need money. But I don't know when I'll be back'.

'I will wait for you for as long as it takes you to stay at the front and write for your editor.'

'I may be gone for weeks – months even,' he warned. 'I may not even return to Basra if the army moves forward.'

'I will still wait.' She moved over him pressing him down into the mattress. 'Even when I am no more than dust blowing across the desert I will still be waiting for you.'

Basra, mid-morning, Monday 3rd January 1916

Michael stood in the doorway of Abdul's coffee shop. He studied the paddle steamer bound for Ali Gharbi and wondered if it was strong enough to withstand the river currents. There was more rust than paint above the water-line, which begged the question: what was concealed below by the muddied waters of the Shatt al-Arab. The engines coughed and wheezed as though they were in the final stages of pneumonia, and although there were queues of men and animals waiting to board, the level of the river hovered well above the Plimsoll line.

215

The wharf area around the craft was bedlam. Sepoys and bearers shouting at and to one another as they scurried up and down the gangplanks, hauling supplies, officers' kits and luggage. A third gangplank aft of the vessel was reserved for horses, and Arab syce and Indian bearers were leading the officers' mounts on board and into the make-shift stables on the lower deck.

Michael joined Daoud, who was patiently standing back with the horses he'd bought: a chestnut ex-cavalry mount, sold on when the owner, a captain, had been invalided to India after being wounded at Nasiriyeh, and a handsome black hunter whose owner had been killed in the same battle.

'How are Toffee and Brutus doing, Daoud?' He stroked the hunter's muzzle.

'Better than those skittish grasshoppers, sir.' Daoud indicated a couple of greys that snorted, bucked and reared whenever they were led within kicking distance of the gangplank. 'I wish we could have bought you a third mount, sir. You may need one.'

'You insisted there was nothing suitable for sale.'

'There wasn't, sir,' Daoud protested.

'We might find something upriver.'

'Half-starved nags and walking skeletons, sir,' Daoud prophesied. 'There's no grazing beyond Amara upriver.'

'Your turn.' Michael slapped Brutus's rump as a syce beckoned Daoud forward. He saw Daoud, Toffee, and Brutus on board before making his way back to the coffee shop. Adjabi was leaving the building with a line of Abdul's waiters in tow.

All loaded with his kit.

'Sahib, your attaché case and travelling bag are on a chair at your table. This is the last of your luggage. I will see it safely into the hold. I have reserved a chair on deck for you and a berth in a cabin.'

'Thank you, Adjabi. I'll follow you shortly.'

'I'll guard your chair until you are there to sit on it, Sahib.'

Abdul handed Michael his attaché case and bag. 'It was a pleasure to have you in my humble house, Mr Downe.'

'Thank you for your hospitality, Abdul.'

'I will care for Kalla, keep other men from her door, and feed her only the best food. I will also continue to keep your brother's things safe, Mr Downe. Never fear. I look forward to your return.'

Michael tucked his attaché case under his left arm and shook Abdul's hand. He glanced up the stairs and decided against returning to his room to say a last goodbye to Kalla. Tears and hysteria he could have coped with but her dry-eyed anguish was difficult to bear.

He returned to the quay and sensed someone watching him. He looked around and he caught the eye of a man crouching in the stern of a mahaila, one of the high-masted, colourfully painted, low-slung native boats that plied the river. The vessel was berthed above the paddle steamer and the man was ignoring the shouts of his fellow crewman as he continued to blatantly stare in his direction.

Charles's description of Harry's orderly echoed

217

through Michael's mind.

'*He's Arab, huge, with the face of a brigand.*'

It was difficult to gauge the man's height as he wasn't standing, but his handsome, hawk-nosed features certainly resembled the *Boys' Own* adventure books' illustrations of a brigand. Had he been the figure in Harry's room? The one who'd emptied the chest of the sovereigns?

The man knew he was watching him, yet made no attempt to avert his eyes. Michael looked around for Abdul. He retreated to the door and called his name.

'I thought you'd be on board by now, Mr Downe.'

'There's a man watching me. Could he be my brother's...' Michael recalled Abdul's reaction when Charles had referred to Harry's "orderly" '...friend?'

'If someone is staring at you, Mr Downe, he could be an acquaintance of your brother who recognises the family similarity.'

'Please, Abdul, take a look at the man.'

Abdul reluctantly left his backgammon board and joined Michael in the doorway.

'He's on board that mahaila.' As Michael spoke, a short wiry man on the quayside untied the ropes that had secured the boat and flung them to a man on board.

Michael ran up the quay, before he reached the mooring, the boat was in the centre of the river, its sail halfway up the mast fluttering in the wind. All he could see of the man he'd been watching was a rapidly diminishing shadow moving around the deck.

'Was it Harry's friend?' he demanded of Abdul when he returned.

Abdul shrugged. 'All Arabs look the same, Mr Downe.' A smile curled the corners of his mouth when he repeated a stock phrase British officers resorted to, whenever they described natives of every land other than Britain.

The whistle blew on the paddle steamer. Adjabi appeared at the top of the gangplank and waved to Michael.

'You will continue to ask if anyone has seen my sister-in-law?'

'Yes, Mr Downe, as I promised,' Abdul assured him. 'You don't want to miss your boat.'

Michael ran up the gangplank.

'I will take you to your chair, Sahib. I have placed it next to Major Chalmers and his friend Captain Heal.' Adjabi led Michael on to the forward deck.

'Scribbler, meet Martin Heal. Join us,' Richard held up a bottle of beer when he saw Michael.

'Thank you.' Michael took the beer but kept his eye on the sail of the mahaila as he sat on the rattan chair between Richard and Martin.

'You see Charles this morning?' Richard handed Michael a glass.

'No, I said my goodbyes last night.'

'Would you believe he was trying to get himself posted to one of the command boats?'

'Yes.' Michael continued to watch the dot that was the mahaila.

'We will be in time for this show, won't we?' Martin demanded. 'Only there were rumours...'

'There are always rumours,' Richard cut in.

219

'Everything in good time, as the vicar said to the tart.'

Michael glanced at him.

'The waiting's always the worst.' Richard slurred and Michael realised he was drunk. Either he'd started early, or hadn't finished drinking since the night before. 'Gives a man time to think of all the good chaps who've gone before him.' He lifted his glass to Michael. 'Men like your brother.'

'You knew him well?'

'Everyone knew Harry Downe. War's a damned sight less interesting since he's been gone.'

Chapter Seventeen

Confluence of Tigris and Euphrates below Qurna, leading to Shatt al-Hal, Tuesday 4th January 1916

Although Mitkhal knew the mahaila couldn't possibly out-race the paddle steamer, he resented Zabba's cousin, Habid's, decision to leave the main waterway of the Tigris before dawn on their second day out of Basra. They turned up one of the side channels below Qurna and sailed into the network of ancient waterways and canals that had been hacked through the marshes by the engineers of ancient civilizations long lost to human memory.

Mitkhal had lost sight of the steamer at sunset on the first day but logic hadn't prevented him from hoping that the vessel would stop to take supplies and men on board at Qurna and they'd catch up with it on the voyage to Ali Gharbi.

With the Tigris behind them, Habid set a course for the Shatt al-Hai, a river that diverged from the Tigris south of Kut al Amara. Given the number of military vessels plying the Tigris between Basra and Ali Gharbi it was a sensible decision but Mitkhal wasn't in a mood to be sensible.

Stunned by the similarity between Harry's brother and Harry, all too aware of the risks to Harry and Furja should anyone – even Harry's brother – discover that Harry was still alive, Mitkhal wanted to talk to the man and find out if he resembled Harry as much in character as he did in appearance.

'We're heading for Kut by the back door.' Mitkhal stated the obvious as he manned the rudder, negotiating a course through the reed beds. 'This course is safer. Less chance of being held up by British river traffic and the military police.'

'More chance of meeting pirates.'

'I know them and they know me.' Habid pointed to a stall and makeshift wooden smoke house outside a reed and mud village. 'Breakfast?'

Mitkhal adjusted the rudder and took down the sail. He was hungry but his resentment escalated as he sat with his back to the prow watching Habid gossip with the fishermen who crewed the small, canoe-like native mashufs and the sailors from the mahailas who'd also been seduced by the smell of fresh bread and smoking fish.

In Furja's house he'd felt restless – fettered and imprisoned despite his pleasure in fatherhood and Gutne's company. Now he was heading

221

upriver he felt guilty for leaving Harry seriously ill and the women unprotected apart from Farik. Zabba had promised to take care of them but what if Furja's father or husband tracked her down and turned up in Zabba's with a dozen or more well-armed tribesmen?

Would the British officers who patronised Zabba's whorehouse fight them off? The more he considered the situation, the less faith he put in the British military to protect Zabba's brothel or her 'friends' in the secret house. The British had enough to do in fighting the Turks without making enemies of the friendly natives in Basra and he was certain that's how the officers in British Headquarters would categorise Ibn Shalan and his tribesmen. Especially if Shalan brandished the treaty Harry had negotiated with him before the war, a treaty that had secured Shalan's protection for the Anglo-British oil pipeline in exchange for weapons.

For all that Furja was Shalan's daughter and Guthe his sister, Mitkhal knew that, if the sheikh considered circumstances warranted it, he wouldn't hesitate to kill Harry or either of the women or their children. Furja had committed an unpardonable sin in the sheikh's eyes by taking Harry's daughters and fleeing the tent of Ali Mansur, the second husband he had chosen for her.

By flouting Shalan's edicts, Furja, Harry, and their children posed a threat to the sheikh's authority within the tribe, and as Gutne and his son's presence in Furja's house confirmed that he'd helped Furja and her daughters escape Ali

222

Mansur, his and his family's lives would be forfeit too.

Mitkhal narrowed his eyes against the watery winter light and scanned the reed beds. A flock of ducks hurtled upwards. Startled by a wild cat – or human predator? He hadn't forgotten that it was a Marsh Arab, Ibn Muba, who'd betrayed Harry to the Turks and identified him as a British officer.

Marsh Arab, Bedouin, town Arab in the pay of Ibn Shalan, Turk – and British who would no doubt ship Harry back to Britain or at the very least an Indian medical facility if they found him alive. It seemed the entire Middle East was ranged against him and Harry and those they loved.

Habid interrupted his thoughts by splashing through the shallows to the boat. 'These are so good I brought you one. I thought it might chase away the sour expression on your face.' He handed Mitkhal a bread flap filled with smoked fish.

'Thank you.' Mitkhal took it, smelled the fish and fresh bread, and bit into it.

Habid climbed on board and sank down on his haunches beside Mitkhal. 'Word on the bank is the British are preparing to move upstream from Ali Gharbi tomorrow.'

'Towards Kut?' Mitkhal didn't know why he was asking when all the talk in Basra had been gossip and guesswork as to when – not 'if' – the British would muster their forces to relieve their beleaguered troops.

'Towards Kut,' Habid confirmed. 'According to our most excellent cook, Mohammed, who gathers and digests information as birds do bread-

223

crumbs, most of the desert tribes have joined forces with the Turks outside the town.' Habid lifted his bread flap from its palm leaf wrapping and took an enormous bite.

'The Bedouin are not there to fight with the Turk, only to scavenge from the battlefield when the bullets stop flying.'

'Whatever they're there for, they're not inside the town walls with the British, which means things don't look too well for the British inter-lopers.'

'They haven't looked well for the British since the battle of Nasiriyeh,' Mitkhal reached for his water bottle.

'From where I'm standing, I regard British and Turk the same. Both have no business here. They should return to their own countries and leave this land to those who have always lived here.'

'The Marsh Arabs? The Bedouin? The Bani Lam, the Shias, the Sunnis...' Mitkhal paused to take another bite.

'At least we'd be fighting and killing our own kind who were born and bred here.' Habid looked out over the riverbank. 'Allah only gave us enough land to bury our own, not the hordes intent on colonising us.'

Mitkhal thought of Shalan, Furja, and Gutne. He'd been mad to leave them for horses ... then he recalled the expression on Harry's face when he realised Dorset was real, not just a dream.

'What do you think, Mitkhal?'

Mitkhal looked across at Habid and realised he'd been too lost in his own thoughts to listen to him. 'You're right, all the interlopers should leave.'

'And then?'

'We can start quarrelling amongst ourselves as to who should govern us.'

Habid laughed. 'You are a born diplomat, my friend. Zabba said you were going upriver to look for horses?'

'I am.' Mitkhal was wary, wondering what else Zabba had told Habid.

'The British look after their animals but upriver...' Habid shook his head. 'There's no grazing. Animals soon become skinny and sicken. You want good horses pay a visit one dark night to the British Military stables in Basra. But take your gun, because their sentries are well armed, and if you're wise you'll collect friends who also have guns to go with you.'

'I'm not insane enough to try to steal livestock from Kut. The horses I want belong to a friend. He was taken ill and was forced to leave them behind when he travelled downriver by boat.'

'These horses. They're inside Kut?'

'Close by,' Mitkhal hedged.

'Let me know before we're in sight of whoever's guarding them, so I can kick you off the boat.'

Mitkhal smiled. 'I will.'

'You give me your word?'

'You have it.'

'You may not value your own head more than that of a horse, my friend. But I value mine.' Habid tossed the palm leaf that had been wrapped around the bread flap he'd eaten overboard. 'Unfurl the sail. With Allah's grace and this wind we may be out of the marshes by the next sunrise.'

Lansing Memorial Mission, Basra, Tuesday 4th January 1916

'Come in,' Maud called in response to a knock at the door.

Mrs Butler bustled in with a tea tray.

'Mrs Butler, good morning.' Maud set aside the book she'd been reading. 'How kind of you to bring me tea.'

'I thought you might enjoy a mid-morning drink and as I was making it I realised so would I.' Mrs Butler set the tray on the desk and glanced into the cot, which the nursemaid, Badia, had as usual pulled close to her in the alcove. 'He looks so angelic sleeping there. Reverend Butler was only saying this morning that you'd hardly know there was a baby in the house. I thought I heard him crying once in the night but I couldn't be sure whether it was him or one of the cats.'

'It was him, but once Badia fed him he soon fell back to sleep.' Maud turned to the nursemaid who was sitting head down, working her way through a pile of mending, apparently oblivious to the conversation, although she was beginning to wonder just how much the woman under-stood.

'Reverend Butler and I talked this morning,' Mrs Butler announced, as though she rarely com-municated with her husband. She busied herself with pouring tea and spooning sugar and lemon slices into the cups. Maud sensed her hostess was embarrassed by the information she'd been en-trusted to impart and decided to pre-empt her.

'You and Reverend Butler have been very kind, Mrs Butler, but now Robin has arrived, it's time I made plans to move on and set up my own establishment.'

Mrs Butler finally met Maud's gaze and there was unmistakeable relief on her face. 'We wouldn't hear of you leaving us until your baby is at least six weeks old, Maud.'

'That is very kind of you. It will give me time to look for suitable accommodation, and, unless you allow me to poach Badia, a nursemaid.'

'Surely you don't intend to settle here in Basra? Angela told us you have no family or friends in Great Britain but a war widow in your position will attract sympathy and social connections. You must think of Robin; there will be better schools and more opportunities for him in Britain.'

'I don't know a soul in Britain, Mrs Butler. As for choosing somewhere to live there, I would be reduced to placing a pin in a map.'

'There's Captain Mason's family.'

'Robin isn't Captain Mason's child. It would be embarrassing for his parents and me if I were to settle close to John's family home.'

Although Theo had informed her and the Reverend that Maud's child was the result of an attack, Mrs Butler was used to "refined society" where all unpleasantness – if it had to be referred to at all – was cloaked in euphemisms. Maud's honesty shocked her, rendering her momentarily speechless.

She sank down on a chair and waited for her hand to stop shaking before handing Maud her tea.

'If I'm being too personal, please, just tell me to mind my own business, but has Captain Mason left you well provided for?'

'He has, Mrs Butler. Captain Tom Mason mentioned an annuity that John had taken out, payable on his death, and I'm also entitled to a military widow's pension. As neither can be claimed by any other member of John's family, I intend to make enquiries about them.'

'If you really have no friends in Britain I could ask if there is a sinecure or position in one of the Lansing's other charitable institutions that may suit you. Possibly one in America.'

'It's very kind of you, Mrs Butler, but as I said, I have no plans other than finding alternative accommodation as soon as I've recovered from Robin's birth.'

'But if you move elsewhere in Basra, Maud, I'd feel as though we're ... well ... not to put too fine a point on it ... throwing you out.'

'Considering all you have done for me, you'd be doing nothing of the kind. Mrs Butler. It really is time for me to build an independent life for myself and my child.'

'Mrs Butler, ma'am, Mrs Mason.' A maid hovered outside the door. 'There's a military gentleman here to see Mrs Mason. Shall I show him in here?'

'Not in Mrs Mason's bedroom, girl. Take him into the drawing room, offer him tea, and tell him I'll be along presently.'

'I'll go with you.' Maud rose from her chair.

'Are you certain you're strong enough, my dear?'

'Quite certain, Mrs Butler.' Maud followed her out of the door and into the drawing room.

A man rose to his feet when she and Mrs Butler entered. The breath caught in Maud's throat. It wasn't just the uniform, a major's, the same rank as John. It was also his features. He resembled Geoffrey Brooke. The first lover she had taken after her marriage.

'I'm Mrs Butler.'

'Mrs Butler.' He shook her hand. 'Major Brooke, stationed at Basra HQ.' He turned to Maud. 'You must be.'

'Mrs Mason, Major Brooke.' Maud shook his hand and sat down.

'It's good of you to see me, Mrs Mason. My condolences on the death of your husband. I heard of your indisposition,' he added delicately.

'Thank you, Major Brooke, I'll soon be quite well again.'

'I knew your husband, Mrs Mason. I was at school with him, Charles Reid, and Harry Downe.'

'You had a brother, Geoffrey, Major Brooke.'

'A younger brother. He was killed at Ahwaz last June.'

'I met him in India.

'Good Lord, did you? He never said, but then he wrote infrequently.'

Maud knew from the tone of Major Brooke's voice he was lying. And that was without the way he was looking at her, cool, appraising, as though he were visualizing her naked.

'You're here on business, Major?' Mrs Butler prompted.

'At the behest of HQ and Mrs Mason's father-in-law who contacted HQ with regard to an annuity Major John Mason set up payable to his widow on his death. With reference to your military war widow's pension, Mrs Mason, HQ sent out the usual forms that had to be returned but we haven't as yet received them.'

'They haven't been returned because I haven't received them, Major Brooke.'

'I suspected there might be a mix-up. HQ has been at sixes and sevens since Nasiriyeh. I've brought a set with me. If you can spare the time, Mrs Mason, I could assist you to fill them in now.' He turned to Mrs Butler. 'We will require a witness to Mrs Mason's signature.'

'Of course, Major Brooke.' Mrs Butler watched a maid bring in a fresh tray of tea. 'Reverend Butler always says it's as well to settle business matters as quickly as possible. I'll just fetch my spectacles.'

Reginald Brooke opened his attaché case and removed a file. He waited until Mrs Butler's back was turned before winking at Maud. He then proceeded to caress her fingers under the pretence of giving her the forms. It was a suggestive touch she remembered only too well.

He was more self-assured and less diffident than his brother Geoffrey, but his designs and intentions were exactly the same.

Chapter Eighteen

Qurna, Tuesday 4th January 1916

'Qurna!'

The cry resounded around the steamer, waking Michael. The sound was accompanied by a cacophony of raised voices in languages he couldn't even begin to understand. Stiff, cramped, he stretched out in his berth, only to graze his knuckles on the board above his head and bruise his toes when his feet hit the bottom.

'Good morning, Sahib.' Adjabi swam into view beside him, cup of tea in hand. 'I have bread and fruit for breakfast. Shall I bring a tray here or will you eat on deck?'

Michael breathed in the stale cabin air, rank with male perspiration and night odours. 'On deck please, Adjabi.' He curled himself as small as he could. By resting his chin on his chest he managed to roll out of the bunk without hitting his head, unlike Richard, who landed on his knees and elbows on the floor with the aplomb of an unexploded shell.

'There's sand grouse on the river bank. Hundreds of them.' Martin Heal burst in, dressed and looking more awake than any man had a right to be after the beer and wine he'd downed the night before. 'I've sent my bearer into the hold to rummage for my hunting rifles. You two coming?'

'How long will we be berthed here?' Richard made a face as he rubbed his elbows.

'A while,' Martin hedged.

'You sure about that?' Michael checked. 'I'd hate to be left behind.'

'A party from the ranks have left for the bazaar and the padre's organising a sightseeing trip on shore. Apparently Qurna is, or rather was, the Garden of Eden, and the Tree of Knowledge of Good and Evil is still to be seen.'

'What about Eve?' Michael questioned.

'Unless she's draped in a black tent she isn't around, and before you ask I haven't checked the place for serpents. Although we've been advised to hang on to our wallets and anything else we're carrying that can be easily lifted.'

'I was stationed here for a couple of months last year. Believe me, Michael, there's nothing left of the Garden of Eden. Although I can vouch for the pickpockets. They're here in abundance.' Richard felt under his berth for his shoes.

'If you want to borrow my camera, you can have your picture taken at the confluence of the Tigris and Euphrates.' Martin held it up. 'Padre just took mine.'

'I think I'll give everything a miss except breakfast, but if you bag a sand grouse for me, I'll join you for dinner.' Richard finally found his shoes and rummaged for his washing kit.

'Wonderful,' Martin complained. 'I do all the work...'

'I'll supply the wine. Two bottles if you bag one for Downe as well.'

'In that case I forgive you. Coming shooting?'

Martin invited Michael.

'Not before breakfast,' Michael picked up his towel.

'Neither of you have a sense of adventure.'

'We'll get adventure enough when we reach Ali Gharbi. For the moment I'll settle for ablutions and breakfast on deck, if it's all the same to you, Martin.' Richard walked to the door.

'I'll be with you shortly.' Michael pulled his shirt on over his trousers and without stopping to fasten the buttons or put on a collar he walked out on to the lower deck.

The quayside was teeming with natives ferrying and offering wares. He felt as though a coloured illustration from the Bible had been brought to life. Rain was falling in a steady, light veil that coated him and everything in sight. The atmosphere was as humid as a Turkish bath, the overwhelming stench one of sewage laced with a whiff of exotic spices that proffered the promise of pleasant surroundings – if you could find them.

The river bank was lined with palm trees and bushes, beyond them were mile after endless mile of date groves. He looked inland over the rooftops of the mud brick houses. Some had open-sided tents pitched on top to keep out the rain and beneath their shades rudimentary tables were set with bowls and pitchers, presumably in preparation for breakfast.

The din escalated. He looked down. Swarms of men and boys were clamouring below the steamer, hands outstretched as they scrambled for coppers being thrown by the ranks.

'Make the most of the greenery here, Downe.' Damp, smelling of carbolic soap, Richard joined him at the rail. 'Beyond those date groves is a treeless waste of swamp and desert.'

'Will we reach Ali Gharbi tomorrow?'

Richard gave him a pitying look. 'Only if this vessel grows wings? The captain was bathing alongside me. He hopes to berth at Ezra's Tomb tonight. If we make good speed he's hoping we'll reach Amara by mid-afternoon tomorrow. He's expecting a long slow haul from there to Ali Gharbi because we'll have to take on supplies and tow lighters.'

'So two to three more days?' Michael failed to hide his disappointment.

'More like five or six, but if Martin shoots a tenth as well as he boasts we'll dine well every night on sand grouse.'

'And if he's unlucky?'

'My bearer's a whizz with bully beef.'

Kut, Tuesday 4th January 1916

John stood in the doorway of the General Hospital, which catered for non-commissioned officers and ranks, and peered out at the rain-soaked street. He'd spent the morning in surgery, prising bullets from heads, shoulders, necks and upper arms. Not all the operations had been successful. Trying to blot images of the cold dead eyes and grey flaccid bodies of his failures from mind, he cradled a tin mug of tea and watched a dozen or so boys kick a battered empty biscuit tin

234

around the muddy street.

A neatly moulded dome of mud halfway down the street faced a similar moulded dome at the Tigris end, and, as approximately half the boys yelled in delight whenever the tin collided with one or the other, he presumed they were make-shift goals.

He looked towards the river. Thirty yards away the heads of sentries poked above the parapet of the trenches that had been dug alongside the bank, and he had to suppress the urge to run to them and order them to keep down. The inter-mittent crack of rifle shots rang out peppering the air as the Turkish snipers sought targets.

Engrossed in their game, the boys swerved and kicked. They were oblivious to the shots as they were to the rain that soaked through their thin cotton shirts and mixed with the dirt, turning it into a glutinous mess that coated their bare feet as thickly as woollen socks.

'Hardy blighters, these native kids.' Knight joined John in the doorway.

'I envy their capacity to ignore their surroun-dings. I wish I could forget mine for a couple of hours.'

'Perhaps you should take up foot, or should I say tin, ball,' Knight suggested.

'They're too good to let me play. I was always useless at team games.'

A shot whistled towards them. It embedded itself in the wall, next to Knight's head.

John shouted to attract the boys' attention and pointed further up the street. One of them walked over and held out his hand.

'Cheeky, hardy blighters,' Knight amended.

John dug his hand in his pocket and pulled out a rupee. The boy shook his head and lifted his hand higher. John dug deeper and added another rupee. He held up both coins in front of the boy.

The boy continued to stand looking at them.

John pointed away from the river and although he knew the boy couldn't understand him, said, 'you won't get them until you move further up the street.'

The boy smiled and shook his head to signify he hadn't understood.

Knight added another rupee to the two in John's hand.

The boy snatched them, smiled his thanks, turned, and fell face downwards into the mud. His friends raced over.

John kneeled and examined the back of the boy's head. He turned him gently. The boy's dark eyes, wide, lifeless, stared up at him.

John looked up at the boys. 'Someone should fetch his mother.'

The boys didn't move.

'Mother? Mama?'

Two boys raced off. John picked the corpse up out of the mud. 'Matthews?'

'Sir.' John's orderly appeared in the doorway. He summed up the situation at a glance.

'Wash the boy and see that he's laid out properly. I think his people will be along shortly.'

'Yes, sir.'

'Damn and blast, what's going on up there?' Knight unbuckled his revolver and ducked into the building as another volley of shots echoed from the river end of the street.

John slammed open the door of the hospital and shouted to the remaining boys. He waved them inside the building.

Perry, who'd been visiting Cleck-Heaton, was on the stairs. He stared as the urchins flooded in and at Knight's suggestion huddled beneath the staircase.

'What the hell do you think you're doing, Mason, Knight?'

'Saving the lives of local children, sir,' John replied unabashed.

'You can't bring the filthy animals in here!'

'You'd rather they were shot by snipers and left in the street?'

'Frankly, yes. God knows what diseases they're carrying. This is a hospital...'

'I'm aware of that, Colonel Perry. I'm also aware of the directive from HQ that good relations are to be fostered with the locals.'

'Not when it endangers the health of our sick and wounded.'

'With due respect, sir... Quiet!' John heard the sound of boots squelching. He opened the door a crack and saw Crabbe leading a squad from the Oxfordshire and Buckinghamshire Light Infantry. They were marching close to the wall of the building opposite, heading towards the river.

'If you've your medical bag and revolver, Mason, we've no medic with us.' Crabbe shouted.

'Knight, take care of the boys and bolt this door after us. Dira,' John called in direction of the ward, 'bring my medical bag.' He unbuckled his holster and palmed his revolver.

Sergeant Greening took the bag from Dira and slipped out into the street joining John as he caught up with Crabbe.

'I shouted to Dira...'

'Escort to be with prisoner at all times.' Greening patted his rifle. 'Orderlies aren't armed, sir.'

'Glad to have you with us, sergeant. Sepoys are trying to desert,' Crabbe informed John.

'It's becoming a habit with them,' John muttered.

'Not en masse it isn't. Runner came into HQ from the dugout at the end of this avenue. More than twenty were spotted trying to make their way across the wreck of a mahaila in the river to the Turkish lines. Johnny Turk snipers haven't realised what they're up to. They're trying to pick them off.'

'The idiots just blew out the brains of an innocent local boy who was playing outside the hospital.'

'War doesn't recognise bystanders.' Crabbe ducked as two bullets scudded past. He waited a few seconds, when there was no follow up he signalled to his squad. 'Take cover in the trenches.'

Crabbe leapt down over the parapet only when the last man was in. John and Greening tumbled alongside him. They looked up to see Philip Ashman, revolver in hand, standing on a firing step sandbag, peering over the edge of the trench.

'Good of you gentlemen to join us.'

John crouched beside a sapper with a scalp wound.

'My mate's worse, sir.' The man pointed to a

lance corporal with blood pouring from his neck.

Greening handed John the medical bag.

Crabbe climbed on the firing step beside Ashman and borrowed his field glasses.

'I counted seventeen sepoys on the wreck of the mahaila and four in the river. One's floating face down so I think we can discount him,' Ashman reported.

'We court-martialled six this morning for trying to break through the lines last night.' Crabbe returned Ashman's glasses. 'Bloody fools.'

'You defended them?' John asked.

'Sat in judgement.'

'Couldn't you get out of it?'

'No chance. Have you any idea how many are being held in the glasshouse waiting to be processed? It's as much as HQ can do to keep up with the "would-be" deserters and mutineers. Looters, "conduct unbecoming", and fighting on duty have been sitting in the cells since we moved into the town. Be grateful you're a doctor, or you too would be sentencing sepoys to be shot at sunset.'

'How many?' John asked.

'With the ones we sentenced this morning, eight tonight, that's if the sun sets behind this bloody rain.'

'I thought miscreants were shot at dawn.' Philip angled his field glasses on the parapet again.

'Sunset saves a meal and in our present situation every ounce of food counts.' Crabbe took a last look at the sepoys clambering over the mahaila that had been sunk on General Townshend's orders when they'd dug into the town. 'A gun would shift those blighters from that wreck, Ashman. Where's the nearest, or failing that, a howitzer?'

'Captain Smythe's gone to find out, sir.'

A deafening blast rent the air. Crabbe joined Ashman. 'Looks like Smythe found a gun.'

'Any casualties?' John placed a last stitch in the neck wound.

'Three are moving in this direction. Wouldn't it be kinder and less time consuming to shoot them or let them drown?' Crabbe looked down at John.

'Not if you're a doctor who's taken the Hippocratic Oath. Sergeant Greening, round up stretcher-bearers to take these to the hospital.'

Turkish lines outside Kut, Thursday 6th January 1916

'Yakasub village,' Habid pointed in the direction of the liquorice factory.

Mitkhal noticed the village was the only area outside of the loop of the Tigris to be flying the British flag. Surrounded by a plethora of Turkish flags, the whole of its perimeter on the landward side was encircled by heavily manned Turkish defences, piquets, posts, and lines.

'You want to get into Kut, Mitkhal, that's your best option. There's a boat bridge in front of the village that spans the river.'

'I'd have to breach the Turkish lines to get into the village and the British gunship *Sumana* has its sights trained on the bridge. I doubt they'd allow me to stand on it long enough to explain my peaceful intention,' Mitkhal observed.

Habid had berthed his mahaila at the confluence of the Shatt al-Hai and Tigris, out of sight of the river traffic on the Tigris. They secured the boat and paid a local tribesman to guard it before making their way as close to Kut as they dared. Thousands of Arab irregulars had transformed the entire area on the Turkish-held right bank into a camping ground. Men smoked, gossiped, and chewed sunflower seeds as they huddled around dung fires that belched acrid smoke beneath blackened awnings erected to keep off the worst of the rain. Strings of tethered camels and horses bellowed and moaned behind them. Young boys raced from one tribal camp to another carrying messages and begging dates and bread flaps.

'The desert must be empty.' Mitkhal surveyed the heaving, noisy mass of humanity.

'The smell of loot attracts the Bedawi.' Clouds obscured the moon and stars, but the camp fires lent enough illumination to navigate a path. 'This way.' Habid walked confidently ahead.

Mitkhal followed. The rain had mixed with the dust and thousands of feet had churned the mess into a sea of cloying mud that sucked at their feet.

'Looking for one man here is like searching for one duck in the marshes at the height of the breeding season. But when I was last here my cousin laid claim to a spot in the fork between the two rivers.' Habid stopped again and looked around.

A thickset, heavily built man with a manicured beard rose from the mass around him and waved.

'There he is. Greetings, Qadir.' Habid slapped

Mitkhal's shoulders and led him into his cousin's camp. It was the largest in the vicinity. Mitkhal stopped counting armed men of fighting age when he reached forty. Some of the guns slung over their shoulders were old, single-shot muskets but the knives at their belts gleamed with reflected firelight without a single spot of rust to mar their blades.

'This is my good friend, Mitkhal.' Habid pushed Mitkhal forward.

'Then you are my good friend too, Mitkhal,' Qadir embraced him. 'Sit, eat.' He indicated a prime spot in front of the fire. Mitkhal sat on the ground. Someone pushed a bread flap into his hand, someone else handed him a fistful of dates.

He sat back, ate, and listened.

'We will stay here one more week, no longer,' Qadir declared. 'If the Turks do not attack within seven days I don't believe they ever will. As for the British,' he shrugged 'they are too comfortable in the town to want to break out. They have roofs over their heads and stoves in their quarters. In one week the rains will be here in earnest, giving them even less reason to leave the comfort of the houses they have stolen, to attack the Turks shivering in their trenches. War is best fought at the beginning of the summer. We will return then.'

'So, it hasn't been a profitable visit for you this time?' Habid offered Qadir his tobacco pouch.

Qadir rose. 'Walk with me, cousin.'

'Did you have trouble in the marshes?' the man at Mitkhal's elbow asked.

'None.'

The man nodded. 'Habid has always been able

242

to deal with the Marsh Arabs. Curse their thieving hands.'

'You've had problems with them?'

'My brother had a boat. I helped him sail it. We made a living until they killed my brother and stole it.'

'Mitkhal?' Qadir beckoned. Together they walked away from the camp towards a watering hole on the bank.

'Tomorrow I'll take delivery of Habid's goods. His men will load them on my boat. With the grace of Allah I will head back downstream by sunset.'

'Through the marshes?' Mitkhal asked.

'Back through the marshes,' Qadir confirmed. 'The boy you were talking to, Rabi, will be coming with us, and we'll have enough guns and ammunition to frighten off even the most intrepid of the thieving Marsh breed. Will you be ready to travel with us?'

'I have no way of knowing if I'll locate the horses by then, but if I do I'll be here before sunset?'

'With the horses.'

'I don't intend to return without them if they're alive.'

'You'll steal them from the British?' Qadir's eyes gleamed in the darkness.

'The horses are mine. No man can steal what is rightfully his.'

'My boat is not made to carry horses.'

'What boat is? We could hide them under the awning,' Mitkhal suggested.

'And if we're stopped?'

'Who is there to stop us?'

243

'The British, the Turk, the Marsh Arabs...'

'The British and the Turk are too wise to venture into the marshes, and even if they did, they're too reliant on Arab boatmen to bring them supplies to risk shooting us. They know our deaths would make other captains wary of serving them. As for the Marsh Arabs, they can be bribed,' Mitkhal declared.

'And if the Marsh Arabs want more money than you can give them?'

Mitkhal's hands strayed to his gun. 'I'd shoot them before they shot us.'

'These horses, they are good-looking?'

'They were. If I find them I suspect they will be thinner than when I last saw them.'

'How much money will you pay me to wait until you find them?' Habid asked.

'Ten sovereigns if you wait until tomorrow night for me, if I have the horses, an extra hundred for their passage.'

'Gold sovereigns.'

'British gold sovereigns,' Mitkhal reiterated.

'In advance.' Habid held out his hand.'

'One in advance, so you can see the quality of my coin. The rest are inside Kut,' Mitkhal lied. 'If I find the horses you will receive the coins tomorrow night.'

Habid took the coin Mitkhal handed him and bit it. 'And if the British kill you?'

'You will have to be content with the five sovereigns I paid you for my passage and that single sovereign, my friend.'

'Your horses. Are they as magnificent as that beast?' Mitkhal looked up to see a grey thundering through the camps. Oblivious to men and fires it was charging directly towards him.

'Devon!' As he breathed the name, a sharp pain tore into his left arm. He felt his blood, warm, wet, trickling down over his hand. He looked up. Ali Mansur was staring at him.

Chapter Nineteen

Turkish lines outside Kut, Thursday 6th January 1916

'Bastard!' Ali Mansur pushed his face close to Mitkhal's. He spat in his eye. 'You stole my wife.'

Blood flowed, soaking Mitkhal's gumbaz when Ali Mansur pulled the broad-bladed knife from Mitkhal's arm. Ali Mansur lifted his knife again and aimed the blade at Mitkhal's chest. Mitkhal feinted. He tried and failed to lift his left arm. It hung cold and unresponsive at his side. He reached for his own knife with his right hand, yanked it free from his belt and stepped back to face his assailant.

The world blurred. A buzzing filled his ears. He was aware of Ibn Shalan's men closing in at Ali Mansur's back. Of Devon's breath, warm on his neck. Of the rough feel of the rope trailing from Devon's muzzle brushing his cheek.

He saw Habid and Qadir wrench out their knives, and sensed them moving in on either side of him. A man behind Ali Mansur primed his

245

rifle and aimed the barrel. Before the man could fire, one of Qadir's men snatched the rifle from him. Four more of Qadir's men bore down on Ali Mansur, grasping his arms they pinned them tight to his sides.

Ali Mansur screamed. 'Didn't you hear me? This man stole my wife. I have the right to kill a thief.'

The pain in Mitkhal's arm escalated but he deliberately kept his voice soft, low in contrast to Ali Mansur. 'A man can only steal the possessions of another. You did not own your wife.'

'A man owns the wife that is freely given by her father. I owned Furja. You stole her from my tent and spirited her away.'

'You saw me spirit her away?' Mitkhal challenged.

'You took care I saw no more than a shadow that consigned me to oblivion and left me with a headache.'

'So you were asleep when she left?'

'You knocked me out, Mitkhal.'

'Look at me, Ali Mansur.' Mitkhal drew himself up to his full height. 'I am no shadow.'

Habid laughed but no one joined him.

'You and your wife were nowhere to be found after my wife disappeared,' Ali Mansur snarled.

'I took my wife and left the tribe because I could not trust you. This,' Mitkhal indicated his slashed and bleeding arm, 'suggests I was right to do so. Perhaps your wife also distrusted you.'

'If every man whose wife ran from him blamed another for stealing her and demanded the right to kill whoever he suspects, the desert would be awash with blood and there would be no men left and a surfeit of childless wives.' Unlike Habid's words, Qadir's were greeted with laughter, which only served to further incense Ali Mansur.

Devon nuzzled the back of Mitkhal's head.

'First my wife, Mitkhal. Now my horse.' Ali Mansur struggled to free his arms, but Qadir's men held him fast.

'I did not steal your wife, Ali Mansur, but if you want to talk about stealing horses, I accuse you of taking mine. Devon sought me out because she knows her true master.'

'You abandoned the beast when you took my wife.' Ali Mansur succeeded in freeing his right arm. He reached up to Devon. The horse reared and kicked, catching Ali Mansur's hand with a hoof.

Ali Mansur screamed. One of Ibn Shalan's men lunged upwards with a knife, intending to strike the mare, but Mitkhal deflected the thrust. The man lost control, his hand jerked back and the honed blade slid easily, cleanly, into Ali Mansur's throat.

Ali Mansur opened his mouth. A bestial gurgling filled the air as blood flowed from the wound. He stood poised, swaying on his feet for what was only seconds yet seemed like an eternity to Mitkhal, before his eyes darkened, rolled upwards and he crashed, face down to the ground.

Ibn Shalan's men hurled themselves on to Qadir's men.

Habid grabbed Mitkhal and Devon. 'He's dead! Go!'

Mitkhal jumped on Devon's back. Having no

saddle or bridle, he guided the horse towards the river with his knees. Devon remembered his voice and touch and needed no persuasion. Driven by the cries behind him Mitkhal dug his heels into the mare's flanks and trusted her to avoid the closely packed camps of Arabs. Deciding the Turks posed a lesser threat than his fellow countrymen, he set a course for the Turkish lines.

The camps of the Arabs irregulars grew sparser and disappeared altogether once he had the Turkish trenches in his sights. Behind the trenches, little more than narrow black slits in the unrelenting flat landscape, lay the pockmarked desolation of no-man's-land. Scarred by craters, festooned with ragged swathes of barbed wire, it stretched to the faint lights that burned in the British-occupied village of Yakasub.

To his right the river gleamed like gunmetal. Berthed in front of the village, he could make out the velvet black outline of the gunship *Sumana*. Alongside the vessel the dark shadow of a bridge boat dulled the shine of the water. The bridge led to the opposite bank and the square outlines of the mud brick buildings of Kut.

Mitkhal could still hear Ibn Shalan's and Qadir's men shouting but their cries were faint, muted by distance. Around him, all was quiet, but he knew it wouldn't remain that way if he tried to get any closer to the Turkish defences. He guided Devon to the right and into the shallows of the Tigris.

When the mare was hock-deep she bent her head to drink. Mitkhal slid from her back. The only regret he'd had about leaving Ibn Shalan's camp with Gutne, Furja, and the children was abandoning Devon. It wasn't just that the mare was too large to be conveyed on the small mahaila he'd paid to carry them down to Basra. The horse was simply too recognisable. From the moment Harry had shipped his four polo ponies Dorset, Somerset, Devon, and Norfolk, into Basra from India, they'd been as coveted and admired by the Arabs as much as they'd been among Harry's fellow officers.

A generous wedding present, along with Norfolk, from Harry, Devon was known as one of Harry's greys, and he'd been anxious not to attract attention from anyone who might recognise the mare and pass on information which would lead Ali Mansur or Ibn Shalan to him or Furja.

Devon nuzzled him in the back, pushing him further into the water. His left arm was aching unbearably. He stroked Devon's nose with his right hand, wishing he had sugar to give her. 'Where are your stable mates, girl?'

The horse whinnied as if she'd understood what he'd said.

Norfolk's whereabouts were no mystery. He'd presented the mare to Ibn Shalan along with the sovereigns Harry had given him to pay Gutne's bride price. He didn't doubt Shalan kept Norfolk close. He hadn't seen the sheikh when Ali Mansur had attacked him and suspected the promise of battlefield loot hadn't been strong enough to tempt Shalan from his beloved Karun Valley.

That left Dorset and Somerset. Were they still in Kut? Or had Harry entrusted them to a fellow officer who'd taken them along with the cavalry when they'd retreated to Ali Gharbi before the Turks had tightened the noose around the town? Was he risking his neck on a fool's errand? Were Harry's horses safe downstream?

Or – he grimaced at the thought – had they been slaughtered to fill an officer's plate in Kut?

He examined his arm. Ali Mansur's knife had cut through the muscle and the wound was still pumping blood. He pulled off his headdress, tied the cloth kafieh tightly around the gaping wound and strapped up his arm with the rope agal he used to hold his kafieh in place. He turned to Devon. The mare's coat gleamed silver even in the moonless darkness. He picked up a handful of mud and spread it over the horse's flanks and back. It was slow work one-handed but he used the time to think out his next move.

Kut was close. All he had to do was swim Devon across the Tigris, a simple matter of three – or depending on which part of the river he chose – maybe four hundred yards and he'd be on the opposite shore. He and Harry had swum further through the marshes on many occasions.

Whether he'd reach Kut alive was another matter. He'd not only have to avoid the bullets the Turks and the sentries on the *Sumana* fired his way, but also those of the British sappers manning the defences of the village on the bank opposite Kut and the defences of Kut itself. He'd never missed Harry more. No matter how stacked the odds against them, Harry always found a way to laugh and joke his way through.

Devon shook her head when he plastered the mess too close to her eyes.

'Sorry, old girl,' he murmured in English, unconsciously adopting the soothing voice Harry used to address his horses. 'I know this mud doesn't look or feel good but we have to lie low for a while.'

When he'd covered Devon with as much of the sediment as would stick, he crouched and waited. He had no way of measuring time but when he looked at the camps of the Arab irregulars he noticed their fires had begun to die down.

Men were rolling themselves into blankets and lying alongside the fires, although at least one man in every group remained sitting, knife in hand and rifle cradled in his arms. He continued to wait, watching the dying embers of the dung fires and the shadowy shapes of the men around them. When all was silent he took out his tobacco pouch and rolled a cigarette. He pushed it between his lips but he didn't dare light it.

The moon and stars remained obscured by clouds. The only light came from the flickering fires at ground level. The air was freezing, heavy with moisture, and he wondered how long it would be before the rainy season broke in full force.

A snatch of conversation drifted towards him from the nearest camp. He recognised the dialect as Bani Lam. The voice was young. The tone, adolescent, boasting of brave deeds to be accomplished in battle, coupled with generous estimates of the number of Turkish and British cavalry horses, weapons, gold sovereigns and silver rupees that would be lying on the battlefield waiting to be picked up after the Turks attacked Kut and the

251

cowardly British surrendered.

He knew, from the sorties he'd planned and carried out with Harry, that the hour before dawn was the best to mount an attack, infiltrate an enemy position, or catch a man off-guard. The spirit and eyelids were at their lowest, the body's senses less alert.

When the boy fell silent he walked Devon closer to the Turkish lines. He saw the shadow of a man's head as he moved down the trench towards the Tigris. At the river end, the Turkish soldier climbed out from his underground bunker and headed for the bank.

Devon whinnied, but the man ignored the sound and continued walking. The sound of water falling into water echoed in the air. As Mitkhal had suspected, the man was relieving himself.

Mitkhal listened hard but heard no other movement. He removed the knife from the sheath at his waist and moved lightly on the balls of his feet. The man was adjusting his clothes, his face turned to the river and Kut across the water.

Mitkhal wrapped his forearm across the man's neck and squeezed. When the man began to choke, he released his hold long enough to free his hand and slice his blade through the man's windpipe. The man slumped, a dead weight. He eased the corpse down into the water. It sank below the bank. Air bubbles broke on the surface, but the sound was no louder than the noise fish made when they rose.

Mitkhal kicked the body into mid-stream, watched it bob downstream, grabbed Devon's rope and pulled the mare into the river. Lying along the horse's back he headed upstream towards the village of Yakasub and the *Sumana*. He urged Devon on, whispering into her ear, waiting for the moment when the ground would give way and horse would begin to swim. The current was stronger than he'd anticipated and it reached him sooner than he'd thought it would, taking him unawares. When he was close enough to see the guns of the Turkish sentries manning their redoubts the first shot rang out.

He grabbed Devon's mane and guided the mare into the deep water between the *Sumana* and Kut. Shots splashed into the river beside him. He realised the sentries on deck of the *Sumana* were shooting at him as well as the Turks. He took a deep breath and shouted, as loud as he could, 'Harry Downe.'

A voice he recognised bellowed across the deck. 'Harry Downe is dead.'

'It's Mitkhal, Harry's orderly. I need to get into Kut.'

Lieutenant Grace snapped, 'Hold your fire! Mitkhal, can you get on the bridge?'

'No, I have my horse with me.'

'I'll radio ahead. We'll keep the bastards on the bank busy. Stay alongside the boat bridge. Good luck.'

Mitkhal cursed as the current dragged him and Devon downstream away from the protection of Yakasub and the *Sumana*. He kicked the horse's flanks, wrapped the fingers of his right hand deep into her mane, and clung on. Devon began to make headway, slow at first then gradually almost imperceptibly, the buildings of Kut drew into focus.

Devon sought firm ground and floundered. If his fingers hadn't been so firmly entwined in the mare's mane, Mitkhal would have floated away. He hauled himself back on the horse as another bullet fell short behind them.

'Grab the rope, Mitkhal.'

He squinted into the darkness. He couldn't make out the features but he recognised the voice.

'Major Crabbe?'

'Ignore the welcoming party behind me. After a couple of months in Kut they distrust all Arabs. You can convince them otherwise when you reach shore.'

Mitkhal kept the fingers of his right hand firmly embedded in Devon's mane. He trusted the horse more than Crabbe's rope, especially after Crabbe's veiled warning.

The horse floundered, found her feet, floundered again, and finally stepped on firm ground.

Crabbe helped him from the horse's back.

'Welcome to Kut, Mitkhal. Let's get you somewhere warm and dry.' He noticed the blood stains on the kafieh wrapped around his upper arm. 'Where you can get medical attention.'

Chapter Twenty

'Good to see you, Mitkhal. It's been a long time. How have you been keeping?' Crabbe offered Mitkhal his hand.

Mitkhal shook it. The situation was peculiarly British. No one other than an English officer would ignore his wet, dripping, bleeding state and offer to touch him with bare hands when he'd just crawled out of a fouled, freezing, and filthy river.

'You remember Lieutenant Bowditch?' Crabbe indicated his companion.

Mitkhal nodded to the naval officer.

'Put Lieutenant Colonel Downe's friend's mount in the Dorsets' stable,' Crabbe ordered a sapper. 'See it gets a good rub down and as much feed as we can afford to give it. And warn the duty orderly that no one, absolutely no one, is to take the horse from the stable unless I or Captain Smythe is present.'

'Sir.' The sapper reached for the rope Mitkhal was holding.

Devon stubbornly held her ground.

'Go with him, Devon,' Mitkhal handed the sapper the rope and patted the mare's rump. Slowly, somewhat reluctantly, Devon walked off with the private.

'This way.' Crabbe led Mitkhal down a narrow

255

alley away from the river. 'HQ woke me when they received a radio message from Grace on the *Sumana*. I sent my bearer to wake Mason and Smythe and told them to meet us in the officers' hospital. Not because I expected you to be wounded, but the stove there is kept lit day and night and I thought you'd be cold after a ducking.'

'Mitkhal, good to see you.' John left the dressing room to meet them when he heard Crabbe open the door of the building. 'Dira, bring coffee for five, please, and any food you can forage.'

Dira disappeared. John handed Mitkhal a clean pair of Indian cotton pyjamas, a towel, and a woollen robe. 'There's a bathroom through there stocked with soap and antiseptic. I'd use both if I were you after a ducking in the Tigris. The Turks built their latrines upstream with the intention of contaminating our water supply. Fortunately, we have access to a small reservoir in the town for drinking purposes. I'll get bandages and dress your wound as soon as you're clean. Leave your wet clothes in the bathroom. Dira will see to them. We'll be in here when you're through.' John pushed open the door to the dressing room.

The bathroom was basic but there was a tub large enough for Mitkhal to stand in and plenty of jugs of water. He stripped off his sodden clothes and untied the headdress from his arm. The wound was still bleeding and the raw flesh stung as if mosquitoes were banqueting on his muscle. He washed and cleaned the wound as best he could. After drying himself, he put on the cotton trousers. Wary of getting blood on the robe and pyjama shirt he carried them into the dressing room.

It was warm, stiflingly so, after the cold night air and icy river but Mitkhal was grateful for the heat. Peter, John, Crabbe, and David Knight were sitting around the stove, drinking coffee. John pulled out a chair for Mitkhal and examined his arm.

'That gash is deep. It needs stitching. How did it happen?'

'I fell on a Bedouin knife.'

'That sounds suspiciously like one of Harry's excuses. I suggest you learn to tread more carefully around tribesmen.' John probed the wound, pulled a trolley towards him, and prepared a syringe.

Mitkhal eyed it suspiciously. 'If that's to numb the pain I'd prefer brandy.'

'Take mine.' Peter handed over his flask.

'How many Arab irregulars are with the Turks?' Crabbe asked.

Mitkhal drank from the flask. 'Four, maybe five thousand.'

'Are they all prepared to fight on the Turkish side?' Peter asked.

'You should know the Arab by now, Captain Smythe. The only side they fight on is their own. Your generals call their technique hit and run. Harry translated it to pose and retreat. The Arabs pose with weapons where they can be seen to greatest effect, but only in areas where there's no danger of meeting armed opposition. The retreat begins the moment they sniff a blade or a bullet.' Mitkhal eyed Peter. None of the men looked well. All were pale and thin but Peter had a hacking cough and there was a wild, haunted look in his eyes that suggested more was troubling him than physical ill-health.

'Sorry,' John apologised when Mitkhal winced. 'Are you sure you won't change your mind about the anaesthetic? This cut needs at least another twelve stitches.'

'I'm fine.' Mitkhal's assertion didn't prevent him from taking Peter's flask when he offered it a second time.

'You know Harry's dead?' Crabbe asked the question uppermost in all the officers' minds.

Mitkhal stared down at the cracked tiles on the floor. They were blue and red with an abstract pattern that resembled the ancient one that floored the mosque in Basra. He was an accomplished liar but these men loved and valued Harry as much as he did. It wasn't easy to sit in front of them, knowing how much they were suffering at the thought of Harry's brutalised and tortured corpse being thrown into an unmarked grave alongside other nameless victims of the Turks.

'I know about Harry,' Mitkhal found his voice unaccountably hoarse.

'You weren't with him when he was captured?' Crabbe asked.

'No.'

'Why? You two went everywhere together,' Crabbe persisted.

'Harry asked me to take care of his wife and children. We expected him to join us. When he didn't, I went to look for him and discovered the Turks had captured him.'

John fastened one stitch and reached for

another. 'Harry told me his father-in-law forced him to divorce his wife.'

'He did, shortly after war broke out,' Mitkhal acknowledged. 'Sheikh Ibn Shalan knew, as did everyone within the tribe, that Harry and Furja's marriage would be seen as an alliance between the tribe and the British. It put the tribe at risk of an attack by the Turks. The only way to protect the tribe, Furja and her daughters, not only from the Turks, but would-be assassins sympathetic to the Turks within the tribe, was for Harry to divorce her.'

'I can't imagine Harry doing anything he didn't want to.' Peter was incredulous.

'Harry had no choice,' Mitkhal explained. 'He was a British officer. His life was at the disposal of his superiors. He could hardly take his native wife and children into battle with him. Ibn Shalan promised Harry that after the divorce he'd do his best to protect Furja and their children. After Harry left, Ibn Shalan decided the best way to care for his daughter and grandchildren was to marry her to one of his tribesmen.'

'Furja agreed?' John, who knew Furja, was shocked.

'Only to protect her children. If she'd refused, her father and the tribe would have cast her and her daughters out into the desert. They wouldn't have lasted long without food or water.'

'Did Harry know she'd remarried?'

'Why do you think he asked me to take care of them?' Mitkhal met John's probing gaze.

'You took her from her husband?'

'She wasn't happy with him. It didn't help that

she was carrying Harry's child. She was terrified the child would be born fair and her husband would take his anger out on all three of her children. So, yes, I helped her and her children to leave her husband's tent.'

'Did her husband follow you?'

'He was killed in a fight.' Mitkhal felt that at least that wasn't a lie.

'Are Furja and Harry's children safe now?' John looked intently at Mitkhal.

'They are safe.' Mitkhal repeated.

'Where?'

'The fewer people who know that the better, Major Mason.' Mitkhal watched John insert another stitch into his muscle.

Crabbe broke the silence that had fallen over the room. 'To get back to our situation here. We have aerial photographs from our planes. But anything you can tell us about the Turkish positions might be helpful.'

'I can give you a rough estimate of the number and deployment of Turkish troops. But I didn't have time to make a study. I only arrived here a few hours ago.'

'What's it like in Ali Gharbi? Is the relief column ready to move out and break the siege?' Crabbe opened a pack of Camel cigarettes and offered them around.

'I've no idea. I travelled up the Shatt al-Hai.'

'Through the marshes?' Knight spoke for the first time. 'I'm amazed you lived to tell the tale.'

'The Marsh Arabs are human – just,' Mitkhal qualified. 'They're friendly enough if you offer them coins. They prefer gold to silver.'

260

'You risked a great deal to come here,' Crabbe observed suspiciously.

'I came for Harry's horses. I was too late to help Harry but I know what he thought of them. They'd make fine breeding stock for Harry's wife and children. Are they here?'

'They're here,' Crabbe made a wry face.

'Are they all right?' Mitkhal enquired anxiously.

'Thin, like the rest of us,' John declared. 'Colonel Perry has them shut up in the Norfolks' stables. Animal feed is as short as ours.'

'Good job you came now, we're almost out of mules and donkeys. If we're not relieved in the next week or two we'll have to start on the horses,' Knight observed.

'We tried to get Dorset and Somerset moved into the Dorsets' stable,' Peter explained. 'Problem is, Perry outranks us.'

'Harry always did wind up Perry the wrong way, but this time the colonel's being stubborn to annoy me.' John took the blame on himself.

'Hardly. Bastard decided to have it in for the pair of you.' Crabbe topped up their cups from the coffee pot and added tots of whisky from his flask.

Dira knocked, and handed Mitkhal a bowl of bully beef stew. 'I'm sorry, I could not find anything better for your guest, Sahib,' he apologised to John.

Mitkhal took the bowl with his free hand and set it on the table. 'This is fine and very welcome after what I've been eating for the past few days, thank you.'

'You've put a cot up in my room for my guest?'

261

John asked.

'I have, Sahib. And found extra blankets.'

'Thank you, Dira. You can go to bed now. We'll clear up here.'

'Yes, Sahib.'

'So,' Crabbe asked the questions no one else wanted to, 'are you still fighting for the British, Mitkhal?'

'When it won't interfere with my responsibilities.' Mitkhal dug a spoon into the stew.

'Harry's wife and daughters?'

'And my own wife and son.'

'A boy. Congratulations.' Peter smiled.

'Harry has a son too.'

'Did he see him before he died?' John asked.

Mitkhal shook his head.

'He is Harry's son?' John pressed.

'No doubt about it. Blond hair, blue eyes that are beginning to turn grey. He looks just like his twin sisters. Furja was right to leave the husband her father found for her. He would have killed her and the baby if he'd seen him.'

'Hard to imagine Harry with three children.' Peter rose to his feet.

'Harder to imagine him dead.' Knight left his chair and picked up their mugs and the coffee pot. 'I'll clear up here, John. Mitkhal's sleeping on his feet. It's late, and I doubt the Turkish snipers will allow us poor overworked doctors to lie in tomorrow morning so I suggest we all head for bed.'

'The brigadier will want to see you in morning, Mitkhal,' Crabbe said.

'After I've seen Harry's horses.'

'It'll be impossible to prise them away from Perry,' Peter warned.

'Impossible is a word I, like Harry, refuse to recognise, Captain Smythe.' He glanced at the clock on the wall. 'In a few hours it will be light. Perhaps it might be better to visit them now.'

'I'll come with you,' Peter volunteered.

'Neither of you are going. I'll have a word with the brigadier in the morning. If anyone can get Harry's horses away from Perry, he can.' Crabbe joined Peter at the door.

John bandaged Mitkhal's arm and secured the dressings. He handed him the shirt and dressing gown. 'I'd wear both in bed if I were you. It's cold here at night.'

'Cold everywhere, not just Kut, Captain Mason.'

'Could you call me John?' John led the way into the hall and up the stairs. He opened the door of his room. Dira had made his bed and laid a cot out for Mitkhal. 'Basic but clean.'

'Thank you.' Mitkhal put on the shirt and dressing gown and lay on bed. 'This is soft after the boards I've been sleeping on for the past few nights. It's kind of you to put me up in your room. But any corner would have done. I know how officers look down on your kind for hob-nobbing with the natives.'

'No one looked down on Harry and he "hob-nobbed" with more natives than any officer.'

'Harry could get away with it.'

'Harry could get away with anything,' John agreed. 'I asked you to share my room because I wanted to talk to you in private. Have you seen my wife or Mrs Smythe?'

'No. I haven't visited the mission since last February.'

'You haven't been in Basra?'

'I've been looking after Harry's and my own family.'

John sat on his bed. Seeing Mitkhal grimace in pain he unscrewed the top of his brandy flask and handed it to him. 'My wife believes I'm dead.'

'Do you want me to visit her and tell her you're alive?'

'Good God, no! To cut a long story short, I was court-martialled and found guilty of killing an officer and refusing to obey orders while under fire.'

'Perry accused you?'

'You know us better than we know ourselves, Mitkhal. Crabbe managed to get the sentence postponed and a review of my case to be held after we're relieved or surrender. My wife received notification of my death from fever after the court martial. It's how the army explains the deaths of those they sentence to be shot. The brass believes it best to keep the truth from the family concerned.'

'I'm sorry for your problems, John.'

'I didn't mean to pour my troubles out on you, but I don't want you tell anyone outside of Kut that I'm alive. I asked Maud for a divorce, so I doubt my death affected her. The best thing I can do is let her carry on living her life.'

'Your family in England?'

'If I survive the war they'll have a surprise, hopefully a pleasant one. If I die...' John shrugged.

'And Major Reid?'

'We heard he's alive. Crabbe wrote to him about Harry. We thought he'd be in India.'

'He's in Basra?'

'Have you seen him?'

'Only at a distance. He didn't see me, and I thought it best not to draw attention to myself by approaching him.'

'For Furja and the children's sake.'

'Harry entrusted me with their safe keeping.'

'Harry had a lot of friends, Mitkhal. Friends who will see it as their duty to care for his wife and children. I'm not in a position to help while I remain cooped up here, but should I survive it will be a different matter.'

'I will watch over them.'

'How can you while you are here?'

'They are with trusted friends who will not betray their whereabouts.'

'They'll need money to live on.'

'Harry left them enough.'

'And the children's education?' John questioned.

'Harry told me about the time he spent in an English boarding school. From what he said, I hardly think they would take his Arab children.'

'You're probably right, Mitkhal, but things may be different after the war.'

'Different enough for the British to allow the Arabs to govern their own country?'

'We can all hope and that goes for the British soldiers as well. None of us want to be here.'

'Hope is not enough to live on.'

'No it isn't.' John pulled his strong box from under his bed and unlocked it. He removed two small parcels and handed the smallest to Mit-khal. 'There's an amulet in there Furja gave me. It contains the words of the prophet'

'You must keep it.' Mitkhal handed it back to him. 'It would be bad luck to return it to Furja while you are alive.'

John took it. 'This,' he gave Mitkhal the second box. 'Contains gold and pearls Harry gave me as a wedding present. He said he won them gam-bling.'

'You doubted him?'

'No. Please, give them to Furja. Anything could happen here and I don't want to hand the enemy anything of value.'

Mitkhal shook his head. 'You are a doctor. You could exchange these with a Turk for drugs that might save a man's life.'

'I didn't think of that.' John replaced it in the box.

'The relief column could arrive tomorrow...'

John interrupted Mitkhal. 'And be decimated by the Turks.'

Mitkhal realised there was no point in trying to reassure John. 'It could,' he agreed.

Chapter Twenty-one

Ali Gharbi, evening Thursday 6th January 1916

'The Western Front looked chaotic but there was always an underlying thread of organisation hidden within the madness. Things always came together whenever we had a show with the Hun. This feels different,' Boris picked up the mug of tea his bearer had brought him. 'The guns the Sussex Territorials hauled on the boats yesterday morning looked as though they'd been taken from a museum commemorating the Indian mutiny. Where are the bombs, rifle grenades, range finders, Verey lights, periscopic rifles...'

'In France,' Tim Levitt suggested.

Boris picked up his binoculars from the camping table set in front of the tent they shared with Tom Mason. 'Fat lot of good they're doing there.' He scanned the munition boxes being carried up the gangplanks for recognisable markings.

'What you have to remember is the War Office isn't running this show. The India Office is, and they have shallower pockets.'

'That doesn't give them the right to palm us off with equipment Warren Hastings would have rejected as antiquated a century ago?'

'Take my advice, Boris. Calm down, eat a cracknel, enjoy your tea and your last relaxing supper for a while, and stop trying to monitor

267

what is and isn't being loaded on the steamers.'

'Twelve months in India and you've become Indian Army to the core. Your entire life revolves around tea.' Boris was scathing.

'If we're talking Indian Army we're talking tiffin, not tea.'

'For the record, I hate cracknels. There's no taste to them. I'd give anything for a plate of macaroons.'

'Wouldn't we all,' Tim agreed. 'As for what awaits us upriver, I talked to a naval officer in the mess over breakfast this morning. He was upstream two days ago within four miles of Sheikh Saad. He said he didn't get as much as a sniff of a Turk. No sign of them or their trenches.'

'Then he wasn't looking. I assure you they're there. My CO showed me the aerial recon photographs this morning,' Boris contradicted him. 'He said no British sapper digs a slit trench like a Turk. They're there, and the Johnny Turks will all be squashed inside like a tin full of sardines, only with their heads and bayonets pointed up. Ready and waiting to slit the bellies of our horses as we jump over them.'

'There's Tom leaving the supply tent. Bring cha for Captain Mason and extra biscuits,' Tim shouted to his bearer.

'Why the thunderous face, Mason?' Boris asked when Tom joined them.

'Did you know they've appointed only one Medical Officer to a brigade?'

'Heard it in the briefing this afternoon. Problem is we don't have any more to go round,' Boris said.

Tim offered Tom the plate of biscuits.

Tom didn't even notice. 'It's insanity for thirteen and a half thousand men to go into battle without medical cover and that's without taking into account the seven thousand or so in Kut – if we get through. The reports I've read suggest they're not in the best of shape...'

'Which brigade have you been posted to?' Boris interrupted.

'I haven't. I've been ordered to stay here, monitor supplies, and set up a hospital tent – if one arrives. Should we get, and I quote, "unforeseen seriously wounded", I've been ordered to oversee their evacuation to Basra.'

'I've heard command isn't expecting many casualties.' Tim helped himself to a cracknel.

'With only two hundred and fifty hospital beds, no tents, no hospital ships, and only enough lint, bandages, and supplies for the aforementioned 250 beds, I hope they're right. Although I'd like to know what intelligence they're using to base their forecast.' Tom pulled up a camp chair and sat down.

Boris looked around to make sure there were no ranks listening in. 'No doubt they'll soon pass on the order that no member of the force is to allow himself to get wounded.'

'Have they told the Turks to use toy guns that fire corks?' Tom enquired acidly.

'If they were communicating with the Turks we wouldn't be here enjoying this delightful Cooks' Tour courtesy of the War Office.'

Tim's bearer turned up with an extra mug for Tom and a fresh pot of tea.

'And if the casualties aren't light?' Tom snapped.

'May the Lord help us, although despite all the communications sent heavenwards from officers and rank and file, no celestial force has helped us so far in this sideshow.' Boris glanced back into the tent as his bearer picked up his kit bag. 'All packed?'

'All packed, Sahib. This is the last of your luggage.'

Boris glanced at his watch. 'When you've loaded that into the hold, stay on board. We're due to sail in ten minutes, although given my experience of the timetable of this expedition that probably means an hour.'

'Yes, Sahib.'

'If they hitch any more barges to that steamer it'll take for ever for us to get upriver and by then it will be over,' Tim complained.

'I doubt it. I have a feeling this particular show is going to last a while,' Boris left his chair when the whistle blew on the steamer. 'Just look at the way the brigades have been bundled together.' He watched the men walk up the gangplank. 'I doubt there's a platoon where everyone has a nodding acquaintance with their fellows, let alone one that trained together. But,' he raised his eyebrows, 'what choice does Lieutenant General Aylmer have but to rush to the rescue when Townshend radioed out that his food and supplies will run out by mid-January.'

'Will a week be enough to get him and command out of Kut?' Tim asked. When neither Boris nor Tom answered, he added, 'Do we really know what we're up against?'

'I know what command is telling us we're up against.' Boris who'd been briefed on the battle plans by his CO, replied. 'There are approximately 4,500 Turks on the right bank at Sheikh Saad and 9,500 on the left. They were reinforced yesterday by 2,000 troops that the Turks pulled from the siege at Kut. In addition we've the usual rag-tag and bobtail horde of irregular Arabs that no one's even bothered to count to contend with. But...' he gave a grim smile '...we have a secret weapon.'

'We do?' Tim drew closer to Boris.

Boris lowered his voice. 'We have a mashuf bridge built of native boats that will enable us to move swiftly from one bank to another and fight on both sides of the river.'

'Given the bridges the engineers have built that I've seen, it would be quicker to swim across the river,' Tom declared.

A sergeant bellowed from the deck of the paddle steamer. His voice carried above the braying of the mules penned in to wait for a later transport and the cries of the bearers as they tossed kit bags on board.

'Get a move on, you idle bastards. No time for dilly-dallying with men starving in Kut.'

Tom shook Boris's hand before turning to Tim. 'Good luck. Both of you. This place is going to be as dull as ditchwater without you.'

'With luck we'll break through Johnny Turk's lines and reach Kut in a day or two. Then all we'll have to do is send our chaps downstream and follow them. We could be back here by next weekend, so don't drink all the medicinal brandy,'

271

Boris cautioned Tom.

'Nice thought, Boris, but a little bird's told me that once we relieve Kut we'll be receiving further orders,' Tom warned.

'Baghdad?' Tim whispered.

'The powers that be think a victory there will make a nice headline for my cousin and all the other scribblers to send back home.'

'We're a long way from Baghdad,' Tim mused.

'Only a couple of hundred miles and some twenty or thirty thousand Turks.' Boris slapped Tom's back. 'See you.'

'Yes, see you,' Tom repeated. He watched Boris and Tim walk up the gangplank.

Kut al Amara, Friday 7th January 1916

'Mitkhal, isn't it?' The brigadier rose to his feet when Crabbe ushered the Arab into his office shortly after dawn.

'Yes, sir.'

'Please, take a seat. You too, Crabbe. I knew Lieutenant Colonel Downe. I also know how highly he thought of you, Mitkhal. Major Crabbe said you're here to pick up Lieutenant Colonel Downe's horses.'

'For his widow, sir.' Mitkhal was becoming increasingly adept at subverting the truth.

The brigadier addressed Crabbe. 'They're in the Norfolks' stables?'

'Colonel Perry put them there for safekeeping, sir,' Crabbe lied.

The brigadier sat forward in his chair and

linked his fingers. 'Then there'll be no problem releasing them into Lieutenant Colonel Downe's aide's care?'

'None whatsoever, sir. Provided you give us a written order.'

'I'll see to it.' The brigadier hesitated. 'I take it you will be taking the horses downstream, Mitkhal?'

'Yes, sir.'

'To the Karun Valley?'

'No, sir.'

'Isn't that where Lieutenant Colonel Downe's widow resides with her father?'

'No, sir.'

'But she is downstream?'

'As it isn't only the Turks who'd like to lay their hands on Lieutenant Colonel Downe's widow, I'd rather keep her exact whereabouts secret, sir.'

'You're right to be cautious,' the brigadier agreed. 'Can I assume she is south of Ali Gharbi?'

'You can, sir,' Mitkhal acknowledged.

'How do you propose to take out the horses? There are two of them?' the brigadier looked to Crabbe for confirmation.

'Three, sir. I rode in here on my own horse,' Mitkhal answered. 'I intend to take them out the way I came in. The boat that brought me here will set sail at sunset.'

'You sailed here through the Turkish lines?'

'Through the camp of Arab irregulars, sir.'

'You came up the Tigris?'

'The Shatt al-Hai.'

'Through the marshes?'

'Yes, sir.'

273

'I've seen Lieutenant Colonel Downe's horses. Do you think you'll get them past the thieving Marsh Arabs?'

'I can but try, sir.'

'I have a proposition for you, Mitkhal. It's common knowledge that we are in contact with HQ Basra and the Relief Force by wireless. What isn't common knowledge yet, and I trust you not to repeat this, is that hostilities broke out this morning between Lieutenant General Aylmer's Relief Force and the Turks at Sheikh Saad. The Turks have pulled troops from the siege lines to engage our forces. Now would be a good time to attempt to sail down the Tigris, not the Shatt al-Hai, with your horses.'

'I have no boat,' Mitkhal pointed out.

'We have a mahaila large enough to take three horses.'

'You'll give it to me?'

'With pleasure. As for crew, you'll be accompanied by a British officer. There are certain ... important documents we'd like to send downstream. Documents that cannot under any circumstances fall into the enemy's hand.'

'You want me to carry them?'

'The officer will, but we would appreciate you escorting him downstream.'

Mitkhal stared at the brigadier.

'I realise what I'm asking you to do would almost certainly prove fatal should you fall into Turkish hands. I can't order you to accompany our...'

'Spy?'

'I won't lie to you. He'll be dressed in Arab

274

clothes and, if caught by the Turks, shot. If Lieutenant Colonel Downe had lived...'

'You would have ordered him, not me and your spy, to carry the documents downstream?'

'I would have,' the brigadier conceded.

'Just as you ordered him to leave Kut dressed as a native and spy on the Turkish positions the day he was captured and tortured.'

'Tortured? The ghulam with him said he was killed when the first shots were fired.'

'He was wrong, Brigadier.'

'The Turks tortured Harry?' The colour drained from Crabbe's face.

'They tortured him.' Mitkhal reiterated.

'How do you know?'

'I saw his body.' Mitkhal scraped his chair over the floor tiles as he rose. 'I will escort your courier downstream, Brigadier, provided you find me a mahaila large enough to take the horses.'

'When would you like to leave?'

'Three hours before dawn tomorrow. Now, I'd like to see the horses.'

Chapter Twenty-two

Sheikh Saad, Friday 7th January 1916

'I wish this damned mist would shift.'

As if the gods heard Boris, the fog drifted upwards to reveal a solid wall of Arab camelry and cavalry ranged in front of the Turkish lines. At the

275

sight of the British cavalry drawn up in battle order they uttered bloodcurdling whoops.

'What are they saying?' Boris asked.

'Off-hand I'd translate it as they're not pleased to see us,' his CO replied.

'There are thousands of them.'

'Probably no more than two or three.' The CO lifted his hand in preparation to give the signal to mount.

'If they're out to intimidate, they're succeeding.

'Soon as we charge they'll melt into the landscape. Arabs never stand and fight. Always hit and run, hit and run, hit and run, followed by run and run and run and run. So ignore the cabaret, it's nothing more than wind and bluster.'

'Prepare to mount!' The order was passed down the lines. 'Mount!'

The British cavalry assembled on the left flank of the Relief Force steadied their horses before swinging in one quick synchronised movement upwards, and into their saddles.

'The Black Watch are going in,' a voice on their right cried as the bagpipes started up.

'Without artillery support over a bare open plain...' Realising what he was saying could be construed as criticism of command, Boris took a deep breath.

'Get ready...'

The rest of the order was drowned by Turkish gunfire. Boris reined in his horse and watched rows of the Black Watch advance only to fall at the first volley.

Cries of 'Stretcher-bearer!' resounded in the air. High-pitched, urgent, they could be heard even above the noise of artillery.

'Advance!'

The cavalry moved out in a solid line. Their mounts trotted into a steady canter picking their way past the British wounded as they headed for the Turkish trenches.

Boris gripped his sabre, spurred his horse and tried not to look at the men lying on the ground as he galloped past. Tom Mason's warnings about lack of medical facilities echoed in his mind when he spotted two stretcher-bearers stepping into no-man's-land from the trenches that housed the 35th Brigade.

'Turks ahead!' The CO's voice was carried by the wind.

Boris tugged his reins, swerving to avoid two privates on the ground. There was no way of knowing if they were alive or dead.

As his CO had predicted, the Arab camelry and cavalry were falling back either side of the advance. As they dispersed they reminded Boris of the cockroaches that had scurried under the skirting boards whenever he'd carried a light into his father's cellar.

The first Turkish trench loomed ahead. He jumped his horse over an enemy gun battery, whirled around and thrust down at a gunner's head. The blade sliced cleanly almost but not quite severing the man's head from his body. There was no time to think.

Only react.

To his left and right were his comrades. Ahead the Turks and their guns. His horse thundered over the hard ground towards the Turkish artillery.

Guns he needed to silence for men who hadn't made it as far as him.

'Take Lieutenant Colonel Downe's aide to the Norfolks' stable, corporal,' the brigadier ordered.

'Sir.' The corporal snapped to attention in the doorway of the brigadier's office.

'If you wait for me there, Mitkhal. I'll be along with the paperwork that will be needed to release Harry's horses into your care,' Crabbe said.

Mitkhal turned to the brigadier. 'Thank you for allowing me to take Harry's horses to his widow, sir.'

'I'll see you before you leave, Mitkhal, and it's me who will be thanking you if you get the dispatches to Ali Gharbi before the Relief Force reaches here.'

Mitkhal left. The brigadier motioned Crabbe back into his chair.

'Do you have any ideas on the courier?'

'Yes, sir.'

'I thought you might.'

'Smythe, sir,' Crabbe said decisively. 'He hasn't recovered from the leg wound he took when he demolished Sandes's bridge or the bullet in his shoulder. He can't seem to shake off that hacking cough...'

'So you send him out undercover with a native. The Turks will hear them coming from a mile away.'

'That's the idea, sir. You know how terrified the

Turks are of tuberculosis.'

'With good reason considering a third of the POWs we took before Nasiriyeh were infected.'

'Exactly, sir. They'll hear Smythe cough and give him as wide a berth as the river will allow.'

'Does he have TB?'

'Not according to Mason or Knight, sir. He's had a couple of bouts of pneumonia which have worn him down physically and Mason has been concerned that he isn't recovering from his wounds as well as he should.'

'So by making him a courier we'll be killing two birds with one stone, informing Nixon and Aylmer of our dispositions inside the town before they get here so they'll know how best to disperse their troops; and getting Smythe out so he can continue on to Basra, decent medical care and no doubt a stretch of leave that he can spend with his wife.'

'Yes, sir.'

'You're somewhat transparent at times, Crabbe.'

'Yes, sir.'

The brigadier pulled a notepad towards him and scribbled an order. He tore it off and handed it to Crabbe. 'That should get Harry's horses out of Perry's clutches. If Perry kicks up a fuss refer him to me.'

'Yes, sir.'

'I'll have the dispatches ready by nightfall. We'll go over them before I hand them to Smythe. Do you want to give him the good news or shall I?'

'I thought I'd ask Mason to do the honours, sir.'

'Good idea. Might be better coming from a medic. Off with you, Crabbe. I have work to do

279

even if you don't.'

'Sir.'

Crabbe left HQ and went directly to the hospital. He couldn't have timed it better. John had finished his morning rounds and was drinking tea with Knight in his cubicle.

'Snipers starting late today?' Crabbe joined them.

'Night sentries reported Turkish troops being pulled from the lines and moving downstream in columns. Show must be starting down there soon, if it hasn't already.' Knight filled another mug with tea and handed it to Crabbe.

'I came to give you the news.'

'Perry won't hand Harry's horses over to Mitkhal?' John suggested.

Crabbe held up the paper the brigadier had given him. 'No, I have the order here, signed by the brigadier.'

'If Perry ignores it?' John asked.

'I don't think even Perry would cross the brigadier. I'm here because we need a courier to get the brigadier's dispatches through the lines. I suggested Smythe.'

'Through the lines with Mitkhal,' John guessed.

'As far as Ali Gharbi, but once Smythe reaches there I doubt anyone will begrudge him a few days with his wife in Basra.'

'If he lives to see Ali Gharbi,' John qualified.

'You think Smythe will be up for it?' Knight moved his chair to face Crabbe.

'I think he'll listen to a doctor who tells him it's his duty.'

'He's feverish and has a cough...' John began.

'The brigadier knows. We think it will put the Turks off questioning him, if he's dressed in Arab robes and headdress.'

'And if it doesn't, Smythe will be shot as a spy.'

'Mitkhal knows how to avoid Turks.'

'I would have said the same of Harry until they murdered him. When is Mitkhal leaving?' John asked.

'Tomorrow before dawn. Will you tell Smythe or shall I?'

'Tell? A mission like this has to be voluntary. The one to do the asking should be the brigadier.'

'The brigadier thought the request might be better coming from a medic able to point out the benefits of a rest in a Basra hospital.'

'Really?' John was openly sceptical. 'You've already told the brigadier I'll talk to Smythe, haven't you?'

'If I have, it's your fault for always being so accommodating.'

'Thank you, Crabbe,' John snapped.

'I ordered Smythe back to bed after I dressed his wound this morning,' Knight opened the stove and tossed in a cake of dried dung.

'It's infected?'

'Not looking good, but what do you expect on this diet? Half the men I treated this morning have wounds and sores that are failing to heal and bleed when pressed.'

'I'll find him.' John left his chair.

'I'll walk with you as far as the Norfolks' stables.' Crabbe followed John out of the building. 'Have you asked Mitkhal to call on Maud?' he asked when they were in the street.

'No.'

'Mitkhal's not returning to Basra?'

'You heard him last night. He's not prepared to say where he's based.'

'You're not giving him a letter for Maud or your family that can be sent on?'

'No, Crabbe.' John stopped walking. 'Believe me, I'm grateful to you for defending me, and rescuing me from a firing squad. If it wasn't for you I'd be mouldering in the cemetery, but you're a realist. You're aware just how precarious our situation is.'

'Your family believe you're dead, man!'

'If I survive they'll be surprised. If I don't, they won't have two telegrams to contend with.'

'And there's me thinking you'd be delighted to spread some sweetness and light among your nearest and dearest.'

'One lot of sweetness and light will have to be enough for you, Crabbe, and even that's dependent on me persuading Peter to accompany Mitkhal.'

'These are the Norfolks' stables.' Unsure how to address Mitkhal, the corporal stood back to allow him to enter the building first.

Mitkhal ducked under the doorway and walked into a long, low-built barn that had obviously been built for storage. There were no stalls and no water troughs. The horses had canvas water buckets slung around their heads and a stable hand was filling them from a hose connected to a water pump.

Thoroughbred officers' mounts were ranged in

lines facing one another. Before Mitkhal's eyes had time to adjust to the windowless gloom, Dorset saw him, whinnied, and stamped her hooves. Mitkhal turned and saw the two greys tethered next to one another. He walked over to the mare. She nuzzled his abba in search of sugar lumps.

'Sorry, old girls, I've nothing for you,' he murmured.

Somerset, who'd always been more reticent than Dorset about coming forward, nudged his elbow alongside her stablemate.

'They're beautiful horses,' the corporal who'd escorted him to the stables ventured.

'They are,' Mitkhal agreed.

'They know you.'

'They haven't forgotten me.' Mitkhal thought of the greeting they'd give Harry – if he managed to avoid horse thieves and transport them downstream.

Footsteps echoed over the mud brick floor.

'Hey, you there! Native boy!'

Mitkhal didn't turn his head.

'What do you think you're doing there with Colonel Perry's horses?' a square-built, thickset sergeant demanded.

'The brigadier sent him, sergeant,' the corporal answered. 'These are Lieutenant Colonel Downe's horses.'

'Lieutenant Colonel Downe's dead and I was talking to the raghead, not you.' The sergeant tugged at Mitkhal's head cloth. Mitkhal turned and yanked it from the sergeant's hands.

The sergeant pushed his face into Mitkhal's. 'I'm talking to you, cloth ears. What are you doing with Colonel Perry's mounts?'

'The brigadier...' the corporal began.

'I don't care what the brigadier said. He has no jurisdiction in this stable. And neither have you. Hampshires, aren't you?' The sergeant shoved the corporal. He lost his balance and reeled into the line of horses. The two tethered next to Dorset reared. They struck out with their hooves and one caught the corporal in the chest.

He gasped and fainted. Mitkhal scooped him up.

'Take your friend and clear off out of here, you bastard,' the sergeant tugged a crop from his belt and raised it to Mitkhal. 'Hit me and you'll regret it.'

The vehemence in Mitkhal's voice momentarily stayed the sergeant's hand. 'So you do have a tongue in your head, raghead.'

Mitkhal set the corporal down on a pile of sacks of grain. Next to them was a small sack covered with greenish dust that had a peculiar distinctive odour. Mitkhal touched it.

'No bloody raghead tells me what to do!'

Mitkhal whirled and caught the crop before it struck him. He wrenched it from the sergeant's hands and snapped it across his knee.

'What the hell's going on here?' Colonel Perry stood in the doorway blocking the limited light that percolated into the building.

'This raghead was messing with your horses. He assaulted me.'

'Did he now?' Perry advanced. 'It's Harry Downe's tame Arab, isn't it?'

Mitkhal stood his ground and stared at Perry.

Perry bellowed an order. Half a dozen men ran into the building. 'Disarm this native, escort him to a cell. If he gives you any trouble, show him who's in charge of his country now.'

Chapter Twenty-three

Basra, Friday 7th January 1916

'Who is that man Reverend Butler and Maud are talking to in the garden?' Theo asked Mrs Butler when he and Dr Picard arrived at the mission for lunch.

'Major Brooke from HQ. He came to tell Maud he's finalised the paperwork for her widow's pension and the annuity Major Mason arranged for her. Apparently the Brooke family are business acquaintances of Dr Mason's father. After Major Brooke visited Maud last week he telegraphed Dr Mason and offered to put her affairs in order.'

'That was good of him.' Theo watched Major Brooke clasp Maud's hand and kept his suspicions about the major's motives to himself. 'I trust Maud has been left well provided for.'

Reverend Butler left Maud and the major and entered the dining room through the French windows. 'Sorry, my dear,' he apologised to his wife, 'I couldn't persuade Major Brooke to stay for lunch as he has a meeting at HQ. As for Maud, Theo, she is now an extremely wealthy lady. I was aware Major Mason had independent means, but I didn't realise the extent of his family's wealth.'

'Major Brooke apprised you of Maud's financial affairs, Reverend?' Theo was surprised.

'Maud asked me to sit with them while the major explained the details. Like all women she's incapable of understanding simple accounts.' Reverend Butler took his place at the head of the table.

'Sorry I'm late, but my lesson on Greek mythology overran.' Angela rushed in.

'Your pupils still want Troy to win the Trojan War?' Theo teased her.

'They can't understand why a war was named after the losing side.'

'Go on, admit it, you wanted the Trojans to win too when you first read the Iliad.'

'You have to concede, Troy is a more romantic name than Sparta.'

'Romantic maybe, but hardly moral, especially when you consider the city state produced men like Paris who stole another man's wife.' Theo took his chair between the Reverend and Dr Picard.

'Morality seems to have bypassed most of Greek myths.'

'May I suggest because they were penned before the Christian era, Angela.' The Reverend folded his hands together. 'Grace.'

Dr Picard, Mrs Butler, and Theo rose to their feet. Angela remained standing behind her chair and bowed her head.

'Thank you, Lord, for the food we are about to eat and all your blessings. Amen.'

Grateful to the reverend for keeping the lunchtime grace short, Angela picked up the tray that had been set up for Maud on the sideboard and began filling the water glass and soup bowl. 'I'll take this to Maud.'

'Tell her we're looking forward to her joining us at meals as soon as she feels up to it.' Mrs Butler passed the bread plate down the table.

'You heard anything interesting at the hospital?' Reverend Butler asked Theo and Dr Picard.

'Like what?' Theo helped himself to bread.

'Like something's happening upriver?'

Angela froze.

'Not that we've heard. In fact Sister Margaret observed this morning that given the lack of new casualties the fighting appears to have stopped,' Dr Picard observed.

'I called in the Basra Club this morning to put up notices about our chess club for officers. The steward informed me that one of the subalterns from HQ let slip that hostilities have broken out between the Turks and the British upriver. In fact he...' the Reverend started nervously when Angela dropped the tray. It shattered in a welter of cracked wood, broken glass, shards of porcelain and rivulets of soup and water.

'Sit down before you fall down.' Theo grabbed Angela by the shoulders and led her to her chair.

'I'm sorry. I didn't think,' Reverend Butler blurted apologetically. 'But even if the subaltern and steward are right, and hostilities have broken out, the fighting can't possibly be anywhere near Kut. Besides, the account's probably an exaggeration based on the actions of a few marauding Arabs who decided to attack the British at Ali

Gharbi...' Reverend Butler faltered. Even he realised the more he said, the less credible he sounded.

'Please, let me do that,' Angela said to the maid, who'd brought in a bucket and cloths to clear the mess.

'I wouldn't hear of it, my dear.' Mrs Butler patted Angela's hand. 'Don't worry about Maud. I'll take in her tray.'

Theo checked Angela's pulse. 'You need to lie down.'

'No, I have to teach...'

'I'll take your class this afternoon. It's not their day for Bible studies but timetables should never be too rigid.' Mrs Butler went to the sideboard and arranged another tray. 'Go with your brother, dear. I'll send you in some soup.'

'Please don't. I'm not an invalid.'

'A sandwich and some water then.'

'Come on, sis.' Theo helped Angela to her feet.

'No, really, I'm fine,' Angela protested.

'We can see how fine you are by your chalk-white cheeks. No more arguing, you're going to lie down.' Theo propelled his sister into the hall.

'I can walk without supervision, please eat your lunch,' she pleaded.

'Not until I see you on your bed.' Theo watched her lie down before returning to the dining room where Reverend Butler was holding forth on the steward of the Basra Club's predictions on how long it would take to relieve Kut.

'Everyone's agreed it has to be days rather than weeks. So many troops are being shipped in from the Western Front and India they'll overcome the

Turks by sheer weight of numbers. As you've seen first-hand,' he looked to Dr Picard and Theo, 'the average Turkish soldier is a very poor specimen. Disease-ridden and cowardly.'

'The disease can be put down to poor nutrition, if not outright starvation. As for cowardice, I'm not sure how I'd react if I were subjected to a constant artillery barrage.' Dr Picard leaned back so the maid could clear his soup bowl.

'But you agree the British will soon overcome the Turk and drive them from this land,' Reverend Butler pressed.

'As I have no idea of the conditions upstream I wouldn't like to hazard a guess as to the outcome of this war.'

'The British have never failed to triumph,' Reverend Butler countered.

'For all our sakes, I hope you're right, Reverend.' Bored by the speculative conversation, Dr Picard looked at Theo. 'Given the rumours we'd better return to the hospital and check our stocks of dressings and medicines in preparation for another influx of POWs.'

'I'll be with you as soon as I've finished this meal and checked on Angela.'

'What about pudding, Theo?' Mrs Butler smiled. 'It's your favourite. Madeira with custard.'

'Save me some for later, please, Mrs Butler.'

'I'll make sure the cook sets it aside.'

As he finished his meal, Theo considered Maud's new-found wealth and independence. She'd received rich compensation for the loss of the husband she'd betrayed and who would have divorced her for infidelity had he lived. If Peter

Smythe died tomorrow, all Angela would be left with was a military pension, which she'd lose if she remarried. Unlike John Mason, who'd had independent means, all Peter could leave his widow was the memory of his love – and no one could live on that.

And him? He glanced at Dr Picard. Would that be him thirty years from now? After a lifetime of working for the Mission, Picard had little more than the clothes he stood up in, the goodwill of the patients he'd tended, and the fare back to France. If he didn't last as long as Dr Picard, no doubt the mission would purchase him an 'economy grave' as it had done for his missionary parents when they'd succumbed to disease.

When he left Basra, whether it was tomorrow or years from now, he'd be hard put to scrape the fare back to the USA for both him and Angela if she was widowed – which was a likely prospect if conditions in Kut were anything like as foul as he'd heard.

They'd return to the States as paupers, without a house to live in and no funds for him to buy into a medical practice. Whereas Maud, who'd borne a bastard and treated her husband abominably had been left comfortably off. He and Angela for all their hard work would be left destitute.

He finished his meat and hid as much of the mashed potatoes as he could beneath his knife and fork. 'Please excuse me.'

'Would you like me to send the maid in with coffee?'

'Just for Angela, please, Mrs Butler, I'll have mine at the hospital. I'll be with you in ten minutes, Dr Picard.'

'I'll order the carriage.'

Theo found Angela still lying on her bed staring up at the ceiling.

He pulled a chair up and reached for his pipe. 'Mind if I smoke?'

'You know I don't.'

'In your bedroom?'

'You can open the window when you leave.'

He took his tobacco pouch from his pocket and unclipped it. 'I don't have to ask if you're worried about Peter. Remember what I told you before Nasiriyeh, sis. Peter's a survivor. He'll be fine." He saw no point in upsetting her by relating the rumours he'd heard about conditions in the besieged town.

Her eyes were dark, anguished. 'How can you be so sure?'

'Because I know Peter.'

'So do I, and better than you. It's easy for us to be blasé about what Peter and the others are suffering in Kut from the comfort of this mission and the certainty that Mrs Butler's table will groan with food every mealtime. But the troops in Kut are starving. I've heard they've been reduced to eating mules and horses...'

'The Relief Force will get them out before they die from malnutrition, Angela,' Theo interrupted.

'How can you be so sure?' Her voice rose precariously. 'Even if they break through it will mean more fighting. Peter could be wounded or killed like Harry. Even if he survives the fighting, he could get fever like Major Mason...'

'Or he could be back here with you within a few

291

days. You have to stop worrying about what might never happen, Angela, and start taking care of yourself. If you don't, you'll wear yourself to a shadow and Peter will have no one to come back to. Try to rest.'

'I'm not ill. I can't possibly lie in bed all day and do nothing.'

'Then go and sit in the garden with Maud and enjoy the last few dry days. The rainy season will be upon us before we know it and that will put an end to walks and sitting outside.'

'I suppose I could spend some time with Maud. She asked me to help her find a house she could rent – or possibly even buy.'

'In Basra?'

'Yes.'

'I thought she'd want to go back to England.'

'She's never been there. She was born in India and stayed there with her parents until her father was posted here. I suppose that's why she's reluctant to leave. With John dead, he's all the family she has and until the siege is raised...'

'Stop thinking about Kut, Angela,' Theo lit his pipe and blew a smoke ring at the ceiling. 'When the siege is raised, they'll all be back here. Peter, Maud's father ... all of them.'

'Not all of them, Theo. Not Harry, Stephen Amey and John, and all the others like them who've been buried in an early grave.'

Kut al Amara, Friday 7th January 1916

Peter narrowed his eyes and closed his fists as he

faced John. 'You want me to leave you – all of you, now of all times when you're penned like rats in a trap waiting for the rat-catcher?'

'The point of this mission is to deflect the rat-catcher. The brigadier and Crabbe asked me if you were fit enough.'

'They only asked because they know I'm ill. They want to send me downriver so I can be put out to grass like a lame mule. Don't they?' Peter demanded suspiciously.

'They asked for my opinion because you're the obvious choice for the job. You can find your way around our defences blindfolded at night thanks to your morale-boosting trips to the front lines with Crabbe. You know Major Sandes's defensive avenues better than the back of your hand. You can report on the state of mind of our troops, British and Indian, but most important of all you know Mitkhal. You trust him because Harry trusted him. You know how he thinks and how he'll react under fire.'

'I thought...'

'You'd been chosen because you can't stop coughing and your wounds aren't healing?'

'Frankly, yes.'

'Your cough is one of the reasons that makes you the perfect courier.'

'Because you want to send me to the hospital in Basra?'

'Because the Turks will assume you're infected with tuberculosis and give you a wide berth. We're hoping that, accompanied by Mitkhal, who can do the talking for both of you, and dressed in Arab robes you'll be waved through Turkish lines.'

293

'The brigadier really believes I'm the best man for the job?' Peter still sought reassurance.

'If you were in his position, who would you send?'

'A political officer who speaks fluent Arabic, and understands, thinks and behaves like a Bedouin.'

'Harry's dead and Leachman and Wilson are in Ali Gharbi. You're all we have, Smythe. Will you do it?'

Peter walked away from the window. 'Do I have a choice?'

'Do any of us in this man's war? But that's enough philosophy. Shall we go and tell Crabbe and the brigadier that you've volunteered?'

Crabbe was in the brigadier's office when the corporal who'd been ordered to escort Mitkhal to the Norfolks' stables staggered in with the assistance of two sappers who'd found him unconscious, lying on a dung heap behind the stables. As soon as they'd brought him round he'd asked to be taken to the brigadier's office. Before he finished speaking, Crabbe sent a message to Sergeant Lane, ordering him to meet him at the Norfolks' stables with two dozen armed Dorsets.

Leaving the brigadier to assemble his dispatches, Crabbe sent the injured corporal to the hospital and headed for the stable.

The square thickset sergeant was lounging in the doorway. He snapped to attention when he saw Crabbe. 'This stable has been requisitioned by the Norfolks ... sir. It's been declared off limits to all other regiments.'

'An Arab visited here earlier. A high-ranking

294

emissary of the brigadier who sent him to examine the horses. He was accompanied by a corporal.'

'I don't know anything about any Arab – sir.'

'How long have you been on duty here?'

'Since six this morning – sir.'

'Then you were here.'

'I could have been in the tack room or checking the grain supplies.'

'Who else was on duty here?' Crabbe questioned.

'Perkins and Lamb – sir.'

'Where are they now?'

'I don't know – sir.'

Crabbe stepped up to the sergeant.

The escort of Dorsets arrived and assembled behind him. Sergeant Lane ordered them to present arms. The sergeant retreated into the stable.

'Sergeant Lane. With me.' Crabbe entered the stable.

'Sir, I protest...'

'Protest all you like, Sergeant...' when the sergeant didn't answer, Crabbe pushed his face very close. 'Your name?'

'Pickering, sir.'

'Remember that name, Sergeant Lane.'

'I will, Major Crabbe, sir.'

Crabbe checked the lines of officers' mounts. There were three greys, none of which resembled Dorset or Somerset. 'There were two other greys stabled here a few days ago. Where are they now?'

Pickering stammered, 'I don't know, sir.'

'Sergeant Lane, take twelve men and escort Sergeant Pickering to the brigadier's office. Tell the brigadier I'll be along presently.'

'Sir.'

'I don't know where Colonel Perry took the horses or the Arab, sir...'

'You admit that the Arab and the horses were here?' Crabbe asked.

Sergeant Pickering fell silent as Sergeant Lane and his men closed around him.

Crabbe turned to the remaining men. 'Accompany me to the Norfolks' mess.'

'Pleasure, sir,' a corporal answered.

Private Evans muttered, 'It's lovely watching our betters fall out.'

'One more word from you, Evans, and you'll find yourself in one of the mud huts with iron bars for windows.'

'Yes, Major Crabbe.'

'Move!'

Chapter Twenty-four

Kut al Amara, Friday 7th January 1916

Mitkhal groped slowly into consciousness. Pain sliced through his head when he moved. Something was hanging over his face curtaining his vision. His muscles ached and there was an agonising gnawing in his stomach. He retched and wiped his face. When he drew his hands away they were wet, sticky. He blinked, forced his eyes open and saw that his fingers were covered in blood.

A narrow strip of grey light shone high above his

head, marking the line between wall and ceiling. He was lying on a damp floor, slimed with stinking sewage. He crawled to a corner. Fighting pain he leaned against the sodden mud brick wall.

He remembered Perry ordering a platoon to drag him from the stable. He pictured the thickset, bullnecked sergeant, laughing at his pain, saliva dripping off his chin as he spat at him. The whoops of excitement when the ranks obeyed the order to beat and kick him. The sense of impotence as he attempted to fight off a dozen men single-handed.

He rubbed his eyes, made an effort to focus and take stock of his surroundings. The thin strip of light and the damp suggested he was in a cellar. On the wall opposite was a wooden door heavily studded with massive metal nails. There was a keyhole but no latch. He tried and failed to stand upright, which left him no option but to crawl. It seemed to take forever to reach the door. When he did, he pushed at the base. It was stuck fast.

Exhausted, he turned his back to the door, stretched out his legs and leaned against it. It was dry in comparison to the wall.

He flexed his muscles, explored his damaged body and considered his predicament. He reached inside his abba. He was in luck. They hadn't thought to search him. He pulled out a wooden baton and pressed a concealed button at the base. A slim stiletto blade sprang out. He eased it back into the handle and tucked it inside his gumbaz. He had one surprise in store for whoever opened the door.

Crabbe marched his escort to the Norfolks' mess and halted them.

'Corporal, inside with me. The rest of you, wait here.' He turned to the guard on duty. 'Step aside.'

'Sir, this is the Norfolks' mess...'

'I'm aware of the location. I'm on official business.'

The man stepped aside.

Crabbe walked into the dining room. Colonel Perry was sitting at a table playing bridge with a major and two colonels.

'Major Crabbe,' Perry stared at Crabbe. 'To what do we owe this intrusion?'

'I am here to escort you to HQ, sir.'

'As you see I'm busy.'

'Too busy to answer a summons from the brigadier? He's questioning a Sergeant Pickering from the Norfolks' stables about a pair of grey horses you stabled there.'

'The only horses I stabled with the Norfolks were my own.'

'Sergeant Pickering was under the impression they were Lieutenant Colonel Downe's horses, sir.'

'Lieutenant Colonel Downe is dead,' Perry snapped.

'The brigadier is aware that fact, sir. A representative has arrived from his widow to claim his horses.'

'Those horses were given to me in recompense for my polo ponies, which Downe used in our campaign in the Hammar Marshes.'

Crabbe remembered Harry using Perry's polo

298

ponies to swim in the marshes. He also remembered the horses surviving. 'You have documented evidence to that effect, Colonel Perry?'

'Don't be ridiculous. Gentlemen don't need documented evidence. But then a man of your low antecedents wouldn't realise that.'

'In which case would you please come with me, sir? The horses are missing and the brigadier is anxious to find them.'

'Tell the brigadier I'll be along shortly.'

'The matter is urgent, sir.'

'I said I'll be along presently.'

'Shall I inform the brigadier and General Townshend that you consider a game of bridge more important than military matters, sir?'

'I'm off duty...' Perry hesitated. 'General Townshend?'

Crabbe strayed into the realms of fiction. 'Is overseeing the matter personally, Colonel Perry.' He waited while Perry left his chair. 'After you, Colonel Perry.'

He followed him out of the mess.

Lansing Memorial Mission, Basra, Friday 7th January 1916

'Letter for you, Ma'am Mason.' The maid handed Maud an envelope. She turned it over and glanced at the address on the back.

'I'll leave you to read it and get us some tea.' Angela rose from the garden bench.

'It's from Reggie Brooke so it's hardly personal. He probably forgot to mention some boring bit or other about the annuity. I know I should be more interested in my affairs, but I'd rather sit on an ant hill than look at a column of figures.'

'I don't know about sitting on an ant hill but account books send me to sleep,' Angela agreed. 'My father insisted I study basic bookkeeping so I'd learn to manage my own finances and never spend more money than I had. He needn't have bothered. Growing up as the daughter of missionaries meant I rarely saw a penny that wasn't destined for essentials. Not that I'm complaining. Peter's captain's pay was riches compared to what I was used to living on, but after uniform and mess bills have been paid there's very little surplus to enter into our accounts. It certainly saves worrying about investments we can't afford to make. Would you like cake or biscuits with your tea?'

'Cake would be nice. I saw the cook putting a lemon drizzle out earlier to cool.'

Maud waited until Angela disappeared through the kitchen door before opening the envelope. As she'd expected from Reggie's smiles, winks, and the pressure of his fingers on hers whenever he handed her a document, it wasn't a business letter.

Dear Maud,

Thank you so much for seeing me earlier today. I trust you found the meeting beneficial. If you require any more assistance, I can always be found at 1.00 p.m. on a Monday afternoon in number 6 private room above the Parisienne Ladies' Fashion store.

I look forward to meeting you there, and await such a time as you can make it.

Reginald Brooke (Major)

When Maud re-read the letter she had to concede Reginald was more careful and discreet than his younger brother Geoffrey. When she'd had an affair with Geoffrey in India, he'd thrown caution to the wind. Sending her daily missives protesting his love and doing all he could, short of shouting out his feelings for her publicly, to persuade her to leave John and run off with him. She presumed, given that it was wartime, for as long as the war department would grant him leave.

If Reggie's letter fell into the wrong hands, someone who didn't know any better might assume he was doing no more than offering to help organize her personal affairs. As for the Parisienne Fashion Store, it was managed by a Frenchwoman whose knowledge of France extended only as far as that country's colonies. She'd heard rumours that Madame Odette rented out the rooms above the shop by the hour before she'd moved into the Lansing. After she'd moved, Mrs Butler took care that no scurrilous rumours of any kind were aired in the mission.

She considered her position carefully. Thanks to John's foresight, she was now financially secure, although she felt guilty for taking her husband's money after the cavalier way she'd treated him and her marriage vows.

The world, as the saying went, 'was her oyster'. She had enough money to go wherever she chose, and rent or buy a house. John had made provision for her to withdraw a lump sum from the annuity provided it was used for a house purchase, but there wasn't a single person or place in the world that would welcome her and her bastard.

British military society was small and claustro-phobic but its tentacles reached far, wide, and deep in Britain. No matter how small or remote a village she settled in, she knew that sooner or later rumours about her infidelity and Robin's birth would surface. India was out of the question after her adulterous affairs, affairs that given the constant exchange of army personal between the two posts had become common knowledge in Basra.

'I brought you tea.'

Theo set a tray on the garden table.

'Only two cups, I thought Angela was making it?'

'She was but Major Reid is here. Hostilities have broken out upstream and he wanted Angela to hear the facts first hand.'

'That's good of him.' She made an effort not to sound sarcastic.

'Peter's popular and you know how it is. Officers tend to look out for their brother officers' wives.'

'I remember,' she snapped.

He recalled the gossip in Basra when Charles Reid had dragged Maud back to Basra from India and let the subject drop. 'I called back to get overnight things for myself and Dr Picard. We've decided to sleep in the hospital in case Turkish POW casualties are already on their way downstream.'

'Surely if hostilities have just broken out they'll take at least three or four days to reach here.'

'That depends on where there's been fighting. If the Turks have occupied the marshes and attacked Qurna, wounded could arrive at the Lansing within the next few hours.' He sat next to her on the bench. 'I asked Charles if he'd like to join us but he wanted to talk to Angela privately.'

'He hasn't brought bad news, I hope,' Maud said anxiously.

'No, I checked with him before I took him to Angela. Anyway,' he poured two cups of tea and handed her one. 'I'm glad I have you to myself, there's something I'd like to ask you.'

'If you want me to resume my nursing career in the Lansing, the answer has to be no. Much as I liked nursing and was tempted to try to make a career of it, Mrs Butler is right. I can't risk carrying infection back to my child.'

'I agree.'

'That was a short discussion.'

'On one topic. Angela said you're thinking of renting or buying a property in Basra.'

'Hopefully renting. I don't want to stay here indefinitely.'

'You want to stay until Kut is relieved and your father returns?'

'With everything that's been happening I'm ashamed to say I haven't given my father a thought, other than in my prayers that he'll survive the siege at Kut. Whatever the outcome of the fighting upriver, or for that matter the war, my father will want to continue his military career. He's always enjoyed life in the mess more than domestic life. The one certainty I have is that he won't want to live with me.'

'Then why stay in Basra?'

'Because I have nowhere else to go,' she said simply.

'Surely there must be someone.'

'Why don't you say it, Theo? An old lover who'll take me back? I assure you there's no one, and no English-speaking country that won't have heard the British military gossip about me, apart from possibly New Zealand, South Africa, or Australia. And I don't feel adventurous enough to travel to any of those with a child.'

'There is one other place you could go, Maud. America.'

'I know no one in America.'

'You know me.'

'You want a mistress? I warn you, I'm soiled goods and I have a child in tow.'

'You're also wealthy. A thousand pounds a year wealthy with a military widow's pension to boot.'

'You want my money?'

'I'm offering you marriage and respectability in America in return for your money, Maud.'

'Marriage!' Stunned, she stared at him in disbelief.

'I'm sorry. I've shocked you.'

'You've never evinced the slightest interest in me.'

'This is not a romantic proposal but a business proposition. I never planned to work for the Lansing Memorial. I came to fetch my sister after our parents died. Newly qualified, it took every cent I had to get here. I wasn't in a position to turn down the post of doctor in the Lansing Memorial Hospital when it was offered, and after three years I've just about saved enough for my fare home. It takes money to set up a medical practice in the States. I don't have any, but you do.'

'You want to use my money to buy into a medical practice?'

'And buy or rent a comfortable house for you and your son. What do you say, Maud? I'm a qualified doctor, a hard worker with excellent prospects. I'm prepared to take you and your son on, give you my name and treat both of you with the respect you'd command from everyone in your new status as my wife and child.'

'I've been married. Even taking financial considerations into account it's a great deal more than a business proposition.'

'Ordinarily I'd agree with you.'

'But not in this case?'

'I'm trying to be honest.'

'You've succeeded, Theo. To the point of brutality.'

'You want romance?'

'Not from you.'

'Given your reputation, I think it would be optimistic of you to expect it from anyone, Maud.'

She took a deep breath and kept her temper in check. 'You'd want us to live as man and wife?'

'That would be entirely up to you.'

'You'd want to share my bed?'

'It's what married couples do.'

'Sexual intercourse would be part of our "business arrangement"?'

'I wouldn't force you, if that's what you're asking. If what I've heard is true, you like novelty and adventure in your private life. I have no objection to either because, as it happens, so do I. But I promise you, Maud, I would never rape you or coerce you into doing anything you didn't want to do. However, should you decide to marry me, the one thing – the only thing – I would expect from you is fidelity. I'm not as generous or forbearing as John Mason. If you were unfaithful to me, I'd throw you into the street without a cent. No payment, no insurance, and no annuity for you to draw on. You could live in the gutter for the rest of your life as far as I'm concerned.'

'Thank you for making that perfectly clear.'

'It's my only condition.'

'That and unlimited access to my money.'

'A husband is legally entitled to use his wife's money to maintain his family as he sees fit.'

'Leaving his wife penniless.'

'Leaving his wife a generous allowance for housekeeping and personal expenses.'

'If I marry I will lose my army widow's pension.'

'But not the annuity?' he checked quickly.

She looked him in the eye. 'No, not the annuity.'

'Think about what I said.' He replaced his cup on the tray and reached out to take hers.

'I don't need to think about your offer, Theo.'

'Don't be hasty. We'll talk again at the end of the month. If you refuse me, then I promise I'll never mention the subject again.'

Chapter Twenty-five

Kut al Amara, Friday 7th January 1916

Crabbe paced uneasily outside the brigadier's office. He listened hard but the silence inside was absolute. Resisting the impulse to knock on the door, he pushed his hands deep into his trouser pockets and walked to the east end of the corridor.

Sergeant Lane entered the building.

Crabbe beckoned to him and led him past the office doors to a secluded alcove. 'Has Pickering told you where they've taken Mitkhal or the horses?'

'He's refusing to talk, sir. Going by the amount of blood on him, he's been involved in a ruckus but he wouldn't say whether it was with a horse or a man. You don't think he'd kill Lieutenant Colonel Downe's orderly or his horses do you, sir? I've seen the horses. They're magnificent specimens. It would be a crying shame to slaughter them.'

'At the moment we don't know anything, other than the horses and Lieutenant Colonel Downe's orderly are missing.'

The door to the brigadier's office opened. His adjutant appeared. 'Major Crabbe?'

'Wait here, sergeant.' Crabbe marched into the office.

Colonel Perry was standing in front of the brigadier's desk. The brigadier was sitting back in his chair watching him.

'Thank you for joining us, Major Crabbe.'

'Sir.'

'I understand you have the duty sergeant from the Norfolks' stable under guard?'

'In the Dorsets' guard house, sir.'

'Interrogate him using whatever methods you deem fit and necessary to ascertain the whereabouts of Lieutenant Colonel Downe's orderly and his horses.'

'Yes, sir.'

'Your orders.' The brigadier handed him a sheaf of forms. 'These give you access to every building and authorize you to conduct a thorough search of the town and the environs. The moment the orderly or the horses are found inform me.'

'Yes, sir.'

'Do you have any suggestions as to which quarter Major Crabbe should commence his search, Colonel Perry?'

'None. As I have repeatedly told you, sir, I have no idea as to the location of the horses or the orderly.'

'You have no thoughts whatsoever on where they might be?' the brigadier pressed.

'As I have already said, sir, I stabled the horses with the Norfolks and entrusted them to the care of the duty sergeant. I last saw them two days ago. They were tethered to the line of officers' mounts and in reasonable condition considering the reduced livestock rations.'

'Mitkhal?' Crabbe demanded.

'I haven't seen Downe's Arab in months.'

'Months?' Crabbe queried.

'At least a month, maybe two before the battle of Ctesiphon.'

The brigadier moved in his chair. 'Ensure the men search meticulously, Crabbe. Start in the stables and work out. Keep me posted.'

'Sir.' Crabbe left the office and closed the door behind him. He found Sergeant Lane in the street outside, smoking. The moment the man saw him he dropped his cigarette, ground the stub to dust beneath his boot, and snapped to attention.

'I need volunteers for search parties. Two platoons would be good, four better. You've left Sergeant Pickering in the Dorsets' guard house?'

'Yes, sir.'

'Meet me there as soon as you've organised the search parties. Tell them to begin with the stables. When they've finished they are to wait there for a supervising officer to arrive.'

'Sir.'

Ali Gharbi, Friday 7th January 1916

Tom was bored, restless and tired. He'd been kept awake most of the night – not by the intermittent boom of the guns which he'd learned to ignore on the Western Front – but by the thought of wounded men lying neglected and unattended upriver.

After breakfast he carried a camp chair outside his tent which seemed ridiculously large since Boris and Tim had left, and sat, scanning an

309

ancient copy of the *Westminster Gazette*. He turned the pages, read the first paragraph of a short story and realised he hadn't absorbed a single word.

He looked around. Sappers and sepoys were moving in and around the camp in every direction; hauling boxes of tinned beef and ammunition into and out of the supply tents. Clerks were filling out dockets clipped to boards. Messengers were delivering yellow envelopes to the brigade offices, envelopes he presumed held communiqués that had arrived over the wireless. Despite the bustle he couldn't help feeling that the men were only going through the motions, trying to look busy because it was preferable to sitting around thinking about what was happening upriver.

'Sahib?' Sami ran towards him. 'Boat coming in, Sahib.'

Tom rose to his feet. Inertia had exhausted him more than a twenty-four hour surgical shift in a French field hospital. 'Wounded from upriver?'

'No, Sahib. Fresh troops from downriver and France. I have seen many bearers on board I know.'

'You're sure nothing is coming down from upriver?' Tom wondered what was holding up the wounded. Because one thing he was certain of was that gunfire and shelling generated catastrophic injuries.

'Nothing, Sahib. If you don't need me I'll go to meet the boat. Sahib Downe and Adjabi might be on board.'

'They might at that, Sami. I'll walk to the river with you as I've nothing better to do.'

When they reached the bank, Tom instinctively

310

looked upstream, but the only signs of life were the flocks of wild geese, grouse, and ducks that flew upwards, filling the air when they heard the noise of the steamer. He watched the paddle boat wend its way upriver. The upper decks were crowded with officers, the lower with ranks. He spotted Michael in the prow. It wasn't difficult. He was the only man in mufti. He went to meet his cousin as he walked down the gangplank.

'Good journey?' he asked.

'Strange journey. There isn't a tree, bush, blade of grass, or weed between here and Amara.'

'I noticed.'

'What do the locals and wildlife live on?'

'Fish?' Tom suggested. 'It's good to have you here.'

'I wish I could say it's good to be here.' Michael studied the shoreline. 'They told me Qurna was the Garden of Eden. I take it this is the wilderness?'

'Very possibly.'

'According to the wireless, fighting has broken out upstream.'

'We heard the guns. They've been firing most of the night.'

A man ran out of the wireless room along the deck of the steamer. He was shouting. 'All medical personnel ordered upriver.'

'Sami...' Tom saw his bearer running back towards his tent.

'I am collecting your things, Sahib,' Sami shouted.

'If there's action upstream, that's where I'm going.' Michael saw Daoud leading the horses

311

back on board and waved to Adjabi. 'Put my kit back in the hold, we're staying on board.'

'But I haven't seen Sami, Sahib.'

'You soon will. Find him and give him a hand to haul my things on board.' Tom stepped on to the gangplank. 'The fact they're looking for medics doesn't bode well. I wish they'd let me move out with the main force.'

'They're letting you move out now when you're rested.'

'Rested?' Tom repeated. 'You know the worst things about war. Resting, waiting, and boredom. Sometimes I wish the generals would push everyone harder. That way whatever's coming will come sooner and we can just put an end to it and go home.'

Kut al Amara, Friday 7th January 1916

Crabbe went directly from HQ to the General Hospital.

'Mason or Smythe around?' he asked Knight, who was pulling a bullet out of the first in a queue of sniper victims.

'Operating,' Knight glared at his patient. 'Move again, private, and I'll put you on a charge.'

'You hurt me, sir.'

'Hurt? You'll know the meaning of "hurt" if you move again. Sit still, that's an order.'

'Yes, sir.' The man grimaced as Knight continued to probe his arm with a scalpel.

'You need a medical man?' Knight asked Crabbe.

'I need advice from a medical man and I need to find Smythe. I've a job for him.'

Knight concentrated, frowned, ignored his patient's scream and finally yanked out the bullet. 'Clean up this wound, Matthews. I'm taking a five-minute break. I'll be outside if you need me.'

Crabbe opened the door, filched a pack of cigarettes from his pocket and offered Knight one. 'Have you heard Mitkhal's disappeared?'

'How the hell can he disappear when we're hemmed in on all sides?'

'Brigadier's convinced Perry arranged it. Harry's horses are missing too.'

'When you say the brigadier's convinced Perry had something to do with it, you mean you convinced the brigadier Perry had a hand in it.' Knight took a cigarette and pushed it into his mouth.

'The brigadier didn't take much convincing.'

'Has anyone tackled Perry?'

'He's with the brigadier now.' Crabbe struck a Lucifer and lit their cigarettes. 'Perry's playing the "I know nothing" card. He insists he placed the horses in the care of the duty sergeant in the Norfolks' stables, and hasn't checked them in two days.'

'And Mitkhal?'

'Perry says he hasn't seen him in months.'

'You believe him?' Dizzy from the effect of smoke in his lungs, Knight leaned against the wall.

'No.'

'Tried beating the truth out of him?'

'I'd have no compunction but the brigadier has.

Perry's a dunderhead but unfortunately a senior dunderhead. However, we have the duty sergeant in custody.'

'So,' Knight gave a grim smile. 'You intend to beat Mitkhal and the horses' whereabouts out of him.'

'He prides himself on being strong and silent.'

'Hence the advice from a medical officer. You want hints on how to persuade him?'

'He was covered in blood when we found him. There's no way of knowing whether it's the horses or Mitkhal's, but either way time is of the essence.'

'In that case it's just as well John's in surgery.'

Crabbe gave Knight a quizzical look.

'He has reservations about using torture to glean information.'

'You don't?'

'Depends on the cause.' Knight pushed open the door. 'Matthews, send Gagan out here. Tell him to bring his bag.'

'Who's Gagan?'

'An Indian veterinary who cares for the horses. If you're looking for Smythe you should find him in his quarters. John ordered him to rest in preparation for his little adventure.'

Crabbe found Peter playing chess with Alf Grace in the Dorsets' mess. As both were off duty they volunteered to supervise the search teams and set off for the Norfolks' stables. He took Gagan and met Sergeant Lane outside the Dorsets' guard house.

'Captain Smythe and Lieutenant Grace are

supervising the search around the stables,' Crabbe informed Lane.

'I mustered four platoons, sir and ordered three to the Norfolks' stables. I told them to send a runner if they find anything.'

'Good, man.' Crabbe nodded. 'Follow me.'

He led the way into the small courtyard that fronted the warehouse they'd requisitioned as a temporary prison. Two guards were stationed at the door of a single-storey mud brick building.

'Sergeant Lane, Gagan, inside with me. The rest of you, remain here.'

The guard opened the door and Crabbe stepped inside.

'Evans, in the absence of anyone senior, you're ranking private. Platoon at ease. If anyone arrives, alert me immediately.' Lane followed Crabbe.

The interior of the building was dark, gloomy. The only light came from a small barred un-glazed window that looked out on the courtyard wall.

A corporal and a private were sitting at a table cleaning their guns. They jumped to attention when they saw Crabbe.

'I'm here to interrogate the prisoner.'

The corporal picked up the keys from the table and unlocked the door.

Crabbe entered the cell with Gagan and Sergeant Lane.

'You'll need this, sir.' The corporal handed Crabbe an oil lamp.

'Lock the door behind us. Ignore any noises and don't let anyone in.'

'Sir.'

The door closed with a thud behind them. The bolts grated home. Crabbe examined the cell. Barely six-foot-square, a two-foot-wide wood plank ran the full length of the wall behind the door. As a grey army blanket was folded on it, he assumed it did duty as a bed. Another shelf a foot long and barely half a foot wide had been nailed above a bucket in the opposite corner.

Crabbe handed Sergeant Lane the oil lamp, took a roughly drawn map of Kut from his pocket, held it up and faced the occupant.

Pickering rose slowly from the bed board. His wrists were locked in handcuffs, his ankles in chains.

'He was reluctant to accompany us here, sir,' Sergeant Lane said by way of an explanation.

'So I see, Sergeant. Do you have anything to tell us, Pickering?'

'About what, sir?' The prisoner coughed, cleared his throat and spat a gob of phlegm, blood, and a tooth into the pail.

'Can you look at this map and pinpoint the location of Lieutenant Colonel Downe's orderly, or his horses?'

'No, sir.'

'Not even if I tell you that Colonel Perry is speaking to the brigadier at this moment?'

'No, sir.'

'This is the last time I will ask you. Sergeant Pickering. Do you know the location of the horses or the Arab orderly who came looking for them?'

'No, sir.'

'Time to get out your instruments, Gagan.'

The Indian lifted his bag on to the bed shelf

and opened it. Sergeant Lane set the lamp down next to it. Gagan lifted out one glittering, gleaming metal tool after another. Crabbe studied them before picking one up. He held it in front of the prisoner.

'Do know what these are?'

'No, sir.'

You don't know very much do you?'

'No, sir.'

'They're castrating irons. Sergeant Lane, would you please assist the prisoner to remove his trousers?'

Chapter Twenty-six

Sheikh Saad, Friday 7th January 1916

'Dear God!' Tom stood at the rail of the steamer and stared at the bank. From the edge of the sluggish, corpse- and debris-ridden muddy waters, to the horizon, the ground was carpeted with filthy, blood-stained men. More unpalatable even than the stench were the cries of the dying and wounded. The few men capable of kneeling were ministering to those lying prone. Driven by thirst some had crawled to the river. They were balanced, leaning over the bank, lowering in water bottles by their straps in an attempt to fill them. Given the increased number of floating corpses in the vicinity it was a dangerous exercise.

Streams of men wearing soiled and bloody field

dressings were staggering in from the north-west to join the hellish scene. Crude wooden springless carts juddered, shuddered, and bumped over the rough terrain among them, every movement eliciting screams from the cargo heaped indiscriminately on the bare metal grids that floored the vehicles. In their wake lay a trail of broken men who'd thrown themselves out of the carts because they could no longer stand the pain from the jolts.

Some lay where they landed, others were crawling riverwards on their hands and knees. Behind them the walking wounded limped in using their rifles as crutches. Others leaned on their comrades, the fittest propping up those in a worse state.

'The guns are firing. The battle must still be raging.' Michael felt as though he was watching a real-life illustration of Dante's *Inferno*.

'I thought nothing could be worse than the Western Front. I was wrong.' A short dark-haired man joined Tom and Michael at the rail. He turned to Tom. 'You're the other one.'

'The other what?' Tom couldn't tear his gaze away from the bank where he was already assessing the condition of the nearest men.

'The other doctor.'

'There are only two of us on board?' Tom was incredulous. 'They were calling for medics.'

'Two doctors, the rest are stretcher-bearers and army-trained field medics.'

Tom shouted for his bearer. Sami and Adjabi came running. Tom barked orders. 'Round up all the bearers on board. Send them to the hold. Tell them to find the hospital tents. Carry them on to the bank, clear an area to erect them, and put up the Red Cross flags. Get my bag. I'll need it the moment we berth. Check the medical supplies and see they're ferried to the tents. When that's done, both of you find me. It's time to train you as medical orderlies.

'What can I do?' Michael asked.

'Take charge of the non-medical personnel. Tell them to distribute whatever comfort they can, especially water. Preferably clean, not river, although I doubt the water we're carrying will last long given the number of wounded. If there's a field kitchen on board, set it up. If another boat comes in and we've enough manpower, detail someone to collect ID tags and bury the corpses, but for the moment, insist everyone forgets the dead and dying and concentrate on the living who stand a chance.'

Michael was horrified. 'I'm not qualified to decide who should live.'

'Do you think I am?' Tom sank his head in his hands. When he looked up his eyes were cold, hard. 'Now I understand why John's letters seemed odd. It's bad enough waging war when there are medical facilities. When there aren't...'

The ship's engine cut out. The gangplank went down. Tom and the dark-haired doctor ran down from the deck and disappeared into the seething mass of humanity.

Daoud joined Michael. 'Permission to help with the hospital tents, sir.'

Michael nodded.

'Beg your pardon, sir.' A private from the Hampshire's accosted Michael the moment be stepped on firm ground.

'You don't have to call me sir. I'm a civilian.'

'Then what you doing here, Mr Civilian?' A private lurched towards them. Blood seeped from a bandage covering one eye and most of his forehead. His remaining eye glared balefully at Michael. For the first time Michael sensed what it would be like to face troops trained to hate enough to kill.

'I'm a war correspondent.'

'Scribbler,' the man said scornfully.

'Drink?' Michael took his water bottle from his pack and offered it to the man.

He snatched it from Michael's hands, unscrewed the top, and gulped the water.

'I'm Michael Downe. We've only just arrived,' he indicated the steamer, 'but there are doctors with us.' He didn't dare mention how few.

'Do you know where the field ambulances are, sir?' the private who'd first spoken to him asked. 'We – that is those of us who can walk. We've been looking all night.'

'The hospital tents are going up now. Looks like someone's thought of food,' he added when he saw half a dozen bearers carrying crates of bully beef. 'Private...?'

'Locke, sir.'

'If you make your way to where they're pitching the hospital tent, someone should see to you.'

'Thank you, sir, but there are a lot worse off than me, so if it's all the same to you I think I'll rest here for a bit. Don't suppose you've anything to eat on you? It's just that none of us have eaten anything since yesterday morning.'

Michael dug in his pocket and came up with half a bag of crackers left over from his last meal. 'That's all I have, but there should be more as soon as they sort out the kitchen.'

'Thank you, Mr Downe, sir. You're very kind.'

Michael was glad Locke had the sense to push the crackers into his pocket, out of sight of the others. He retrieved his water bottle from the one-eyed private. It was empty. Not knowing what else to do he headed for the field kitchen the Indian bearers were setting up to check if they had drinking water he could distribute.

'There's more than you can see here,' a voice whispered hoarsely up at him.

'Pardon?' Michael looked down on a sergeant wearing the insignia of the Black Watch.

'Good to see you, Downe. Even in mufti.' The man's skin was grey, his eyes beginning to glaze. Blood seeped from his shirt. Michael realised he'd mistaken him for Harry.

'There's close on a thousand Indian sick and wounded behind the village of Sheikh Saad. Poor beggars can't understand what's going on. No hospitals, no food, no care ... not that any of us understand.'

'Where are you wounded?' Michael asked.

'Guts.' The man lifted his shirt, displaying a wide gash and protruding intestines. 'But there's plenty worse off than me.'

The whistle blew on the steamer. Michael saw the crew carrying some of the wounded on board. He remembered what Tom had said. 'Concentrate on the living and those who stand a chance.'

'Sami?' He shouted to Tom's bearer who was

hauling a box of lint down the gangplank. 'Give me a hand over here.'

'You should see to the men...'

'I'm seeing to you. That boat's going downriver. You'll stand a better chance in the hospital in Amara. We'll never relieve Kut if we lose our sergeants.'

Kut al Amara, Friday 7th January 1916

Crabbe left the guardhouse and headed for the stables. Peter was standing on the corner of Number 1 Avenue and Spink Road, the thoroughfare that led to the front lines.

'No luck. You?' Peter shouted when he saw Crabbe approach.

'Where are the platoons?' Crabbe questioned.

'Searching every building on this avenue.'

'Call one in.'

'The stable sergeant talked?'

'For his sake I hope he wasn't lying. I've left Gagan and Sergeant Lane with him in case he suddenly remembers more than he's told us so far.'

'Where are we headed?' Peter struggled to keep pace with Crabbe.

'The cellar of the Norfolks' non-com officers' mess.'

Mitkhal heard footsteps outside the cellar door. He pulled the knife from his gumbaz and flicked the blade. He tensed his muscles and tried to stand.

The gloomy cellar swam around him and the floor rose to meet him. He stumbled and collapsed to the sound of bolts being drawn back on the door.

It creaked open.

'Put that bloody knife away. I'm here to free you, not fight.' Crabbe bent over Mitkhal and grabbed his shoulders. 'Smythe, give me a hand. We need to get him to the hospital.'

'Dear Lord, you're worse than Harry was. Will you please sit still for two minutes so I can stitch this eyebrow?' John pushed Mitkhal back down on to the spare cot in his room.

'I feel odd.'

'You're entitled to after the beating that sergeant gave you.' Crabbe and Peter had stayed while John had examined Mitkhal and dressed his wounds.

'You've a lump the size of a duck egg on your head and you're exhibiting signs of concussion,' John diagnosed.

'Just a lump on my head? Nothing else is broken?' Mitkhal spoke slowly, hesitantly, like a drunk.

'Your spine's bruised, which is why you're having trouble walking, but your limbs are intact. There, finished.' John dropped the instruments he'd used back on the tray. 'If the morphine I gave you isn't working yet, it soon will. Then you'll have no choice but to rest.'

Mitkhal raised himself up on one elbow.

'I said rest...'

'Have you found Harry's horses?'

'No,' Crabbe answered Mitkhal. 'But we have four platoons out looking.'

Mitkhal stared out of the window. 'The sun is setting.'

'Night usually follows day.' John pushed an extra pillow beneath Mitkhal's head.

'The captain won't wait. The boat will leave...'

'We have boats and we have other ways of getting you downstream. First rest...'

'The horses...'

'One thing at a time. Close your eyes...'

'I have to get the horses ... have to ... for Harry ... Harry needs them...'

'Did he say Harry?' Crabbe asked.

'He doesn't know what he's saying. He won't remember much of what happened when he wakes tomorrow. What have you done with the sergeant who beat him?' John checked Mitkhal's pulse.

'Turned him over to the brigadier,' Crabbe replied. 'I don't envy him. The brigadier's convening a court martial.'

'What charge?'

'Attempted murder of a friendly native and ally.'

'You still have search parties out looking for the horses?' John checked.

'And watching Perry, and all the streets and thoroughfares, in case Perry tries to have them moved.'

'Do you think Perry had them killed?'

'I found no trace of their hides among those of the slaughtered mules and horses,' Peter went to the door. 'If you'll excuse me, tomorrow is another day and I want to rise early to carry on searching.'

'Sleep well. Can you spare me a moment?' John asked Crabbe when he went to follow Peter.

'Any time.'

'I heard you took a veterinary with you when you interrogated the sergeant.'

'I did.'

'Strange choice.'

'Not at all. He proved useful except in one respect.'

'What was that?'

'He helped us find Mitkhal but failed to implicate Perry in Mitkhal's beating or the disappearance of the horses. But, that's not to say I won't use him again. I'm still hoping to strike lucky with that man.'

'Don't try too hard, Crabbe. I'm proof that Perry can bear a grudge longer and more viciously than most.'

'That's exactly why I'm determined to see him get his comeuppance. Sleep well, John.'

Furja's house, Basra, Saturday 8th January 1916

Furja sat nursing her son but she was watching her husband. His fever had broken leaving him weaker than her baby. She set Shalan in his cot when she saw Hasan's eye flicker but he fell back comatose, deep in sleep before she'd even settled the child.

She covered Shalan with his baby blanket and went to Hasan. She laid her hand on his forehead. It was cool. As the doctor had promised the fever had abated, but she knew Hasan wouldn't begin to recover until he woke and started eating and drinking again.

'Furja.' Gutne was at the door with Bantu. 'Zabba wants to talk to us. Bring Shalan to my room, Bantu will sit with Hasan and fetch you if there is a change.'

Furja picked up her baby and went into Gutne's quarters where Zabba was talking to Hari and Aza.

'I haven't seen those dolls before,' she smiled at her twin daughters.

'Auntie Zabba gave them to us.' Hari held up hers so Furja could admire it. Aza, who hardly spoke because she was content to allow Hari to do the talking for her, followed suit. 'Lucky girls. You can go out on the terrace to play with them if you want.'

They didn't need a second invitation.

'You may be bringing them up in the town, Furja, but you can see the girls are Bedouin. They hate being confined. Already they love the feel of air on their skin, even in winter. Thank you.' Zabba took the tea Gutne handed her.

'I have no choice but to bring them up in a town, while their father is ill and most of the world wants to hunt us down.'

'That is why I'm here.'

'You've heard something? My father ... the Turks...'

'Abdul sent a message. Your father has let it be known that he is offering a reward to anyone who can tell him your whereabouts.'

326

'How large?' Furja shook her head when Gutne offered her tea.

'A thousand gold English sovereigns.'

Furja set her baby down on the cushions beside her. 'How many people know we're here beside you, Zabba?'

'Two of my servants and all of yours.'

'Your servants?'

'Would die sooner than betray my trust. I trust them with my life. Yours?'

Furja thought for a moment. 'Farik is my father's slave. Bantu belongs to Mitkhal.'

'Bantu never leaves the house,' Gutne pointed out.

'But Farik does.'

'Do you think Farik would betray you?' Zabba asked.

'Not for money. Out of loyalty to my father, perhaps,' Furja murmured. 'Abdul told you about the reward. Did he tell you where my father is?'

'He doesn't know, other than he left the Karun Valley some weeks ago.'

'Is Ali Mansur with him?'

'Abdul didn't mention Ali Mansur.'

Furja left her cushion and walked to the window.

'What do you want to do, Furja?' Gutne asked.

'Find my father and try to reason with him. Ask him to withdraw his reward.'

'Aren't you forgetting that you disobeyed him, and in leaving the husband he chose for you, you've dishonoured him? He could kill you,' Zabba warned.

'He could, but look at us, Zabba. We are living

like hens in a coop too frightened to leave because if the Turks find out Hasan is alive they'll send men to kill him. If the British discover he's alive they'll take him back and make him work for them no matter how ill he is ... and...'

'Your father?' Gutne said what Furja couldn't bring herself to say. 'You shamed your husband and your father when you left Ali Mansur. As Zabba said, they could kill you and not just you, your children and everyone who helped you to leave the tribe. Mitkhal, our baby, and me wouldn't live more than an hour after you, Hasan, and your children were slaughtered.'

Furja's eyes flashed in anger. 'You think I don't know that?'

'The first thing you must do, Furja, is remain calm. There's no sense in curdling your baby's milk.' Zabba sipped her tea. 'The next is to keep Farik here. Tell him you're afraid that the Turks or the British have heard that your husband is alive and you need him here to protect you. Tell him I heard rumours and offered the use of my servants to bring you whatever you need.'

'How long can we stay locked up here?' Furja raged.

'The war will not go on for ever.' Zabba lifted Furja's baby from the cushion and caressed him. 'As for your father, wait and see what he will do when no one takes up his offer of a thousand English sovereigns. He may see sense when he realises his gold cannot buy treachery. Time is on your side, Furja. You may be imprisoned here, but it is a comfortable prison. You have your husband, your children, Gutne, and her family. My

328

advice to you, is don't do anything in haste. Mitkhal will return soon. Talk to him. He may have a better plan than simply waiting.'

Chapter Twenty-seven

Sheikh Saad, Saturday 8th January 1916

Tom spoke to Michael three times before Michael moved and looked at him through blank, uncomprehending eyes.

'You're exhausted. Go outside and breathe in what passes for fresh air in this part of the world,' Tom ordered.

'I'm no more exhausted than you,' Michael protested.

'I'm accustomed to working long shifts in a field hospital. You're not.'

'How do you stand it?' Michael looked around the hospital tent. Men's bodies carpeted the entire canvas floor with barely a footstep width between them. A few were mercifully silent. Most were not. Their cries of pain and pleas for water, food, and attention rose, an ever-heightening crescendo he was finding unbearable.

Tom shrugged. 'You get used to it.'

'I'll never get used to it.' Michael looked down at the man he'd been trying to drip-feed from a water bottle. His blackened head had lolled limply to one side.

'He's dead,' Tom declared. 'Stretcher-bearer!'

He turned back to Michael. 'You're not helping anyone the state you're in. Go, clear your head. It's started raining again, that should wake you up.'

Michael rose slowly. Long hours spent crouching over bodies on the floor had played havoc with his thigh muscles.

Stepping gingerly between bodies, he headed for the tent opening, passing Sami and Adjabi who were filling water bottles from a tank they'd brought off the ship. Daoud was handing the bottles out to bearers who were taking them to the patients.

'If anyone wants me I'll be outside, Adjabi, I won't be far.'

'Can I get you anything, Sahib?'

The irony of his bearer's question wasn't lost on Michael. In the middle of chaos where there wasn't even enough drinking water for the dying, his bearer was still a loyal, dutiful servant.

There was nothing he could do other than play the role of considerate employer. 'Nothing, thank you, Adjabi. I'll be back soon.' He went outside and stepped to the side of the tent, out of the path of the stretcher-bearers who were ferrying men in and corpses out.

He gazed at the river. Behind the slanting masts of the native mahailas and the smoking stacks of the transport steamers, snow crusted the distant peaks of the Pusht-i-Kuh. The rays of the dying sun had tinged it a beautiful pale pink, the colour of the petals of his mother's favourite rose in the gardens at Clyneswood. Although his mouth was as dry as a tinderbox he reached for his cigarettes from force of habit and lit one. Drawing on it, he turned left and walked towards the lines of braying mules, spitting camels and ammunition dumps running parallel to the river.

Behind them a large square had been marked out with sticks and string. Pockmarked with holes, six feet by two, it was a giant version of the silverware drawers in the butler's pantry at home. He walked to the edge of the first hole and looked down.

A corpse wrapped head to toe in a concealing grey army blanket lay in the bottom. Misted with light, silvery raindrops, it reminded Michael of an Egyptian mummy. Pinned to the front was a jagged-edged page torn from a notebook. He crouched down and read the scrawled name:

Captain Tim Levitt, 6th Indian Cavalry.

Outside the cordoned off area was a pile of rough planking torn from packing cases. Two sepoys were sitting alongside it, hammering the lathes into rough crosses. When they'd finished one, they handed them to a British corporal who been given the task of painting names on the rough memorials.

Michael offered him and the sepoys cigarettes.

'If you're here for the service...' the corporal noted Michael's civilian clothes and added, 'sir, the padre won't be along for an hour or two. We've a bit of work to do before he can start.'

'I'm taking a break from the hospital.' Michael sat on the ground beside the corporal and leaned against a packing case that hadn't yet been torn apart.

He turned aside from the sight of a fatigue party making its way towards them with a stretcher heaped with three copses and looked back at Tim Levitt's remains.

'They're not letting up, are they?' the corporal said to no one in particular.

Shells were bursting on the sunset-streaked horizon, their crimson, opal, and violet lights mingling with the dying shades of the day. The sharp staccato of shrapnel cracked against the deep boom of the guns in a noisy symphony that reminded Michael of childhood fireworks.

'Friend of yours, sir?' The corporal indicated Tim's grave.

'No. Came over in the boat with a cavalry officer from the same regiment, I just hope he's not dead too.'

'What's his name and rank, sir?'

'Captain Boris Bell, 6th cavalry.'

The corporal referred to his list. 'No one of that name among these dead, sir. This the first time you've seen battlefield graves?'

'You can tell?'

'There's an expression a man wears when he looks at the last resting place of men he was talking to and joking with only a few hours before. I call it "the how long will it be before I'm in a hole like that" look.'

'It's that obvious?'

'You know what they say?'

Michael sensed what was coming but he asked anyway. 'What?'

'War is a much overrated pastime.'

'Corporal?' One of the sepoys pointed to a

stream of wounded, pouring towards them. Darkness was falling and the pale stark faces of the injured were thrown into sharp relief by the lamps they carried.

'The living need us, more than these dead. Round up as many able-bodied sepoys as you can find,' the corporal ordered the Indians.

Michael had never possessed any artistic talent. He'd never wished for any until that moment but he longed to capture the numb, defeated faces of the men stumbling into the grossly inadequate medical facility.

The travelling desk his editor had given him was with the rest of his kit – wherever Adjabi had stowed it for safekeeping. He reached inside his pocket and pulled out his small notebook. A stub of pencil was tucked between its pages. There were many who needed help, much for him to do, but he had to capture the moment and what he was seeing and feeling before his memory was overwhelmed by another influx of broken men.

He moved close to a lantern and started writing.

Kut al Amara, early hours Sunday 9th January 1916

Crabbe could almost taste the whisky – good Scotch whisky. He watched the orderly uncork the bottle and lift it above the tray of glittering glasses then someone started banging. He looked down the table and prepared to chastise the subaltern who dared to disturb the hallowed moment, but the scene faded and the banging continued.

He woke with a start and opened his eyes. The room was in darkness.

'Major Crabbe, sir?'

He stumbled from his bed only just managing to regain his balance when his foot became tangled in the sheet. He wrenched open his door. The duty orderly was outside. He handed him a candle.

'Brigadier's called a meeting, sir.'

'At,' Crabbe turned and squinted at the window. 'Dawn's not broken.'

'It's coming up to four o'clock, sir.'

'Tell the brigadier I'll be down as soon as I've dressed.' Crabbe shouted for his bearer before closing the door. The man came running. Crabbe went to the washstand, tipped water from the jug into the basin and splashed his face. He ran his hands over his stubble. He needed to shave but as the brigadier had decided to call a meeting in the middle of the night he could damn well take him as he was.

When he felt more human he began to dress.

'You know what this is about?' he asked his bearer.

'The relief column or so I've heard, Sahib.'

'General Aylmer's close?'

'All I know is the wireless has been red-hot crackling all night and messengers have been running to and from the wireless room to HQ, Sahib.'

'So something must be happening.'

'I don't know if it's good or bad something, Sahib, but it's certainly something.'

When his bearer approved of his appearance,

Crabbe ran down the stairs and crossed the street to HQ. He knocked at the brigadier's office door. It was opened by an adjutant. The brigadier dismissed his aide, and asked Crabbe to close the door.

'My bearer said the wireless has been red hot. Are we about to be relieved, sir?'

'Not soon.' The brigadier was pale from lack of sleep. 'The Turks are in retreat downriver but the battle at Sheikh Saad was an absolute bloody shambles. Over 4,000 casualties and 417 dead.'

'Good God.'

'He's not being very good to us at the moment, Crabbe. More than 90 British officers have been wounded, and the medical facilities are non-existent. Most of the hospital ships are still at sea. From the dispatch it appears facilities for our casualties were on a par with the Crimea, which proves the criminal inefficiency of the India Office. Sooner this sideshow is put under the auspices of the War Office in London the better. Problem as I see it, is General Aylmer pushed his men forward before they were ready. Between me and you,' the brigadier lowered his voice although there was no one else in the room, 'Townshend telegraphed that we only had supplies to last us until mid-January.'

'We've all advised him to search the town for foodstuffs. You only have to look at the locals, sir, to see they're eating better than our men.'

'After hearing General Aylmer's and General Younghusband's casualty figures, Townshend's finally capitulated. A search of all local housing is to be conducted at 0700 hours this morning.

Colonel Perry's been ordered to oversee the one in the native areas between second and third avenues. I'd appreciate it if you'd keep an eye.'

'I will, sir.'

'What's happening with Downe's orderly?'

'Mason is caring for him in his own quarters.'

'Will he be fit to leave within twenty-four hours?'

'I'll let you know Mason's verdict, sir.'

'Townshend wants a report on the Turkish positions around Kut. Initial estimates from officers in the front line suggests their strength is around 11,000 fighting men. Townshend is convinced if Aylmer pushes through and joins forces with us we can overcome them.'

'Doesn't he realise most of our men and officers are sick and the native troops demoralised and half-starved, and that's without taking account our Muslim sepoys who are loath to fight brother Muslims.'

'You haven't been to many of Townshend's Durbars, have you, Crabbe?'

'I haven't been to any, sir.'

'Should you be invited, remember the general is not an admirer of free and candid speech. When I left, he was berating Aylmer and Younghusband for wasting their troops by sending them across open ground in the face of a full Turkish fusillade. We've paid a high price for the few miles of country the Relief Force has taken. A price that needn't have been paid if we'd ransacked Kut for foodstuffs and stockpiled them before the siege was raised. As it is, I'm afraid this search is too little, too late.'

'I'll check the measures Colonel Perry has ordered, and collate the reports the regiment has made on Turkish troop dispositions facing the Dorset lines, sir.'

'Thank you. I know you'll be busy but don't forget to inform me if Harry Downe's orderly is fit enough to go downstream tonight. If he is, we'll need to find a boat and brief men to create a diversion. Should we be in a position to go ahead, you'd better send Smythe to me. One good thing about going downriver is he can always drop the dispatches into the water if the Turks ambush the boat. I hate the thought of sending out a sick man, Crabbe, but if we're going to be relieved it's imperative that information gets to Aylmer as soon as possible.'

'Yes, sir.' Crabbe went to the door and hesitated.

'Thought of something else, Crabbe?'

'Medical aid and reinforcements for the Relief Force, sir?'

'We've been assured they're being sent upriver.'

'Being sent – not already sent?'

'I'm afraid so.'

'Sufficient field hospitals?'

'We can hope they're on their way.'

'Seasoned troops, or raw recruits in the Relief Force, sir?' Crabbe watched the brigadier's face.

'If it's the latter, Crabbe, I doubt Aylmer and Younghusband will break through. Time perhaps, for us all to start making contingency plans to sit out the rest of this war in a Turkish prison camp.'

Crabbe left the brigadier and closeted himself in

his own office. He summoned the company clerk and two hapless lieutenants who'd drawn night duty and set them to work collating all the reports the Dorsets had made on Turkish troop placements. Leaving them to their task, he went to the mess. Two platoons were standing outside awaiting orders. Inside he saw Colonel Perry and two captains studying plans of the native quarter. He managed to leave the building without Perry spotting him and headed for the hospital.

John and Knight were breakfasting on fish and coarse native flatbread in Knight's alcove.

'Mud fish and sawdust bread?' Knight offered Crabbe a plate.

Crabbe's stomach revolted at the thought. 'Tea would be good if there's any in the pot.'

John poured him a glass.

Crabbe looked at it suspiciously.

'It's what passes for clean here,' John joked.

'Thank you.' Crabbe took it and sat on a stool. 'How's Mitkhal?'

'Asleep, when I left my room. I think I may have overdone the morphine. The problem is the man's the size of an ox. He fought the effects for so long I kept increasing the dose. What's the flap?'

'You've heard?'

'The rumour that wireless didn't stop all night? Hasn't everyone?'

Crabbe looked over his shoulder, checked that no one was within listening distance and passed on the information the brigadier had given him.

John pushed the remains of his breakfast to the

side of his plate. 'I'll check on Mitkhal now.'

'I'll find Smythe.' Crabbe finished his tea.

'And look for Downe's horses,' Knight added. 'I can't see that Arab going without them.'

Chapter Twenty-eight

Kut al Amara, Sunday 9th January 1916

'You're concussed,' John remonstrated with Mitkhal when the Arab staggered from his cot.

'It's not the first time. I'll get over it.' Mitkhal sank back down and held his head in his hands.

'Like Harry, you're adept at ignoring medical advice. You should rest...'

Mitkhal was in no mood to discuss his condition. He interrupted John. 'Harry's horses?'

'Crabbe and Peter have had platoons out all night looking for them.'

'I think I know where they could be.' Mitkhal placed his feet flat on the floor, rose and fought to maintain his balance.

John pulled a chair out from a table. 'I brought you breakfast.' He pointed to a tray. 'Oat cakes made from mule feed and a slice of the mule that would have eaten the feed if we hadn't been hungry enough to eat him. The tea's weak, brewed from twice dried leaves, but I did manage to track down half a spoonful of real sugar.'

'It's good of you to forage for me, Major Mason.' Mitkhal was glad to sit down again.

'The least I could do, and it's John, Mitkhal, now you're no longer attached to the Expeditionary Force. While you eat I'll send a message to Peter and Crabbe asking them to meet us here. They might have some news about the horses.'

Mitkhal studied one of the oatcakes before tentatively biting into it. It had the taste and consistency of river sand. Not wanting to appear unappreciative, he waited for John to leave before pushing the plate aside. He sipped the tea which, sugar aside, was as bad as John had warned. Feeling stronger he went to the travelling washstand, washed his hands and face, and reached for his gumbaz and abba which had been washed by John's bearer. He'd finished dressing and was lacing his boots when John returned with Crabbe and Peter.

Peter didn't bother with pleasantries or enquiries after Mitkhal's health. 'John said you might have an idea where Harry's horses might be?'

'I don't think they'll be far. Have you searched the stable?'

'We've looked in the stable half a dozen times and everywhere in the town. Even the attics, roofs, and cellars,' Peter asserted irritably.

'But not in the right place.' Mitkhal slipped his abba over his gumbaz. 'Shall we go, gentleman?'

'Much as I'd like to join you, unfortunately the Turkish snipers are already at work. There's a queue at the dressing station. You're taking a platoon with you, for protection?' John checked with Crabbe.

'Two,' Crabbe answered.

A corporal had taken over command from Sergeant Pickering in the Norfolks' stables. He, and the two privates who were assisting him, snapped to attention when Crabbe stepped over the stoop followed by Peter and Mitkhal. Peter was careful to leave the stable door open and ordered their armed escort to remain in view of those inside the building.

'We're here to search for Lieutenant Colonel Downe's horses,' Crabbe informed the corporal.

'I received an order from the CO to assist you, sir.'

Peter walked up to the two greys he'd examined the day before and peered closely at them.

'No matter how often you look at those greys you can't turn them into Dorset and Somerset,' Crabbe commented.

'More's the pity,' Peter muttered.

Mitkhal looked for the sack of henna he'd seen the day before. There was no sign of it. He stood in front of the lines of horses and whistled. Two rusty brown horses in the darkest corner of the stable, started neighing and pawing the cobbles.

Mitkhal went to them. Both horses pushed their noses at him, nuzzling his abba as soon as he was within reach. He stroked their noses. 'I'm sorry, I'm not Harry and I have no sugar for you, not this time. But there will be later.'

Peter joined him. 'You knew their coats had been dyed?'

'I saw a sack of henna before the sergeant attacked me. It's a strange thing to keep next to sacks of feed in a stable.'

'Corporal, groom these horses, wash them, and

341

restore them to their original colour,' Crabbe ordered.

'No,' Mitkhal countermanded. 'Not if I'm taking them downstream. In fact we should find the henna and dye Norfolk. She's in the Dorsets' stables?' he checked.

'She is. I'll arrange it,' Peter volunteered.

'I'll take these to join her. They'll be glad to see their old stablemate.' Mitkhal untied Somerset's and Dorset's halters from the rope. 'I'll be happier when these two are in Harry's regimental stables.'

Kut al Amara, early hours Monday 10th January 1916

The rainy season had broken with a vengeance. The heavens had opened and water was sheeting into the Tigris. The sentries squelched as they patrolled the barricades. Most of the trenches were knee deep in water and ankle deep in the "drier" sections. Off-duty troops lying in their berths in the trenches coughed painfully, making sounds the medics feared were symptoms of early-onset pneumonia.

'I have to check the wounded, so I'll leave you here.' John stopped at the entrance to the fort the Dorsets had commandeered which contained an aid station for minor injuries. He extended his hand to Mitkhal. 'You won't forget what I told you about keeping my presence here quiet.'

'No.'

'Good luck with returning the horses to Furja.

Tell her I still carry the keepsake she gave me. The words of the prophet have kept this ferenghi alive so far and that I hope to live to see Harry's children and tell them about him.'

'Take care, Harry's cousin.' Mitkhal gripped John's shoulders.

'We'll take care of one another.' Crabbe waved them on towards the river. He lifted his watch to a sentry's lantern. 'Five minutes to the fusillade. We need to be on the other side of the old boat bridge within ten minutes.'

They continued to move forward, slipping and sliding in the mud. Hampered by his unaccustomed Arab skirts and headdress, Peter tried not to consider what might happen to him if he fell into Turkish hands. He was conscious of the tarpaulin-wrapped dispatches bandaged to his chest, and his fair skin and blue eyes. Then he realised – this was what Harry had faced every time he'd gone out dressed as a native.

'This is as far as we go.' Crabbe herded Mitkhal, Smythe, and the grooms who were leading the horses into a redoubt on the British side of the defences next to the old boat bridge.

'There's the mahaila. Can you see it?' Crabbe pointed. Mitkhal peered into the night. A shell burst overheard. The first of the British barrage. The outline of a native boat gleamed silver in its glare.

'I see it.'

A Turkish gun blasted into life in response to the British fusillade.

'Good luck.' Crabbe gripped Peter's hand, then Mitkhal's.

The guns continued to resound deafeningly around them.

'Go!'

Mitkhal took Dorset's and Norfolk's reins leaving Somerset for Peter. Instinctively ducking although the blasts were behind him, he splashed downstream through the mud.

Basra, Monday 10th January 1916

Colonel Allan examined Charles's leg. 'Stand and drop your stick.'

Charles laid it on the chair he'd been sitting on.

'At attention. At ease. Pick up your stick before you fall down. Walk to the door. Turn. Walk back. Attention again. I've seen enough. Put your trousers on.' He reached for his pen, dipped it in the ink bottle, and made a note on Charles's medical record.

'You're discharging me?' Charles fastened his braces over his shirt.

'The infection you picked up in your wound ran deep. It affected the bones. In my opinion you'll experience weakness there for the rest of your life. That means you'll never be classified A1 fit again. You'll be invalided out.'

'Have you heard what's happening upriver?' Charles interrupted.

'There's no chance of me avoiding hearing what's happening upriver given the way every convalescent officer I examine demands I mark him fit for active duty. But, before you ask, you're most certainly not fit for duty.'

344

'I'm fit enough to go upstream on the General's staff. Nixon's asked to be relieved because of ill-health.'

'Yes, I've heard that too.'

'I've been offered a place by his replacement General Sir Percy Lake.'

'Offered or volunteered?' Allan probed.

'Does it make a difference?'

'When you volunteered you didn't consider that the last thing a CO needs is an unfit officer on his staff?'

'General Lake will need all the men he can get who have experience of the Turk and the terrain. I'll be on Gorringe's staff. He's requisitioned Gerard Leachman's boat, the *Lewis Pelly*. All I'll have to do is sit on board and direct operations.'

'Really?' Colonel Allan raised a sceptical eyebrow, 'and if the Turks shell the *Lewis Pelly* and you end up in the Tigris?'

'Everyone knows the Turks would never shell the staff...'

'Because they're too damned useful to the Turks making a balls-up of British operations from the rear. Yes, I've heard that one too.' Allan shook his head.

Charles finished lacing his boots and sat down. He tried not to allow his relief at being able to take the weight off his leg to show.

'That wound of yours still isn't totally healed. I'll not answer for your health if you take a ducking in the river. Aside from the sewage, it's thick with corpses...'

'All the more reason for me to go upstream. The Relief Force needs every man.'

345

'Only because Command is wasting men on a colossal scale.' Colonel Allan dropped his pen. 'You wouldn't have been put on the discharge list from the hospital if it wasn't for the flood of casualties coming down from the battles of Sheikh Sand and the Wadi. God alone knows how many more slaughters there'll be before we reach Kut. That's if we do. When I think of the conditions the men have described ... being forced to march over open ground to face artillery ... the sick and dying being left in the open because there are no medical facilities, and that's without what the poor starving beggars in Kut are suffering. You're insane for wanting to join them, Reid.'

'I have friends with the Relief Force and in Kut, sir.'

'That's the crux of the problem. We all have friends with both forces, which is why we keep putting up with these bloody awful conditions that are killing more men than the Turks. Your quarters all right?' Allan abruptly changed the subject when he heard footsteps outside the door.

'The quarters are excellent. I'm in Major Chalmers's bungalow with his cousin.'

'I thought his cousin went upstream.'

'Another cousin, sir. Captain Anthony Bell, Boris Bell's brother. You will sign me off as fit for duty, won't you, sir?' Charles pleaded.

'I'll sign you as fit for light duties only and don't try arguing your way out of that one. Take on more than you can cope with and it won't only be your life on the line but the lives of everyone with the Expeditionary Force you come into contact with.' Colonel Allan reached for another form from the piles on his desk. 'If your leg starts acting up don't be too proud to forego the stick for crutches.'

'Yes, sir.' Charles took the papers the colonel handed him. 'Thank you, sir.'

'All the thanks I want is to see you back here in one piece after Kut has been relieved, Reid. Take care of yourself, and get Townshend and his men out.'

'I'll do my best, sir.'

Charles left Allan's office and walked down the corridor. The hospital and the verandas were crowded with a fresh influx of wounded men. Clean, with newly applied dressings they were in better shape than he'd been when he'd arrived in Basra after a hellish journey on a filthy boat packed indiscriminately with wounded and dysentery cases.

'Charlie Reid?' Reggie Brooke walked up to him. 'What on earth are you doing here?'

'What one generally does in a hospital. Getting my wounds seen to.' Charles, John, and Harry had been at school with Reggie Brooke, but he hadn't been a special friend, which probably had something to do with Harry using Reggie's bed as a mortuary for the remains of the reptiles dissected in the biology lab. Reggie had declared war on Harry. He and John had been dragged into the conflict, but to Reggie's annoyance most of the victories had been Harry's.

Charles looked Reggie up and down. 'You appear to be remarkably fit considering where you are.'

'Collating intelligence from the wounded.'

'You're not going upstream?'

'Intelligence, based in HQ.'

'Wangled yourself a cushy number, Brooke? You haven't changed.'

'Neither have you, Charlie. Still playing the hero?'

A nurse came out of a side ward behind them. 'Excuse me, sir.' She tapped Charles's shoulder.

Her accent was Welsh. She was dark-eyed and, from what little he could see of her hair beneath her sister's veil, dark-haired. She was also extremely pretty. He gave her a rare smile. 'Hello, Sister.'

'Are you Major Charles Reid?'

'That depends on who's asking. And you are Sister...'

'Jones, Major.'

'No Christian name?' he prompted hopefully.

'Are you Major Charles Reid?' she repeated impatiently.

'Yes. Who's asking?'

'Major Boris Bell. He heard your name and said you're a friend of his cousin.'

'I am. Major Bell is wounded?'

She capitulated when she saw the look of concern on Charles's face. 'He's just arrived on a transport with the first of the injured from Sheikh Saad via Amara. The doctor's examining him now, but he should be free in ten minutes. If you wait on the veranda, I'll come and get you.'

'Thank you.' Charles turned back to Reginald. 'I would say see you around, Reggie, but I won't if you're staying in HQ.'

'You're going on active service?' Reggie looked

pointedly at Charles's stick.

'We can't all skive in HQ.'

The veranda was crowded. Charles sat on the first free seat he came across. A young lieutenant, bandaged from his waist to his throat, was propped in a wheelchair next to him.

'You caught a packet,' Charles commented.

'Sheikh Saad, sir.'

'I heard it was bloody.'

'It was worse than bloody, sir. I'm with the Leicesters. We lost sixteen officers and 298 rank and file in the first attack.'

Charles pulled his chair closer. 'Tell me about it, Lieutenant...'

'Grove, sir.'

Charles sat back and listened while the young man talked. He could have been describing the battle of Ctesiphon and Charles wondered if anything had changed since he'd been wounded.

Chapter Twenty-nine

Basra Military Hospital, Monday 10th January 1916

Sister Jones stood in the doorway of the veranda. 'You can see Major Bell now, Major Reid.'

'Thank you, Sister. I'm sorry to leave you, Lieutenant Grove. I've enjoyed our talk. I'll call in and see you again tomorrow if I'm not sent upstream.'

Charles left his chair.

'If you are sent upriver, good luck, sir, you'll need it,' Grove called after him.

'You're going to join the Relief Force?' Sister Jones commented.

'I hope to.' Charles couldn't help smiling at her. She was the most attractive woman he'd seen since he'd left England.

'With that leg?'

'I've wangled myself a cushy staff position.'

'With a bath chair for you to sit in and a runner to carry your messages?'

'I'm not that incapacitated,' Charles protested.

'Long John Silver was quicker on a peg leg.' Her smile took the sting from her words. 'Major Bell is on the right at the end of the ward.'

'Thank you. Before you go, would you consider having dinner with me in the Basra Club tonight? I'll book a table. Shall we say eight o'clock?'

'You can say eight o'clock, Major Reid, but I don't make a habit of dining with strange men.'

'I could give you a full biography.'

'Now?'

'I'd be delighted.'

'I'm working.'

'Tonight?'

'I'm dining with a friend.'

'A fellow nurse?'

'That could be construed as a personal question.'

'Please bring your friend. It would be my pleasure to meet her.'

'Or him. You're certain you want to buy us both dinner?'

'It would be my pleasure, whether it's a her or him. Shall I pick you up here?'

'You're very sure of yourself, Major Reid. What if my friend takes a dislike to you?'

'I'll take care to be at my most charming.'

'We'll both meet you at the Basra Club at eight o'clock,' she said decisively.

'The table will be booked under the name of Reid. I'll be waiting.'

'As Major Bell is now. He's in pain and he's exhausted. Five minutes. Not a second more.'

Charles watched her walk away before turning into the ward.

Boris was propped up in bed, looking out of the window.

'I'm your cousin's friend, Charles Reid.' Charles shook Boris's hand.

'Thank you for coming to see me. I heard someone call your name and I thought there couldn't be two Charles Reids in Basra.'

'It was an old schoolboy acquaintance.' Charles made a face. 'HQ Wallah, as we say in the Indian army.'

'It's good of you to wait until the quack finished with me. Do you know if Richard's all right?'

'His name isn't on any of the lists that have come down so far. I know because I read them as soon as they're posted. Your brother Anthony is bunking with me in Richard's bungalow now.'

'I knew he was shipping in from India.'

'I'll tell him you're here.'

'Thank you.' Boris grimaced in pain. 'I won't be happy until I know Richard's made it.'

'Like all Indian officers he knows how to look

after himself,' Charles reassured.

'Before this show I would have said we all did. Be glad you weren't with us. They wasted men. Absolutely wasted them. It was a complete shambles. Townshend's put so much pressure on the brass they had men advancing into Turkish artillery without covering fire. I saw 400 men and sixteen officers go against the Turks. Only one man and one officer made it within ten yards of the Turkish lines, and the officer fell before he reached the Turkish first line.'

'You've heard General Nixon's gone?'

'Ill health someone said – I'd like to believe it's guilty conscience.'

'Sir Percy Lake's taking over.'

'He can't possibly do a worse job.' Boris was bitter.

'I managed to get myself posted on to Gorringe's staff.'

'You're a brave man. Have you any idea what the men think of him?'

'My close friend, John Mason, marched with him across the desert in the Karun campaign.'

'He lived to tell the tale?'

'For a short while.' Charles wondered if he'd ever become accustomed to speaking about his two closest friends in the past tense. 'As to working under Gorringe's command, I have friends in Kut.'

'That's the problem. We all have friends in Kut or with the Expeditionary Force. We fight for our friends and the man next to us, while the Generals treat us as expendable. I've wondered if they even consider us as human.'

'You lost close friends?' Charles guessed.

'The best.'

'How much damage have you done to yourself?' Charles felt a need to change the subject.

'Broke both my legs when my horse went down under me. Dislocated my shoulder and caught a bullet in the sole of my foot crawling back to our lines.'

'So you'll be back up the lines by the end of the week.'

Boris laughed. 'That depends on how desperate Lake is.'

'Major Reid,' Sister Jones stood at the foot of Boris's bed. 'I warned you not to tire my patient. I said five minutes, you've been here fifteen.'

'My apologies, Sister.'

'Visiting hours are between four and five o'clock, Major Reid. You may return tomorrow.'

'Yes, Sister.'

'Don't suppose there's any more of that iced orange juice standing around in a jug anywhere?' Boris asked.

'I'll look.' She faced Charles. 'You still here, Major Reid?'

'I'm going.' He winked at her and limped away feeling brighter than he'd done in months.

Lansing Memorial Mission, Basra, Monday 10th January 1916

Mrs Butler followed Maud into the hall and watched her pin on her hat.

'I wish you'd allow one of us to go with you,

Maud,' she protested.

'No, really, Mrs Butler. You're all so busy, Angela with her teaching and you with your Ladies' Guild meeting. I'm perfectly well and quite capable of visiting a dress shop and picking up a few necessities for myself and Robin.'

'At least take a servant?'

'There's really no need, Mrs Butler. The groom knows where the shop is, the nursemaid is best left with the baby, and I'll probably be an age. I've never been able to make up my mind quickly in a dress shop and I need so much. I've put on so much weight having Robin I haven't a thing that fits me. Now the rainy season is upon us, it will bring the cold weather. I need at least three winter day dresses, besides essentials and things for Robin. While I'm in town I'll take the opportunity to call into Headquarters and see if they have a list of properties suitable for widows to rent. There must be other women in my position who are no longer eligible for military quarters.'

Maud was so used to Mrs Butler protesting that there was no hurry for her to move out of the mission that she was taken aback when she didn't contradict her.

'As you say, dear, there must be other widows. It will be nice for you to have the company of someone in the same position as yourself.'

'Same position as yourself.' The words burned. Maud knew Mrs Butler was aware that she'd been ostracised by the military wives and also that most widows returned to England quickly after their husband had been killed.

'Is that the carriage, dear?' Mrs Butler's voice,

354

as soft and gentle as ever, intruded on Maud's thoughts.

'It is. Thank you so much for allowing me to borrow it along with the groom.'

'Not at all, dear. You've given the nursemaid instructions on caring for Robin?'

'Of course. She's as capable of looking after him as I am. Are you sure there's nothing I can get you from town?'

'Nothing, but thank you for asking, dear. The cook did all the marketing this morning.'

'Then I'll be off.' Maud left the house and climbed into the carriage. 'Parisienne Fashion Store,' she ordered the groom.

Cold, she pulled her mourning cloak closer and lifted the hood. It was Monday afternoon. She'd arrive at the shop earlier than Reginald had stipulated, but she really did need to do some shopping.

She'd spent considerable time mulling over her past and thinking about her future. She recalled a quarrel between her parents when her father had insisted the only course open to her was that of military wife, simply because colonial army life was all she knew.

Much as she hated to agree with him, he was right. The only life she knew was the one she'd been raised in and she'd decided when Reggie Brooke made her an offer of marriage, she'd take it.

Reggie was the same rank as John, and Geoffrey had told her that he and his brother had inherited independent fortunes from their grandfather. There was a family estate in Wiltshire that included a Georgian manor house, built and lavishly furnished with money a Brooke great-grandfather had made from the East India company in the eighteenth century.

The house in Wiltshire would have to wait until after the war. Before then she'd play the dutiful service wife, more loyally and less scandalously than she had with John. Reggie Brooke and his name would give her respectability and a social standing few other wives could ignore. They'd have to invite her to their social functions. To exclude her would be to snub Reggie. Given time she'd live down the memory of her marriage to John and the scandal of her adulterous affairs.

She doubted the Brookes were as wealthy as the Masons but they were an older family. She'd never craved respectability until she'd lost it. But it wasn't too late to regain it. It simply couldn't be.

Pleased with her scheming she looked around. They were almost at the shop. She gathered her bag and umbrella.

'Parisienne Fashion Store, Mrs Mason.'

'Wait here for me.' She alighted from the carriage, and head high entered the shop. To her dismay, her mother's former maid, Harriet Greening, was at the counter with another sergeant's wife, examining bales of brushed cotton.

Maud acknowledged Harriet, 'I trust you are keeping well.'

'I am, Mrs Mason, thank you.'

Maud waited for a reciprocal enquiry as to her health. When none was forthcoming she addressed one of the female Jewish assistants.

'I would like to see your ready-made day dresses, silk suitable for evening gowns, and cotton and muslin for baby nightdresses and napkins. Could you arrange to have them brought up to one of your private rooms?'

'Of course, Mrs Mason. Number five is free. Would you like tea?'

'Not at the moment, thank you. Possibly later.' Maud climbed the stairs, aware of the line of assistants trailing behind her, including one who'd been serving Harriet.

She spent the next half-hour choosing fabric for nightgowns for Robin and silk evening gowns for herself. She picked out two ready-made day dresses and was examining an array of silk stockings and underclothes when she was disturbed by a knock at the door.

'Enter.'

'Enjoying shopping?'

'I am.' She forced a smile. She couldn't help but compare Reggie to her other lovers. He wasn't as good-looking as Geoffrey, or as tall, broad, or handsome as John, or as dashing and exotic as Miguel D'Arbez...

He interrupted her thoughts. 'I've completed my purchases and ordered tea to be served in my room next door. Number six. Would you care to join me?'

'That's uncommonly kind of you, Major. I'll join you as soon as I finish here.'

'I'll order for two.' He closed the door behind him.

Maud picked up the finest – and most expensive – pair of silk stockings. 'I'll take six of these, please, and two Ivania corsets in white, three of these embroidered muslin nightgowns and three embroidered silk petticoats and matching skirt knickers.'

'And the overall you wanted, ma'am?' the girl ventured.

Maud glanced at the half a dozen the assistant had brought for her inspection. 'The casement cloth.' She pointed at random. She could never get excited at the purchase of the mundane. She'd avoided owning an overall until that moment. But as a new mother it was proving necessary to hold her baby on occasion, and as she'd discovered in the ruination of two of her drawn threadwork muslin blouses, babies are messy. 'My driver's waiting outside in the carriage. If you wrap everything, he'll collect the parcels. I'm having tea with the major and I may be some time.'

'Yes, ma'am.' The assistant curtsied. She began to separate Maud's purchases from the discarded pile.

Maud entered the room next door.

Reggie was presiding behind a fully laden tea table crammed with English delicacies: scones, jam, butter, fairy cakes, jumbles, and cinnamon buns as well as chicken and cucumber sandwiches, a pot of tea, and bottle of brandy.

She gave him a wide-eyed smile. 'Thank you, this looks delicious.'

'Doesn't it just. I trust your finances are still in order?'

'They are fine, thank you. The first payments of both the annuity and the pension have arrived in my account, hence the shopping.'

'So you are officially an independent lady.'

'I think I've been that for some time.'

'Sit down.' He patted the sofa beside him. 'Tea or brandy, or both?'

'Both, please.'

He poured brandy into a glass and handed it to her, then poured the tea. 'Help yourself to sandwiches and cake.'

'Thank you. I had no idea they laid on such sumptuous teas. This is quite cosy.'

'Domestic even.' He raised his eyebrows.

'Will you be going upriver?'

'Good Lord, no, not if I can help it. Someone has to stay behind to run the office. Besides, one hero in the family is enough. I'm not anxious to be lowered into a soldier's grave before my time like poor Geoffrey. Did you know he wrote to me about you?'

'You didn't mention it when you visited the Lansing?' she answered warily.

'Only because we weren't alone.'

'What exactly did he write?' she probed.

'He said he became acquainted with you in India and that you shared some amusing times.' He unbuttoned his tunic, went to the door, and turned the key in the lock.

'What are you doing?'

'Setting the scene for us to enjoy some amusing times.' He returned to his seat on the sofa and slipped his arm around her shoulders. He pulled her close and kissed her, a lingering lascivious kiss that ended when he pushed his tongue deep into her throat and she struggled free. It was only after she moved away that she realised that while he'd been kissing her he'd unfastened all the buttons on her blouse.

'There's a bed behind the curtain, why don't we make ourselves more comfortable.' He slid his hand down to her ankle and slipped it up the length of her leg until it rested on a stocking top. His fingers inched inside her French knickers, delicately teasing and tantalizing.

Maud couldn't conceal her mounting excitement. She felt as though her pregnancy had lasted for ever. It had been a long time since a man had found her attractive enough to want to make love to her.

He kissed her neck. 'The bed,' he murmured.

'I've only just had a child.'

'You'd never think it to look at you, Mrs Mason.'

She visualized the wedding ring he'd give her. The mantle of respectability marriage would confer. No military wife would be able to 'cut' or ignore her. Not even one who knew her history like Harriet.

She allowed him to lead her to the bed.

Chapter Thirty

The Tigris River at Umm-El-Hannah, Monday 10th January 1916

Peter crouched in the bow of the mahaila as Mitkhal steered downstream. The canvas awning couldn't keep off the rain. His head cloth was saturated and water trickled into his gumbaz and abba until he felt the fishes couldn't be any wetter. A few miles ahead the battle raged, blinding and deafening. Shells burst high in the air on the left bank between the Turkish and British lines. Well behind the area of conflict, half-hidden by drifts of smoke, they occasionally made out the outlines of British command vessels.

'We'll never get past the Turkish lines.' Peter had to shout to make himself heard above the artillery.

Mitkhal shook his head to signify he hadn't understood.

Peter stared despondently at the mayhem. It reminded him of what lay ahead of the beleaguered force in Kut if – or what was more likely, when – the Turks chose to close in. It also brought home to him the importance of the dispatches he carried. Maps that would enable the Relief Force to plan their moves street by street as well as utilise the defences Townshend's engineers had built within the town.

361

Mitkhal steered the mahaila close to the right bank. He was aiming for a wharf that served a village about half a mile inland. When he reached it, he dropped the sail and anchor and picked up leather buckets.

'I'll water the horses,' he shouted close to Peter's ear.'When I've seen to them we'll carry on downstream on this side of the river.'

'And the Turkish guns?'

'Are directed at the British lines, not native boats.'

There was a blissful unexpected lull in the firing.

Peter took a deep breath. 'Thank God, I can hear myself. They must be recalibrating.'

'Whatever they're doing, they won't be doing it for long, so make the most of the quiet.'

'What if the British fall back and the Turks advance? We'll never get past this stretch of river.' Peter didn't want to play devil's advocate, but the area between them and the Relief Force appeared to be impassable.

'We'll have to wait until nightfall, sail on under cover of darkness until we're in British waters, then cross to the left bank and ride into camp. We'll make it if we're not detained as Turkish spies.' Mitkhal checked the buckets. They were empty. He refilled them and continued watering the horses.

'We – you'll come with me? I thought you were in a hurry to take the horses downstream.'

The guns started up again. 'I am, but Harry – wherever he is in the next life–' Mitkhal shouted hastily, realising he was referring to Harry as if he were alive, 'would never forgive me for abandoning you so close to enemy territory.'

Peter crawled forward and peered over the prow. 'I'm betting General Aylmer or his staff are on that boat.' He indicated a steamer.

'That boat has guns and I suspect it will send us, this mahaila and the horses to kingdom come if I sail close to it.' Mitkhal emptied the buckets, and pulled up the anchor. 'Our best course is to hug this bank.'

Peter continued to crouch, wet and miserable, on deck. He noticed a line of low-slung bellums that had been dragged up on the bank. Similar to British canoes, they'd been fitted with guns and used by the Dorsets in the marsh campaign the year before. 'As soon as the battle eases, and it will when darkness falls, I could change out of native dress, put on my uniform, take one of those, and head for the British lines. If I get stopped by a British ship so much the better.'

'Before we make any plans we need to get away from this noise.' Mitkhal unfurled the sail and picked up the wind.

Parisienne Ladies Fashion, Basra, Monday 10th January 1916

'That was an enjoyable way to while away half an hour. I'd like to make a habit of it.' Reginald kissed Maud's breasts and nipples before rolling away from her.

Maud smiled but she couldn't suppress the thought that Reginald's lovemaking had been perfunctory compared to his brother's boyish raw enthusiasm. And neither Geoffrey nor Reggie was as skilled, practised, and adept at satisfying her as John.

She realised that although she'd made love to dozens, possibly even scores, of men since she'd first been unfaithful to John, she still persisted in using her dead husband as a yardstick to measure all the others.

Reginald left the bed, walked naked to the table, poured two brandies, returned, and gave her one. She sat up, deliberately allowing the sheet to fall away and expose her breasts and legs.

Reginald sat beside her and slid his hands between her thighs. 'Will you be able to get away every Monday afternoon?'

'Possibly,' she said cautiously, 'after I've moved out of the mission.'

'You're moving? You surprise me. I thought you had it cosy there. Servants to look after you and your baby. Use of a groom and carriage...'

'It's an American Baptist mission, Reggie. I'm neither American nor a Presbyterian. I was only invited to move in for a few weeks as a temporary measure after Colonel Hale died of fever and his widow returned to England.'

'You seem at home there.'

'Home! It's a working mission, not a family house. I have a baby that cries in the night and disrupts the household.'

'Put that way, I understand why you have to move. Where are you thinking of going?'

'I intend to call in at HQ and see if they have a list of properties suitable for widows to rent.'

'I may be able to help you there. Fellow I know has a widow friend who lives in a house five minutes' walk from HQ. Damned handy – for him that is. He can see her anytime he likes. He said the place is too large for her. Four bedrooms, two sitting rooms, enormous garden that needs a full-time gardener. I could have a word for you if you like. Arrange for you to see the place. If it's suitable you could move in there and I could see more of you.' He kissed her lightly on the lips. 'As frequently as duty allows.'

'This friend of yours,' she frowned. 'What exactly is his relationship to this widow?'

'They're good friends.'

'As in "mistress" good friends?'

'I would never have you pegged as a prude. Not after what we've just done.'

'I have my reputation and a child to think about, Reggie. The last thing I can afford to do is attract gossip by moving in with an officer's mistress. I'm shocked you should even suggest it.' Maud pulled the sheet from the bed, wrapped it around her, carried her brandy to the table next to the sofa, and gathered her clothes.

'Sorry. I wasn't thinking straight. Given your annuity as well as your pension you can easily afford your own establishment. I'll help you look.'

'And the future, Reggie?'

'The future, Maud? We're in the middle of a war.'

'I wasn't talking about the war but our future.'

'Give me a crystal ball and I'll forecast a great many fun afternoons like this for both of us, and once you have your own place, evenings.' Reginald smiled.

Her anger heightened. She could feel her cheeks burning. 'You want me as a mistress?'

'I prefer lover, it sums up the way I feel about you. Tell you the truth, I was jealous as hell when Geoffrey wrote to me about you. I thought he was exaggerating. Now I know he most certainly wasn't.'

A picture came unbidden to her mind of Geoffrey as he'd been the last time she'd seen him. So young, so alive, as he'd begged her to divorce John and live with him. A preposterous idea. Doubly so in the middle of a war.

Reginald misread the expression on her face. 'Geoffrey's not here any more, Maud, but I am.'

'What exactly did Geoffrey write about me?'

'That when it came to bed work you were as good as any whore. Totally uninhibited, which I'm glad to say is true.' He walked over to the sofa and pulled the sheet away from her.

She made no attempt to cover herself.

'Geoffrey asked me to marry him.'

'That is something my parents would never have allowed. Besides, weren't you married at the time?'

'John was alive. Geoffrey asked me to divorce him.'

'I have no idea what circles you move in but it would have been unthinkable for Geoffrey to marry a divorced woman. The family would have disowned him. Not just my parents, but my uncles, aunts, and cousins He'd have been ostracised by everyone who mattered.'

'Geoffrey was almost of age.'

'Not financially. My grandfather stipulated that his grandchildren's trust funds remain under family control until we're thirty.' He stared at her. 'You really thought Geoffrey would marry you?'

'He asked me. If he'd survived John's death, I would have considered accepting his proposal.'

'Considered accepting ... our future ... Maud? Darling little Maud!' he started to laugh. 'You didn't think I had marriage in mind when I invited you here, did you?'

'What else?'

'My dear Mrs Mason, quite aside from the fact that I'm very happily married, I have more sense than Geoffrey. I could never saddle myself with a woman with your reputation. Don't you know you're the talk of Basra?'

The room turned red before Maud's eyes. She picked up her brandy glass and flung the contents into Reggie's face.

He retreated to the bed. 'Look, I'm sorry if you misunderstood me...'

'Misunderstood! You visited me as one of my dead husband's fellow officers. You offered to help me with the paperwork for his pension and the annuity...'

'Keep your voice down. They'll hear you in the other rooms. I offered to help you because I like you. I really do.'

'You wanted to get into my knickers.'

'So the rumours are right. Scratch the surface and the whore appears.'

'You bastard!' she raised her voice to screaming pitch.

He wrapped his hand around her throat. 'Quiet!' he hissed. 'Or you'll have the military police in here. Neither of us can afford a scandal but of the two of us I'd say I'd survive it somewhat better than you, wouldn't you?'

The Basra Club, Monday 10th January 1916

Charles and Anthony rose to their feet when Sister Jones entered the dining room with a grey-haired, middle-aged woman.

Anthony's face fell. He leaned close to Charles and whispered, 'You conniving devil, Reid. This is above and beyond the call of duty. She's brought the bloody matron with her.'

'Indeed she has, Lieutenant Bell. I'm Matron Howard. You may call me Matron.' She offered first Charles then Anthony her hand. 'I take it you are Major Reid. I'm already acquainted with Lieutenant Bell. We sailed to the Gulf on the same transport.'

The waiters pulled out chairs for the ladies and took their wraps. When they were seated, Charles and Anthony returned to their chairs and the waiters handed them the menu cards.

'I don't often have the opportunity to dine at the Basra Club, Lieutenant Bell. I trust you're not too disappointed with Sister Jones's choice of companion?'

'Not at all,' Anthony lied.

Charles watched Sister Jones through the preliminaries of choosing and ordering the meal. Her hair was as dark as he'd expected, although he was surprised by how curly it was. She had a dimple in her right cheek, and when she smiled there was a look in her eyes he felt would chase away his darkest mood.

'So, Major Reid,' Matron eyed him suspiciously. 'You have designs on Sister Jones?'

'Only for companionship,' Charles explained. 'I hope to be posted to active service soon.'

'You're limping.'

'Which is why I've wangled a berth on General Gorringe's staff boat.

'You have no red tabs on your collar.'

'My tailor is adding them.' Charles nodded assent to the wine waiter when he showed him a bottle of Chianti.

'And when you've won all your battles and return downstream?' The matron watched the wine waiter fill her glass.

'Hopefully we'll have sent the Turks packing out of Mesopotamia and we'll all be making plans to return to England.'

'So, your invitation to Sister Jones was made purely with the intention of enjoying her companionship for one evening.'

'It was.' Charles winked at Sister Jones when the matron wasn't looking.

Matron leaned closer to Anthony and lowered her voice conspiratorially. 'As we're here purely to enjoy companionship, Lieutenant Bell, what would you like to talk about?'

'Whatever you want, Matron.' Anthony placed the onus on the matron.

'Well, as neither of us has seen the latest theatrical offerings in the West End, they're off-topic. Are you interested in medical matters?'

'Not at all,' Anthony demurred.

'The human body and its ailments and re-cuperative powers is fascinating. Are you sure you don't want me to enlighten you?'

'Quite sure, thank you.'

'There's always literature. Are you fond of Henry Fielding, Charles Dickens, or would you prefer something more philosophical like Hazlitt's essays? Then there's Trollope's England or the cut and thrust of Dumas' swordplay in the *Musketeers*.'

Charles saw Sister Jones watching him. They both burst into laughter.

Sensing he was the butt of a joke, Anthony looked from one to the other.

'Have you a favourite author?' Matron con-tinued, ignoring Charles and Sister Jones.

'I'm fond of Dumas.'

'As am I, Lieutenant Bell. Have you read *The Count of Monte Cristo*?'

Grateful to the matron for engaging Anthony in conversation, Charles lifted his glass to the sister.'

'Do you have a Christian name or would you prefer me to continue calling you Sister?'

'It's Katherine, but my family and friends call me Kitty.'

'Are you counting me as a friend?'

She touched her glass to his. 'You could be.'

His heartbeat quickened. After Emily's death he'd never expected to as much look at another woman again. Emily had gone from this life and his. He'd been forced to accept that much. But he couldn't help feeling that he was somehow being disloyal to her and the memory of what they'd shared by inviting Kitty to dine with him.

Had he done so only because he was about to return to active service, and wanted someone, even someone he'd only just met, to shed a tear when they heard the news of his death?

Chapter Thirty-one

Lansing Memorial Mission, Basra, 10th January 1916

'I'm so glad to see you at table, Maud,' Mrs Butler commented when Maud joined the family for dinner that evening.

'Thank you.' Maud didn't know what else to say. Every time Mrs Butler spoke to her she felt as though what her hostess was really saying was, 'How soon are you moving out of the Lansing Memorial, Maud?'

'Did you have a successful shopping trip?'

'Very, thank you, Mrs Butler.' Maud forced a smile when she recalled the ugly scene and words she'd exchanged with Reggie Brooke. 'I returned with everything I set out to buy.'

'That's successful.' As usual, Angela rushed into the dining room after everyone else was seated.

'Busy day at school?' Theo shook out his napkin.

'My pupils never cease to surprise me. They actually remembered most of the last geometry lesson I taught them, including the theorem. Any news from upriver?'

'The stream of Turkish POWs has turned into a flood. Theo and I will have to return to the hospital as soon as we've eaten.' Dr Picard broke a slice of bread over his soup. 'They're in the most appalling state. There's been no attempt to tend to their wounds and they're all half-starved and infested with lice and fleas.'

'I hope you deloused and disinfected yourselves before leaving the hospital,' Mrs Butler folded her hands in preparation for her husband to say grace.

'As always,' Theo confirmed. 'You're quiet, Maud. You didn't pick up any gossip in town?'

'There wasn't any gossip in the shops. Have many British wounded come downriver?'

'Steamers full,' Theo answered. 'From the number of casualties and the severity of their wounds it doesn't look as though things are going very well up there for your countrymen. If it's any consolation, from what the Black Watch POW escort told us, General Lake is using everyone and everything he has at his disposal to reach Kut. He's determined to relieve the force before they run out of food. I dread to think what the final casualty lists will be.'

'I suspect more than the numbers trapped in Kut.' Dr Picard fell silent when Reverend Butler tapped his glass as a prelude to grace.

After grace was said and the maids began handing out dishes, Maud stopped listening to the conversation. Preoccupied with Reggie Brooke and the way he'd treated her, she gave up even attempting to nod in the correct places.

She looked down the table at Theo. He was short and stocky, bordering on overweight. No more than an inch, maybe two, taller than her. Compared to John, Geoffrey, and her Portuguese lover, Miguel D'Arbez, who'd all been exceptionally tall and good-looking, his features were bland, nondescript, half-hidden behind round spectacles that did nothing to enhance his appearance.

Could she marry Theo? Live with him? Sleep with him in the same bed – and bear his children?

The one experience she wasn't anxious to repeat after Robin's birth was childbearing. It curtailed social interaction, ruined the figure and there was no consolation at the end. Only a miserable squalling child that required constant attention, leaked everywhere, and ruined gowns.

'Maud? Maud? Maud, are you all right?'

She looked up to see everyone watching her.

'You all right, Maud?' Angela repeated.

'I'm sorry,' she apologised. 'I was miles away.'

'Penny for your thoughts?' Theo enquired.

'I was wondering how many more men will die before this war is over,' she lied.

'That I'm afraid is more in the generals' hands than God's.' Reverend Butler left the table. 'Thank you, my dear, that was an excellent dinner. If you'll excuse me, I have a confirmation class to attend to.'

'Yes, thank you, Mrs Butler. I have marking to do,' Angela looked at Maud, 'cocoa later?'

'That would be lovely, Angela. Thank you for dinner, Mrs Butler. If you'll excuse me I must check on Robin.' Maud watched Theo refill and pick up his coffee cup.

'Thank you, Mrs Butler. That was just what I needed after a day in the hospital. If you'll excuse me I'll drink this in the smoking room.'

'I have letters to write, Theo. Will you be ready to return to the hospital in half hour?' Dr Picard asked.

'Whenever you're ready, Dr Picard.'

Maud went to her room. The nursemaid was sewing, the baby sleeping in his cot.

She looked down at him for a few minutes. Much as she'd tried to ignore the resemblance between the child and his father she couldn't. Robin was a miniature version of Charles Reid and she hated him for it. Not because she hated Charles – which she did – but because the child was a living reminder of her infidelity and betrayal of John.

She checked her hair in the mirror, dabbed scent on her neck and wrists, looked at her rouge and powder pots and hesitated. Mrs Butler and Angela would notice she was wearing cosmetics and as they never wore any she decided the demure look would have to do. The baby started to grizzle. The nursemaid bent over the cot.

'See to him,' Maud ordered abruptly before leaving the room.

Maud found Theo where he said he'd be, flicking through an old copy of the *New York Times*.

'You were quiet at dinner, are you well?' he asked.

'Quite well.' she sat in a chair opposite him. 'Do you have time to talk?'

He glanced at his watch. 'Dr Picard said he'd be

half an hour, but knowing him that means at least an hour, so the short answer is, yes, I have time to talk.'

'I've been thinking about your proposal.'

Theo set the paper aside. 'And?'

'I accept.'

'What brought about this change?'

'My maid Harriet was in the dress shop.'

'She ignored you?'

'She said "hello" but nothing more.'

'Polite even when ostracising. British military society knows how to close its doors.'

'There's more.' She steeled herself. 'There was an officer in the shop.'

'Reggie Brooke.'

Maud's blood ran cold. She wondered who Theo had spoken to and how much he knew. Were the shop assistants indiscreet? Did they sell information about what went on in the upstairs rooms? 'How do you know it was Reggie?'

'I saw he was interested in you the last time he was here. Did you meet him by appointment?'

'Not exactly.'

'Explain.'

'He told me he was generally there on Monday afternoons.'

He sat forward in his chair. 'So you knew he'd be there, and went with the intention of persuading him to marry you. To that end you made love to him?'

She was too taken aback by Theo's blunt assertion to do more than sit and stare.

'Don't look shocked, Maud. It's common knowledge the Parisienne Ladies' Fashion store is what's known colloquially in the States as a cathouse.'

She finally found her voice. 'I thought Reggie wanted to marry me.'

He gave a mirthless laugh. 'You really thought Major Brooke would ignore your reputation and marry you? That was optimism bordering on the fanciful, Maud. So now the one hope – as it turns out false hope – that you had a marriage prospect in British military society has been dashed, you've decided to accept my proposal. But only after you slept with the said officer in a last-ditch attempt to get him to marry you?'

'That is not the way I would put it.'

'Then how would you put it, Maud?'

'If you're withdrawing your offer I wouldn't blame you.'

'I should hope not after the way you've be-haved. If there's blame to be apportioned it falls squarely on you.'

'If you want to make me crawl...'

'I have no interest in humiliating you, Maud. But neither have I any interest in marrying a whore who can't keep her legs closed around men. The one thing I applaud, to a point,' he qualified, 'is your honesty. The question is, who else knows about your exploits this afternoon other than Reggie Brooke and the staff of the dress shop?'

'I have no idea.'

'I have a suggestion. Wait a month, if no gossip circulates within that time the chances are it won't. At the end of that time, I'll examine you to make sure you're not carrying Reggie's child. If

376

you are, you and your money can go to England, India, or purgatory as far as I'm concerned.'

'And if I'm not?'

'You can service me so I can sample the delights of your flesh that you distribute so freely. If I'm satisfied with your performance I'll marry you on condition you sign over your annuity and any other assets you're holding to me.'

'If I did that and you left me, I'd have nothing to live on.'

'You have my word that I won't leave you after we're married, provided your antics don't incite further gossip and you remain faithful. My last and final offer, Maud. What do you say?'

She pictured Reggie's face, cold, contemptuous as he'd last looked at her. Harriet turning away from her in the shop. She didn't need to think about what she was about to say.

'Yes, Theo.'

'You'll give up everything you own to marry me?'

'Yes.'

'Why?'

'Because I'm finding it very hard to live without respectability.'

Charles helped Kitty from the landau he'd hired to carry them from the Basra Club to their quarters. They waved goodbye to Matron Howard and Anthony Bell when the driver headed for Matron's house behind the hospital. Charles walked Kitty to the door of the bungalow she shared with three other nurses.

'I can't believe Anthony and Matron are still

talking about *The Three Musketeers*.'

'They've inspired me to look for a copy so I can re-read it,' Charles followed her on to her veranda. 'Are you free tomorrow?'

'Aren't you going upstream tomorrow?' she asked.

'Now we've met properly I'm hoping my orders will come through the day after tomorrow, or if I'm really lucky the end of the week.'

'If they come through sooner?'

'I'll send a message to the hospital.'

'I'm on days this week so I'll be free from seven o'clock – make that eight if you want to see me at my best.'

'We could dine in the Basra Club again. Just the two of us if you think I can be trusted to behave like a gentleman.'

'Only one problem, I doubt I'll be ready to eat the Club's idea of a dinner after what I've eaten tonight.'

'What about supper?'

'In one of the private rooms?' she replied.

'I wasn't going to suggest that,' he protested.

'I suspected you wouldn't, which is why I did. You can pick me up here at eight without a carriage. I enjoy walking in the fresh air after spending a day on the ward.'

'In the rain?'

'You melt in water?'

'No, but...'

'Bring an umbrella.' She took a key from her reticule and slipped it into the lock before turning back to him. 'May I ask you a question?'

'Anything, as long as you realise I'm bound by

the limitations of the Official Secrets Act as applied by the India Office.'

'Are you married?'

He smiled. 'No, people keep telling me I have to win the war first.'

'Good.' She stood on tiptoe and kissed his cheek. 'It's pleasant getting to know you, Major Reid.'

Charles walked up to his bungalow to find Anthony sitting on the veranda smoking a cigar under an umbrella.

'Bit wet out here to smoke, isn't it?'

'Your bearer's inside sending clouds of dust from one side of the bungalow to the other,' Anthony complained.

'My bearer's too lazy to disturb a cloud of dust.'

'Your old bearer was. This is a new old bearer who's just returned from India.'

'Chatta Ram?'

'I think that's what he said his name was. I decided it was diplomatic to retreat for the sake of my sinuses. Smoke?' he offered Charles a cigar.

'Is this a peace offering for wanting to bite my head off when Kitty brought Matron to dinner?'

'It's Kitty now, is it?'

'I'm seeing her again tomorrow night.' Charles struck a match, lit Anthony's cigar and then his own.'

'You're not wasting time.'

'No one has time to waste in a war. If you'll excuse me I'd better go and see my bearer, we have a lot to catch up on.'

'If you had any thoughts on keeping your old

bearer this one has already sent him packing.'

'Excellent, saves me the job of firing him.'

'I take it you prefer this bearer?'

'I was wounded at Nasiriyeh. Chatta Ram carried me to the river, ignored the direct orders of medical officers who told him I was past saving, and stayed with me on a hellish seventeen-day journey downstream, on the *Mejiidieh*. I was out of it, but later I was told there was no cover from the wind or rain. More than half the wounded had dysentery and the boat was covered with faeces, urine, flies, and vermin. By the time we arrived at Basra more than half the wounded had died where they lay. Medics directed the removal of those they considered had a chance. I wasn't one of them. Again Chatta Ram ignored the orders of superior officers, carried me off the boat, and placed me on one of the hospital trans-fer carts. It wasn't until I came round that I dis-covered he'd been wounded himself and sent back to India to recuperate.'

'If you want to get rid of him...'

'No chance, Anthony, but feel free to take the bearer Chatta Ram sent away.'

'He's even worse than the one I have.'

Charles found Chatta Ram in his bedroom. He'd laid out Charles's kit and uniform and was examining it.

'You walked through the door and began work right away?' Charles propped his stick in a corner and sat on one of the wickerwork chairs.

'From the sorry state of your uniform, your last bearer appeared to be less than conscientious, Sahib.'

'Lieutenant Bell tells me he is now my ex-bearer.'

'I gave him notice because he was negligent in his duties.'

'He's not you. But I doubt many bearers would carry their officer on their back for miles if he'd been wounded, as well as argue with superiors who consider the officer past saving. I owe you my life, Chatta Ram. If I haven't thanked you until now, it was only because I lacked the means.'

'Any bearer would have done the same,' Chatta Ram demurred.

'I doubt it, but most brothers would have.'

'You shouldn't talk like that, Sahib.'

'There's no one to overhear us.'

'Now. But it might lead you to drop your guard when there is.'

'There's a bottle of brandy and glasses in the living room. Why don't you bring it in so we can drink as well as talk?'

'And if Lieutenant Bell should hear us?'

'I told him we have a lot to catch up on.'

Chatta Ram left and returned with the bottle and two glasses. He placed them on the table in front of Charles.

'Please, sit down.'

'Someone could look through the window and see us.'

'Pull the blind. Then they'll only see shadows. Besides, it is allowed for officers to talk to their bearers.' Charles took the bottle and filled two glasses. 'How is our mother?'

'Getting old.'

'Your father?' Charles didn't want to know but

felt he should ask.

'Died last November, before I returned home.'

'I'm sorry.'

'Your father?' Chatta Ram asked.

'Fine, as far as I know. Running the war from the War Office in London, not the India Office, so we can't blame him for the shortage of equipment, boats, and supplies that's crippling the Relief Force.' Charles filled the brandy balloons and pushed one towards Chatta Ram.

Chatta Ram picked it up and looked at it. 'I can't drink with you.'

'I thought we'd just established that we can do what we like in secret.'

Chatta Ram studied Charles. 'You've changed.'

'If you mean that coming close to death has softened some of the officer starch that went into my make-up, you'd be right. Cheers,' he touched his glass to Chatta's. 'This is a new experience for me. I've never had a brother before.'

'From what I saw you were as close to Harry Downe and John Mason as any man to his brother, Sahib...'

'Charles,' Charles contradicted.

'No, it has to be "sahib". If we're overheard conversing like this it would go bad for both of us. I would be thrown out of the army and so would you. Some of the older officers know what our mother did. It was a huge scandal at the time.'

'Which my father kept from me. But after this war things will be different. The old social barriers will be broken down.'

'Some, maybe,' Chatta Ram agreed. 'Too many of your class are being killed here and in France not to make a difference. The shortage of men may encourage the ordinary sapper to try to work his way up the social tree and into a better position in life. But nothing will change for the likes of me or you, Sahib.'

'In terms of our relationship, it will. I promise you.' Charles replenished both their glasses.

'Enough for you to introduce me to your father, Sahib?' A ghost of a smile played at the corners of Chatta Ram's mouth.

'Not that much,' Charles qualified, 'but who knows where any of us will be, or what we'll be doing when this war is over.'

Chapter Thirty-two

Chitab's Fort, The Wadi, early hours before dawn Tuesday 11th January 1916

The river ran noisily below Peter. The surrounding air was so inundated he felt as though he were breathing in water not air. Above him, rain fell with the force of hailstones. It permeated everything, drenching every inch of his body, coating the boards of the mahaila and soaking his and Mitkhal's robes until they dripped whenever they moved.

The guns had fallen silent. Only the cries of the wounded rent the air, piteous and pathetic. Occasionally Peter spotted the flash of a lantern as an officer or stretcher-bearer searched the battlefield for survivors. He couldn't see any fires and assumed if any had been lit after the battle the braziers had been placed inside tents out of the rain.

'Now would be a good time for me to swim back to the bellums,' he suggested to Mitkhal.

'If you want a bellum I'll sail back.'

'No need. I couldn't possibly get any wetter than I am now.'

'Give it another half hour and the sentries on the bank will look for shelter and we'll be able to sail across to the British side.'

'What sentries?'

Mitkhal tapped the binoculars slung around Peter's neck. Peter lifted them to his eyes. 'I can't see a thing.'

'Shadows on the bank.'

'I'll take your word for it.'

'Listen. You can hear their footsteps in the mud.'

Peter strained his ears but he could only hear the sound of the river and the rain. After the deafening din of the battle the rhythm proved hypnotic. His eyelids grew heavy despite the wet and the cold.

He was catapulted out of sleep when Mitkhal shook him.

'Put on your uniform. We'll hit the left bank in five minutes. The sentries may not listen to you, but they definitely won't listen to me.'

Peter reached for the cloth bag that contained his uniform. Like everything else it was sodden. His trousers clung uncomfortably to his legs when he pulled them on but when he tried to put on his shirt and tunic, he felt as though he'd entered into a wrestling match.

Just before they hit the bank, the sound of rifles being cocked was accompanied by a, 'Halt who goes there!'

'Captain Smythe, 2nd Battalion the Dorsets out of Kut al Amara. Take me to your CO.'

A lantern was lifted high. Its light shone directly into Peter's eyes blinding him. 'Sentry, this is my orderly. Take care of him and the horses.'

The sentry hesitated.

'That is a direct order from a superior, Private.'

'Yes, sir. I'll summon an escort to take you to the Duty Officer, sir.'

'On the double, Private.' Peter shook Mitkhal's hand. 'Thank you. I wouldn't have made it without you.' He joined his escort and disappeared into the darkness.

Mitkhal untied the horses and led them off the boat. 'Have you anywhere dry I can stable these?' he asked the remaining sentry.

'You'll be lucky, mate. There's nowhere dry for us let alone the livestock but we can get your animals some feed. Good-looking horses.' The sentry lifted his lantern higher. 'They're an odd colour. Never seen beasts streaked brown and white before.'

Mitkhal ran his hand over Dorset's flanks then held it up to the light. It was dyed orange with henna. 'We didn't want them gleaming in the dark.'

'I say, these are Harry Downe's horses, aren't they?' The sentry was a corporal, Harry a lieutenant colonel who'd never taken any notice of rank when it came to making friends. 'You selling them, mate?' he asked Mitkhal. 'Because if you are I know an officer...'

'I'm taking them to his widow.'

'Hope she appreciates them.'

'She has a son who will when he's old enough to ride them.'

'Here, I'll help you.' The corporal took Norfolk's rein. Mitkhal looked around as he followed him through the camp. Wounded men lay everywhere on the muddy ground.

His and Peter's trip this far down river had been easy. Too easy. Mitkhal had a feeling that the stretch between the British camp and Basra would be anything but. If a British corporal had recognised the quality of the horseflesh on his mahaila, how many Arabs would cast a covetous eye – and try to snatch them?

Chitab's Fort, The Wadi, early morning Tuesday 11th January 1916

By tacit agreement, the guns remained silent. Both sides took the opportunity to attend to their wounded and clear and bury their dead.

A bearer gave Mitkhal a tin of bully beef and a stool. Conscious of the attention he, or rather Harry's horses, was attracting, he tethered the horses to a post, sat within arm's reach of them and ate.

'Dear Lord, that's Dorset, Norfolk, and Somerset. I'd know them anywhere.'

Mitkhal didn't have to look far for the man who'd spoken. The voice had been uncannily like

Harry's, the speaker his brother.

He hunched further under the grey army blanket he'd scavenged to keep the worst of the rain from his shoulders and pulled up a corner to cover his face.

Michael approached the horses and held out his hand. 'What have they done to you, you poor things?'

'Dyed them to try and keep thieving Arab hands off them, sir,' the private who'd stuck to Mitkhal like a turd to an army boot answered.

'Are they in your care?'

'No, sir.' The private moved aside so Michael could see Mitkhal sitting on a canvas stool behind him.

Even with the blanket partially covering his face Michael recognised him as the Arab he'd seen sail from the wharf outside Abdul's. He approached him and held out his hand.

'How do you do, I'm Michael Downe. The brother of Harry Downe who used to own these horses.'

'I know who you are, sir.' Mitkhal gave Michael a cold clammy handshake.

'You're my brother's friend Mitkhal.' It was a statement not a question.

'I worked with Lieutenant Colonel Downe, sir,' Mitkhal answered evasively.

'You're caring for these horses?'

'I'm taking them to Lieutenant Colonel Downe's widow.'

'Harry shipped four horses from England to India,' Michael continued to stroke Dorset's nose and Mitkhal realised the mare wasn't only

Harry's favourite. 'He had another he named Devon. Is she dead?'

'He gave Devon to his father-in-law.'

'Sheikh Ibn Shalan.'

'You know his name.' Mitkhal was surprised.

'I spoke to people in Basra who'd known Harry. He wrote home almost every week when he first arrived here but after the war broke out, he hardly sent any letters.'

'He was too busy.'

'You said you were taking these to Harry's widow?'

Mitkhal nodded assent.

'Is she in Basra?'

'Downriver.' Much as Michael resembled Harry, Mitkhal was conscious that the fewer people who knew Harry was still alive the safer, he, Furja, and their children would be.

'I'd really like to meet her.'

'She is in hiding, Mr Downe.'

'From the Turks?'

'Many people would like to find Harry's wife and children.'

'I know he has twin girls.' Michael desperately wanted to gain Mitkhal's trust. He lacked his brother's charisma and talent for making friends but from the suspicious way the Arab was eyeing him, he felt as though he were facing a wall of hostility.

'He has a son as well,' Mitkhal revealed,

'That's wonderful. I'm their uncle. I would like to do everything I can for them.'

'You're with the Relief Force?'

Mitkhal hadn't commented on Michael's civilian

clothes but Michael sensed he'd noticed them. 'I'm a reporter for a newspaper.'

'Then you'll be too busy to see them until after the war is over.'

'Depending on where they are, I probably will,' Michael admitted. 'How can I get in touch with her?'

'You could leave a message for me in a coffee shop on the wharf at Basra. It's owned by a man called Abdul.'

'I have a room in Abdul's. I asked him to find you. He didn't.'

'Abdul is discreet. He wouldn't have admitted he knew me until I told him it was all right to acknowledge our acquaintance. He knows where to contact me, although it may take a week or two. Longer if I'm in the desert.'

'You'll be able to pass a message on to Harry's wife?'

'Eventually.' Mitkhal looked Michael in the eye. 'This is a big country, Mr Downe.'

'As I've discovered.' Michael saw a sergeant rise from a canvas stool and grabbed it before anyone else could. He pulled it close to Mitkhal and sat down. 'I heard my brother was killed by the Turks.'

'He was.' Mitkhal felt that wasn't exactly a lie. Harry Downe had been killed by the Turks, Hasan Mahmoud lived on.

'Harry and I were close. If there's anything you can tell me about his time here I'd appreciate the information.'

'What would you like me to tell you about him, Mr Downe?'

'Was he happily married?'

'He loved his wife and children.'

'I spoke to Charles Reid. He said that when Harry was dressed as an Arab he was indistinguishable from a native.'

'He took the trouble to learn our language and our ways,' Mitkhal agreed.

'Was he happier as an Arab than a British soldier?'

'That's a strange question to ask me, Mr Downe. I knew the Arab.'

'You also knew the British soldier.'

'Not well. British officers do not allow natives in the mess or their living quarters.'

Peter Smythe walked up to Mitkhal. 'I've been looking for you. Thank you for waiting. I know you're anxious to carry on downstream.'

'You're ready to leave.' Mitkhal set his empty bully beef tin on the ground.

'General Aylmer asked me to stay with the Relief Force. As I've just left Kut and know the layout in the town, he thinks I'll be of some value. Are you still intent on going down river?'

'Yes,' Mitkhal replied.

'As far as Basra and the Lansing Memorial?'

'I could do.'

Too engrossed in his own affairs to be aware of his surroundings or Michael sitting next to Mitkhal, Peter thrust his hand inside his shirt and pulled out a folded sheet of paper. 'This is a letter for my wife. Tell Angela I'm sorry I couldn't find an envelope, and tell her ... tell her I wanted to go downstream and see her but it's vital we get everyone holed up in Kut out before they starve to death, and that means me travelling back upstream. Tell her I love her and I think of her all the time.'

Mitkhal took the letter which was already damp and tucked it into his gumbaz.

'You've come from inside Kut?' Michael asked.

Peter finally turned to him. 'Good God!'

Accustomed to the reaction his appearance elicited among Harry's friends, Michael held out his hand. 'I'm Harry Downe's brother. I'm a reporter, for the *Daily Mirror*. If you could give me a first-hand account of what it's like for our troops inside Kut, I'd guarantee you the front page.'

'The force would appreciate the front page, but I'd want you to leave my name off it.'

'An anonymous gallant officer who dared to breach the Turkish blockade?' Michael suggested.

'Sounds good, although I'm not in the least gallant. You could be Harry's twin brother.'

'So people keep telling me. You knew him well?'

'Captain Smythe was one of your brother's closest friends, Mr Downe. If you'll excuse me, I have to leave if I'm to make headway before dark.' Mitkhal untied the horses.

'You're riding out?' Michael asked when Mitkhal untied the horses.

'No, I have a boat tied at the temporary dock.'

'I'll walk with you. Can you spare me some time in about half hour?' Michael asked Peter.

'If there's anything resembling a mess tent here, that's where you'll find me. I'm ravenous.'

'Indians have set up a kitchen of sorts in the north-east corner of the camp,' Mitkhal advised.

'You will give Angela that letter and tell I love

her, Mitkhal?'

'I promise, Peter. See you downstream?'

'Soon I hope. Good luck, Mitkhal.'

The Christian name terms weren't lost on Michael. One conversation between Peter and Mitkhal had been enough to convince him that Mitkhal was anything but a subservient orderly.

'I know my brother thought a great deal of you. I was hoping I could be your friend as well.' Michael took Somerset's rein, leaving Mitkhal with Dorset and Norfolk.

'It's difficult to find time for friendships during a war, Mr Downe.'

'Please call me, Michael.'

Mitkhal led the horses on to the makeshift dock the engineers had cobbled together. From there he led them one by one on to the mahaila and under the canvas cover that had been thrown over a makeshift wooden frame.

'You'll mention me to my sister-in-law, when you give her the horses and tell her I'd like to see her.'

'I will.' Mitkhal lashed the canvas cover closed. He lifted the anchor and the sail, waved to Michael and the vessel scudded out into the river. The current carried it swiftly downstream.

Michael stood on the riverbank and watched the sail grow gradually smaller before turning and walking back to the camp.

Michael found Peter ensconced in a camp chair outside the kitchen tent. He'd given up trying to shelter from the rain and was eating bully beef from a tin and nursing a packet of crackers.

'Dessert,' he joked, holding the crackers out to Michael as he approached. 'Want me to see if I can track some down for you?'

'No thanks, four hard biscuits and one tin of bully beef a day is my limit.'

'Here you go, Sahibs. Just made a fresh pot.' Adjabi emerged from the tent with two mugs of tea. He handed one to Michael and gave the other to Peter.

'Thank you, Adjabi. Can you ask Daoud to bring me my travelling desk please?' Michael wiped the rain from his eyes and took the chair next to Peter. 'I can't believe you actually escaped from Kut.'

'I was there last night.'

'What are conditions really like there? Thank you.' Michael took his desk from Adjabi and opened it. He pulled out a small notebook and pencil and closed it quickly before rain soaked the contents.

'Grim,' Peter said succinctly.

'Is it true you're short of ammunition?'

'Ammunition is the one thing we have plenty of. Pity we can't eat it. But we're short of everything else. Warm clothes, fuel, fodder for the animals, food for the men, and medical supplies. I think it was hearing about the shortage of animal feed that drove Mitkhal upstream. He was worried, with good reason, that Harry's horses would be slaughtered for food.'

'How did he hear that the horses were being killed?'

'We radioed HQ in Basra before Christmas that we were slaughtering our animals. We had over 3,000 horses and mules at the beginning of the

393

siege, and we started with the mules. When the Indian sepoys refused to eat their flesh we began slaughtering the cavalry horses. General Townshend radioed out to Hindu, Sikh, and Muslim leaders asking if they could be given dispensation to eat horse and mule flesh. Dispensation was given but the sepoys still refused to eat the meat so the oats and barley intended for the livestock went to the sepoys.'

'Yet Harry's horses survived until Mitkhal arrived.'

'One of the worst experiences of my life was losing Harry. I wasn't alone in valuing his friendship. All his friends – and he has hundreds if not thousands in Kut – conspired to keep his horses safe.'

'How long can Townshend and the garrison hold out?'

'You'll have to wait for an answer to that question. Command keeps changing their mind. When I left, they were finally organising a search of the town for hidden food stocks. Something some of the senior officers had been pleading for since the beginning of the siege. Our troops are a damned sight thinner than the natives in the town.'

'So, the force is short of food, clothes...'

'Decent accommodation. Most of the men have been living in trenches since we dug them the first week of the siege. That makes for freezing cold, damp misery in this weather. The one thing we're not short of is lice. The fleas are bad but nothing like as foul as the lice. They get into everything, clothes, shoes, hair, corners of your body you didn't know you possessed. So if I were you I'd move your chair further away from mine.'

Unsure whether Peter was joking, Michael did as he suggested.

'How long have you been here, Mr Downe?'

'My name is Michael. Since the end of December.'

'Then you've seen this country at its best. After the cold, wet, lice and fleas, come the mosquitoes. Just when you think nothing could possibly be worse than the sandflies and mosquitoes, the hot weather hits. And I mean hits. The good news is, it shrivels mosquitoes and flies, the bad, it shrivels men.'

Michael stopped scribbling. 'Thank you. You've given me an insight into this country. I've been looking for an old Gulf hand to do that since I arrived here.'

'Sahib,' Adjabi appeared again with the teapot in his hand. 'More cha, Sahib?'

'Please.' Michael held out his cup.'

'Sami is packing up Captain Mason's things, Sahib. They are sending him upstream to open an aid station closer to the battlefield.'

'When is he going?' Michael asked.

'As soon as his transport is ready.'

'That could mean tomorrow morning,' Michael quipped.

'Mason, no relation of John Mason by chance?' Peter asked.

'His brother. You knew John Mason as well as Harry?' Michael looked at Peter. There was a strange expression on Peter's face he couldn't quite decipher.

Chapter Thirty-three

Chitab's Fort, The Wadi, Tuesday 11th January 1916

Tom tossed his washing kit and hairbrushes into his personal bag. He had no idea of the location of his tent or his army kit, or even if he still possessed them. If Sami had found time to stow them somewhere, all well and good; if he hadn't, the loss of kit was trivial in comparison to the amount of death and suffering in the Relief Force.

Ordered upstream twice after Sheikh Saad, overwhelmed by the pressing needs of the wounded, he hadn't slept more than an hour or two at a stretch since he'd docked at Sheikh Saad, and then only on makeshift mattresses in field hospitals. He was so bone-weary he had a problem standing upright. He'd even caught himself daydreaming about sleep.

'Tom?'

He looked up to see Michael with a captain from the Dorsets.

'This is Peter Smythe. He knew Harry and John. He's just left Kut.'

'Kut – you escaped?' Tom shook Peter's hand.

'Both of you make it sound as if I've done something heroic. My superiors planned it and I was taken out by an exceptionally brave Arab auxiliary.'

396

'If you don't mind me saying so, you look in one piece compared to the wounded I've been treating, but positively skeletal.'

'I assure you I'm in better shape than most of the Kut garrison,' Peter protested.

'Do they all have hacking coughs?' Tom asked when Peter started coughing and couldn't stop.

'It's the reason I was sent out of Kut. Brass thought if the Turks stopped us they'd assume I was tubercular and wouldn't bother to search me.'

'Take off your shirt and tunic. I'll check you out.'

'No need. Your brother said...' Peter faltered. He couldn't believe he'd been so stupid as to forget the promise he'd made John. He was furious with himself. Physically and emotionally exhausted he'd dropped his guard. An inexcusable error. Then he remembered the promise he'd made John had only been in relation to Maud. Surely John wouldn't want his brother to carry on believing he was dead when he wasn't...

'My brother!' Tom repeated.

Peter would have given a great deal to take his words back but it was too late. 'I promised John I wouldn't tell anyone he's alive. Problem is I'm too bloody tired to think straight.'

'Sit down.' Tom pushed a camp chair towards him. 'You've seen my brother. Major John Mason.'

'Yes,' Peter admitted reluctantly.

'You know him well enough to recognise him?'

Peter sank down on the chair. He looked from Tom to Michael. 'It's a long story.'

The Tigris below the Wadi, Wednesday 11th January 1916

Mitkhal kept a careful eye on both banks as he steered downriver. The horses were well hidden from casual observers under the canvas cover. With the British and Turks occupied with fighting one another upriver, the lower reaches of the Tigris would soon become infested by pirates. That's if they weren't already.

He had sailed the river many times, in British boats with Harry, and in native boats, occasionally with Harry but more often with Arab captains. He knew isolated places, remote from the nearest inhabited hamlet, where he could drop anchor when he needed to water the horses or rest. The only question was, would it be better to choose a spot away from civilisation in the hope pirates hadn't discovered it or risk berthing close to a village where he could appeal for help should he need it?

Whether or not assistance would be forthcoming from people who'd learned to mistrust outsiders from the tribe was another matter.

He pulled his dripping kafieh and agal from his head and squeezed them out one-handed, keeping his right hand firmly on the tiller. He was placing his head cloth back on his head when a movement on the left bank caught his eye. A stationary figure on horseback was watching the boat.

Both face and figure were swathed in black. Blurred by distance and the heavy downpour it was impossible to recognise more than a human shape astride the animal. The mount appeared to be similar to a chestnut ridden by of one of Shalan's trusted advisors, but similar didn't mean it was the same horse.

Mitkhal wondered if the beating he'd taken had affected his judgement. Had he dropped his guard in the British camp? There'd been any number of Arab irregulars around. What if one or more of them had recognised Harry's horses? Watched him load them on to the mahaila and decided to bide their time until he stopped to sleep or water the horses and then steal them? Or was the man simply a lone traveller gauging the distance he'd travelled by the bends in the river?

Was he seeing a threat where there was none? Or was the man a scout for a party of thieves travelling inland out of his sights. Was he one of Ibn Shalan's men?

He checked his bearings and headed out into the centre of the river. Keeping his course steady, he pulled his revolver from his abba. He kept it fully loaded but he still opened the chamber and counted the bullets before returning it to the concealed pocket. He didn't have to look at his stiletto blade. He could feel it strapped tight against his leg.

He'd make as much headway as he could before dark. Then, when he did berth, he'd sleep with one eye open.

Chitab's Fort, The Wadi, Tuesday 11th January 1916

'I know John well. He asked me not to tell anyone

399

he was alive for the best of motives,' Peter insisted. 'You just said I look skeletal. I know I do, but no one in Kut looks good, and John has been seriously ill. None of us thought he'd survive the fever he contracted after crossing the desert from Karun to Amara. He wouldn't have if Harry hadn't pulled strings to get him on a boat bound for Basra.' Peter tactfully managed to avoid all mention of John's addiction to alcohol that had probably done as much as, if not more than, the cross-country trek to wreck his health.

'You said the death sentence on John has been lifted...' Tom began.

'Postponed pending a review after Kut has been relieved,' Peter corrected.

'Surely the brass would have allowed him to send a wireless message to his family out of Kut if he'd asked.'

'They would have,' Peter agreed, 'but as I said, John didn't want to raise hopes that could be dashed again. It's anyone guess what will happen to the garrison. If the Relief Force reaches the town and the Turks put up a fight they could all be wiped out. And if, heaven forbid, the Relief Force doesn't get through and they're all marched into captivity, there's no guarantee any of them will survive. You promise most solemnly not to tell John's wife he's alive?' Peter pleaded in the hope of limiting the damage he'd done. 'John was most insistent on that point.'

'I've no reason to call on my sister-in-law again so I can safely promise you that much. But I still find it difficult to believe he would allow our mother, father, sister, and me to believe he's dead when he isn't.'

'Knowing John's alive gives us all the more reason to carry on fighting until we reach Kut.' Michael offered his cigarettes to Peter and Tom.

'I'd give anything to see my brother alive and well.' Tom was too choked by emotion to say more.

'With luck you may not have to give anything to see him – and soon.' Michael turned to Adjabi. 'There's news?'

'The bearers say there will be an enormous battle tomorrow, Sahib. If we win that, the next battle will be at Kut.'

'I hope you're right, Adjabi. Regret staying with us, when you could have gone downstream to a decent hospital and your wife, Peter?' Michael asked.

Peter rose to his feet. 'No regrets. I have many good friends in Kut.'

Tigris, early hours of Saturday 15th January 1916

Mitkhal couldn't sleep. His insomnia was down to more than the hard boards he was lying on, or the wet clothes that clung uncomfortably, chafing his body. Travelling downriver at the height of the rainy season was never easy, but this particular trip seemed endless. Partly due to the sheer monotony of the rain and boredom coupled with exhaustion. A result of the pain he still suffered from the beating the sappers in the Norfolks' stable had given him.

Having to care for the three horses as well as

navigate and steer the boat without assistance hadn't helped. Neither had his mounting concern for Gutne, Furja, and the children.

Dorset whinnied and all three horses moved nervously, their hooves clattering over the deck of the mahaila. Wet, shivering, bones aching, Mitkhal clambered slowly upright, pushed aside the canvas and ducked under the tarpaulin.

'What's the matter, girl?' He reached out and stroked Dorset's nose. 'You're dancing as if someone's lit a fire beneath you.'

The horse whinnied again, backing up as far as the ropes would allow. A lamp shone suddenly, unbearably bright behind Mitkhal's head, blinding him. Footsteps resounded over the boards. Mitkhal reached for his gun and crouched in preparation to pull out his knife.

'Give me your gun, Mitkhal, or I'll shoot the horses.' Ibn Shalan and two of his henchman moved on deck. Both men pointed the rifles they were carrying at Mitkhal's head.

Mitkhal knew when he was beaten. He handed Shalan his gun. He rose slowly, leaving his knife where it was.

'My men will care for the horses. Come, we'll go on to my boat and talk. It's dry in the cabin and I have coffee brewing.'

With armed men at his back, Mitkhal had no choice but to follow.

Shalan's mahaila was larger than the one the British had given him and Peter. The cabin was small, but dry as Shalan had promised. The coffee was freshly brewed and hot.

'Sit,' Shalan indicated a cushion.

Mitkhal took it and the coffee a slave handed him.

'How is my daughter?'

'Well when I last saw her. She has a son, she named him Shalan.' Mitkhal hoped the news would please the sheikh. If it did, Shalan showed no sign of it. But the sheikh had always been a master at controlling his feelings – except anger. And even then Mitkhal suspected he only allowed it to show when it suited, to intimidate the object of his annoyance.

'A son. Hasan's son?'

Mitkhal looked at Shalan but he had the sense to keep quiet.

'Of course.' He stroked his thin beard. 'That's why Furja left the tribe and that's why you helped her. To return her to her English husband.'

Mitkhal finally spoke. 'Harry Downe is dead.'

'Don't lie to me, you tribeless bastard. You were seen carrying him out of the Turkish camp outside Kut. You hired a boat to take you downriver. And you carried him into Zabba's house.'

'I carried a body into Zabba's house.' Mitkhal kept his voice soft, low. Almost as low as Shalan's.

Shalan pulled out his tobacco pouch. He removed a pack of papers and began to roll a cigarette. Mitkhal had seen him do the same thing many times. It passed the time while Shalan counted off minutes designed to unnerve his audience and prompt them to say things they hadn't meant to, just to fill the silence.

Shalan finally finished rolling his cigarette. He looked at it. 'You killed Ali Mansur.'

403

'A blade wielded by one of your men killed Ali Mansur.'

'He was not aiming for Ali Mansur.'

'He was aiming for Norfolk. I deflected the blade.'

'You admit you started a fight between my men and those of Habid in which several of my men were killed.'

'Your men started the fight, not me.' Mitkhal contradicted.

'You did not stay until the end of the fight.' Shalan's eyes, dark, probing looked directly into Mitkhal's.

'No.'

'Because you went into Kut al Amara.'

'I had business there and with the Turks sitting outside it seemed best to go in under cover of darkness.'

'So you still work for the British.'

'I work for myself, my family, and Furja. You know I went into Kut. You've seen the mahaila they gave me and the horses I brought out. You know they were Harry Downe's horses. You've admired them often enough.'

'You want the horses for yourself?'

'For Furja and Harry's children. Harry always said if they were used for breeding they'd found a fine bloodline.'

'You were seen leaving Kut with a British officer. You helped him evade the Turks.'

'In return for the horses.'

'So you still work for the British.'

Mitkhal shrugged. 'I told you, I work for myself, but like all Arabs, including you, I work for the

British when it suits me.'

'You are on good terms with them?'

'Obviously they talk to me or I would not be sailing a boat they gave me.'

'Gave you?'

'I didn't have one. It was the easiest way to travel downstream. Not just for me but for the British officer.'

'I lost twelve men outside Kut beside Ali Mansur.'

'The fighting was heated,' Mitkhal agreed.

'I also lost twenty horses and guns I could not afford to lose.'

'There were Arabs of many tribes camped outside Kut. The Bani Lam, the Bakhtairi Khans ... there is no love between them and your tribe.'

'And you and my daughter? Do either of you have any love for the tribe?'

Mitkhal chose his words with care because he couldn't see where Ibn Shalan was leading the conversation. 'I and your daughter have a great deal of love for the tribe.'

'My daughter wants to return to the tribe?'

'Not if it means her death and the death of her children.'

'You and Gutne?'

'We like being alive.'

'I need more guns and ammunition to replace the ones that were stolen from my men at Kut by the Bani Lam and Habid's men. Two hundred new rifles with a corresponding amount of ammunition should be sufficient. We also need more horses, a minimum of fifty, because many of ours have been stolen by the Bani Lam who raid our camps mercilessly. This war has made it difficult to find grazing for our goats. My people are hungry, we need replacement herds. Four would be good, eight better.'

Mitkhal chose to deliberately misunderstand Shalan. 'Why tell me?'

'Because you have the ear of the British. I have kept my part of the bargain I negotiated with Hasan before the war. My men guard the British oil pipeline, but without horses and more guns and ammunition we won't be able to do so in future.'

'We all need things, getting them is the problem.'

'The British know you. They trust you. As do I. You can go to them and negotiate for us.'

'And offer them what in return for their guns, ammunition, horses, and goats?'

'The safety of their pipeline. A guarantee that my men will keep the Karun Valley free from Turks, and the tribes that support the Turks. You may have to remind the British that while they fight their way to Kut, the Karim Valley is at their back. It would be in their interest to have a friend watch it for them.'

'And what would I get for taking your proposal to the British?' Mitkhal asked boldly.

'My hand in friendship. My protection when you return to the tribe.'

'Ali Mansur had brothers, sisters, a mother.'

'They will be compensated. His sisters will be found husbands.'

'Your protection...'

'Extends to all of you. Mitkhal. You, Gutne,

your son, Furja, her children and Hasan.'

Shalan rose to his feet. 'Don't look surprised. You would never have left the women to fetch horses if Hasan hadn't lived. You wanted them for him – not Furja.'

'He doesn't remember his life as a British officer.'

'I know.' Shalan opened the door of the cabin. 'Farik is my slave, not Furja's. He heard I offered a reward for information as to her whereabouts, and found a way to reach me, even when he was not allowed to leave Furja's house. Norfolk is on the bank waiting for you. Sir Percy Cox has travelled upstream to the British lines on Lieutenant Colonel Leachman's boat, the *Lewis Pelly*. You can speak to him about the guns, horses, ammunition and goats.'

'The mahaila, Dorset, Somerset...'

'I will take them to Furja's house and wait for you in Basra.'

Mitkhal followed Shalan on deck. Norfolk, saddled and bridled was on the bank. His bags were across the mare's back.

Shalan pointed to the gang plank. 'See you in Basra, Mitkhal.'

Mitkhal remembered Peter's letter to his wife. He could hardly ask Shalan to carry it to the mission.

He walked on to the bank, pulled his robe close, and mounted his horse.

Chapter Thirty-four

The Battle of Umm-El-Hannah, Friday 21st January 1916

Michael stood on the firing step inside the front line trench, home to, and held by the Black Watch. He was soaked to his skin as were the men around him. The rain was insidious, constant, freezing and could permeate a dozen layers, even those guaranteed waterproof. A shell exploded a hundred yards ahead. He found it difficult to resist the urge to dive for cover.

He gazed at the backs of the British troops advancing towards the Turkish lines on his right. As in every battle since he'd joined the Indian Expeditionary Force, they'd been ordered out over a flat plain with no more defences than the covering fire that could be provided by their comrades "stood down" in the trenches behind them.

He slid down and sat on the cold, clammy sandbag. His notebook and pencil were in his pocket but he didn't need them. He already knew that the sights and sounds he'd seen and heard since he'd stepped on Mesopotamian soil would be seared on his mind for the rest of his life.

'Not making notes for the paper, sir?' a corporal asked. 'The readers of the *Mirror* will be disappointed.'

'I have it all up here.' Michael tapped his forehead.

'So do I, sir, and, frankly, I wish I didn't. Seems to me none of us will be able to forget this mess-up in a hurry. That's if any of us are lucky enough to make it back home,' a private commented.

The sound of a whistle shrilled above the artillery barrage. High-pitched, ominous, the sound stiffened the backs of the lines of waiting men. An officer halfway down the line held up his fingers and dropped them one by one. The atmosphere was tense, expectant. When the officer had counted to ten, he blew his whistle a second time.

The men moved as one, climbing up and out of the trench. Michael returned to his post on the firing step, and watched them follow their officers directly into the path of the Turkish guns.

A shell exploded in front of the corporal he'd spoken to. The shock sent his body spinning in the air. When he landed his legs were more than six feet from his body but his torso continued to shudder and scream.

Unable to stomach the nightmarish scene, Michael slid back to the floor of the trench and clapped his hands over his ears, more to drown out the cries of the wounded than the booming of artillery and staccato of rifle shot.

A stretcher fell on his head, its pole hitting him on the arm. A medic stumbled in behind it, carrying a wounded sergeant on his back.

'Sorry, sir. Hope I didn't hurt you.' The man laid the sergeant on the muddy floor.

'I'm fine.' Michael splashed towards them. 'Can I help?'

'You can if you've any water to spare.' The medic looked up at the rain. 'Seems like even God is joking with us. Talk about "water, water, everywhere, and not a drop to drink." That isn't thick with dirt, that is.'

Michael handed over his water bottle. The stretcher-bearer moistened the lips of the sergeant who tried to grab the bottle.

'Dare not give you any more, Sergeant,' the stretcher-bearer warned. 'Not when you've a stomach wound.'

Michael noticed the sergeant's shirt and tunic had been slashed open and his torso covered by a field dressing. The linen was saturated, stained by a bubbling flow of blood. Michael tried to give the sergeant an encouraging smile. He couldn't manage a sincere one. Every soldier who'd been near a field ambulance knew the worst wounds for attracting infection were those in the abdomen.

'Fancy bandaging,' Michael complimented the medic for the sake of saying something.

'Not mine, sir. I couldn't do anything as good as that. There's a doctor out there from the Indian Medical Service. He's taken bullets in his left arm and right side but is still attending to the wounded and refusing to go to the clearing station. My mate's helping him. Not often you come across a useful toff.'

'First time I've heard anyone referred to as a "useful toff".' Michael repeated the expression.

'That's because you meet so few of them, present company excepted, sir.' The medic took Michael's water bottle when Michael offered it again and drank. 'You take command now. They're a right load of useless toffs, sitting well behind the lines or in their boats at a nice safe distance from the shells, bullets and fighting. Ordering us poor sappers to do the impossible and march up to the Turks as if we'd been issued with invisible protective armour.'

The sergeant groaned.

'Well it was nice chatting to you, sir, but the sooner I get this non-com to the Field Ambulance the sooner I can get back to my mate. There are a lot of men out there who need us, and if that doctor's taken another bullet we might persuade him to come in. Do you mind if I leave the stretcher here until I come back?'

'Be my guest. It's not as if it will be in the way of anyone.' Michael propped it up beneath a torn piece of mud-stained tarpaulin. 'How far back is the Field Ambulance?'

'Behind the third line manned by the 37th Dogras and 6th Jats. You're not wounded, are you, sir?'

'No. You've put me to shame. I'm a war correspondent but I can't write in the rain so I may as well go out there and see if I can help.'

'Here take this, sir. I would say it would help you to avoid pot shots but it didn't do much for my mate.' The medic handed over a red-cross armband.

'Thank you.' Michael took it and pushed it into his pocket. He linked his hands to give the stretcher-bearer a leg up out of the trench. When the medic was on top he lifted the sergeant out of the mud and handed him up.

411

The guns fell quiet but not for long. Michael glanced at the packs and detritus left by the men who were fighting and wondered how many would return to collect their belongings.

He took the armband, pulled it on over the sleeve of his jacket, returned to the firing step and lifted his binoculars.

There were more Connaught Rangers and Hampshires lying in the mud than there were advancing. All the wounded were coated in clay and thick mud, most shivering. He continued to scan the field. He spotted Tom kneeling over a man on the ground, an orderly beside him. When Tom turned and delved into his knapsack, Michael saw that his sleeve was bloodstained. When he turned back he saw stains on his left side.

'So you're the idiot doctor who wouldn't leave the injured to go to the Field Hospital to have your own wounds tended to.' Michael packed his binoculars into his knapsack, dropped it next to the packs on the ground and climbed over the top. He turned to see Daoud beside him.

'I go where you go, sir.'

Kut al Amara, Tuesday 25th January 1916

The brigadier faced Colonel Perry across his desk. 'I don't want a list of the foodstuffs you found in the natives' secret storerooms, what I require is an estimate of how long we can hold out.'

'The supply department...'

The brigadier had no compunction about interrupting Perry. 'Colonel, when you took stock

412

shortly after our arrival on the 3rd December last year, you stated the garrison had one month's rations. Accordingly, General Townshend radioed your estimation to command in Basra and General Nixon was given to orders to expedite the Relief Force at all costs. Four days later on the 7th December you doubled the time limit to sixty days.'

'It took time to assemble all our stocks and calculate...'

The brigadier held up his hand to silence Perry. 'I'm not finished. On the 11th of December you estimated the local population could feed themselves for three months and all ranks in the garrison could remain on full rations, except for meat, for a further fifty-nine days.' The brigadier picked up a file. 'You signed off on the report, Colonel Perry.'

'It was founded on intelligence available to me at the time, sir.'

'Based on your predictions, Lieutenant General Aylmer pressed on with the relief operation although he was far from ready. As a result he lost 600 men on the 6th January and over 4,000 on the 7th. On the 16th of January you declared there was a twenty-one day supply of half-rations for the British and an eighteen-day supply of half rations for the Indians, which would take the garrison through until the 18th February. On the 22nd January you announced there were 22 days of half-rations for the British troops, but that there was more food available in the town. It is the 25th January today, is it not?'

'It is, sir,' Perry squirmed.

413

'Now you tell me that following your house-to-house searches you have eighty-four days' half-rations left which should keep the garrison fed until the 17th April, and in addition you have 3000 horses and mules that can be slaughtered?'

'That I entirely attribute to my own and my junior officers' laudable efforts, sir...'

'Laudable. Did you listen when I recounted the casualty figures for the Relief Force? The last three days alone run into thousands of men Aylmer and the Expeditionary Force can ill afford to lose.'

'With all due respect, sir. The men under my command conducted a thorough house-to-house search...'

'Have you any conception of the number of complaints this office has received from your "thorough search", Perry?'

The silence in the room grew intense.

'Do me, and yourself, a favour, Perry. Check every item of our food stock. Every item,' the brigadier repeated forcefully. 'Bring me a full and comprehensive list by six this evening, with a platoon of men who can show your successor exactly where each and every item is being stored.'

Perry's colour heightened to that of ripe burgundy but he managed an unemotional, 'Yes, sir.'

'I want you to supervise this search personally. Not from the Norfolks' officers' mess while you play bridge. In fact you can give the bridge parties a miss from now on. You won't have time when you take up your new duties.'

'New duties, sir?'

'To personally supervise the slaughtering of all

mules, donkeys, and horses for consumption by the men. You are to examine them prior to slaughter for signs of disease. Watch the butchering and ensure each regiment receives a fair share of the meat. That will be all, Colonel.'

British Expeditionary Force camp outside Umm-El-Hannah, Wednesday 26th January 1916

Michael left Daoud in the Indian field kitchen and negotiated his way around the wounded laid out on the floor of the aid station. An orderly had assured him that Captain Mason was in the top left-hand corner of the tent, along with the other wounded awaiting non-urgent surgery.

He looked down at the faces of the men lying on the canvas. Most were mercifully unconscious, those who were awake were showing signs of pain but few were complaining. Possibly because there was no one to complain to, as all the available orderlies and doctors were busy assessing the stream of wounded still pouring in from the battle-field.

'Michael?'

The voice was weak. He looked down. Tom gazed up at him.

'They said you were here, I've been looking for over an hour.' Michael crouched down, balancing precariously on the balls of his feet, he steadied himself with his hands lest he topple on one of the men lying around him.

'They've just brought me in from outside.'

'Damn the India Office for not giving the

medical service tents and supplies.'

'The doctors are doing what they can. I was stupid to get shot...' Tom gasped for breath and his eyes rolled.

'Medic!' Michael shouted. He looked around. The only movement came from the men lying groaning on the ground.

'Medic!' he repeated. He'd never felt so impotent. Wishing he'd studied medicine like his cousins, he took out his water bottle, upended it on his handkerchief, and bathed Tom's face.

There was a bandage on Tom's arm, but whoever had tied it hadn't bothered to remove Tom's shirt. Another bandage was wound around his torso. Then he noticed a third wound in Tom's neck. He took his handkerchief and bathed it.

'Put pressure on it to stop the bleeding.'

An Indian orderly stood over him. The man looked as though he was sleeping on his feet.

'This man is a doctor and he needs a doctor now,' Michael protested.

'All the doctors are operating.' The orderly bent over Tom and examined the wound. 'I'll put a stitch in it, it should hold until he gets down-river.'

'Downriver! You can't move a man in this state.'

'It's his best chance. A medic will be on board in case of further emergency. There,' the orderly fastened off the stitch he'd put in Tom's neck.

'Damn...'

'Please, sir. These men are sick, don't make so much noise. Believe me, your friend is better off than most. He will be cared for on the boat and in a few days he will be at Amara. There is a proper

416

hospital there. With nurses and everything. Excuse me, sir.' The orderly moved on.

Michael's thigh muscles were cramped and aching. He wanted to move but he also felt there was no way he could desert his cousin. He had no idea how long he crouched there. The light beneath the canvas turned from light to mid- then dark grey. The pounding of the rain above grew heavier, the rivulets of water running down the inside of the walls, thicker.

A lamp shed a glow into the darkness. He sensed movement further down the tent; cold rain needled in as the tent flaps opened and closed.

'You still here, Mikey?' Tom mumbled.

'I thought you were out of it.'

'Not quite.'

'They're taking you downstream.'

'Best place. Out of this.'

The men in front of Tom were carried out. The stretcher-bearers returned and took the men either side of him.

'Sorry, sir, we have to take the captain now.' A medic set a stretcher beside Tom.

Michael grasped Tom's hand. 'As a doctor I expect you to take care of yourself.'

'Get John out of Kut?'

'I'll try, and I'll make a point of looking you up next time I'm in Amara.'

'With John.'

Michael recognised the signs of delirium.

'We'll come together.'

'Really have to go, sir.'

Michael nodded to the medics. He sat back, stretched his legs in front of him, and watched as they carried Tom out. For the first time since he'd entered the tent he listened – really listened to the moans and cries of the remaining men. One word was intelligible above all others. 'Water.'

He reached for his water bottle and unscrewed the top. It was empty. He continued to sit and wait while the circulation returned. So much thirst to quench and so few people to do it.

Chapter Thirty-five

Basra wharf, Wednesday 16th February 1916

Restless, Georgiana paced the deck and watched the dock inch gradually closer. It was swarming with lines of British troops drawn up in formation. Behind them sepoys were ferrying supplies to and from vessels. Doctors and nurses were supervising the unloading of wounded from hospital ships and on to hospital transports.

She ran a practised eye over the walking wounded. Most looked as though they should be lying on a stretcher or at least propped up in a chair. She couldn't hazard a guess at the condition of the men on stretchers.

Clary joined her. 'I missed you at breakfast.'

'The snorer in our cabin kept me awake most of the night so I decided to eat early. Besides, I was anxious to catch a first glimpse of the town. Harry wrote to me about it in detail when he was sent here as punishment back in 1912. I've been

418

longing to see it ever since.'

'First impressions?'

'The country's flatter and greener than I thought it would be but that could be down to the time of year. Trust us to arrive at the height of the rainy season.' She stuck her hand out from under her umbrella. 'One of the crew said we'll be close enough to drop the gangplank in ten minutes.'

'It looks every bit as cold, wet, and miserable as London.'

Georgiana looked at her. 'Clary, what's the matter?'

'The senior nursing officer posted a list on the board five minutes ago. Apparently the fighting's escalated. There's been an enormous influx of wounded.'

'I saw some of them being unloaded on the quayside.'

'Not all, apparently. Some have been taken to hospitals upriver and that's where half of us are going, including me.'

'You're not disembarking?' Georgiana was as disappointed as Clarissa.

'Not here.'

'I'm so sorry. I suppose it was optimistic of me to hope that we'd both be in Basra and could continue as we've have done in London. Arranging to see one another on our days off and spending our free time together. You will write?'

'I promise,' Clary said solemnly.

'You have the address of the Lansing Memorial Hospital?'

'You've given it to me three times.'

A thud announced that the gangplanks had

been dropped. Georgiana balanced her umbrella in her left hand and hugged Clarissa. She looked down at her military issue kitbag and small case.

A middle-aged captain appeared at her elbow.

'If you are disembarking, madam, may I and my bearer help you with your luggage?'

'Thank you, Captain. You're very kind.' Georgiana picked up her case. The captain directed his bearer to pick up Georgiana's kitbag. The Indian shouldered it along with the captain's.

'You have a husband with the forces in Basra?' the captain enquired as they walked ashore.

'No. I've been given a post at the Lansing Memorial Hospital.'

'The American mission?' He asked in surprise.

'Yes.' She looked up and down the quayside but could see no sign of vehicles for hire. 'Are you stationed in Basra, Captain?'

'Horace Maytree.' He shook her hand. 'I am. I've just returned from a spell of leave in India. My wife made me promise that I'd look for accommodation here for both of us, but, I ask you, does this look like the sort of place you'd want to take your wife?'

'I don't know, Captain. I don't have a wife,' she smiled. 'Is there any transport I can hire to take me to the Lansing Memorial?'

'There should be, but this isn't the kind of country where a lady should travel alone.'

'I'm accustomed to being independent, Captain Maytree.'

'Please, for my own peace of mind, allow me to assist you.' He spoke to his bearer in Hindustani. The man dropped the kitbags and scurried off.

'I really don't want to put you to any trouble.'

'You're not. I need to hire a carriage to get to my own bungalow and the Lansing isn't far out of my way.' His bearer returned with a carriage and an Arab driver.

Captain Maytree helped Georgiana inside, handed her the suitcase and left the kitbags for his bearer to load.

'I find it odd that a British lady would want to travel halfway across the world to work in an American mission,' he commented after they set off.

'I have a brother with the British Expeditionary Force. I'm worried about him and taking a job with the Lansing Memorial was the only way to reach here.'

'An officer?'

'Lieutenant Colonel Harry Downe.'

'The political officer?'

'You know him?'

'Not personally, but everyone with the Expeditionary Force has heard of Harry Downe's exploits. He's quite the hero.' He coughed nervously. 'You have heard...'

'That he's posted missing presumed dead. Yes, but I refuse to believe it and I won't until I see his body, Captain Maytree.'

'In which case I wish you luck, Miss...'

'Downe, Dr Downe.'

'Pleased to make your acquaintance, Dr Downe.'

She looked out at the high mud brick walls of the town's buildings.

'This area's not a pretty sight but the outskirts

of the town are quite attractive. If you look ahead you'll see villas set in gardens. The large white building just coming into sight now is the Lansing Memorial Hospital. As you see, and I promised, it's no more than a few minutes' drive from the British compound.' Captain Maytree pointed to a building hemmed in on all sides by rough wooden carts filled with wounded Turkish soldiers. 'I'll ask the drivers to move some of these carts on so we can drop you at the door.'

'No, please I'll walk.' As soon as the cart slowed, Georgiana opened the door and stepped down. She thrust her hand into her pocket. 'I must pay for the carriage...'

'I wouldn't hear of it,' the captain looked up as a nursing sister approached. 'I have a feeling we're about to be confronted.'

'This is a hospital with strict visiting times. If you come to visit anyone, please return at a time when we're not busy...'

'I'm Dr Downe. Please find someone to take my luggage and stow it where it can be retrieved later. You are...?'

'Sister Margaret.' The nurse was so shocked by a female doctor it was as much as she could do to mutter her name.

Georgiana looked down at a patient who was lying, choking in the back of a cart. 'Please, find me an apron – an overall would be better and a medical kit? This man's windpipe needs stitching urgently, if he's to survive.'

She pulled off and pocketed her gloves before exerting pressure on a severed blood vessel. 'Apron and medical kit?' she repeated.

'Right away,' Sister Margaret shouted to an orderly.

British Camp outside Umm-El-Hannah, Wednesday 16th February 1916

Mitkhal plodded slowly into the British camp. The constant rain, tramp of feet and wagon traffic had turned the ground to sludge. After seeing Norfolk struggle hock deep in the glutinous mess, he'd dismounted and walked the mare the last few miles. Arab auxiliaries had congregated beneath a wind-torn, open-sided canvas shelter on the edge of camp. They'd lit a brazier inside. It smouldered low in the waterlogged atmosphere, belching out black smoke. He searched for a familiar face, and recognised Daoud, one of Cox's senior auxiliaries.

'Mitkhal, my friend.' Daoud left the fire to greet him. 'I don't know which looks worse, you or your horse.' He took Norfolk's rein and called over a syce. 'Treat this horse like royalty. Give it plenty of feed, a rub down, and as dry a stable spot as you can find in this marsh. Don't worry, Mitkhal, she'll be well looked after.' He handed Mitkhal a camp chair.

Mitkhal took the chair, lifted his saddlebags from Norfolk's back, and slung them over his shoulder. 'Thank you.'

'Didn't expect to see you back here so soon,' Daoud commented.

'I need to see the Chief Political Officer urgently.'

'You have news?'

'News that won't wait,' Mitkhal made it clear he'd said as much as he was going to.

'All the political officers are on the chief's boat. I'll find a bellum to take you there but the meeting has just started so they won't be free for an hour or so. Are you hungry?'

Mitkhal recalled eating fish and flatbread but couldn't recall whether it had been that morning or the day before. 'I could eat.'

Within minutes Daoud had organised a mug of tea, a bowl of bully beef stew, and a bellum to ferry Mitkhal to the staff boat.

'I can't promise you that you will see Sir Percival Cox quickly, but what I can promise you, is that he'll find it more difficult to ignore you, once you're on board.

British staff boat moored on the Tigris outside Umm-El-Hannah, Wednesday 16th February 1916

Sir Percy Cox looked down the table at his assembled political officers. Over half were dressed in Arab robes, including Michael Downe, who'd just returned from a trip upriver to meet one of the sheiks camped just outside the Turkish lines. Despite his similarity to his brother, unlike Harry he looked ill at ease in native dress. The archetypal Englishman masquerading in fancy dress for a ball.

'So, to begin.' Cox closed the file in front of him and surveyed the men around the table in the cramped captain's quarters. 'I can't stress enough that what I'm about to tell you is highly confidential, and can never be mentioned or alluded to outside of this room. General Townshend is seeking approval from Lord Kitchener and the War Cabinet for an attempt to be made to buy the freedom of the garrison in Kut from the Turks.'

'At what price, sir?' Michael asked.

'One million pounds and five guns.'

'General Townshend has one million pounds with him in Kut?' a major asked.

Cox sat back in his chair. 'According to my sources in the India Office, neither he, nor the India Office, has anywhere close to that amount of money.'

'It's a bluff?' Michael ventured.

'On the contrary, I believe General Townshend made the offer on the assumption that either the India Office or the War Cabinet will provide the funds should the time come for them to be paid. What I want you gentlemen to do is contact every influential sheikh you know, friendly, duplicitous, or hostile and without going into details, canvass their opinion on such a bribe being paid to the Turks in return for free passage out of Kut for the beleaguered garrison.'

'I can tell you now, sir, what the reaction of every decent Arab with integrity will be,' one of the senior political officers said. 'The British would lose the respect of the native population and our prestige in Mesopotamia and the Near East would hit rock bottom. We would be called cowards, and rightly so. Men stand and fight for their beliefs. Only cowards would try to bribe themselves out of a siege situation where the odds are stacked against them.'

Cox didn't comment. He turned to Michael. 'Mr Downe, you have just returned from a conversation with the leaders of the Arab auxiliaries who've attached themselves to the Relief Force. Have you an opinion on this matter?'

'Only to agree with what's already been said, sir,' Michael demurred. 'From what I've been told by the old Gulf hands, when Force D landed here in the autumn of 1914 the Arabs regarded us as invincible, which is why so many sheikhs flocked to our side. Now, most of the sheikhs I've spoken to regard the British as vulnerable which is why so many have retreated to the side lines to await the outcome of events rather than fight alongside us. You say that General Townshend has sought approval from the British War Cabinet and Lord Kitchener. Is he likely to get it?'

'Is Michael Downe the war correspondent asking that question or Michael Downe, intelligence gatherer for the British Expeditionary Force?' Cox asked pointedly.

'I gave you my word when I took this post, sir, that everything said within the confines of the Political Office is confidential. All my dispatches are heavily censored and I have sent my editor nothing that has not been approved by yourself or senior staff of the Relief Force.'

'Point taken, Downe. Please accept my apologies. Like everyone else in the force, I'm tired. Recent setbacks have affected me more than I would wish. Has anyone else a comment they wish to make?' He looked down the table. 'No? Carry on the good work, gentlemen. No one knows more than myself that it's not easy in view of the recent setbacks to convince the native population that we will be victorious but I assure you, we will win this war. On all fronts. Dismissed, gentlemen.'

Chairs were scraped back over the board planking and the officers began to file out of the door.

'A word please, Mr Downe,' Cox said as Michael stood in line to follow the others. He waited until they were alone before continuing. 'I wanted to thank you for the sterling work you've done among the natives in such a short time.'

'Any success I've had in gathering information is due to Daoud, sir, not me.'

'It's you in your brother's clothes that loosens their tongue, Downe. I've heard people of all races and colours say that Harry Downe was more Arab than the Arabs. He understood the Arab mind better than any of us and with understanding came mutual respect. How I miss him.'

'I'm finding it hard to live without him, sir,' Michael couldn't bring himself to say more.

'It's going to be hard to win this war without him.' Cox changed the subject. 'I'm sorry if I offended you earlier by the suggestion that you would print confidential information.'

'No offence taken, sir.'

They were disturbed by a knock at the door. An adjutant opened it.

'Lieutenant Colonel Downe's orderly, Mitkhal, is here, sir. He's asking for an audience. He says it's urgent.'

'Show him in, captain.'

'Yes, sir.'

Michael went to the door.

'No need to leave, Downe. I understand you've already met your brother's orderly.'

'Briefly, sir.'

'Now's your chance to renew the acquaintance.'

Chapter Thirty-six

Lansing Memorial Hospital, Basra, Wednesday 16th February 1916

Georgiana stepped around the burial party who were headed towards the room Dr Picard had designated temporary mortuary. Fourteen Turkish soldiers had been laid out on the floor in the four hours since her arrival. Testimony to their deplorable condition on arrival.

Already she felt a murderous rage towards the inept British doctors who'd allowed the transfer of dying, wounded, vulnerable POWs in conditions of filth and degradation an animal shouldn't be subjected to.

Theo left the theatre and joined her on the ward. He pulled off his blood-stained gown and took a clean one a volunteer nursing assistant handed him. 'How are you coping, Dr Downe? You haven't stopped since you walked through the door.'

'My disgust is sustaining me. Just looked at this man.' She uncovered the arm of the patient she'd been tending. It was black with putrefaction, and covered with large blisters. This man's wound hasn't been dressed in the ten days it took him to reach here.'

'How do you know?'

'Because his sergeant,' she pointed to the man lying on the makeshift bed on the floor next to him, 'speaks French, and I understand enough to make out what he's saying. How could British doctors allow Turkish POWs to be treated like this? If this man's wound had been properly cleaned after it was inflicted it would have healed. Instead his arm will have to be amputated...'

Theo interrupted her. 'Time to take a break. We'll talk about this in the kitchen. Sister Margaret?' Theo called to the senior nursing sister. 'Put this man on the list for immediate surgery ... and before you protest, I know immediate doesn't necessarily mean within twenty-four hours. Angela,' he addressed his sister who'd handed her class over to Mrs Butler, yet again, so she could help out at the hospital. 'We're having tea.'

'That means you want me to make it?'

'Thank you for volunteering. But as you've finished dressing that leg wound I thought you could do with a break.'

He ushered Georgiana into the kitchen and ferreted around the shelves. 'There should be some cookies here...'

'Mrs Butler sent down cheese sandwiches. They're in the tin.' Angela joined Georgiana at the sink where she was washing her hands. 'Hello, Dr Downe, I'm Angela Smythe.'

'I'm Georgie. Dr Wallace and Dr Picard told me you know my brother.'

'Your brother? He's with the British Force?'

'Dr Downe is Harry's twin sister.' Theo set two cheese sandwiches on a plate, sat on the edge of the table and proceeded to eat them. 'Excuse me for not standing on ceremony, Dr Downe, or may I call you Georgie too?'

'You may.'

'I'm ravenous. Twenty-four hour shifts do that to me.'

'We met your other brother...'

'Michael?' Georgiana dried her hands and took the plate of sandwiches Theo handed her.

'He wasn't here long before leaving for upriver to join John Mason's brother Tom. I brought you in here...'

'Because we both needed a break,' Georgiana suggested to Theo.

'That, and because I wanted to tell you how much I admire you. You haven't stopped since you walked through the door.'

'I hate to disappoint you but I took ten minutes to wash my face and cool my temper in the nurses' room an hour ago.'

'I'm trying to tell you, if you'll allow me to get a word in edgewise, that the abysmal condition of the POWs is not down to the Relief Force Medical Service.'

'It isn't?' She took the tea Angela handed her. 'Thank you. If it isn't down to them, whose fault is it?'

'The India Office. They haven't sent the Expeditionary Force enough supplies of anything. Hospital tents, equipment, dressings, doctors, orderlies, antiseptic, drugs, the list of what they don't have is endless and the little they do receive is invariably sent late, often too late to be of use. Believe me, the Turkish POWs have fared no worse than the British wounded. I'm sure Colonel Allan would be delighted to show you around the British Military Hospital to prove my point.'

Georgiana's temper rose. 'Are you telling me that our troops are being ordered into battle without medical facilities to care for the wounded?'

'Yes.'

'Dear God! No wonder my aunt said John's letters seemed strange.'

'I'm sorry you've been thrown in the deep end here, but we'll manage if you take a proper break. Mrs Butler has sent down three messages demanding Dr Picard and I send you to the mission so you can unpack and rest.'

'I'm perfectly fine. I'm used to working long shifts in the London hospitals, and that man's arm needs amputating. If it's gas gangrene...'

'Pity help us if it spreads among the other patients.'

'I'll operate as soon as I've scrubbed up.' Georgiana ate the last of the cheese sandwich and returned to the sink.'

'You – operate?' Theo looked at her questioningly.

'I'm a surgeon, Dr Wallace. Didn't they tell you?'

British staff boat moored on the Tigris outside Umm El-Hannah, Wednesday 16th February 1916

'What exactly did Sheikh Ibn Shalan ask for?'

431

Cox unscrewed an ink well, pulled a notepad towards him and picked up a pen.

Because Cox had been constantly on the move, it had taken Mitkhal a full month to track the man down. Time he'd used to evaluate the weaknesses and strengths of both the British and Turkish positions.

'Four hundred new rifles with a corresponding amount of ammunition. A minimum of one hundred horses, and sixteen herds of goats.' Mitkhal had doubled Ibn Shalan's demands on the premise that if the British acquiesced to the full amount, which he doubted, he'd dovetail the extra into his own and Harry's personal holdings. If they beat him down as he expected, it gave him a reasonable margin to bargain with.

The political officer offered no reaction to Mitkhal's demands other than to carry on writing. He finished, read what he'd written, and signed his name at the foot of the page with a flourish. He handed the paper to Mitkhal.

'This is an order for everything you asked for. Four hundred new rifles with a corresponding amount of ammunition, fifty horses – and frankly you'll be lucky to get those – and sixteen herds of goats, to be given to you on production of this note. No further confirmation needed or to be asked for. Present this at Basra HQ and you should have the goods within twenty-four hours.'

Mitkhal tried not to look surprised as he took the paper and folded it into his saddlebag. 'Thank you, sir.'

'No need to thank me. With all that's going on here we can't afford to risk an insurrection at our back. If Ibn Shalan can keep the peace in Ahwaz, the Karun Valley, and the area around the Kerkha river, in return for livestock and guns, it will be a cheaper price to pay than British and Indian blood. I take it you will need assistance to convey the goods from Basra to the Karun Valley?'

'No, sir. Ibn Shalan is waiting for me in Basra. He and his men will arrange the transportation.'

'You'll be travelling with them?'

'I will be returning to the Karun Valley with my wife, our son, and Lieutenant Colonel Downe's wife and children.'

'You've had enough of war?'

'Ibn Shalan will keep the Karun Valley peaceful. It's time for me settle down with my family.'

'I wish you well, Mitkhal, but should we fail to relieve the garrison in Kut in the next two weeks there is one last thing that I would ask you to do for the sake of Hariy's friends besieged there.'

'Which is?' Mitkhal asked warily.

'If the food runs out completely, we will attempt to send a ship through the Turkish lines with supplies to buy more time for the Relief Force to reach the town. Captain Smythe told me you captained the mahaila you sailed out of Kut.'

'I did.'

'Do you think you could sail back in?'

'The Turkish defences are formidable, Lieutenant Colonel Cox.'

'Having you on board whichever vessel is chosen to break the blockade could mean the difference between success and failure.'

'When will the attempt be made?'

'When supplies in Kut are close to running out

and the last attempt to break through by land has failed.'

Mitkhal looked down at the table momentarily before meeting Cox's eye. 'I will do what I can to help navigate your boat.'

'Before then...'

'Yes,' Mitkhal prompted.

'There are a few errands you could run between here, the Turkish lines and Kut. Do it before you pick up the goods in Basra and I'll pay you a fee, as well as Ibn Shalan. That's if you'd care to volunteer.'

Mitkhal met Cox's steady gaze. 'How much?'

British Military Hospital, Amara, Tuesday 29th February 1916

Clarissa carried a box of patients' files into the surgical ward in preparation for the doctors' ward round. To her annoyance Major Chalmers had left his bed – yet again – in direct contradiction of his doctor's orders. Balancing precariously on crutches he'd 'borrowed' from another patient he was heading for the stove where his fellow patients had congregated.

'Major Chalmers! What do you think you're doing?' she demanded in her most authoritative matron imitation.

He gave her a wry smile. 'Racing to the teapot before it's emptied.'

'If Matron sees you "racing" it will be my head, not yours, on the chopping block.' Clarissa saw Richard sway and slipped her arm around his waist. She walked him back to his bed.

'How am I ever going to get fighting fit and back to the Relief Force if you keep me in bed? I'm as weak as a baby.'

'Your weakness has everything to do with your wound and the infection that set in on your voyage down here. Your fever only abated yesterday and your temperature was still higher than normal this morning.' Clarissa folded back the bedclothes and Richard slumped down on the mattress, accidentally dropping his purloined crutches. Clarissa lifted his legs up on to the bed and pulled off his slippers.

'You make me feel like a two-year-old,' Richard complained.

'You behave like a two-year-old.' She ignored the laughter of the men gathered around the stove.

She placed his hospital issue slippers in his locker, pulled up the sheet and blanket and tucked them firmly around him.

Richard would never have admitted it but the only emotion he felt was relief as he sank back on his thin mattress. The pieces of shrapnel embedded in his thigh and pelvis were causing him excruciating pain. The doctors had warned it might not be possible to remove all of them and they wouldn't even attempt to until he'd built up his strength, which was why they'd ordered complete bed rest. Bored, furious at his weakness, he sneaked out of bed whenever the nurses' backs were turned to test his walking ability.

Clarissa pulled up the sheet and blanket covered him to the chin and tucked him firmly in.

'I can't move,' he protested.

'That's the idea. Leave your bed again and I'll look for shackles. I believe the Turks may have left some behind.'

'The doctors wouldn't allow you to use them.'

'This doctor would.' Dr Evans, a short, round, middle-aged Welshman said from the doorway. 'Another batch of wounded are coming down from upriver, Nurse Amey. Matron has ordered all doctors and nurses to meet the convoy.'

'On my way, Dr Evans.'

'Not before you've set the largest orderly available to guard Major Chalmers, I hope.'

Clarissa instructed the orderlies to watch the ward, went to the nurses' cloakroom and slipped on an all-enveloping canvas overall that completely covered her uniform. She'd only been working in Amara a few days but this would be her fourth hospital ship, and if it was anything like as grim and unsanitary as the others she'd need protection.

'You ready, Amey?' Molly Gallivan called from the hallway.

'Coming.' She pushed open the ward door one last time. Richard Chalmers was still lying almost to attention in his bed, just as she'd left him.

'Make sure no patient does anything he's not supposed to,' she warned the Indian orderlies. 'If Major Chalmers tries to move, there's a set of surgical restraining straps in the supplies' cupboard. You have my permission to use them.'

'I pity your husband, Nurse Amey, whoever he'll be,' Richard shouted as she closed the door.

Clarissa lined up with the other nurses and they walked alongside the carts that had been har-

436

nessed the moment the hospital ship had been sighted.

'Holy Mary, mother of God.' Molly Gallivan, Clarissa's cubicle mate in the nurses' quarters crossed herself as a ship drew close to the wharf. 'The smell is enough to knock out a hogman. This is going to be every bit as bad as the last ship.'

Clarissa reached out and grabbed Molly's hand as the engine cut and the gangplank was dropped.

The decks and sides were festooned with a thick dense brown layer of faeces.

'Damn them, why don't they put the dysentery cases on the lower decks?' Dr Evans demanded.

'We do, sir.' An exhausted medic stumbled down the gangplank. 'Dysentery only started spreading on our second day out.'

'Cut off the field dressings and soiled clothes; leave them on deck to be burned.' Dr Evans ran on board the ship. 'Nurses! Stretcher-bearers! Orderlies.'

Clarissa followed him. He handed her a soft-leaded pencil.

'You know what to do?'

'Place a cross on the forehead of those most likely to survive, sir.'

'Good girl.'

'Major?' A man slumped against the door of a cabin called weakly to Major Evans. 'Captain Price, Indian Medical Service, sir. We're just the first.'

'The first what?'

'The first boat, sir. There are three behind us.'

Chapter Thirty-seven

Furja's house, Basra, Thursday 2nd March 1916

'All down! I did it!' Hari jumped up in excitement as her lemon 'ball' knocked down the tower
she and Aza had built out of wooden food bowls
and utensils they'd sneaked out of the kitchen.

'I think it's time to give the bowls and everything else back to Bantu before you break them.'
Furja stroked her daughters' hair.

'One more,' Hari begged.

'Only if you let Aza take two turns to your last
one.'

Hari reluctantly handed Aza the bruised lemon.

Furja picked up the dolls Hari and Aza had left
on a stool and looked through the open arches of
the covered terrace that ran the entire length of the
house. On summer evenings and early mornings it
was a cool and pleasant place to sit. Halfway between living area and courtyard garden it was
everyone's preferred place. In winter and during
the rainy season it was grey and miserable.

The rain poured down in sheets almost as dense
as the black cloth of the Bedouin tent she'd been
raised in. She carried the toys into the sitting
room and opened the door to her bedroom.

Hasan was sleeping again. But his face was no
longer flushed with fever and his breathing was
soft, regular, without nightmarish thrashings.

Three days ago the doctor had told her that he was certain that her husband would recover as much as anyone with his serious injuries could. She was still finding it difficult to believe him.

A knock at the door separating her house from Zabba's interrupted her reverie. She closed the bedroom door, and placed the dolls in the girls' toy box. Farik opened an umbrella, and darted out of the shelter of the terrace to the courtyard door. Furja watched him open it and smiled, ready to welcome Zabba. Her father stood framed in the doorway.

They stared at one another as a full minute ticked past. Shalan was the first to break the silence.

'Isn't my daughter going to invite me into her house?'

Furja steeled herself. 'Of course, Father. Will you honour me by entering and drinking tea?'

He walked through the door and into the terrace.

She turned to her daughters. Hari had fallen unnaturally silent and Aza was hiding behind her sister's skirts – as she always did whenever she felt unsure of a situation – or a stranger.

'Hari, take your sister to Aunt Gutne. You can play in her room.'

Hari craned her neck and gave Ibn Shalan a tentative shy look before grasping Aza's hand and leading her away. Furja called to Farik to bring refreshments and showed her father into the sitting room.

'Please sit down.' She waited until her father had taken his seat before curling on a cushion at his feet.

Farik brought in a tray of coffee and almond and date cakes. He set them on a low table. Furja poured her father coffee, sweetened it to his taste, handed him the cup, and set a selection of the cakes on a plate which she placed before him.

'I've brought Dorset and Somerset back to you. They are in Zabba's stable.'

Furja's blood ran cold. 'Mitkhal...'

'Is well, Furja.'

'You've seen him?'

'When he gave me the horses. I sent him upstream to the British.'

'Why?' she asked suspiciously.

'I needed an ambassador.'

'And as you no longer have Harry to call on you decided to send Mitkhal. Into a British camp when they are in the middle of fighting the Turks.'

Shalan bit into an almond cake. 'This is very good. Did you make it?'

'Gutne, who's worried sick about Mitkhal, did,' Furja replied.

'Why? Mitkhal can look after himself.'

'Why did he "give" you the horses?' Furja didn't attempt to hide her scepticism.

'They were an encumbrance. Mitkhal had brought them out of Kut but he had Norfolk as well and when I asked him to contact the British on behalf of the tribe I offered to bring them here.'

'Mitkhal had Norfolk ... but Ali Mansur...' Furja fell silent. The last person she wanted to discuss with her father was the husband he'd foisted on her against her will.

'Ali Mansur is dead, Furja.'

440

She looked her father in the eye.

'No tears?'

'I didn't wish him ill.'

'You didn't wish to remain with him.'

'I already had a husband.'

'How is he?'

'Dead.'

'Don't lie to me, Furja.'

'It's not a lie, Father. My English husband is dead. He was tortured to death by the Turks.'

'You believe Hasan no longer remembers his past.'

'You can see for yourself.' She left the cushion and opened the bedroom door.

British Military Hospital, Amara, Thursday 2nd March 1916

Clarissa picked up the leg Doctor Evans had just amputated, wrapped it in brown paper and carried it out of the operating theatre. She set it on a trolley that was already loaded with a motley collection of bloody covered body parts.

'You look about done in, Sister, if you don't mind me saying so.' An orderly dumped a zinc bucket of blood- and pus-soaked dressings on the lower shelf of the trolley.

'It's the end of a double shift. I haven't stopped since the last ship docked.'

'Which one was that, Sister?'

'First thing yesterday morning – I think. It all seems rather blurry.' She frowned. 'Another ship's docked?'

441

'Half an hour ago. We've orders to leave everyone on board while we load one that's just come up from Basra with our walking wounded. Hospital's ready to burst at the seams and the doctors are refusing to look at another case.'

'That's hard on the men on the boat.'

'If it's like the last one, there won't be many fit enough to save.'

'I hope you're wrong.' She pulled down her surgical mask. 'I'd better get to the ward and see how many beds we can clear.'

She went to the nurses' cloakroom, peeled off her surgical gown, gloves and mask, dumped them in the linen bin and scrubbed her hands with antiseptic. They were red raw. She surveyed the cracked skin around her nails and wondered if she'd ever manage to restore them to their pre-war glory.

'You know another's ship come in,' Molly said when she returned to the ward.

'An orderly just told me.'

'Given the number of men who have passed through here in the last few days I don't believe there can be anyone left in the Relief Force to fight the Turks.' Molly helped a patient into a wheelchair.

'Basra for Blighty,' he smiled hopefully.

'Never know your luck, lieutenant. War could be over before your wounds have healed.'

'If my return to Blighty is dependent on the peace treaties being signed, I'll be here for the next decade,' he prophesied gloomily.

Clarissa fixed a smile to her face. She was finding it harder to remain cheerful in the sight of so much suffering. Richard Chalmers was sitting in a wheelchair next to his bed playing cards with three other men. They'd all pulled chairs around Richard's empty locker and were using it as a table.

'You're leaving us, Major Chalmers?' she said in surprise.

'Told you I was fitter than you thought. I'll be back upstream fighting fit at the beginning of next month.'

'I don't know about fighting fit, but you might well be back upstream if you give the nursing staff in Basra as much trouble as you've given us. I can't honestly say I'm sorry to see you go.'

Richard adopted a theatrical pose worthy of a melodrama. Hand on heart, he declaimed, 'If the doctors weren't tossing me out of this place, like an unwanted rodent, I would never dream of leaving you, Sister Amey.'

An orderly walked in and shouted, 'Everyone for downstream bound for Basra to the harbour.'

Despite her weariness and mood, Clarissa couldn't help laughing. 'I'll power your chariot, Major Chalmers, as soon as I've put on my overall. Come on, everyone, the sooner you leave the sooner we can unload another vessel.'

The orderlies did their best to cover both the nurses and the patients with umbrellas as they navigated the chaos of the dockside. An orderly took Richard Chalmers's wheelchair from Clarissa as they approached the downstream vessel.

'This is as far as I go, Major Chalmers,' Clarissa shouted to make herself heard above the crowd and the rain.

'Kiss goodbye?' he demanded.

Clarissa looked around. Major Evans and two of the junior doctors were already boarding the vessel that had come down from upstream. It was just as foul as the others and she could feel her stomach churning, revolting at the thought of having to board it. She placed her fingers on her lips and placed them on Richard's cheek.

'That's no good, Sister. I want a proper kiss to remember you by.' He grabbed her arm, pulled her down with a strength she wasn't expecting, and kissed her firmly on the mouth, to the amusement and catcalls of his fellow officers.

'If you were fit, I'd slap your face for that Major Chalmers,' she said when he finally released her.

'If I was fit I'd carry you aboard and marry you in Basra, Sister Amey.'

'Sister Amey,' Major Evans called to her, 'when you've quite finished flirting we need your assistance here.'

'On my way, Major.' She took a deep breath before boarding the upstream vessel. After ruining one pair of shoes on the first boat she trod carefully in an effort to avoid the worst of the mess.

The major handed her the inevitable soft-leaded pencils. She slipped them into her pocket turned and looked down on Tom. She froze. His skin was translucent, as dry as parchment. She crouched next to him and held her own breath until she could be certain he was still breathing.

'Is he dead, Sister Amey?' Familiarity with death had blunted all their sensibilities, Major Evans's more than most.

'No, sir. Not yet.'

He looked more closely at her. 'Do you know this man?'

Clarissa made a superhuman effort to pull herself together. 'Yes, sir. His name is Captain Thomas Mason. He's a doctor.'

'Relative?'

She ventured into the realms of fiction. 'My fiancée, sir.'

'We need all the doctors we can lay our hands on. Get him into the hospital and cleaned up. If he needs surgery, tell whoever's on duty in theatre to put him at the top of the list.'

Clarissa rose to her feet and shouted, 'Stretcher-bearers.'

Furja's house, Basra, Thursday 2nd March 1916

Hasan woke with a start to see his wife and father-in-law looking down at him. Disorientated, he struggled to sit up and face Ibn Shalan.

'My father has brought Dorset and Somerset. They are in Zabba's stables.'

'Mitkhal went to fetch them.'

'Mitkhal is well and sends you greetings, Hasan, I sent him upstream on business.'

'What kind of business?'

'We need more guns, ammunition, and horses to guard the ferenghi pipeline.'

'You expect Mitkhal to steal them?'

'I expect the British to give them to him. It is in their interest to give us what we need to watch their back, when they fight the Turk that stands

445

between them and their men in Kut al Amara.'

Hasan left the bed. 'I want to see the horses.'

'I'll go with you.' Ibn Shalan studied Hasan. The marks of torture on Hasan's face were obvious. The hollow, scar-encrusted eye socket where his right eye had been, the dark circular burn marks on his neck, cheeks, and forehead where cigarettes had been stubbed. The bandaged stump that ended at his right wrist. But the extent of Hasan's sufferings was most noticeable when he moved. Slowly, stiffly, jerking his arms and legs as if he were an old man.

'I'll go ahead and ask Zabba to clear everyone from the passage that leads to the courtyard and the stables.'

'Ask my men to do it,' Ibn Shalan ordered Furja.

Hasan went to the bowl on the table, splashed his face and hands, and put on his kafieh and agal. He took his abba from a chair and slipped it on over his gumbaz.

'You don't trust me.' Shalan had stated a fact not asked a question.

'No. For myself I don't care. But if you should try to hurt Furja, our children or Gutne or Mitkhal...'

'I'm here to invite you – all of you – to return to the tribe.'

'In return for what?'

'Mitkhal's help with the British.'

'Even if I believe that, what about Ali Mansur? He still believes himself to be Furja's husband.'

'Ali Mansur is dead. It's regrettable but a fact.' Shalan shrugged in a gesture Hasan remembered

446

only too well. His father-in-law had frequently resorted to it when enforcing unpalatable decisions.

'How did he die?'

'In a fight with the Bani Lam.'

'Then his relatives will not be baying for my or Mitkhal's blood?'

'Not after I have arranged good marriages for his sisters. Come, Furja is beckoning. We'll go and see your horses.'

Hari and Aza ran out of Gutne's room as soon as they saw their father enter the terrace. Hasan smiled at Aza and offered her his left hand. She grasped it and wrapped her arm around her sister. He was conscious of Gutne and Furja standing behind him. Their concern like their silence hung heavy in the atmosphere.

'Come and see our horses,' he murmured to the girls.

Ibn Shalan went ahead. Furja walked next to Hasan and their daughters. Gutne and Ibn Shalan's men followed them and closed the door behind them. The passageway to the stables was deserted. They walked out into the courtyard. The stable door was open and Hasan led the girls inside.

Dorset and Somerset went to Hasan, burying their heads in his chest.

Furja bit her lips to control the emotion welling inside her.

'Few men could expect such a greeting from their wife,' Ibn Shalan observed dryly. 'You have rivals for your husband's affection, Furja.'

Chapter Thirty-eight

Kut al Amara, Friday 10th March 1916

John took a folded piece of paper from his pocket and handed it to Knight. They were sitting as close to the stove in the dressing room of the hospital as they could get without burning themselves. It was the tail end of a very long day. Turkish snipers had started taking pot shots at the sappers in the forward trenches the moment the sun rose, and as the rains were finally abating, a full hour earlier than a week ago. They only finished firing when darkness blocked their sights. As a result the officers' hospital had been banked up with casualties and the last wounded officer had left for the ward only minutes before.

It was the first break they'd been able to take all day and they were too exhausted to even go in search of an orderly to make them tea. David unfolded the sheet and read the latest directive sent to the medics from General Townshend.

'Finally, Alphonse is taking our advice and killing a large number of horses to reduce the quantity of grain the animals are eating to free up enough to increase the rations of the sepoys.' John rubbed the circulation back into his hands.

'It's a short-term measure,' David commented. 'The garrison can only eat the horses once.'

'As most of the Indian troops are refusing to eat

mule, donkey, or horseflesh, we have to increase their grain rations somehow and I can't think of another way. How many Indians have you seen close to the last stages of malnutrition in the last couple of weeks?'

'Too many,' David admitted. 'If only the idiots would eat horse.'

'Townshend and HQ have done all they can to persuade them. Hunger is the last and most persuasive force. The problem is, even if some of the sepoys change their mind at this late stage they'll be too weak to digest meat, so an increased grain ration is the only solution.'

'It will be hard on the cavalry officers. Given the choice most would shoot their wives in preference to their horses.' David became serious. 'The death rate from disease is escalating alarmingly. How much longer do you think we can hold out?'

'Last time I spoke to Crabbe he said HQ were estimating a month. I told him if it takes that long I seriously doubt any of us will be worth rescuing.'

The door opened and Mitkhal walked in, saddlebags slung over his shoulder and carrying two large boxes.

'Good Lord, Mitkhal. Where did you pop up from?' David asked.

'Turkish lines.'

'They letting you come and go as you like?' John pushed a chair in the Arab's direction.

'To a point.' He handed John a hamper. 'Food from the Relief Force stores.'

John opened it. 'Good Lord, tinned beef, chicken, ham, biscuits, cheese, rice ... we have to

449

keep this for the sick.'

'No you don't. I knew you'd want to give everything away, John, so I filled the mahaila with supplies. It's not as full as when I left the British lines, because I had to give a couple of boxes to the Turks as payment for allowing me to pass through their defences.' He pulled up a chair and sat next to them. 'They asked me carry a communiqué to General Townshend from Halil Bey.'

'Halil suggested we surrender?' John guessed.

'That's what they told me, but the message was sealed, so I can't say for certain.' Mitkhal opened the second box, which held a dozen bottles of brandy. He took out two and handed them to David.

'I was about to go in search for an orderly to make tea but this is better.' David left his chair and took three tin mugs from a shelf. He filled them and handed them around. As he returned to his chair, Warren Crabbe walked in.

'Is that what I think it is?' he asked.

'Brandy, courtesy of Mitkhal.'

'Get yourself a mug,' David held out the bottle.

'Thank you.' Crabbe fetched one and a chair and joined them. 'What wind blew you in, Mitkhal? Not that you're unwelcome.'

'If you're asking about supplies, I brought a load in.' Mitkhal indicated the boxes at John's feet.

Crabbe set his attaché case on the floor and lifted his mug. 'To our brave Arab ally. Without his largesse this bloody awful siege would be bloody insupportable.'

'Who are you trying to impress, Crabbe?' Knight indicated the attaché case.

'No one. Alphonse has written another of his morale-boosting letters to the men in the hope that it will stiffen their resolve along with their backs. I've been given two hundred copies to distribute through the town and the trenches.'

'If he set foot in a trench and talked to some of the men who haven't been able to leave them since we dug in here in December, he might accomplish more in the way of raising spirits,' David griped.

'Given that everyone knows that the Relief Force were rebuffed by the Turks at the Dujeila Redoubt yesterday, he probably decided it would be more circumspect to stay in his quarters.' Crabbe opened his case and handed David a copy of Townshend's communiqué.

'Do we know the casualty figures from the last Relief Force push?' John asked Mitkhal.

'Three and a half thousand,' Mitkhal answered.

'That takes the Relief Force's casualties to fourteen thousand,' Crabbe murmured.

'Fourteen thousand casualties to free less than ten thousand trapped men, and we're still sitting here, bathing our sniper wounds, and fighting disease and boredom.' Knight picked up the brandy bottle. 'Before you suggest the wounded need this more than us, John, we're not machines. We deserve a rest before the onslaught of whatever tomorrow brings.'

'I'll drink to that.' Crabbe raised his mug. 'Rest for all medical officers.'

'You'll drink to anything, Crabbe,' Knight topped up Crabbe's mug first.

'How long are you staying, Mitkhal?' John asked.

'I'll be leaving at dawn. Halil Bey wants an answer to his dispatch by tomorrow.'

'Who did you give it to?' Crabbe asked.

'The brigadier.'

'Then you'll have your answer first thing.'

'If you don't mind I'll leave you to your brandy. I have a pass from the Turks that should get me through their river blockade tomorrow, but some of their sentries are trigger-happy and I'll need my wits about me. May I sleep in your room again, John?'

'I told Dira to leave your bed made up. I'll come up with you.'

'Trouble with you, John, you've no stamina.' Crabbe raised his mug. 'There was a time when you could drink until dawn.'

'That was when I could look forward to three square meals a day.'

'Point taken.' Knight pushed the cork back into the brandy bottle. 'Have you seen the way the flies are breeding in the trenches now the hot weather's on its way? It won't be long before fever strikes.'

'Now you've said it, we can expect the first case tomorrow.' John led the way out and up the stairs. He opened the door to his room. Mitkhal followed him and sat on the only chair. John sank down on the bed.

'Before you fall asleep,' Mitkhal opened his saddlebags and took out a couple of dozen packs of cigarettes, two bottles of brandy, half a dozen lemons, and a dozen oranges.

'Is it Christmas?' John lifted an orange and smelled it.

452

'The Bakhtairi Khans had some of last year's harvest going spare.'

'You expect me to believe that?' John raised his eyebrows. 'There isn't a piece of fruit or a corner of vegetable to be had for love or money in this town, and I doubt there's much in the Turkish lines.'

'None,' Mitkhal countered. 'Arab irregulars aren't into sharing with armies that have invaded their lands. 'I suppose it's too much to hope you'll keep those oranges and eat them yourself.'

'The patients...'

'Those oranges won't go far among hundreds of men and you and Knight look worse than those in your care. How long is it since any of you have eaten fruit or vegetables other than the grass and weeds the cooks harvest and cook?'

'I was going to have a word with you about those. Have you any idea which plants are poisonous and which aren't? Four men died last week. We think a particular plant was to blame.'

'I'll talk to a cook before I leave. You need to keep strong, John,' Mitkhal continued his lecture. 'No one knows what the future will bring...'

John interrupted him. 'You know something don't you?'

Mitkhal met his steady gaze.

'Come on, out with it?'

'Discounting Arab irregulars, the Turks have 13,000 troops and 34 guns at Sannaiyat and 21 guns surrounding Kut along with 11,000 troops.'

'The Relief Force has 24,000 men, and a cavalry brigade. Which puts us a cavalry brigade ahead of the Turks.'

'I went up in a reconnaissance flight with one of the Royal Flying Corps. The manpower is the same but the Turks have 55 guns to your 35. They're also better placed,' Mitkhal revealed.

'You think Townshend will be forced to surrender?'

'I do, and so does he, otherwise he wouldn't be trying to bribe his way out of Kut.' Mitkhal told John about the discussion he'd had with the senior political officer. 'If Townshend accepts Halil Bey's offer...'

'He won't,' John predicted, 'not after just issuing the order to kill the horses. If the Relief Force doesn't break through in the next couple of weeks he may rethink, but not yet.' Depressed by the thought of remaining besieged for the foreseeable future, John changed the subject. 'It's strange to see you without Harry. I miss him more every day.'

'So do I.' Mitkhal pulled the cork on one of the bottles. He drank directly from the neck and passed it to John.

'Are you still fighting for the British because Harry was killed by the Turks?'

'I'm fighting for Ibn Shalan, my wife and child, and Harry's wife and children. The tribe needs the guns and horses the British pay us for guarding their pipeline.'

'Furja and the children. They are well?'

'They were the last time I saw them. I intend to return to them as soon as this siege is over.'

'One way or another.' John drank from the bottle, but barely a mouthful. He'd lost his taste for alcohol and brandy in particular.

Clarissa wheeled Tom's chair through the doors of the hospital and under the covered terrace. 'You wanted fresh air, Captain Mason, you have it.' She stopped next to a bench, pressed the brake on the chair with her foot, and sat beside him.

Tom eyed the men around him. 'I was hoping for privacy?'

'In a military hospital in the middle of a war?' She smiled. 'You'd stand a better chance of privacy in a glass case in the Natural History Museum.'

'No doubt labelled, *Captain Mason, idiot medic who didn't duck low enough to avoid Turkish bullets.*' He reached for her hand. She took it, but only after she'd looked around to check there were no senior nurses around. The doctors, recognising Tom as one of them, were more forgiving of his displays of affection.

'Feeling sorry for yourself more than usual today?' she asked.

'I'm not self-pitying. Am I?' he asked, suddenly feeling that he'd been just that.

'No more than usual.'

'I've been a bloody idiot.'

'I'll second that.'

'All that talk before I left London about you having a good time, getting on with your life and not moping over my absence. I didn't mean a word of it.'

'You didn't?' she waited for him to continue.

'I said it because I thought that's how men going off to war should behave. Nonchalant, as if it was no more important than going off to study medicine in London. Then, when I reached Basra and Charles told Michael and me that John and Harry were dead I realised just how fragile and temporary life is.' He gripped her hand hard and turned to her. 'I love you, Clary. I only realised just how much when I thought I was going to die out on that hellish battlefield. Marry me, please?'

Her smile broadened.

'Is that a good or a bad smile?' he asked.

'Neither. I remembered what Georgiana said when she thought I was going to travel here alone.'

'Knowing Georgie, I might regret asking this, but what did she say?'

'"Don't put up with any nonsense from that cousin of mine when you catch up with him." She added that there'd be military chaplains even in Mesopotamia, and I should drag you to the altar.'

'She's right.'

'No she's not, Tom. If I married you I'd have to give up nursing. I've never felt as needed as I am here. You only have to look around. How can I leave these men to return to England to wait for you? Because given the shortage of doctors you will be going back to active duty.'

'And there's me hoping that I would be invalided out.'

'No you aren't. I overheard you talking to Dr Evans about taking a post here as soon as you're fit enough.'

'If I did, at least we'd be in the same hospital. We could put in for leave at the same time, and sneak down to Basra. As Georgie's living in a Baptist mission she could arrange a secret wedding...'

'That would waste valuable time. If we sneaked down to Basra, as you put it, we could book into a hotel and forget the wedding ceremony.'

'You told Evans we were engaged, at least let me buy you a ring.'

'That I will agree to. But you'll have to buy me a chain as well.'

'Chain – this is the twentieth century.'

'Idiot. A small one I can thread through the ring so I can wear it around my neck under my uniform, out of sight of Matron.'

'Fine, I'll settle for an engagement night and a promise you'll marry me the moment the peace treaties are signed. Agree?'

Clarissa looked around at the men on the terrace. Over half of them were missing limbs or eyes. The peace treaties couldn't come quick enough for her. 'Agree,' she murmured, pulling her hand away as he lifted it to his lips. Matron was walking towards them, and if Matron had an inkling of her relationship with Tom, she knew she'd be moved off his ward within the hour.

Chapter Thirty-nine

Relief Force, Sannaiyat, Sunday 23rd April 1916

Michael was sitting in his tent among a welter of scribbled notes he'd made on the communiqués Townshend had sent out via the wireless from Kut. He was trying to shorten them into an easily read form that wouldn't depress the readers of the Daily Mirror. Something, that given the nature of the news from both the besieged and Relief Force, was proving impossible.

He read what he'd written,

The Force sent to relieve General Townshend and his beleaguered troops at Kut al Amara are entrenched close to the Turks. In places barely 150 to 200 yards separate the front lines of the two armies. General Gorringe is determined to break through, but the Relief Force faces even greater difficulties than the well-armed Turks. The end of the rainy season has brought flooding to the Tigris and some of our troops notably the South Wales Borderers have spent days in waterlogged trenches without blankets, waterproof sheets, or firewood. It speaks volumes for the determination of our troops that their spirits remain as high as their determination to break General Townshend's forces out of Kut.

The rations for all ranks British and Indians inside Kut have been reduced to 5 ounces of meal, but General Townshend has sent word to us over the wireless...

Michael looked up as Peter Smythe entered the tent. 'How did the staff meeting go?'

'Same as all the others. If it was possible to bottle hot air, the amount that was expended could have propelled the entire staff over the Turkish heads and into Kut.'

'Any news?' Michael fished.

'None other than what you've probably already heard. Rations have been reduced to five ounces a day inside Kut. We were starving before I left, I can't bear to think of what John and the others are going through now. The staff are talking of Townshend surrendering and that's before Captain Lawrence and Colonel Beach have even reached here to talk over Townshend's idea of bribing the Turks to stand their siege troops down.'

'Do you think they'll allow Lawrence and Beach to talk to the Turks?' Michael pressed him.

'As Kitchener and the war cabinet are backing the idea I don't see how they can refuse.'

'Despite everything Mitkhal and the Arabs have said about offering Halil Bey the money?'

'When have the brass ever taken any notice of anything a native says, even a knowledgeable one. Come to that, when have the brass taken any notice of anyone who speaks sense.' Peter flung himself down on his cot and reached for his cigarettes. 'I'm not Harry, nor do I possess his knowledge of this country and the people, but I understand enough to know Mitkhal's right. The Turkish press and our enemies will make a great deal of this attempt at bribery. We'll lose "face" – that strange concept few Westerners understand. Harry was one of them. I've never missed your brother more. Things would be very different if he were here.'

'He was only one man. Could he really have done anything to sort out this bloody awful mess?' Michael asked.

'He could, and he would have. Harry was brilliant. As a political officer and a man.' Peter looked around the tent. Mitkhal's cot was made up but there was no sign of his saddlebags. 'Where's Mitkhal?'

When Mitkhal had first stayed in camp overnight, Michael and Peter had insisted on him sharing their tent, much to the annoyance of the staff and their fellow officers.

'Airlifting food into Kut with the Royal Flying Corps. From what the Squadron leader told me this morning, the only flour that doesn't land in the Tigris are the bags dropped from whatever plane Mitkhal's in. Unfortunately from the wireless messages coming out of Kut, the airlifted food is too little too late. Why are you asking, did you want him for something?'

'Not me, the brass. They're planning to take in 250 tons of supplies by river.'

'That's suicide.'

'We're of the same opinion. When I tried arguing with the brass they pointed out Mitkhal's sailed mahailas in and out of the town without any trouble.'

'He had to bribe the Turks even to carry messages for Halil Bey, and the entire cargo of the mahaila he sailed couldn't have amounted to an eighth of a ton. The Turks won't look on 250 tons kindly.'

'All of which I said. It fell on deaf ears. They're preparing the *Julnar* at Amara as I speak. To be crewed by twelve volunteers, unmarried ratings only to apply. Captained by Commander Charles Cowley, Royal Naval Reserve.'

'I've heard of him. Isn't he half Armenian?' Michael checked.

'His mother was of that race.'

'Haven't the Turks put a price on his head?'

'You're well-informed. They have. There's no doubt that if they catch him, they'll hang him. Something else I pointed out to the brass that they ignored.'

Relief Force, Fallahiya, Sunday 23rd April 1916

Peter and Michael accompanied Mitkhal when he rode downstream from the British camp at Sannaiyat to Fallahiya where the *Julnar* was berthed. They reached the steamer at six in the morning. Indian sepoys had set up a kitchen on the bank and greeted them with mugs of tea and bowls of bully beef.

'This is way beyond what anyone expects of you, Mitkhal.' Peter said as they all walked down to the bank and stared at the river. 'The ship's engineer, Sub-Lieutenant Reed, and Commander Cowley, know the Tigris. They both worked for the Euphrates and Tigris Steamship company before the war.'

'They don't know the location of the Turkish gun emplacements and sniper burrows.'

'They asked for bachelor volunteers. You have a

461

wife and child, and there's Harry's wife and children...'

'Ibn Shalan will care for them.' He handed Michael Norfolk's reins.

'You want me give the mare to Harry's wife?'

'I doubt you'll find her. If I don't return, keep the horse. Take her back to Harry's home at Clyneswood.'

'You know about Clyneswood?

'Nights can be long and cold in the desert. Take care, both of you.' Mitkhal slung his saddlebags over his shoulder and walked up the gangplank. He didn't want to walk away from Peter and Michael without telling them that Harry lived. But Harry's safety and that of their families was paramount, and Harry wasn't alive. Only Hasan Mahmoud. If he told Michael or Peter about Hasan Mahmoud they would search for him if they survived the war. And the one thing he couldn't predict was how Hasan would react if he was faced with someone from his previous life.

Lansing Memorial Mission, Sunday 23rd April 1916

'It's wonderful to see everyone around the table for once,' Mrs Butler said as soon as her husband had said grace. 'I take it things have quietened in the hospital.'

'The flood of wounded Turkish POWs has dwindled to a steady stream.' Dr Picard watched the maid fill his soup bowl.

'Dr Downe, I know you're needed in the hospital but this is only the second meal you've shared with us since your arrival. I hope Theo and Dr Picard aren't wearing you out?'

'No more than the London Hospital, Mrs Butler, and please call me Georgiana. It reminds me that I have a personality beyond that of doctor.'

'How are you settling in, Dr Downe?'

'As far as the hospital goes I believe I've made myself useful. As for the rest, I'll tell you when I've had time to look around.'

'Useful,' Dr Picard repeated. 'I don't know how we managed without Dr Downe.'

'Have you heard from your brother?' Theo asked.

'Michael seems determined to stay with the Relief Force. I also had a letter from a friend of mine who's working in the military hospital in Amara.'

'A doctor?' Dr Picard asked.

'A nursing sister, Clarissa Amey. She and Captain Tom Mason,' Georgiana looked up from her plate and glanced at Maud, 'have just become engaged. As soon as Tom has recovered from his wounds they intend to visit Basra to buy an engagement ring.'

'They must stay here,' Mrs Butler insisted.

'First he has to recover from his wounds,' Georgiana qualified. 'According to Clary – Clarissa, he was in a bad way when he arrived at Amara.'

'I thought doctors were supposed to stay behind the lines.' Dr Picard commented.

'No one told Tom that. He was treating men in no-man's-land when he was hit.' Georgiana picked up her soup spoon again.

'It would be lovely if Captain Mason recovered

463

in time for your and Theo's wedding, Maud,' Mrs Butler said unthinkingly.

Her remark was met by silence.

'Oh dear, how tactless of me,' Mrs Butler apologised. 'I doubt Captain Mason would want to attend the wedding of his brother's widow.'

'If you'll excuse me, I think I hear Robin crying.' Maud left the table and the room.

'Theo, I'm so sorry.'

'Don't trouble yourself, Mrs Butler. It's just wedding nerves now the date is drawing closer.' Theo handed the maid his soup bowl.

'Is everything organised, Theo?' Mrs Butler asked. 'Because if there's anything I can do, I'd be delighted.'

'We're seeing the solicitor tomorrow morning to draw up the legal agreement.'

'You need to see a solicitor before you can marry in Basra?' Georgiana raised her eyebrows.

'Only if you have a stepson to adopt.' Theo saw no reason to make his financial arrangement with Maud public.

'Of course, how remiss of me.'

The maid cleared the soup bowls and brought in the entrée. Maud returned.

'Robin has settled,' she announced to the room in general.

'Can we talk about the meeting with the solicitor after dinner?' Theo asked.

'Of course.' Maud kept her eyes downcast and concentrated on her meal.

'Would you like a game of chess after dinner?' Angela asked Georgiana shyly. Having seen the way she worked in the hospital and barked orders

464

at the formidable Sister Margaret, she was more than a little in awe of Harry's sister.

'Charles called into the hospital today. He and Kitty are going to a fundraising concert party in aid of war orphans at the Basra Club and he offered to pick me up. Why don't you come too, Angela?'

'I couldn't possibly. I'd feel like a gooseberry.'

'Then we'd be gooseberries together. I haven't met Kitty, but Charles is clearly besotted with her.'

'He still hasn't managed to wangle a posting to the front?' Theo asked.

'From what he said, it's not for the want of trying. But as he can barely stand upright for more than five minutes with a stick, I can understand HQ's reluctance to send him further than the Basra office.'

'That won't please Charles.'

'It hasn't.' Georgiana looked at Angela. 'You will come with us, won't you, please? I think Charles only asked me out of a sense of duty and it would be lovely to have someone to talk to when he and his lady love are billing and cooing.'

'You've talked me into it. Do you think it will be very dressy?'

Maud continued to sit at the table, with, but apart from, the others. Preoccupied with thoughts of her forthcoming wedding she oscillated between the absolute conviction that she was following the only course open to her if she was going to end her pariah status, and the certainty that she was about to make the biggest mistake of her life.

Mrs Butler's reaction to the news that she and Theo were about to marry, had been cool enough to convince her that she wouldn't overcome her tainted reputation while she remained in Basra, even after she changed her name to Wallace.

She listened to Georgiana and Angela discuss clothes. She would have given anything to have been able to turn the clock back to the early days of her marriage to John. If she'd been a faithful wife – if she'd never had an affair with Geoffrey Brooke – if she'd never allowed Miguel D'Arbez to seduce her – if she'd never participated in Miguel's orgies – 'if', the saddest word in the English language.

'You all right, Maud?'

She looked up. Angela, Georgiana, Dr Picard, and the Butlers had left the room. The meal was over.

'I'll see you in my study in ten minutes?'

'Yes.'

'I'll give you a final medical examination. Just to be sure you're ready for all that marriage entails.'

Lovemaking with John had been a beautiful experience. Sex with Geoffrey exciting because it was forbidden. The orgies Miguel had organised had been erotic, stimulating, titillating senses she'd never suspected herself of possessing until Miguel had aroused them. Throughout it all she'd been a willing, even eager, participant.

So was it simply guilt that made her feel so used and degraded whenever Theo 'examined' her?

466

Chapter Forty

Mitkhal sheltered against the bulkhead and reloaded his revolver. The *Julnar* had made good progress since it had set off that morning at 7.00 a.m., making an average speed of six knots, but the last four hours had seen five assaults from Turkish positions new to him. The attacks had been so well orchestrated he could only assume that the *Julnar* had been tracked from Amara by Turkish spies.

He finished reloading, crawled back along the lower deck and peered over the side. All he could see were moving shadows, black shapes against a black background. A shot thudded harmlessly against the side of the vessel below him. He stared at the bank in search of a recognisable shape. A whistling tore through the air. He recognised the sound and flung himself flat next to the rail. A shell crashed on deck, splintering the wood. A scream pierced the air and he knew shell fragments had found a target. It was only when he moved that he realised he was drenched in blood. Another shell tore through the air, illuminating the scene around him. The captain was lying dead on deck next to him.

A rating crawled up to him. 'Lieutenant Commander Cowley's injured.'

Before Mitkhal could answer him the engines gave an unearthly screech and the ship juddered to a halt. The engine continued to make the eerie noise but the boat remained caught in the river unable to make headway.

A broad Welsh accent stated the obvious. 'Something tells me we're stuck.'

Another voice, in heavily-accented English, resounded from the bank. 'Crew of the *Julnar*. You are surrounded. We are holding you fast. You have no choice but to surrender.'

Mitkhal heard snatches of whispered conversation on deck. He pushed his revolver back into his abba and slithered over the deck away from the bank to the river side of the steamboat. As silently as he could, he slipped over the side and into the water.

Kut Al Amara, Friday 28th April 1916

John pulled a sheet over the head of a sapper who was lying on an improvised bed on the damp mud floor of the cellar of the General Hospital. Two days ago he'd expected the man to make a full recovery from the wound in his chest but when he'd pressed the wound that morning it had seeped blood, and he knew it was useless to even hope. Exhaustion and malnutrition had destroyed the body's ability to heal itself. It was a phenomenon the doctors and orderlies in Kut were becoming depressingly familiar with.

He straightened his back and studied the other men in the makeshift temporary ward that had been hastily improvised to alleviate overcrowding. From the look of them it wouldn't be long before another doctor or orderly pulled a sheet over their heads.

The door opened and Crabbe beckoned to him. He waved to signify he'd seen him, went to the orderly who was trying to spoon horsemeat stew into a man's mouth and ordered him to send for a burial party.

Knight and Bowditch were waiting with Crabbe outside the building. John noted the sombre expression on all their faces. 'It's official, we're surrendering.'

'Tomorrow.' Crabbe handed him a sheet of paper. 'Townshend's still hoping that we'll be able to embark for India on condition we never bear arms against the Turk again.'

John took the sheet from him. 'Do you think that's likely?'

Crabbe looked around the deserted street before shaking his head. 'We've been ordered to destroy all our weapons and anything else the enemy could make use of, so what does that tell you?'

'We'll be marched into captivity tomorrow,' John guessed. 'What about the sick and wounded?'

'I asked, and was assured that those in need of medical attention will be examined by Turkish doctors and sent downstream. In exchange for wounded and sick Turkish POWs.'

'Which is probably why Perry's in the officer's hospital now with a fever. I wouldn't have put it past him to get deliberately infected,' Knight said.

'That sight is enough to make a grown man

cry,' Bowditch declared when they reached the riverbank.

Officers were shooting their revolvers into their binoculars to smash the lenses. A bonfire had been built of the wagons and officers and their bearers were throwing saddlery and swords on to it. Larger guns were being dismantled, smashed, and tossed into the Tigris. Ammunition was being dumped by the boxload into the river.

'Where are you going?' Crabbe asked John when he turned his back.

'To get my binoculars and telescope so they can be destroyed. Then I'll check the wounded and make a list of everyone who should be sent downstream.'

'I'll come with you.' Knight handed John a copy of Townshend's latest communication to the troops.

John read the last paragraph.

Whatever has happened, my comrades, you can only be proud of yourselves. We have done our duty to King and Empire. The whole world knows we have done our duty.

I ask you to stand by me with your ready and splendid discipline, shown throughout in the next few days, for the expedition of all service I demand from you. We may possibly go into camp, I hope between the Fort and the town, along the shore whence we can easily embark.

'We're going into captivity, aren't we?' John asked Crabbe who'd decided to accompany them so he could pick up his own weapons and binoculars.

Crabbe nodded.

'For the duration?' Knight asked.

Crabbe nodded again. 'But one of you will have to accompany the wounded downstream.'

'You're the weakest, you should go,' Knight said to John.

'I'll toss you for it. Tails you stay and I go.'

'Agreed.'

John took a sovereign from his pocket and tossed it in the air. 'Sorry, Knight, you drew the short straw.'

'That's not fair...'

'You agreed,' John said. 'Too late to argue now.'

Crabbe almost asked to see the sovereign John had used. Later he wished he had. Because he knew Harry had given John a two-headed sovereign for one of his birthdays. He wondered, not for the first time, if John had a death wish...

Lansing Memorial Hospital, Basra, Wednesday 24th May 1916

Georgiana stared wide-eyed at Charles. 'Michael's here! In Basra?'

'Not quite yet. His boat will be berthing in the next hour. I came straight here after I heard the wireless transmission he sent to HQ from the boat. We have to pick up Angela...'

'What's that about Angela?' Theo left the ward where he'd been supervising the removal of the POWs judged fit enough to travel upstream.

'Smythe and Michael will soon be berthing in Basra.'

'Peter – but he's in Kut...'

471

'Apparently not. And don't ask questions because I don't know more than I've told you. I sent down to Abdul, ordered a chicken dinner to be prepared for them and Angela. And Georgie too if you can do without her for the next couple of hours.'

'We managed without her before she arrived here. I wouldn't like to say how, but we managed, and I daresay we'll manage an afternoon without her now. Take her with my blessing. Careful with that man,' he warned two orderlies. 'He has a spinal wound, put him on a wooden board.' He looked at Georgiana. 'What are you still doing here?'

'Thank you, Theo.' Georgiana ran to the office to change out of her hospital clothes.

'Don't run or Sister Margaret will imprison you for flouting the rules.'

'Will you be at the wedding tonight?' he asked Charles.

'I'll have to go to the office to make up for taking time off this afternoon.'

'It's all right.' Theo read the expression on Charles's face. 'I understand. Georgie doesn't want to come either. After all, John Mason was her cousin and your close friend, the last thing you'll want to do is watch his widow remarry.'

'I heard you taking my name in vain, Dr Wallace?' Sister Margaret appeared behind him.

'I was hoping you'd help me check out these POWs and tell me which ones are only pretending to be ill.'

Georgiana scurried out of the office, hat, gloves, and hair pins in hand, her hair in disarray.

'We'll need a carriage.'

'It's outside. We'll fetch Angela and go straight from the Mission to the wharf. She should be waiting for us – I sent a message to the school.'

They found Angela, white-faced with strain, pacing in front of the school. The ten minutes it took to drive the wharf crawled past at a snail's pace.

'There they are, still on deck,' Charles shouted. 'How's that for timing.'

Angela jumped out of the carriage, and ran across the wharf without a care as to how high her skirts flew. Georgiana walked to Michael at a more sedate pace.

'You've lost weight, and you're yellow.'

'With red spots,' he informed her gravely. 'But so would you be if you'd had to live among the upriver flies and mosquitoes.' He glanced up at the window of his room in Abdul's and wondered if Kalla was there.

She finally hugged him. 'Thank God you're here and alive.'

'It's good to see you too, Georgie.' Michael released her and shook Charles's hand. 'We've brought an acquaintance of yours down. He's handing over patients to the medics...'

'John?' Georgiana cried. 'He's alive...' she gripped Charles's hand.

'Dr Downe, Georgie, this is Major David Knight, Indian medical officer and a very good friend of John and Harry.' Michael effected the introductions when David Knight joined them.

'I'm sorry I'm not John. But you're right, he is alive, Dr Downe.'

Charles paled. 'Are you sure John's alive?'

'Yes. It's a long story.'

'We have plenty of time to hear it over lunch, Knight. On me.' Charles waved to Abdul, who waved back.

'Let me guess, John insisted on staying with the men going into Turkish captivity in case he was needed,' Georgiana said.

'Not in case, Dr Downe. He'll be needed all right,' David said. 'One of the officers described the Kut garrison as a sick, skeleton army rotten with cholera and disease.'

'Looking at you, I can believe it, Major Knight.'

'Please don't take me as an example of the Kut garrison. I've had over three weeks of full rations and rest and recuperation on the voyage down here.'

'I suppose we couldn't expect anything else of John,' Georgiana declared. 'He's always put others before himself.'

'Chicken dinner in Abdul's on me, ladies, gentlemen.' Charles reminded.

'Is it true the entire Kut garrison has gone into captivity?' Charles asked Michael.

'Did I hear you right, Charles, an officer from HQ asking a journalist for confirmation of news?' Georgiana teased.

'News, like figures, has a habit of getting fudged in HQ,' Charles murmured too low for anyone except Michael to hear.

'From what I've heard around thirteen and half thousand men have been marched into captivity. Four thousand of those are sick or wounded,' Michael added. 'And approximately two thousand died in the garrison during the siege from enemy action or disease.'

'But John is alive.' Charles was having a problem believing the news. He turned to look at the officers leaving the boat. 'That's...'

'Maud's father, Colonel Perry, yes,' Knight confirmed.

'If he's sick or wounded, he doesn't look it,' Charles observed.

'He's a born survivor, a swinger of lead, as the Navy would say,' Knight smiled at Georgiana.

Angela finally moved away from Peter but she didn't relinquish his hand. 'We have to tell Maud that John is alive,' she insisted. 'Right away.'

'Why right away?' Peter asked.

'Because she's supposed to be marrying my brother tonight.'

'Did she even bother to have widow's weeds made?' David asked scathingly.

'Hardly matters,' Michael chipped in. 'She can't marry him now, it would be bigamy.'

'I'll go back to the Lansing and tell Theo.' Angela was already hailing the carriage that had brought them to the wharf.

'I'll go with you. It's good of you stand us a meal and everything, Charles...'

Charles smiled at Peter. 'But you'd prefer to say hello to your wife in private. Perfectly understandable. Go on off, the both of you. Take the carriage, but send it back here when you've finished with it.'

Angela hugged Georgiana and allowed Peter to help her into the carriage.

Abdul had laid out the lunch in the bay window of a private upstairs dining room that overlooked the harbour. The chicken might have been as good as Abdul insisted it was, but none of them took time to savour it.

Sitting next to Michael and holding her brother's hand, Georgiana listened intently as David Knight recounted stories of what it had been like for the men marooned in Kut. Charles listened intently, while Michael pulled out his notebook and questioned David about the details.

Still holding hands with Michael she looked through the window down at the wharf. A family of Arabs were leaving Abdul's and boarding a gaily painted native mahaila, crewed by half a dozen tall, strapping natives in Bedouin garb. A fine, upstanding, grey-bearded man joined them. Behind him were two heavily veiled women, both carrying babies. Two men shepherding tiny twin girls brought up the rear of the party.

'*Harry has twin daughters.*'

Had Charles told her that?

One was possibly the tallest man she'd ever seen but he wasn't the one who'd caught her eye. She relinquished her grasp on Michael's hand and left the table.

The second man was about her height, a patch covered one of his eyes and the scarring around it suggested the socket was empty. His right arm was supported in a sling and ended at his wrist. But it was only when he looked up at her that she knew for certain.

'Georgie?' Michael left his seat and joined her.

He looked down. 'We have to run down...'

'No, Michael.' She gripped his hand, hard. 'Look at the children and the people with him.'

'He's our brother.'

'Not any more, Mikey,' unthinkingly she resorted to his childhood nickname. 'He's not ours. He's made his choice.'

Mitkhal saw Hasan look up at Abdul's window. He saw Georgiana and Michael staring down.

Furja left the cabin and called to Hasan.

Hasan turned, smiled at her and followed her into the cabin but not before Mitkhal saw the look in his remaining eye. And Mitkhal knew. His friend was Hasan Mahmoud but Hasan Mahmoud had not quite forgotten Harry Downe – not yet.

The publishers hope that this book has given you enjoyable reading. Large Print Books are especially designed to be as easy to see and hold as possible. If you wish a complete list of our books please ask at your local library or write directly to:

Magna Large Print Books
Magna House, Long Preston,
Skipton, North Yorkshire.
BD23 4ND

This Large Print Book for the partially sighted, who cannot read normal print, is published under the auspices of

THE ULVERSCROFT FOUNDATION